PRAISE FOR
"WHEN EMPIRES FALL"

When Empires Fall had me hooked from the first page. Katie Jennings does a great job of capturing my imagination and keeping my attention from beginning to end. I felt as though I was a friend of the Vasser family and wanted to visit the hotel. I was so disappointed to get to the last page and not know what happens next. I am looking forward to the next book in this series. Katie Jennings has a five star book that could easily become an award winning movie. Don't pass this one up—it is a true winner.

- Readers' Favorite -

I enjoyed *When Empires Fall*, the fact that you don't know what will happen, you don't know who to love and who to hate, and that it is filled with so much drama. The author did a wonderful job with the flow of the story.

- Christina's Book Review -

This book has it all—murder, intrigue, and romance. Just as in all the great soaps, I was not ready for this episode to be over. I can't wait to get my hands on the nest book. I hope that she deals with Linc and his Louisiana home more.

- Voracious Reader -

Jennings' writing is excellent, the formatting attractive, and the pacing spot on. I found myself drawn into their world, an unwitting player in the drama of their lives. The story carried me along all the way to its dramatic conclusion. I loved this story and look forward to more from this wonderful author. Well done!

- Richard C. Hale, author of "Near Sighted" -

Also By Katie Jennings

So Fell the Sparrow

The Vasser Legacy

When Empires Fall
Rulers of Deception

The Dryad Quartet Series

Breath of Air
Firefight in Darkness
A Life Earthbound
Of Water and Madness

RISE OF THE Notorious

A VASSER LEGACY NOVEL

KATIE JENNINGS

Sapphire Royale
publishing

Cover design by Katie Jennings
Interior book design and eBook design
by Blue Harvest Creative
www.blueharvestcreative.com

Prologue quotation written by William Shakespeare, *Antony and Cleopatra*

Published by
Sapphire Royale Publishing

ISBN-13: 978-0615797328
ISBN-10: 0615797326

Visit the author at:
www.katieajennings.com
www.facebook.com/authorkatiejennings
www.twitter.com/dryadquartet
www.katieajennings.wordpress.com

To those who live for romance and would die for family.

VASSER FAMILY TREE

*DIRECT VASSER LINEAGE ONLY
WITHOUT SPOUSES*

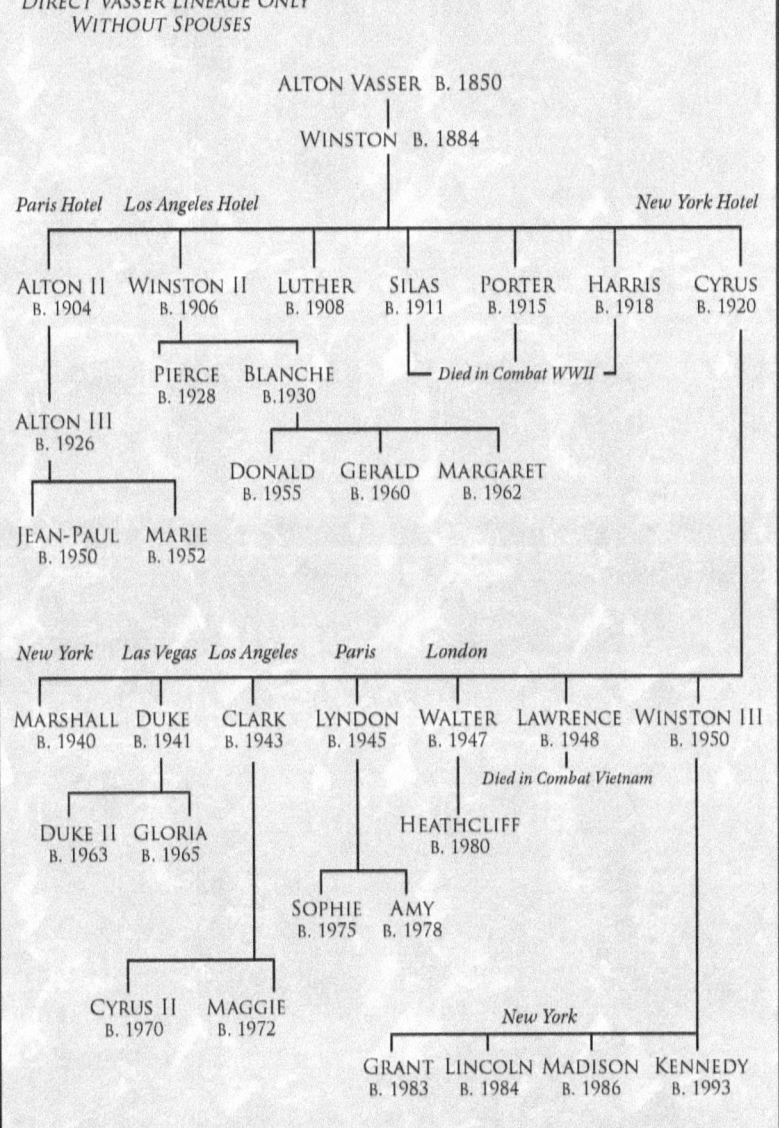

ALTON VASSER B. 1850

WINSTON B. 1884

Paris Hotel   *Los Angeles Hotel*   *New York Hotel*

ALTON II	WINSTON II	LUTHER	SILAS	PORTER	HARRIS	CYRUS
B. 1904	B. 1906	B. 1908	B. 1911	B. 1915	B. 1918	B. 1920

PIERCE   BLANCHE
B. 1928   B.1930

└── Died in Combat WWII ──┘

ALTON III
B. 1926

DONALD   GERALD   MARGARET
B. 1955   B. 1960   B. 1962

JEAN-PAUL   MARIE
B. 1950   B. 1952

New York   *Las Vegas*   *Los Angeles*   *Paris*   *London*

MARSHALL	DUKE	CLARK	LYNDON	WALTER	LAWRENCE	WINSTON III
B. 1940	B. 1941	B. 1943	B. 1945	B. 1947	B. 1948	B. 1950

Died in Combat Vietnam

DUKE II   GLORIA
B. 1963   B. 1965

HEATHCLIFF
B. 1980

SOPHIE   AMY
B. 1975   B. 1978

CYRUS II   MAGGIE   *New York*
B. 1970   B. 1972

GRANT   LINCOLN   MADISON   KENNEDY
B. 1983 B. 1984   B. 1986   B. 1993

PROLOGUE

FINISH, GOOD LADY;
THE BRIGHT DAY IS DONE,
AND WE ARE FOR THE DARK.

LAS VEGAS, NEVADA
JULY 1ˢᵀ 2004

They say only clever creatures can survive the desert heat. After all, the desert is nothing more than a sweltering wasteland that has claimed more lives than it has given, which makes it more of a graveyard than a flourishing habitat. Regardless, man was either foolish enough, or maybe greedy enough, to build a playground in the middle of Hell.

Then they'd had the audacity to call it a fertile plain. *Las Vegas*.

What a glorious contradiction.

Madison Vasser despised the desert with all of her being. She was a creature made for colder climates, for snowdrifts and icy streets. Her ivory skin welcomed a cool winter chill, and scornfully burned under the red-hot desert sun. But, like many others, she had learned to adapt to her new home, as the reward for staying was too great to relinquish.

She was nineteen, she was ambitious, and she was in love.

Her smile was instinctive and more than a little wicked as she sauntered through her family's lavish casino, her golden dress fitted to her curves and cropped short above her knees. Men in the casino faltered and stared as she passed, stunned by her radiance, moved by the passion so clear in her expression. She was a woman who knew what she wanted and was taking it without reservation. There was no *asking*, no *begging*—only ambition and victory. And she was the master of both.

She'd come to Vegas a year before to serve her family's empire. Now, as she walked through the casino, she had to marvel at her grandfather's brilliance to build in the godforsaken desert in the first place. Despite appearances, it really was a powerful city. The money that traded hands was layered thick with hopeful sweat and anxious tears, and the people loved it. They flocked to it, never having fully sated themselves with the escapist thrill of bright lights and lost inhibitions.

The hotel itself thrived, rising like a glittering beacon of refuge out of the dusty sand and drier-than-hell rock. It towered over its neighbors, both larger and taller than anything else within several hundred miles. Cyrus had insisted upon it, had purposely designed it so the sapphire and gold "V" shone boldly and brilliantly from atop the glass walled building for all to see. No one entering Las Vegas would have any doubt who was the top dog in town or who ruled the landscape like a king rules an empire.

The Vasser name was as powerful as it was timeless. And, as her grandfather was apt to say, it was the tower of strength.

She made her way out of the bustling casino and passed by the hotel's premiere French restaurant, *Soleil*, deciding to grab a bottle of wine for later. It was somewhat of an anniversary, as one year had passed since she had arrived in Las Vegas.

Oh, and how things had changed since then.

She may have hated the desert, but there was no denying that it had given her an incredible gift, one she would've gone to Hell and back for.

Wyatt Bailey, the man who'd come from nowhere and shamelessly set fire to her heart.

He'd been virtually nothing when she found him—just a blackjack dealer with a mysterious past working for her uncle—with no car, and a crappy apartment. Despite his shortcomings, she took him under her wing and gave him everything.

Within a few months she got him promoted to pit boss, moved his meager belongings into her suite at the hotel, and bought him a brand new Mercedes SLR and new designer clothes. Most importantly she gave him her heart, and in return, he changed her entire world.

She had never loved any man the way she loved Wyatt, with a fiery passion and a crushing need that consumed her every waking moment until she couldn't stand it unless she was at his side. He was intense and fiercely obsessed with her, emotions she knew only too well as she possessed them herself. They were similar creatures and that was why it was easy to fall in love with him. It barely took more than a touch to become mesmerized with each other, which was exactly how she always hoped love would be.

Smiling again, she swept through the service entrance and into the restaurant's kitchen, her eyes catching sight of Raoul, one of the cooks at the hotel. He was busy whipping up eggs in a large, stainless steel bowl at a furious speed, his dark hair falling into his eyes as he worked.

She and Raoul became fast friends the moment she began working for her Uncle Duke because, like herself, she recognized in him an ambitious and restless spirit. He craved status, power, and the finer things in life as much as she did. Once she had her way, she would see to it they both got what they wanted in this life. Success.

"Darling, I hope that quiche is not for Grant and Erin." Madison smiled as she came up beside him, one hand sliding over his shoulder companionably. "You know she's lactose intolerant."

Raoul stopped whisking and glared down at her, his mouth set in a firm line. "*Sí*, but your brother likes it, no? I will make something else for his woman."

She leaned in to kiss his cheek, coaxing a small smile out of him as she did so. "I can always count on you."

"It's nothing." He brushed her off, reaching for the bowl again to pour the egg into a shallow glass dish layered with pastry dough. "You should go prepare for your brother, *cariño*."

She glanced at the slim, gold watch on her left wrist. "I have a few hours till they fly in. Enough time to have a glass of wine and take a hot bath."

He chuckled and shook his head, sprinkling cheese over the quiche. "There is a nice Moscato in the fridge."

"Fantastic idea." Madison swept over to the kitchen's large wine fridge, opening the glass door and reaching for the Moscato. She checked the date on it and smiled. "Excellent. Wyatt enjoys a good white."

Raoul said nothing as she shut the door and wandered back to him, bottle in hand. "I'll be down in a couple of hours to help you finish with dinner."

"*Hasta siempre*," he murmured without looking at her, his eyes focused instead on the quiche as he finished preparing it.

She paused, her eyes softening as she watched him. It was only when he was feeling emotional that he used that phrase of endearment with her. Just what was bothering him now, she didn't know. But whatever the reason, she would be there for him when he needed her, just as he was always there for her. Loyalty was everything.

"Until forever, darling." She briefly squeezed his shoulder before leaving the kitchen, her focus shifting to her lover, who was waiting upstairs.

Since she began working at the hotel she had lived in one of the suites. Because the arrangement wasn't meant to be permanent, she figured it was best to be close to the action of the hotel instead of living elsewhere in the city. Besides, it didn't get any more luxurious than a suite at the Vasser Hotel.

Wine in hand, she made her way toward the hotel's elevators, her head held high and a smooth confidence to her step. The world was hers for the taking, and she absolutely intended to take. Only what she deserved, of course, but she was going to make her grandfather proud. After all, he had entrusted *her* with his most lucrative secrets, trained *her* to be everything he needed her to be. If it wasn't for him, she would be nothing.

She would never, ever let herself forget that.

The elevator she boarded rose slowly toward the upper floors and she gazed at herself in the mirrored gold doors as she waited. Her long, dark brown hair was meticulously straight, its length falling to nearly her mid-back. Eyes of vibrant amber beneath heavy lids stared back at her, sultry and intense. She was proud of the heritage evident in her appearance, proud that she so greatly resembled the man who she respected above all else. It was all a part of who she was, and who she was becoming.

She was a Vasser, and she would go to the grave defending her family and the empire that was her birthright.

When the elevator came to a stop and the doors slid smoothly open, Madison swept out and strolled down the long hallway, her heeled footsteps muffled by the ornate gold and sapphire carpet. She reached into the small handbag she carried and pulled out her key card just as she came up to the door of her suite.

She slid the card neatly into the slot and pushed the door open, her smile still in place as she entered the room.

"I brought some wine up, darling. I figured we could have some fun before Grant flies in."

She paused, taken aback as she noticed the empty living area and the neatly cleaned bedroom beyond. Frowning, she stalked through the bedroom and into the adjoining bathroom, expecting him to be there.

When she found it empty, her heart began to race in her chest as frustration and anger surged through her. Where the hell was he?

She tore back into the bedroom, headed straight for the dresser and ripped out the drawers. When she noticed his clothes were missing, her breathing became shallow and forced, her chest constricting painfully.

No, it couldn't be. He wouldn't do this.

She stormed into the living room, her hand clenching violently around the wine bottle, her vision hazing with red. That was when she spotted the note, written on the hotel's white and gold stationary, sitting atop the coffee table. Beside it lay the key to the Mercedes she had given him.

Her handbag fell to the floor as she grabbed the note and hastily read the words, gripping it so tightly that she nearly tore it to shreds.

It read simply: *I'm sorry, sweetheart.*

"You godforsaken *bastard*," she snarled, her hand shaking as she crumbled the note into her fist. In a fit of glorious rage, she hurled the wine bottle against the wall, her heart panging at the resounding crash as glass and wine spilled hideously onto the floor.

As the realization that he had left her exploded through her system, she did the only thing that would satisfy the blood lust coursing through her at that very moment. She tore the room to pieces, cursing his name over and over until her throat was dry and her eyes were bright with tears. The fury she unleashed ripped through the suite like a tsunami; its wake leaving chairs upturned, tables pushed over, vases shattered and draperies ripped from windows. Anything she could grab she did, and as she ruined her pretty possessions she vowed to hunt him down and make him pay.

"Stop it, *cariño*." Raoul's voice shot out from the doorway, causing her to falter for the briefest of moments, her chest heaving. In her hands was a priceless Baroque statue, the weapon she intended to use to shatter an equally priceless antique mirror to pieces.

She looked up to meet his dark eyes, and in that instant felt her knees crumble beneath her. Within seconds he was with her, gathering her close, pressing her face into his chest.

"Don't you dare waste tears on him," he grunted, glaring around at the destruction she had made, an odd, prideful gleam in his eyes. Although he knew she was normally cool-headed, when provoked she became a vindictive devil capable of catastrophe. "He is not worth it."

As hard as she tried, her fury could only carry her so far. Her emotions were boiling up to overtake her, cloaking her in misery and abject humiliation. Because that's exactly what this was. Wyatt Bailey had used her, led her to believe he loved her, and then left. For as long as she lived, she'd damn him to the darkest depths of Hell for scorning her.

"How dare he leave me," she spat, despising the crack in her voice as the words sank in and enveloped her in despair. When she spoke again, it was more of a whisper and she hated herself for feeling this awful weakness. "How dare he."

Clutching at Raoul's white dress shirt, she gave in to her emotions and let them drain her dry, her tears painful and horrific.

Never again. Never again would she trust a man with her heart only to have him trample on it this way. She thought of the night only three weeks earlier when she and Wyatt had impulsively gone to a chapel downtown and tied the knot, completely in secret. No one in her family had any idea. Now, it appeared, they never would.

Raoul held her, seeking to comfort even as a satisfied smile came over his face.

Finalmente. At last. Wyatt Bailey was gone.

ONE

While the world destroyed itself with war thousands of miles away, Paul Morgan sat back comfortably in his desk chair and smiled. He had, thanks to his well-connected father, avoided the overseas conflict. It wasn't that he couldn't handle the violence of war or that he was anything less than a true patriot, he just felt his unique skill set was better suited on the home front. And with war crimes on the rise, how could anyone say that he was anything less than necessary?

For him, his job was a simple one. He was a military man who brought other military men to justice.

One thing he knew without a shadow of a doubt was that war was hell. Regardless of this fact, America still expected her men of arms to maintain civility. It was his job to take the cases that were forwarded on from the commanders overseas and see to it that the soldiers who committed war crimes be dealt with accordingly.

It was a job his training as a New York City police officer had primed him for prior to enlisting in the Army to help fight the war. Only, after boot camp, his father had insisted on his removal from the general ranks and his placement in the CID as a warrant officer. It wasn't the position he had been looking for, but now that he was here he couldn't be happier.

While the friends he had made in basic training died bloody deaths upon foreign soil, he rested comfortably in Quantico, ready to investigate them if they made a mistake. Sure, it gave him some sleepless nights, but it would be foolish of him to regret his good fortune.

Not that he didn't have other regrets, of course. In fact, it was becoming much too difficult to not regret one, nagging little thing in particular.

It was the inconvenient string that came attached to the woman he decided to marry three years earlier. Not that he had known at the time that this string would be a burden; he had married her in part for this important string.

His wife was affluent...*very affluent*. Her great uncle had created an American empire, one that had grown into a flourishing, world-renowned business. One that shined like a beacon on the hill for all to admire and envy, eager to feel even some small part of its glory.

It was an empire that was not only monumental, but magnificent and respected.

It was an empire of hotels. The Vasser Hotels.

When he had married her, she had carried the prestigious name Vasser. Now, it appeared that name was going to haunt him until the day he died.

The phone call came unexpectedly days ago; an unwarranted intrusion of the quiet peace in his work environment. It had shattered his resolve, weakened his confidence, and shaken him to the core. How could they ask this of him? How dare they even assume he would play a willing role in the cover-up of something so undeniably heinous?

Yet they had demanded it. Who was he to deny the whims of a force he had no hope of defeating?

His earlier smile faded as sweat began to bead on his forehead. He wiped it away nervously with the handkerchief from the breast pocket of his suit jacket, his nearly colorless blue eyes darting to the door of his office. Any minute now that wench would walk in, primed for their scheduled appointment. What he wouldn't give to throttle her for what she was making him do...what he had no *choice* but to do.

Lazy afternoon sunlight poured in from the window at his back and highlighted the auburn of his neatly combed hair. It pierced through the half-open blinds so that slats of light shone golden on the white wall across from him. Decorating the wall were his awards, achievements, and family photographs. He turned his eyes away from the photograph of his father, feeling sick to his stomach.

If he got caught then it was all over. Everything. He was a doomed man if this ever, *ever* came back to him. He just had to pray with everything he had that the Vassers had the situation on their end under control. If that man ever killed again...Paul shuddered to even think of it.

Blood was going to be on his hands now. Blood of men he had never met, distant relatives of the wife he should have never married. Damn the Vasser name for carrying its prestige and allure. Damn them all for forcing his hand on this godforsaken cover-up!

A sharp, brisk knock on his office door startled him. Struggling for words, he attempted to clear the sudden lump that rose in his throat. He'd be damned if he let that Vasser woman know he feared her...

"Come in." Paul watched as the door slid open and *she* entered...all long, slender legs and vivid red silk. Golden hair was perfectly styled to curl around her soft, angular face that held a coldly detached and ruthless expression. It was like the devil himself had just ascended from Hell disguised as an angel, ready to collect his due.

"Good afternoon, Mr. Morgan. So nice to finally meet you," Stella Vasser purred, a cat-like grin brightening her face as she shut the door, her dark coat draped over her arm. "I appreciate you agreeing to see me to discuss the matter at hand. My family will be eager to learn what the status is on the investigation."

"Don't play coy with me," Paul growled, slamming his fist down upon his metal desk in a wave of sudden fury. "I know why you're really here."

Stella's grin remained, but her expression notably hardened. Her eyes of rich cobalt examined him as a spider would a fly trapped in its web. And, what a web she had weaved. Until she had this particular little fly snared and secured, her husband and her family faced terrible consequences for what had been done. For what Cyrus had done...

"I know you do. However, all pretenses must be carefully maintained." She sauntered forward on sharp heels and took a seat gracefully in one of the armchairs facing his desk. Folding her hands primly in her lap over her coat and purse, she eyed him once more. "My husband anxiously awaits his flight back from France."

"He should have died there," Paul spat viciously.

Stella's stunning red lips curled into an angry snarl. "How dare you say such a vile thing!"

"How dare he commit such vile acts!" Paul cried out, the urge to jump to his feet and leave her and the whole mess behind exploding through him.

"His reasons are none of your concern," she replied through gritted teeth, eyes flashing dangerously. "I don't expect you to understand."

Paul forced himself to be calm, sucking in deep breaths through his nose in an attempt to quell the uneasiness and anger coursing through his veins. The nerve of these people...

"What exactly would you like me to do?" he finally asked, avoiding her cold eyes. He had never met the husband, but he had to be a crazy bastard to marry a woman like this. It irked him that despite everything else about her, he couldn't deny that she was one of the most beautiful creatures he had ever seen.

And when she gazed at him with that ruthless power in her eyes, it made him feel a foot tall.

"I want you to bury it."

He laughed, a dark, forced cackle that was borderline hysterical. "You think it's just that easy?"

"Of course it is. You're in charge, are you not?"

"Damnit, woman, this is the Army!" He threw his hands up into the air, exasperated as he glared at her again. "Incidents of this magnitude do not just get brushed aside!"

"Sure they do." Stella stared him down with all of the conviction she could muster. She had to hold strong, had to protect her husband.

She was his only shot. "This is war, Mr. Morgan. Men die. Record the deaths as casualties of war and we will be done with this."

"And what of the evidence, Mrs. Vasser? It is already a matter of record, as are the witness statements and the commander's report." Paul reached for a manila folder at his side, thrusting it across the desk. It landed before her and she eyed it with amusement.

"It is your word that determines the fate of my husband, not the evidence nor the witness statements. If you choose not to pursue this investigation, then it will be filed away, never to be looked upon again. That is all I ask of you."

"And what happens when it is discovered that I covered up one of the most atrocious war crimes committed against fellow American soldiers in the history of the Army?" he asked, the heat in his voice mixing with a bitterness he couldn't shake. "Will my wife's family somehow protect me when it's my head on the chopping block?"

"We take care of our own," Stella replied easily. "At least those who serve our purpose."

A cold chill settled in his gut at her words, sending a shiver down his spine. He didn't need to ask what was done with those, even inside the family, who did *not* serve their purpose. There were three dead bodies being shipped back from France who would be a testament to *that* violent truth.

"Then consider it done." He settled back against his chair, dejected. There was nothing he could do; he couldn't refuse her request. If the Vasser family fell under the weight of this horror, his wife and consequently he would fall with them. It was a connection he despised, and yet could not ignore.

Because he was now a part of the Vasser family, he had unwittingly become a player in this elaborate cover-up staged by Cyrus Vasser and his cunning wife, Stella. She had assured him the rest of the family knew nothing, which made the truth that much easier to hide. He wondered briefly how Cyrus Vasser's parents would react if they ever found out he murdered his own brothers in cold blood, just to gain control of the family empire. He silently prayed that day would never come.

Stella rose to her feet, extending her hand to his. "Thank you, Mr. Morgan. I will inform my in-laws that the deaths have been ruled an accidental consequence of war. You have our sincerest appreciation. We will not forget this."

He stared at her hand blankly for a moment before accepting it and rising from his seat.

"Have a safe trip back to New York, Mrs. Vasser," he said dully, watching as she turned and swept from the room, the scent of her sultry perfume lingering in the air. He shuddered once as he sank back into his chair.

He was right when he realized this moment would haunt him for the rest of his life. What he didn't know was that it would also haunt, and even attempt to destroy, the life of his unborn son.

If he had known, perhaps he would have crashed and burned with the truth instead of covering it up. It would have been the noble thing to do.

Two

When he pushed through the doors of the conference room and discovered it empty, Grant Vasser let out an impatient sigh. It was typical he was the first to arrive for a meeting but that didn't make it any less irritating.

He continued into the room, carrying his briefcase filled with legal documents, financial statements, reservation statistics, and a small roll of Tums, wondering if he should sit at his usual spot at the head of the table or if he should sit elsewhere. He wasn't sure what this meeting would entail, given the unique events that had sparked it. All he knew was his sister was now in charge of the family and she would want the head spot.

Part of him was eager to let her have it.

Deciding upon the chair directly to the right of the head seat, he set his briefcase down on the table and began to open it, only to pause, his hands hovering over the latches.

He didn't even know what was going to be discussed. He had just brought as much information as he could to be prepared. As general manager, it was his responsibility to be privy to all manner of information about the hotel. But part of him had a feeling that this meeting was not just going to be about sales figures and tanking reservation numbers.

No, he had a feeling that Madison had something important to say. And it was likely to be earth shattering.

With a heavy and tired sigh, he left his briefcase sitting on the table and wandered toward the wide, expansive windows that opened to the view of the city outside. Mid-morning sunlight cascaded down between the buildings of New York, glittering against the glass and steel. It calmed him to take in the beauty of the city he loved, and know that, despite everything, the Vassers still had a place there.

They were going to make it; he had to believe that. The moment he stopped believing in his family was the moment he himself would be destroyed.

It pained him to think of the turmoil they had faced in the last few months, of the chaos that had brought them to their very knees. The scandal that had rocked the solid foundation he had believed in still threatened to bring to ruin everything he, and they, had worked for.

Then again, when something like murder rears its ugly head, what else could be expected? Even when the murder, or rather *murders*, were decades in the past—buried under years of lies and deception, cover-ups and flat out denial.

His grandfather Cyrus had been a killer, the truth resurfacing only when the letters of a dead woman named Rosalie and the eye-witness account of Grant's father, Win, came to light and upended the entire Vasser family. The situation had corroded even further when Cyrus confessed to everything and then committed suicide, leaving Madison in charge and the rest of them in shock and bitter disbelief.

What could be done other than accept the disturbing truth and move on? There was nothing he could do to change the past, but he vowed to make sure he influenced the future. The greatness of the family had to be restored.

It was a legacy several generations old, one that deserved better than to crash and burn in murderous flames. He had no intention of letting it fail, and knew Linc and Madison didn't either. Together, he had to believe that they would succeed.

"You always look so stoic and lonely standing in front of a window like that."

Grant turned and watched as Madison strolled into the room, her dark hair pulled back into a sleek tail and her expression warm. She approached him, a stack of folders in her arms.

He smiled. "Not lonely. And only sometimes stoic."

"Mmm...yes, that secretary of yours has chased the loneliness from your eyes," Madison observed, pleased at the notable difference she could see in her brother's expression. He still looked tired, but any trace of the coldness he had always possessed had vanished.

Grant only continued to smile as he turned his attention back to the city, wondering if he should ask her why she had called specific members of the family together for this meeting. Though he wasn't sure if she would even tell him the truth; it seemed she was keeping a lot of things closer to the vest these days.

"Dad's ashes arrived back from the crematory this morning," he began, keeping his eyes glued to the view outside. "The urn is in my office. I didn't know what you had planned for it."

Madison sighed, fighting to ignore the irritating ache she felt at the mention of their father. "Why don't you keep the ashes? You're more sentimental about that sort of thing than I am."

He nodded, acknowledging her point. "Have you heard anything more from the police about the drugs or who may have tampered with them?"

"No." She bristled, annoyed because she still did not have any answers to give on the odd circumstances of their father's suicide. The police had been reluctant to do an investigation, given that no crime had technically been committed. But the family needed to know what had happened to Win Vasser—even if his suicide had been his own, lucid choice. They still deserved the truth.

Because Grant could sense she didn't want to discuss it any further, he changed the subject, hoping to lighten the mood. "Has our mother tried to convince you to give me the reins, yet?"

Madison looked at him with a knowing smile. "Surprisingly, no. She understands that she must now come to me when she wants something, so she is being reluctantly polite. I think she's just pleased to see one of us be given this opportunity."

"Well, we will stand with you," Grant reminded her, his dark eyes filling with confidence even though he avoided looking at her. "I believe in you, in your ability to fix all of this."

She closed her eyes briefly, absorbing his words and the knowledge of his faith in her. It meant more than she could ever express to him. When she looked at him again, her smile was vivid, her conviction genuine. "Thank you, Grant."

He nodded again, glancing down at the watch on his wrist out of habit.

She mimicked his movement, looking at her own with an impatient frown. "Naturally, everyone else is late. Can't anyone be on time in this family?"

"I'm here, I'm here, calm down. I know this party can't start without me," Linc said suddenly from behind them as he made his way into the conference room, crunching down on a bright green apple and looking more than a little harried. He managed a cagey grin as he approached his siblings, winking at Madison and nodding at Grant. "So what's this meeting about, anyway?"

One of Grant's eyebrows lifted at the question as he turned to his sister, who merely sighed.

"We will get to the purpose of this meeting once everyone is present. I don't care to explain myself twice."

She moved away from them and took her place at the head of the conference table, laying out her files and paperwork on the mahogany surface. Among the contents was her sole purpose for holding the meeting—her grandfather's letter. As of yet, she had kept the list of instructions to herself, but now that the funeral was done there was no need to wait any longer. Her extended family had already begun to leave New York, therefore she was running out of time.

Before her grandfather had pulled the plug on the machines keeping him alive at the hospital, he had written two separate letters, one to her and one to the detective on the case, Don Hughes. She had recently read the contents of the letter for Detective Hughes. It had contained a full and concise confession from Cyrus admitting to the murder of his father, Winston, and the murders of his three brothers in the war. While her letter spelled out the same confession, Cyrus had also included a list of instructions for her to dutifully follow in order to save the family from certain destruction. He knew his actions would harm them in ways they were not prepared for, so he made sure to arm her with a full arsenal and also make her his heir apparent.

It was now up to her to utilize that arsenal and protect the very empire Cyrus had nearly brought to ruin.

Linc shrugged at Grant and took one last bite of his apple before tossing the core free throw style into the trash can by the door. He dropped down into the seat beside Madison, across from where Grant had set his briefcase, and leaned back casually in the plush, black leather chair. Running his hands through his waves of chestnut hair, he let out a long, heavy sigh. "This has been one hell of a week, guys."

"It will be one hell of a year by the time we're done," Madison reminded him, her hands busily shuffling through her paperwork as she organized herself for the meeting. "But we can't let that stop us from moving forward."

"As long as we stick together, it won't," Grant said as he rounded the table and took a seat, eyeing his siblings as he opened his briefcase to pull out the files he had brought. "We are almost through the worst of it. Reservation numbers are starting to improve again as we head into summer, and our fiscal outlook is satisfactory."

"The media is still having a fucking heyday, though," Linc grimaced, rubbing his right temple wearily. "I've been pulling together more ideas on how we can battle back against all the negative spin in the press."

Madison folded her hands in front of her and eyed both of her brothers. "Good, we'll hear them as well as the details of our fiscal situation later in the meeting. Until then, there are other things to discuss. Things that will have to wait until the others arrive."

Just then, they heard Marshall's booming laughter as he pushed open the door, his attention focused on the four men who followed him in.

"You must be out of your goddamn mind, Clark. Mary-Sue Hudson begged *me* to take her to the spring dance, then *settled* with you when I politely turned her down."

"No, brother, it is *you* who are mistaken," Clark Vasser argued, wagging his finger at his older brother. "Mary-Sue only asked you first because she assumed *I* was going to the dance with Victoria Lewis, which was entirely untrue. In fact, if my memory serves, it was *you* who planted that idea in Mary's head so that she would walk right into your trap, only to have you then turn her down like the cruel, cruel man you are."

"You always were a heartbreaking bastard, Marshall," Duke 'Doc' Vasser chuckled, shaking his head. The glasses perched on his nose slipped down and he immediately pushed them up out of habit. "You know Clark's right. I was there; I can attest to it."

"Oh, you old fools don't know what you're talking about." Marshall waved them both off, though his smile was wide and good-natured as he turned to face his niece and nephews. "Good morning, kids! We old folks have arrived for the meeting."

"And not a moment too soon," Duke II sighed, stepping in behind his father, a briefcase and cup of Starbucks' coffee in his hands. "Sorry we're late."

"Only by a few minutes," Madison said as she watched the men take seats at the table before her, her nerves beginning to race under her skin. This was, in essence, the first official meeting she had hosted as head of the family. While the meeting to discuss Cyrus' will had been difficult, she had a feeling this meeting would be no less daunting.

In her experience, men— particularly older men—did not like being told what to do by a woman. Even though these men were her family, they still possessed egos that she knew she was going to have to beat down before the meeting was through. She had no choice. Either she was going to take control of the situation or she would fail. Simple as that.

Grant nodded at Marshall as his uncle lowered into the seat beside him. His gaze drifted to his two other uncles and his two older cousins, Duke II and Cyrus II, known by all of them simply as Duke and Cy. They both had the dark hair common within the Vasser family, but where Cy kept his long to his collar, Duke's was expertly trimmed and feathered with gray. Duke was taller and leaner in his expensive gray suit. Cy had the muscular build of a man with a gym addiction, and the carefree outfit of jeans and a white linen shirt to prove it.

Before his grandfather's death, it had been over five years since Grant had last seen any of these men, and yet here they were, pretending this was some kind of family reunion when in fact he knew there was more on their minds. They didn't approve of Madison being in charge, though there was little any of them could do to change it.

So while they smiled and pretended to enjoy themselves, he noticed the judgment in their eyes when they looked at his sister. As her older brother, he could feel his protective nature rising up to defend her from them.

"Hey Uncle Duke, did you get those tickets to the Knicks game I had sent up to your room?" Linc asked, tapping his fingers against the table restlessly.

Doc beamed at Linc owlishly through his glasses. "I did Linc, thank you. I'm trying to convince my son here to go with me."

"We don't have time," Duke grumbled, shuffling through the file folder he'd brought with him impatiently. "We are in New York on business, dad. You know that."

"Bah," Doc waved his son's comment away, winking at Linc cheerily. "He works so hard he doesn't have a life. That's why he's divorced."

Duke rolled his eyes and shot a mean look at his father. "Can we not talk about this right now? I'm sure no one else cares to hear about my sham of a marriage."

Doc shrugged, his bald head catching the light as he grinned at the others. "He just misses the Vegas heat. Besides, it's so damn cold here. My old bones can't take it anymore."

Madison smiled despite herself, not realizing just how much she had missed her uncle's easy humor. It had been one of the few things that had made Las Vegas bearable for her. "Well, we will make this process as easy as possible so you can get back home."

"I'm in no hurry, dear." Doc glanced over at his brother Clark and winked again. "It's you young people who are so urgent to get a move on."

"The shit's hit the fan, Uncle Duke. We gotta figure out what to do about all of it," Cy put in, leaning back in his chair nonchalantly and turning his attention to Madison. "I'm ready to hear what her *majesty* here has to say and then I'm on the first flight back to L.A."

Linc turned to his cousin, temper flaring. "Seriously, Cy? Is this how it's going to be?"

Cy shrugged, his mouth upturned in a bitter grin as his green eyes sparked with insolence. "It's gonna be however it's gonna be, slick."

He had just rolled over the hill of forty, but despite his age he tended to act like a college frat boy gone wild. Cy drank heavily, a habit that had once or twice gotten him into trouble with the law. But, like his dead Uncle Win, he managed to use his charm and family connections to slip out of jail time and he usually paid the heavy fines with the family money.

He was in charge of running the Vasser Hotel in Los Angeles, but his father, Clark, tended to take care of the majority of the responsibilities despite having been technically retired for five years. Clark continued to make excuses for his only son, as though hoping one day things would change. Of course, they never did.

Clark looked to his son now, sucking on his teeth as he struggled to come up with some sort of excuse to cover for his son's behavior. "Cy's understandably upset, Linc. The news has been a lot for all of us to swallow."

"That doesn't give him the right to come in here and be a jackass," Linc fired back, glaring at his uncle. "And honestly, I think out of all of us sitting here, Mads is the most qualified to run this company. She's the only one with any goddamn sense."

Duke snorted derisively and Cy snickered, but both avoided looking at Madison as she stared pointedly down the table at them.

"Thank you, Linc. I can take it from here." Madison nodded in her brother's direction, keeping her voice level despite the uptick in the beating of her heart. Her own temper was burning, but she knew she had to expect this behavior from her cousins. After all, they had been even closer to being next in line than her brothers.

"Madison, tell me what it is you plan to do about the backlash by veterans against our hotel?" Duke suddenly asked, gazing up at her expectantly. "They are calling our grandfather a traitor, a war criminal. Understandably, they want to boycott our hotels."

She noticed the challenge in his eyes and could sense the authority he felt he had over her. She could also tell that he was trying to box her into a trap he thought she couldn't escape from. It was a pity he underestimated her. He might be nearly twice her age, but that didn't make him superior or smarter.

"I have already asked Uncle Marshall to make the rounds to the various military veteran functions. As a veteran himself, he should be able to showcase our family's history of strong support for the military and convince them that our grandfather's actions do not represent every Vasser, living or dead." One of her eyebrows rose as she eyed him coolly. "Does that answer your question?"

"For now," he muttered, turning back to the paperwork before him and flipping through the pages absently. "And what about the op-ed piece in the *New York Times* proclaiming you are too young and inexperienced to run such a large company?"

Her eyes narrowed, though it was the only sign of irritation she showed. "The day I start running my life based on op-ed pieces will be the day I grow a beard and join the circus, Duke. It isn't going to happen."

Grant cleared his throat, eyeing his sister. "Can we move on, Mads?"

"Gladly." She pulled out copies of the list of instructions from her grandfather and passed them to Linc and Grant to hand down the table. "This is the list I mentioned before that Cyrus gave to me. I want you to have it so we can all be on the same page. My first step is going to be the first thing on that list."

"Corporatize?" Marshall gaped, brows furrowed as he turned to look at her. "Surely you aren't serious?"

"We will need the additional capital and investments that will come from incorporation if we are to implement the second item on the list," Madison informed him, looking at Linc as he pored over the list. "Your idea wasn't so awful, after all."

Linc let out a slow, disbelieving breath before glancing up at her with a quick grin. "Well, damn, there it is. Expand into the middle-class market with three- and four-star hotels. Revamp the company image to be inclusive of this market. I already have all of this figured out, Mads. I can show you."

"You don't need to," she replied, a spark of pride shining in her eyes. "I want you to take charge of this. I'm trusting you with it."

He nodded, looking more excited than she had seen him in weeks. "Great, I won't let you down."

"I know." She looked down the table at the other men, noting the agitation in their expressions as they read over the rest of the list. When Cy let out a sharp, bitter laugh, she knew he'd read the worst of it.

"Trim the fat?" he asked, shooting her a nasty look. "What the hell is that supposed to mean?"

"Exactly what it says," she replied smoothly, not missing a beat. "From here on out, any member of the Vasser family not directly involved in managing or running the hotels will be bought out of their interest in the company. We will no longer put up with leeches like my father draining our company of money."

"And who gets to decide who gets bought out, *your highness*?" Cy demanded, his hands clenching into fists on the table.

"I do." Madison held his gaze, matching his intensity with cool reason. "The fact that you gentlemen are here means you will not be on that list."

"And Walter and Lyndon? They will not be bought out," Marshall declared stubbornly, looking to his brothers for confirmation.

"Your other brothers will not be included in the list either, Uncle Marshall. But some of their children, and their children's children, will be."

"This is *bullshit!*" Cy shouted, nearly jumping out of his seat. If Duke hadn't grabbed his arm to hold him back, he might have crawled over the table to throttle Madison then and there.

"Stop it, Cy. It's done," Duke growled, forcing his cousin back into the chair. He glared over at Madison himself when Cy managed to calm down. "You understand, *honey*, that this is all just a bit more than we can handle right now. Cyrus is barely cold in the ground and here you are barking orders at all of us about trimming the fat and corporatizing. I hope you know that you're going to be making more than a few enemies if you follow this list."

"Then so be it," Madison declared coldly, earning a concerned look from both of her brothers. "Unlike you, I do not wish to dwell on the past and fail when we have the ability to triumph over this. The list will be implemented, and the company will be saved."

Duke slammed his fist down upon the table in a rush of sudden violence. "Says who? A dead man? A murderer?" When she said nothing and only watched him with thinly veiled disinterest, he sucked in a deep breath and fought to compose himself. "I for one think we need to discuss this issue of turning the company upside down further before we make any brash decisions."

"We don't have the time for that," Grant put in, pulling out the sheet of reservation numbers from the stack before him. He slid it across the table toward his cousin. "Take a look for yourself; we're still lower than we should be. We need to act."

Duke scowled as he grabbed the sheet and glanced at it through narrowed, suspicious eyes. Across from him, his father turned to Marshall worriedly.

"I just don't know about all of this...how about you boys?" Doc confessed.

Clark nodded in agreement and looked at Marshall, who inhaled deeply, unsure what to say.

"I will admit that this...list...worries me," he admitted, eyeing his niece warily. "I know you have the best of intentions, dear, but maybe this is too much change all at once."

Madison accepted his words, understanding the hesitation her uncles felt. They were of an older generation, one that clung to its traditions tighter than a vise. Of course it would be hard for them to accept. But that didn't mean she was going to back down.

"I understand. However, we are going to proceed." Madison watched the anger flash over her cousins' faces and the distress befall her uncles, and she steeled herself against it.

"So just what in the hell have all of you been doing up here in New York, huh?" Cy barked out suddenly. "You let this scandal fall on our family and you let things spiral out of control. I wanna know why none of you did anything! Who's responsible for letting it get so bad?"

"Our father is responsible—" Clark began, only to have Marshall interrupt him.

"None of this would have come out had Win just kept his goddamn mouth shut."

"Win was a weak man; we all know that," Doc reasoned.

"Well if the Brady Bunch over here had better control of their daddy, maybe he wouldn't have blabbed to the press," Cy put in, earning an appreciative snicker from Duke and angry glares from Grant and Linc.

"What could we have done to control our father?" Grant asked. "He was a grown man."

"Yeah, and it's not like we knew his secret. We had no idea!" Linc argued, fire in his eyes. "You're passing the blame pretty easy for someone who hasn't been here dealing with this shit first hand."

"Well the entire family is crumbling and I find most of the fault with those of you here in New York," Cy continued, waving off Linc's comment mockingly. "Someone should have known about this; you people talked with Cyrus all of the time! How in the hell—"

"I knew," Madison interrupted, causing the room to fall into instant silence as they all turned to her in shock. She watched them for a moment, part of her amused at how easy it was to get them to shut up with that one, simple admission. "I've known since I was nine years old that Cyrus killed his father. That was when he trusted me with all of his secrets...well, almost all of them."

"I don't understand," Grant managed, eyeing his sister as though she had sprouted horns from her forehead. His heart faltered as the meaning behind her words began to sink in. "You knew?"

"Cyrus told me about the murder when I was a child. He took me under his wing, made me his confidant and his prodigy. I am who I am as a result of his instruction and guidance. But, despite knowing that Winston had been murdered, I was not told the truth behind the reason for it. I was led to believe that Cyrus had killed his father because of the affair, because of Rosalie. I knew nothing of his brothers, nor that it was the real reason behind the murder."

"He *told* you?" Duke snarled. "And yet you did nothing?"

"What should I have done?" she asked defiantly, determined to stand her ground. She still mourned her grandfather, and at that moment desperately wished for his guidance. The tattoo on her wrist burned dark and violent with his memory, with the memory of the deeds she had done for him. Even though she hated to admit it to herself, part of her was afraid of the backlash that might come from this announcement.

When they said nothing, she rose to her feet and planted her hands upon the conference table, her expression filling with power and the same ruthlessness that had made Cyrus a feared and respected man. From the way the men watched her, she could tell they were thinking the same thing she was at that moment. She had, in many ways, become the man himself. She was his legacy.

"You can either accept the truth of our situation or you can bury your heads in the sand. I honestly don't give a damn," she began, righteousness coursing through her veins. She pulled every last bit of Cyrus that was within her and let it fuel her, let it give her strength and purpose. "Either way, I'm going to salvage our reputation and protect the family and the company, with or without your help. You can choose to stand against me, but consider that betrayal carefully before you act on it. I will not forget."

Marshall cleared his throat, blinking at the sudden illusion of seeing his father standing before him instead of his niece. It alarmed him to see her speak just as he would have spoken, to threaten just as he would have threatened. The resemblance was chillingly uncanny. "Dear, if we could just have a few weeks time to adjust. You understand...this is a hard time for all of us. First we lose Cyrus, then Win...let us have time to grieve and accept before we make any drastic decisions."

Madison met her uncle's eyes, hating that her love for him made it difficult to deny him time to grieve the man they had both treasured. Despite everything, she was not cold enough to refuse.

With a deep, measured breath, she continued. "I'm going to allow you a few weeks to grieve and to explore our options regarding this company. But know that I do intend to follow through with this list. You are welcome to stay here at the hotel as long as you like, and I think in time you will see that our options are much more limited than you may believe."

She took her seat and turned to Grant, all business. "I believe we're ready to discuss our fiscal outlook now, darling."

He blinked, still fighting back the shock he'd received from her admission. He shuffled through his papers and unearthed the financial statements, his mind still racing with questions and concerns. Had she really known the truth for all these years?

Despite being deeply disturbed by the idea, he tried to focus on the task at hand and began to explain the numbers to his still shell-shocked family. But at the back of his mind, all he could picture was Madison standing with Cyrus, laughing over his great-grandfather's dead body.

UNABLE TO FOCUS on work after the meeting, Grant made his way down to the hotel's kitchen, seeking comfort. He gave Quinn a few hours leave from answering his phones to assist Raoul, though he hadn't realized just how much he would need her that day. But now, with his sister's words echoing in his mind and the vicious fighting he had witnessed between his family, he knew nothing could chase away his stress better than simply seeing her.

Only, his anxiousness to see his secretary was instantly replaced with alarm as he heard a loud crash beyond the stainless steel kitchen doors in *Cherir*.

"You're doing it all wrong!" Raoul growled heatedly, the heavy steel pan he violently threw down upon the stove shivering from the abrupt assault.

"Actually, I'm not," Quinn argued stubbornly, fisting her hands on her hips. "I know how to properly mince a damn onion, Raoul. I'm not an idiot."

He scowled at her. "You are in *my* kitchen. You will mince how I tell you to mince!"

"That's fine, but you don't have to yell at me." She sighed, still getting used to his rapid-fire mood swings. She wasn't sure if he had always been this way or if it was heightened lately due to stress. Regardless, she was amazed any of the kitchen staff put up with him. "Just show me how you would like me to do it."

"I don't have time for this bullshit!" he barked, his hands itching to reach for another pot to throw. "Why Madison burdens me with this useless girl in my kitchen, I do not know."

"Quinn is here at my request, Raoul," Grant said suddenly from the doorway, his eyes dark and furious despite his level voice. "You do not have free reign to terrorize the staff."

"It's alright, Grant," Quinn began, huffing out an annoyed breath and eyeing Raoul. "He's just having a bad day."

Raoul snorted, running his hands through his dark hair before rounding on Grant, his finger jabbing into the younger man's chest. "Either she learns to take instructions or I kick her out." He stalked from the kitchen, leaving the two of them alone.

"That man is always having a bad day." Grant turned to her, feeling sorry for her having to deal with the crazy Spaniard. "Are you alright?"

"I'm fine." Quinn managed a small smile as she brushed at the white apron she wore, embarrassed he had seen her getting yelled at. "He's just angry because I've invaded his kitchen."

"This is not his kitchen, it is the hotel's kitchen," Grant reminded her. On impulse, he reached out to gently rub a smudge of flour from her cheek with his thumb.

She looked up at him in surprise, her jade eyes warming as they met his. It was rare that he showed her affection this way, but when he did, he was unbelievably kind. "I can handle him. Just give me time to break him in."

"I don't want to hear him yelling at you again," Grant murmured, shifting so he was standing right in front of her, his hand cupping her face and brushing against her loose, ebony curls. His eyes held hers, smoldering with sudden heat spawned by the contact. "I want you to be happy here, Quinn. Happy with me."

She smiled, tilting her head up in invitation as his mouth lowered to hers. Reaching for his practical gray-diamond tie, she tugged him closer until his lips brushed over her own. "A girl in love is always happy."

As she kissed him, her heart filled with joy and the thrill of his hands sliding over her back. When he pushed her up against the stainless steel kitchen island, pressing against her greedily and desperately, her mind whirled with both need and desire.

She began to loosen his tie, her hands snaking under his suit jacket as her mouth roamed from his lips to his jaw to his neck eagerly.

He groaned, the urge to take her consuming him as he buried his face in her hair. But his propriety and sense of duty outweighed the desire, so he rested his forehead against hers with a long, frustrated sigh.

"Why, Mr. Vasser, I do believe this is incredibly inappropriate." Quinn grinned as she nibbled on his lower lip, only to laugh at the tormented look he gave her as he pulled away.

"I want you to come home with me tonight."

"You mean like last night?"

"And the night before." The memory instantly flashed in his mind of her arching beneath him, her dark hair splayed across his bed as her hands fisted in the sheets. It was a memory that did little to cool the fire flooding his system at that moment. "I'll be back to get you at six."

"I'll be here, like always." She reached up to caress his cheek, saddened to notice the exhaustion still lining his features, the stress darkening his eyes. These last several weeks had not been easy on him, and the next few months were not likely to get much better. "Are you feeling okay? You look a bit pale."

His thoughts immediately went back to his sister and he tried to push whatever he was feeling aside. He could tell Quinn, but part of him wanted nothing more than to forget about the horror of it for now. "I'm fine. Go mince some onions and I'll see you this evening."

She laughed again as he pulled away from her, straightening his tie as he left the kitchen. The moment he was gone, however, her concern for him returned. There was definitely something on his mind; she would just have to find a way to ask him about it later. She wanted him to trust her, to know he could come to her with anything.

What had started as nothing more than a mild friendship months earlier had grown into something so much more. Quinn liked to think back to the day she first met him, and how formidable and powerful he had seemed to her. Her quiet, workaholic boss, so capable and determined. While he still exuded that same incredible strength, she knew that she understood him better now. She knew the warmth of his heart, for he had finally given in and shown it to her. Quinn would never be the same now that Grant Vasser of the illustrious Vasser Hotel family had become a part of her life.

With a wistful sigh, she returned to mincing onions, only to pause moments later as she heard the quick snap of heels outside the kitchen. She braced herself for what she knew was coming.

Charlene Vasser strolled into the kitchen, one eyebrow arched as she scanned the room.

"Was my son just here?" she asked, eyeing Quinn imperiously.

Quinn managed a polite smile. "Yep, you just missed him."

Charlene let out a sigh of exasperation. "I would ask you to tell him something for me but you'll probably just forget. I'll find him myself."

With one last condescending look, Charlene left the kitchen in a flurry of sapphire silk, diamonds, and Liz Taylor perfume.

Quinn absorbed Grant's mother's words painfully, appalled at how carelessly rude the woman could be without any provocation. While she knew Charlene did not approve of her nor like her very much, that did not give her an excuse to be cruel.

Raoul was hostile, but he was nothing compared to Charlene. Quinn returned to the onions, unable to forget how out of place she was surrounded by these kings and queens of New York City.

LINC LIT THE cigarette gratefully, sucking in the smoke and releasing it with relish as he shut his eyes. He hadn't smoked since college, but his sister's confession had been just enough to push him over the edge and splurge on a pack of Parliaments. And coupled with the strange text messages Lynette had received from her father just days earlier, he was in a bad place. A bad enough place that he'd take up bad habits just to ease his mind in any way possible.

Walter walked into Linc's office and handed him a Red Bull, his eyes widening as he saw his boss smoking.

"Seriously?" Walter managed, eyes jolting from the cigarette to Linc's face and back again.

Linc opened the Red Bull single-handed and began to gulp down the elixir eagerly, forcing the caffeine into his system. He slammed the can down upon his desk and took another drag on his cigarette.

"I'm in a mood, Wally," Linc said bitterly, tapping out ash into an empty Coke can sitting on his desk. "Did you get the mail?"

"Yeah, there wasn't anything for you." Walter sat down in one of the chairs facing Linc's desk, leaning over conspiratorially. "Dude, if you need something to calm you down, I can get it for you."

Linc snorted out a half laugh, amusement in his eyes. "What, like pot?"

Walter nodded, his eyes serious. "It's better for you than cigarettes, man. Seriously, I'm getting worried about you."

"I appreciate the offer, but I'll be fine." Linc grinned darkly, leaning back in his chair. "You see that interview Jorja-the-whore did on the news this morning?"

"No...what did she say?" Walter looked apprehensive, knowing this was the main subject that had been irritating his boss for the last week. Ever since Win had died, Jorja Hale had been making the rounds with the networks, proclaiming the Vasser family to be at fault for his suicide. It was, for the most part, a load of shit. But even Walter had his doubts over who had tampered with the drugs that Win had consumed before going mad and killing himself.

Linc's eyes flashed with barely controlled rage. "The usual. Though now she's claiming *I* convinced him to do it, which is just ludicrous. She just likes knowing she's twisting the knife in my goddamn back."

"Well, you can't let it get to you," Walter insisted, tapping his hands against his knees restlessly. "Everything will work out, just give it time."

"God, I hope you're right." Linc dropped his cigarette in the Coke can, exhausted. "Why don't you go get me a sandwich or something?"

"Ham or turkey?"

"Roast beef, extra meat. I need a manly sandwich today."

Linc watched as his assistant got to his feet and left, leaving him to brood in peace. He immediately let out a heavy, burdened groan and rubbed his face with his hands.

Not only was Jorja a continual thorn in his side, but this whole business with Lynette and her father was weighing on him as well. They had yet to find out what the hell Shaw had meant with those text messages, but Linc had a bad feeling about them. As much as Lynette wanted to brush the whole thing off, he couldn't let it go. The entire scenario had begun to consume him, and Shaw had now become an enemy.

Hell is coming for the Vassers. You must not be there when it does.

What did Shaw mean? Was he planning some kind of coordinated attack on the family? Or was he just being foreboding for the sake of trying to scare his only daughter away from the Vassers?

Either way, Linc was convinced that Shaw was up to something. And he would not rest until he found out exactly what it was.

MADISON WATCHED, UNSEEING, as the city lights glittered around her. They penetrated through the tinted glass of her black town car as her driver took her home.

Her secret was out—exposed for her family to see, to dissect, to judge. Her brothers now knew the real reason behind her instant rise to the top, and she suspected their trust in her would be greatly diminished from this point on.

Could she blame them? Not really. Had she been in their shoes, she would have been livid, would have felt betrayed and manipulated. Yet, despite her uncles' horror, her cousins' suspicion, and her brothers' disbelief, she would not have changed one thing. Regardless of his crimes, Cyrus had given her everything. So she would deal with this situation and persevere, just as he would have done.

Her thoughts swept back to her cousin Duke, remembering his callous attack of her. He may not have been as obvious as Cy had been, but his intentions were just as clear. Duke felt he deserved the spot she now inhabited as head of the family and he was letting his bitterness over it cloud his judgment.

It pained her to remember that at one time, long ago, they had been friends. Back in Las Vegas, he had been one of her closest confidants, her mentor and her colleague. She had helped him get over the rough patches in his doomed marriage and had welcomed his advice when she needed guidance in her own life.

But the man who sat before her earlier that day was not the same man she had known. No, this man was hardened and bitter, aged and alone. His dark hair was now going gray, his once brilliant blue eyes were dulled and filled with anger. He despised her now, a fact which bothered her more than she wanted it to. After all, she didn't need him to like her, didn't care what he really thought of her. He was just another pawn on the chessboard she had to play, and as much as he tried to fight back against her, his efforts would be in vain.

She'd give him and the others some time to come to terms with everything, but after that, she intended to go through with the plan her grandfather had laid out for her.

There would be no backing down.

As the car pulled up to her town house on the Upper East Side, she spotted a dark figure standing on the stoop outside her door. When she saw him put out his cigarette with his boot, she felt her heart sink.

The last thing she wanted to do at that moment was speak to *him*. Not when she was desperately in need of rest, aching from the events of earlier that day. She just didn't have it in her for a battle of wits or for a war of hearts.

But it appeared she had no choice in the matter.

She thanked her driver as he opened the door for her, wishing him a good night as she walked across the sidewalk and up the stairs to her front door.

"I don't remember inviting you over, Wyatt," she said coldly, eyeing him in the yellow light of a nearby streetlamp.

He smiled cagily at her, the restlessness of his mood sending sparks into the air. "I wanted to see how you're doing, sweetheart."

"Just peachy." She started to push past him, her keys out and ready to unlock her door, only to be stopped as his hand shot out to grab her arm. He turned her toward him until her face was dangerously close to his own, and the dark, primal thrill he saw flash briefly in her eyes had his grin widening.

"Aren't you going to invite me in?" he asked, honing in on her with an intensity she recognized all too well.

"You would like that, wouldn't you?" she spat, wrenching her arm free of his grip. "Why don't you go back to Maine and leave me the hell alone?"

"I can't do that," he told her easily, his hands finding their way into the pockets of his jeans so he could resist the urge to touch her again. To take her. "I have some loose ends to tie up in the city before I go."

"That's always your excuse. How many loose ends could one person possibly have?" She glared at him, hating the fact that she could still feel the burn of his hand on her arm. "Then again, you're the king of unfinished business, aren't you?"

Wyatt's grin faded as bitterness replaced it. Oh, he had a lot of unfinished business where she was concerned. Thinking of it had him changing tactics and backing off, an icy frost replacing the heat in his expression. "You miss me, sweetheart. I know you do."

"I don't have time for this," Madison snapped, crossing her arms. She continued to watch him frigidly, annoyed that her heart, her body, still yearned for him. Her pledge to herself weeks earlier at the fundraiser to manipulate him back into loving her, only so she could break his heart as he had broken hers, flashed in her mind. The fact that he was still here meant that some part of him still wanted her. She pondered over how she could use that against him as he spoke again.

"How's Raoul doing?"

She immediately disliked the lack of emotion on his face. It meant he was hiding something from her. "Why do you care?"

"Just curious." Wyatt shrugged, trying to brush it off as he strolled off her porch and down the steps to the street. He turned to face her, tipping his black fedora in farewell. "I'm moving out of the Waldorf and into the Vasser Hotel in the morning. I'll make sure to drop by and say hi."

Madison's lips parted in surprise as she watched him take off down the street, whistling to himself. Her eyes narrowed in suspicion as she tried to figure out his angle.

The last thing she needed at that moment was another complication, and Wyatt Bailey had always been exactly that. While she had discovered that his reason for coming back into her life had been because of her father, she had to wonder now why he was staying. Win was dead, after all.

It occurred to her that she really didn't know the man as well as she had once thought. If she had, then she would know the reason why he had left her in Las Vegas all those years before.

Why he had left her to ache miserably for eight long years, crushed by the powerful weight of his memory.

THREE

Her knuckles rapped violently against the door, indignation coursing through her as she waited. She stared around impatiently at the empty hallway of the upscale apartment building, her fury building with each and every second that passed.

The police had some nerve interrogating her like some common criminal, especially since she was entirely innocent. And damn the Vassers for ignoring her. She sincerely hoped to see them all burn in Hell for what they had done to poor Win.

The door flew open and the man inside smiled at her, his gold incisor tooth catching the light.

"Miss Jorja Hale," he beamed, stepping back to invite her inside as he ran a hand over his balding head. His accent spoke of his Russian heritage and only irritated her more. "To what do I owe the pleasure?"

"You know why I'm here, Eddie," she spat, sweeping past him on long legs barely covered by a shiny, black leather skirt. The extreme v-neck of her blood red blouse accented her breasts, and she caught Eddie eyeing them hungrily as she turned to face him. "I want to know what the hell you put in the weed you sold me."

His smile faded as his eyes flew back up to her face. "So this *does* have to do with the Vassers."

Jorja rolled her eyes dramatically and threw up her hands. "Hello! Who the fuck do you think I was buying that weed for? Myself? Please. I don't touch that shit."

"I knew it was for Win..." Eddie grumbled, irritation and panic rising within him as he stormed past her to grab a drink from his wet bar. "I didn't know it would kill him."

"The cops are saying it was laced with PCP. Why, Eddie? Why did you do that?"

Eddie turned to her, sipping at the vodka in his glass fervently as his dark eyes narrowed. "I was told to. The Vasser woman, she's a regular client. She comes in for pills...Vicodin, Oxycontin...she told me Win wanted something different. Something special. So when you came in with a request, I obliged."

"Wait, wait, this was *her* doing?" Jorja snapped, blue eyes aflame as her mind started processing this little piece of information. If only she could lead the cops to Eddie, but then they'd know that she was the one who'd bought the drugs in the first place. Regardless, this may be the one edge she finally had on the woman. This could bring them all down.

"She told me to give him something that would, how did she put it? 'Make him jump out of a goddamn window.'" Eddie shrugged, downing the rest of his vodka with relish. "I thought she was just being colorful. It's not my fault he actually killed himself."

"Poor Win." Jorja frowned, her thirst for revenge fueling off the tiny bit of grief she felt for the man she had latched onto and lost. She should have been sunning herself on a beach in Florida by now, not dealing with this mess. Even if it was the last thing she did, she would see to it that the Vassers paid for killing off her last chance of becoming one of them.

"You didn't tell the cops, did you? I can't have them coming back to me. I run a tight business here, lots of important clients that require discretion," Eddie asserted, a glitter of fear in his eyes. "I don't want any trouble."

Jorja managed a tiny grin, her thoughts of revenge calming her. Now that she knew the truth about the drugs, she could figure out a way to use it against the very family she now hated more than anything else in the world.

"No, I told the cops that Win bought his own drugs, that I had nothing to do with it. This won't come back to you, Eddie, I promise." She wandered toward him, placing a soft kiss on his cheek as she brushed up against his body, pleased at how compliant he was once he had a chance to touch her. "Thank you for the information. I'll see you around."

She backed away, amused by the blatant desire in his eyes. Men were easily played.

As she left Eddie's apartment and rode the elevator down to the first floor, she stared at herself in the reflection of the doors. A confident smile lifted her painted lips, cruel and wicked.

There was one, incontrovertible truth that Jorja knew at that moment. One shining beacon of light that gave life to the spirit of her revenge.

Madison Vasser was going to pay, and pay dearly, for what Jorja now knew she had done to Win.

"ALRIGHT, SO THAT confirms what we pretty much already knew. But who's responsible?" Linc asked his sister as he paced in front of her desk impatiently. "My bets are on Jorja."

Madison watched him carefully, noting he had a hard time looking her in the eye. It was clear he still hadn't forgiven her.

"While I can't figure out a motive for it, I'm inclined to agree with you about Jorja," she told him, running her pen along her lower lip in thought. "Maybe these tox results are telling us something about our father that we are just trying to ignore."

"And what is that, exactly?" Linc demanded, coming to a stop before her desk and glaring at her. She saw the distrust in his eyes, could sense he felt detached from her now in a way he had never been before.

"He had many things in his system, Linc. Not just marijuana and PCP. He had taken heavy doses of prescription pain killers. It's entirely plausible that he simply wanted to die."

"So what, you're saying we shouldn't go after Jorja for supplying him with the drugs he used to end his own life?"

"The drugs didn't kill him, though they might have if he lived long enough. It was the belt tied around his neck that did it," Madison reminded him coolly. She remained composed despite the tension in the room.

Linc cursed violently under his breath, his guilt over his father's death rising up to overtake him. He kicked the corner of her glossy mahogany desk, feeling some small measure of satisfaction from the act.

"It's Jorja's fault. I know it is. And that bitch keeps blaming us because she wants to drive all the attention away from herself."

"If she wanted out of the limelight, she wouldn't be on television every day," Madison pointed out, rubbing her temple. "There's not much we can do about her right now, Linc. We have more pressing issues we need to focus on."

"She's spreading garbage about us and you don't think we should do anything?" he growled, throwing up his hands. "I'm sorry, but I'm about an inch away from hunting her down and strangling her."

Madison couldn't help but laugh at his statement, the darkness of the whole situation taking on a humorous note. "I'll hold her down while you do the deed, darling."

He managed a half-hearted smile as well, running his hand through his hair as he turned to face her. When he met her eyes, he tried to see past the haunting truth he'd been struggling to live with since the day before. She was his sister, and would always be his sister, regardless of what she had done. It was time he started remembering that.

"Mads, I don't want to be mad at you anymore," he confessed, tucking his hands into the pockets of his jeans. "Holding grudges just isn't my style. Can we be friends again?"

She nodded, fighting back a smile even as relief coursed through her. His easy acceptance humbled her more than he could ever know. "Of course."

Before he could say anything else, Kennedy poked her head in, a cheerful grin on her face as she spotted Linc.

"Hey, Walter told me you were up here." She came into the room on long, coltish legs, her waves of chestnut hair falling untamed around her shoulders. "I thought maybe we could get lunch?"

Linc managed a smile for her, but his stress was evident on his face. "I really don't have time today, Ken. I'm sorry. We have a lot going on right now that we need to take care of."

"Oh," Kennedy faltered, unused to Linc brushing her off. She glanced at her older sister and could tell she was annoyed at the interruption. Rolling her eyes, she turned back to Linc. "Alright, I'll just go then."

She stormed out, leaving her siblings behind as she made her way back downstairs. As she stood in the elevator, her arms crossed and her lips pursed into a pout, she couldn't help but despise her family. They were always brushing her off like some annoying fly, as though her opinion, her voice, didn't matter. It had only gotten worse when the scandal had hit and when the rest of the family had come in from out of town. She had been pushed to the sidelines, even more than usual, and it really hurt to see even Linc doing it now. He had been the only one to ever give her an ounce of his time and now even he was too busy for her.

Just like her father had been too busy for her...and now he was dead. Something about that had changed her, matured her in a way she wasn't yet ready to accept. The pain of losing him, despite how much he had upset her, had brought out this desperate need within her to be with the family she had left.

None of them had even bothered to see if she was doing okay. They were clearly all too involved with themselves to take notice that she needed them, that she wasn't sure she could handle any of this without them. It was a dark and lonely place, and she had never felt so lost.

Maybe she should just leave; then someone might actually take notice and give a shit about her for once. She felt the pain hit her in the chest like a hammer, mixing viciously with the resentment. If only she could find a way to disappear. Maybe then they would care.

LYNETTE'S HANDS COMBED through Linc's hair, her smile content as she felt him sigh against her, his back to her chest with her legs wrapped around his waist. They lay on her sofa with the television on across the room, though neither of them paid attention to the baseball game currently playing. Linc trailed his fingers down her calf, lost in his own troubled thoughts.

"You're letting this hair of yours get quite long," Lynette commented, lifting a piece of it between her fingers, admiring the warm chestnut color of it as it caught the light of the lamp behind her.

"I don't have time to get a damn haircut," Linc countered, tilting his head back so he could eye her.

"Nor do you have time for a proper shave, either," she mused, reaching out to trace the five o'clock shadow that graced his jawline. "Though I'm not complaining...it gives you a dangerous look."

He snorted, shaking his head as he settled back against her chest. "Is that what you want, Lynette, danger?"

"We all *think* we want the bad boy until we actually have him. Then we have nothing but regret."

"Guess it's a good thing I'm only a bad boy half the time, then," he joked, earning a laugh from her.

"You have the bad boy swagger, Linc, but then there's that heart of gold you carry with you." She patted his cheek lovingly, grinning down at him. "And I wouldn't want you any other way."

"Good, because you're stuck with me," he informed her, enjoying the feel of her soft hands cruising over the skin of his arms. "Have you talked with your dad?"

She tensed against him. "No. And I don't intend to speak to him."

"I need to know what he meant with that text message. It might as well have been a threat against my family, Lynette. We've talked about this."

"You're overreacting," she reasoned, feeling sorry to see him so worked up over something she was convinced meant nothing. "He's not going to do anything to you or your family."

"Then why say it?" he asked, sitting up to face her. "Why make the statement if it means nothing?"

"Because he is angry that I won't follow his advice and leave you." She frowned, her eyebrows furrowed with distress. "With the election coming up next year, he's probably just irritated that I won't distance myself from you. Regardless of how you and I feel, he sees your family as a liability to his election chances."

"Well, who is his opponent? Is he planning on using us against your dad?"

Lynette considered this, biting her bottom lip anxiously. "I don't know his name, but it's possible. Politics is a dirty business."

"I'll have Quinn look into it, find out who he is," Linc decided, distracted by the thought as he ran with it in his head. He laid back down against her, knowing that he was going to have to eventually confront Shaw himself and find out the truth. He was still not convinced that the senator wasn't up to something...

"Is something else wrong?" Lynette asked, brushing a few strands of hair out of his face. "You seem out of it tonight."

Linc thought instantly of his sister and realized that, despite having forgiven her, the issue still weighed heavily on his mind.

"It's not a big deal, not anymore," he began, squeezing her knee affectionately. "Just work stuff."

"Work stuff, huh?" She leaned in to press a kiss to his forehead, her lips lingering over his skin. "You can tell me, Linc. I want you to tell me."

He reached up to run his hands through her copper waves of hair, releasing a long breath as he tried to find the right words to say. "My sister admitted yesterday that she has known since she was nine years old that my grandfather murdered his father."

"Excuse me?" Lynette froze, unsure she heard him right. "Nine years old?"

"Yep." Linc grimaced, the truth of it churning uncomfortably inside of him. "She knew, all this time."

"I see..." Unsure what to say to him, Lynette rested her head against his and stared off at the television, her eyes unseeing. After a long moment, she spoke again. "So what does this all mean?"

"Nothing, really. What's done is done. It doesn't change anything. She's still my sister," Linc told her, feeling defensive. "It hurts that she kept that secret from us, but that was her choice."

"Are you worried about what other secrets she may be keeping from you?"

He said nothing for a moment, considering her question. Part of him felt instant anger at her for even suggesting it, but the other side of him understood it was a valid question worth noting. Was Madison hiding anything else from him?

"I don't know," he said finally, sitting up again and turning to her. His eyes met hers and held, dangerous emotions storming in them. "I don't want to talk about it anymore."

She nodded as he suddenly cupped her face in his hands and leaned in, capturing her mouth with his own. He poured all of his uncertainty, all of his stress and anger into the kiss, needing to forget all of it, if only for a moment. His hands trailed back to grasp at her hair, tipping her head back so he could run his tongue along her exposed neck. When she moaned against him, her hands grasping at his shirt and her body arching toward his, he let himself become consumed by her. For tonight, at least, he didn't have strength left to worry.

QUINN STROLLED DOWN the hallway toward Grant's office, dressed in a flowery skirt and blouse the color of soft pink roses with her hair curled freely around her face. She grinned as she spotted Grant through the open door of his office, busily working away at his desk. It gave her comfort to know that was where she would always find him. Rain or shine, he would be there, tirelessly burning the midnight oil.

Before she could make her way to her desk to set down her purse and the impulse buy vanilla latte she'd picked up that morning, Madison swept out of her own office, looking distracted and distant. On instinct, Quinn paused and smiled cheerfully at the other woman. "Good morning."

Madison's eyebrows shot up as she eyed Quinn curiously, wondering what she could possibly want now. "Good morning." She nodded and attempted to maneuver around to make her way to the elevator, only to have Quinn stop her.

"I know you're busy, but are you doing alright?" Quinn asked, concern shadowing her features. "I know you were close to your grandfather...all of this must be particularly hard on you."

Madison tensed, irritated at the woman's intrusion into what she considered a private matter. "No need to worry about me, darling. I've survived this long without your concern."

To her surprise, Quinn only smiled. "Grant admires you, you know. He may not say it much, or really show it, but I know how much he cares about you."

"He cares because we're family. Simple as that." Madison brushed off the comment, eager to get away. She really didn't have time for whatever it was Quinn was trying to do. "It's been nice chatting, but I have to go."

"I admire you, too." Quinn stopped her again. "I know you're still on the fence about Lynette and me, however, we're here for you regardless. If you ever need anything, a shoulder to cry on, an ear to bend, someone to vent to...you know where to find me."

Leaving it at that, Quinn turned into the office alcove to set her belongings on her desk. She distracted herself with hanging her purse on one of the coat hooks while behind her, Madison tried to make sense of the strange new sensation beating its way into her protected heart.

She had never really had close girl friends before. Her best friends had always been her brothers, her uncle, and her grandfather. Even in her early twenties while in college, she had rarely socialized with girls her age. Instead she had, since she had been young, closed herself off to that kind of friendship.

The truth of it was, she inherently did not trust other people. In rare cases, outsiders could earn her trust, as was the case with Raoul and her assistant, Carrie. But for the most part she avoided close, personal contact with others like the plague.

So what was it about her brother's lover that had gotten under her skin? She still did not trust the woman, and yet part of her craved the easy offer of friendship that seemed to come so naturally. Was it only because she felt so alone now, detached and alienated from the family that had always been her source of strength?

No. If that were true, then she was weaker than Cyrus had raised her to be. She didn't need anything except the family empire, and she was more than a fool if she let herself forget that. Annoyed with herself, Madison left, skipping the elevator and taking the stairs instead.

Quinn silently watched her go, wondering if she had managed to even make a dent in the formidable steel armor Madison protected herself with.

"What was that about?" Grant asked, leaning against the doorway to his office. His eyes shifted from the stairwell back to Quinn.

She flushed with an awkward smile. "I was just worried about her."

"Worried about Madison?" Amusement flashed over his face. "I wasn't aware you cared so much about my sister."

"Why wouldn't I care?" Quinn began, shaking her head sadly. "She matters to you. Therefore she matters to me, too."

He let her words sink in, once again caught off guard by her natural devotion and compassion. He wondered if he would ever get used to it. When he couldn't find anything else to say, Quinn turned back to her desk and sat down, avoiding his eyes.

"I know she may not like me very much, but I do really want to be her friend. I just want her to know that she can rely on me, that I'm here for her. I can't even imagine what she must be going through emotionally right now, with all of this pressure being put on her. It would be enough to drive me crazy." She took a deep breath, chewing her bottom lip thoughtfully. "I really do admire her. She's brilliant, fearless—"

She was cut off as he suddenly held his hand out to her, silently urging her to her feet. She stared at it for a brief moment before rising out of her chair, her eyes meeting his as she accepted his hand. Before she could say anything, he pulled her against him and held her.

"I love you," he murmured, breathing in the scent of vanilla in her hair.

She let out a laugh as she grinned, leaning her head back so she could look at him.

"If I tell you how much I adore and respect Linc, will you kiss me?" she teased playfully, enjoying the sarcastic smile that played over his lips.

"Nice try." He brushed a strand of hair from her face, his hand lingering over her skin as he watched her. He said nothing for a long moment, letting his heart feel what it miraculously had learned to feel again because of her.

"When you look at me that way, I feel like you're looking right into me..." Quinn admitted, her heart racing as she held his gaze. "Does that even make sense? I don't even know what I'm saying..."

"Tell me you love me," he commanded, serious and intense. She trembled from the words, felt her knees giving out from the tone in his voice. This was the power that had drawn her to him in the beginning, the power she couldn't resist.

"I love you," she whispered the words as she kissed him, her hands grasping at his suit jacket. She repeated them again and again as he dragged her into his office and hastily shut the door.

FOUR

I t had been a week since she received the threat. She looked at it now, her eyes skimming over the words as she let her fury flood out the fear that came with instinct. The fear that was natural, but in no way useful to her now.

> *When empires fall, what becomes of the Queen?* *Everything will burn, and so will she.*

The simple typewritten note felt light in Madison's hands but weighed heavily upon her mind, burrowing deep within her and finding home among the things she feared most in this world. Death of a family member. Failure. Exposure. Shame. This threat hit her on all levels, and it was for that reason alone she knew she had to keep it hidden. It would only make it worse for her brothers to find out, to see the outrage and alarm in their eyes as they tried to fathom why anyone would send her such a thing. She couldn't force them to bear this burden with her, not when it was likely to be nothing more than a petty, meaningless act of intimidation.

As someone in the public eye, she had received letters from strangers before. Though none had been this ominous. Yet, as she had decided when it first arrived, she simply did not have time for it. She tucked the letter inside her desk drawer once more, locking it and returning to the paperwork before her.

The lawyers had given her the necessary documents to begin the incorporation of the company, and she perused over the forms, charts, and statistics with tired determination. It wouldn't be an easy change. It would take time and resources to make it happen, coupled with a smart and concise marketing strategy that would hopefully attract investors.

She had to find a way to sell her family's company as a business not built on lies and murder, but one of integrity, respectability, and a commitment to excellence unrivaled by their competitors. That had been the Vasser reputation *before* the scandal, and somehow she would need to find out how to make it that way again.

Despite the outrage from her cousins, she knew that chopping off a few of the greedy hands that frequented the family money jar would be a step in the right direction. The last thing she needed was the burden of a family member who did not want to pull their own weight.

It was merely a matter of deciding who had to go and who could stay. She knew some members of the family would jump at the chance to be bought out with a big cash sum, while others would fight her to the death to protect their own selfish interests. But that was just the nature of the game, and Cyrus would not have requested it of her if he hadn't thought she could make it happen.

Perhaps Duke was right in his prediction that she would make enemies with this list. Except, of course, he didn't know that it appeared she already had. Both within her own family and in the form of a mysterious stranger who enjoyed sending written threats...

Kennedy's face suddenly flashed in her mind, and she wondered just what role her younger sister wanted to play when she finished college. Presuming she wanted to play a role at all—Kennedy might prefer to take the cash and run off to Cancun or the south of France and party for the summer.

Madison had always known just how different she was from her sister. When she was nineteen, she worked in the restaurants at her family's casino in Las Vegas. She put in sixteen hour days learning the business and revamping the department to run more efficiently, the way she wanted.

Madison started her rise to the top at nineteen, but what was Kennedy doing?

That was the fundamental reason Madison knew she would never understand her sister. They were as dramatically different in personality as any two people could be. It was a shame, but she knew that reality was often hard to swallow. That didn't make it any less real.

Because she knew thinking of Las Vegas would only put her in a bad mood, she tried to push it out of her mind as she went back to reading through the documents.

Then she remembered what Wyatt had told her the day before. If he hadn't been lying to her, then he had checked into the hotel that very morning.

She grimaced, a darkness settling over her as she realized just what that meant.

The last time Wyatt Bailey had arrived at one of the Vasser Hotels, her life was turned upside down. She knew, just as surely as she knew her heart beat red with blood, that the same was about to occur to her now.

LAS VEGAS, NEVADA
JULY 1ST 2003

The first thing Madison understood perfectly the moment she set foot in Las Vegas was that the City of Sin could make the Devil feel right at home.

It wasn't because of the scorching, mind-numbing heat, though there was plenty of that to go around. Or the inherent fear of dying in the hot desert sand, helplessly alone in miles and miles of empty wasteland. No, it was the sin that drew the Devil, the sin that burrowed deep within the roots of the city itself and lit up the night sky with vibrant neon lights. It was all around her, everywhere she looked—the booze and the gambling, the easy sex and the drugs, the impulsive violence...oh, what a city it was.

She was ready to take it head on and make Vegas hers before she was through.

Ascending the steps to the glorious Vasser Hotel and Casino was a monumental experience for her. It was her first time visiting, though she already knew so much about the place. She knew the precise number of rooms, the names of the chefs in the hotel kitchen, and the different job titles of the employees who ran the casino. She had extensively researched everything before making the decision to move there.

Thanks to her Uncle Duke, she was being given the chance to prove her worth to the family, to show them what she was capable of. Although her grandfather already knew it, she appreciated the opportunity to succeed on her own terms.

As she approached the glamorous entrance to the casino, its glass doors emblazoned with a giant gold "V" opening to greet her, she felt a satisfied smile bloom over her face.

It was spectacular in every sense of the word.

The carpet was a rich navy blue with bold yellow floral designs weaving throughout, giving the perception of walking on a lake scattered with autumn leaves. A walkway made of splendid travertine in beiges and yellows snaked its way throughout the casino, leading guests through the blackjack, poker and craps tables, beyond the slot machines and directly to the restaurants and bars that flanked the outer edges.

There were people everywhere, excited tourists and habitual gamblers, long-legged women and short, bald men. Money exchanged hands or was shoved into machines left and right, and the joyful ring of change pouring out of slots sang out into the air, joined by laughter, anguished groans, and endless chatter. The music playing in the background was something upbeat and exciting, the kind of music that made guests tap their feet or nod their heads subconsciously to its rhythm.

Her eyes drifted from the crowds to the ceiling. The atrium was a lofty dome in the style of timeless European cathedrals with engraved gold and lustrous bronze. Beyond, the casino ceiling reflected the

French roots of her family, coffered with Baroque detailing, spotted throughout with recessed lighting and security cameras.

Impressed, she wandered through the casino, admiring the brilliant gold of the slot machines and the spotless poker tables filled with colored chips and crisp white cards. Beautiful women adorned in dazzling, sapphire blue dresses roamed around her, serving drinks to patrons and smiling at every turn.

She passed by one of the blackjack tables, her eyes on the table itself as she watched the dealer pass out cards and accept cash bets, tucking the bills neatly into a slot in the table where they disappeared underneath. Fascinated, she paused a few feet away and took in the entire game as it was played, her eyes following every movement made by the players, but most importantly by the dealer.

He had efficient hands, quick and deft with cards, cash, and chips. It amazed her to see the way he moved, the gold cufflinks on his crisp white dress shirt sparkling in the light that illuminated the table.

She smiled as her gaze drifted upward, eager to take in the rest of this man, to study him further. The way he moved...it was the most incredible thing she had ever witnessed. As her eyes rose to his face, a jolt went through her as she noted he was staring at her as well. Those eyes of molten steel, intense and fearless, caught her own and held. A trickster's grin played over his lips as he turned his attention back to the players. Her heart that had momentarily stopped began to suddenly beat again.

Centering herself with a deep, controlled breath, she continued on, though her eyes stayed locked on the dealer. When he looked up to watch her again, she made sure to be the one who turned away. But not before sending him a smoldering look she knew could stop a man's heart at twenty paces. She didn't wait around to see his reaction, but instead moved on and nearly ran straight into her cousin.

"Ah, you've arrived." Duke smiled warmly, holding his arms out in greeting. She embraced him, pleasure in her eyes as she pulled away.

"I see you've been dancing with the Devil down here in Vegas, cousin," she mused, one eyebrow raised teasingly. "I can already tell I'm going to fit right in."

"Yes, they don't call it the Devil's playground for nothing." He chuckled, draping an arm over her shoulders companionably. "Let me show you around, honey. I'll show you how we do things here in the southwest."

"I can hardly wait." She looked up at her cousin, admiring his intelligent blue eyes and handsomely tanned face, framed by meticulously styled dark waves of hair. He reminded her, in many ways, of her brother Linc with his limitless charm and sociable nature. The only difference she could see was that, by contrast with her jeans-wearing, beer-drinking brother, Duke had undeniable class. From his expensive designer shoes to his perfectly pressed black slacks, he exuded importance. With the several hundred dollar watch on his wrist and the crisp, sky blue dress shirt he wore, he demanded attention.

While she could admire the end result, she found the superficiality of it too shallow for her taste. Having been raised by men of substance, it would be interesting to go head-to-head with a man who clearly prioritized his appearance over his job. Then again, he was forty years old with a new wife. Perhaps married life would weed out the bad parts of his nature.

"As you know, our grandfather had this casino first commissioned in 1974," Duke began, admiring their surroundings proudly. "The hotel has undergone three renovations since then, the most recent just two years ago when we expanded into an all inclusive resort. Cyrus demanded that we be the biggest, tallest, and most luxurious casino on the Strip. And so it was done."

"It's beautiful," Madison said, her eyes drinking their fill as she took in the casino fully. "I'm proud to be a part of it now."

"You'll love it here." Duke grinned down at her with a wink. "This city has it all, honey. It grips you by the throat and doesn't let you go. You'll never get lonely and you'll never be hungry for a thrill."

As he spoke they passed by the blackjack tables, and she couldn't resist chancing another look at the dealer. He was busy entertaining some guests, his smile quick and brilliant, his long, bronzed hair framing a face more ruggedly handsome than any she had ever seen.

She knew, then and there, that by the end of the night she would know him. She would accept nothing less.

"Duke, I'd love to play a game of blackjack." Madison smiled, pulling him toward the table casually. "I've never played before."

"If you'd like," Duke replied happily. As they came up to the table and Madison slid into one of the empty seats, he held out his hand to the dealer in greeting. "How's it going, Wyatt?"

"Just fine, sir." The dealer nodded, shaking his boss' hand. "Should I let Sharon know that I spotted you with another woman?"

Duke burst into laughter, his hand companionably resting on Madison's shoulder. "That won't be necessary. This is my cousin, Madison. She's here from New York to help manage the restaurants." He turned his attention back to Madison. "Honey, this is Wyatt Bailey, one of our best dealers."

"One of? I'm hurt, Duke. I thought I was your favorite." Wyatt grinned with a wink before turning his attention to the young woman before him with the dark witchy eyes and vixen smile. "You're a long way from home, sweetheart. You miss New York?"

"Not yet," she told him, her eyes intent on his. "Show me how the game is played, Mr. Bailey. I'm eager to learn."

"I'll bet you are." Wyatt held her gaze as he began shuffling a deck of cards for a new game, his hands effortlessly cruising over the green felt table.

She couldn't help but lower her eyes to watch his movements, captivated. He continued to watch her as he dealt out one card face down, and another face up directly in front of her. She noted the visible card was a ten of spades.

Madison looked up to him for instruction, unsure what to do.

"Take a peek at the upside down card. The goal is for the cards to add up to twenty-one. You can request a third card—a hit—from me, although if you go over twenty-one you lose."

Tilting her card up carefully, she noted it was a five of hearts. Her eyes lifted back to his, her lips curving.

"Hit me."

He found he had to discreetly clear the lump from his throat, a direct result from the blatant sexuality she put into her voice, into her every movement. She was a walking wet-dream. And she was the cousin of his boss, which meant he would be wise to tread lightly where she was concerned.

Sliding a third card smoothly out from the deck, he slapped it down in front of her. When she saw it was a six of diamonds, she couldn't help the excited laugh that bubbled out of her throat.

"I won!" She turned over her hidden card, showing him. Turning to her cousin, she smiled. "Too bad I didn't bet anything."

Duke laughed, patting her on the back cheerfully. "You'd rob the house with luck like that, huh, Wyatt?"

"Indeed." Wyatt gathered her cards and shuffled them back into the deck, his expression amused and a bit strained as he watched her. "That's the curse of Vegas, sweetheart. Beginner's luck makes a gambler of us all."

"If that's true, then you can expect me back tomorrow for round two, Mr. Bailey." She slipped off the chair and hooked her arm in her cousin's, smiling deviously at the dealer once again. "Until then."

Wyatt nodded, watching as his boss led the girl away. He couldn't tear his eyes away from her, haunted by the very way she moved, by the way those lips of hers curved like a demon or an angel, he wasn't sure which. The worst of it was, he wondered if she understood just what impact that sultry look of hers had on a man…

It certainly had an effect on him. It had been years since he'd felt that for a woman, and he'd seen his fair share of them all over the world. None of them could even come close to comparing to her.

Despite the good angel standing on his right shoulder begging him to leave it be, reminding him that she was a Vasser and therefore off limits if he wanted to keep his job complication-free, the bad devil on his left shoulder demanded that he find a way to have her, come hell or high water. He'd always been fond of taking the Devil's advice anyway.

VASSER HOTEL
APRIL 2011

Grant sat back tiredly in his desk chair and wondered when exactly his office had become the Vasser Hotel's complaint department, eagerly awaiting submissions. As if he hadn't had enough to deal with, now he had his cousins trying to convince him to turn against his own sister. The depravity of it grated on his nerves. Clearly, they did not know who they were dealing with.

"I understand your concerns, but they're pointless," Grant told the two men before him impatiently. He held his great-grandfather's fountain pen in his hands, running it through his fingers absently. It was something he usually did when dealing with people he didn't want to deal with.

"I fundamentally do not agree with this list, Grant," Duke began, rising to his feet to pace the room in frustration. "If I were in charge—"

"But you're not in charge," Grant asserted, his eyes narrowing. "Madison is."

"Yeah and she's fucking everything up," Cy put in with a scowl, his arms crossed tightly as he slouched in the chair across from Grant. "I don't care what the goddamn will said, she's not my boss."

"She is, and if you want to maintain your position in this company as we move forward, you will follow her instruction." Grant sighed, feeling a headache coming on. "What do either of you expect me to say? I wasn't thrilled with this arrangement at first, but it is what it is. We have no choice."

"There are ways to open up our options..." Duke muttered, continuing to pace. Before he could elaborate, the door opened and Quinn poked her head in.

"Sorry to interrupt...Madison called and said she's running late from her appointment with the lawyers. She's on her way now."

Grant nodded to her, attempting a smile. "Thank you."

Quinn winked with a grin as she shut the door, enclosing Grant with his two cousins once more.

"She's a cute one," Cy said suddenly, looking from the door to Grant with a sleazy grin.

"She's taken," Grant asserted stiffly, disgusted by the look in his cousin's eyes.

"Wait, are you tappin' that?" Cy asked, eyes widening. When Grant said nothing, he let out a hoot of laughter and settled back into his chair. "Well, damn. Lucky bastard."

"Is that seriously all you can think about?" Duke demanded, confronting Cy impatiently. "If you're just here to get laid then you can hightail it back to L.A. I don't have the patience for this. We have serious business to figure out and you're sniffing after women."

Cy glared up at his cousin bitterly. "I'm not leaving till you leave, Duke. We both have a stake in what happens with the company now, and despite what you may think I do in fact give a damn."

"Well, then start acting like it," Duke growled as he sat back down, rubbing his face with his hands. He was tired, damn tired, and wanted nothing more than a stiff drink.

Grant silently watched his cousins, mentally wishing he had a gun to put to his temple at that very moment. It was painful to deal with their pettiness, their frustration and blatant chauvinism. They were both trying to bully their way to the top, and understanding that fact made him instantly sick of both of them.

At that moment, Madison swept into the office, filling the room instantly with the scent of her perfume. She paused by the door, taking in the sight of her irritated cousins and furious brother.

"Sorry I'm late." She shut the door behind her and continued toward Grant's desk, setting her purse down on its surface. "What did I miss?"

"Not much," Grant grunted, staring up at her cynically. "How did it go with the lawyers?"

"Fine. We will begin the corporatization process in three weeks."

"Seriously? I thought we were taking time to talk this over?" Cy burst out angrily.

"We are. That doesn't change the outcome." She rested her hip against Grant's desk and crossed her arms.

"You want to know what I think?" Duke said suddenly, rising to his feet again and approaching Madison, his handsome face marred with stress and resentment. He pointed his index finger at her, dark anger in his eyes. "You're going to drive this company straight into the ground. You can't handle this, honey, and we all know it. You're too damn young!"

"And you're blinded by jealousy," Madison countered, attempting to keep her voice level despite the enraged emotions rioting inside of her. "You hate that I've been given this opportunity instead of you."

"Damn right I do," Duke muttered, backing away from her. "We go way back, cousin, but that doesn't change anything. If I'm going to be forced to follow you, then you can bet I won't go easily."

He stormed out of the office. Madison watched him go, a fresh chip cracking in her heart.

No, he wasn't that man she'd known all those years before. He'd let himself become consumed by bitterness.

WHEN DARKNESS FELL over the city, Madison sought comfort in the one place she knew she could always find it. *Cherir.*

She interrupted Raoul while he was cleaning up for the day and without a word wrapped her arms around him. He held onto her, startled by her easy affection.

"What is wrong, *cariño*?"

Madison inhaled deeply as she pulled away, her eyes dry despite the sorrow and confusion mulling deep within her heart. She had only ever cried once around him, and that was years ago now. She didn't intend on reliving that experience.

"I hate men," she confessed with a dark laugh. "Except for you, darling. You would never hurt me."

"Who hurt you?" Raoul demanded, fury rising in a hot flash as his temper flared. She reached out to grab his arm before he could take off in search of the perpetrator, her eyes sparkling with pride.

"My gallant knight..." she mused, watching him fondly. "I don't need you to fight my battles for me. I only came down here to vent."

"A knight defends his queen." He frowned, leading her to a nearby bench so they could sit. "Tell me."

"Duke has become quite the asshole," she announced, resting her head on his shoulder with a sigh. "He hates me."

"No, it is not hate in his heart. It is just jealousy."

"Close enough." She shut her eyes tightly, willing back the misery she felt over the whole situation. Despite the isolation she felt from her family and the pressure to succeed, she had little doubt that she could do it. But lately with her grief still simmering under the surface of her cool reserve, she was having a hard time keeping her emotions at bay. "I didn't ask for this, Raoul."

"I know," he murmured, caressing her hair gently. For a long moment he said nothing, lost in his own dark thoughts. When he spoke again, she noted that his voice had taken on a sharp, acidic edge. "I saw Wyatt Bailey sniffing around this place earlier today. Are you staying clear of him, *cariño*? Or do I need to chase him away for you?"

She laughed, her cynical nature rejoicing at the irony of the whole situation. "I don't know what he's doing here. Feel free to chase him off."

"Are you seeing him again?" Raoul asked, snuffing out her laughter in one rapid beat. She pulled away and stared at him incredulously.

"Of course not. I'm not a fool." She shot to her feet, restless irritation in her eyes as she began to pace. "He's up to something, I just haven't figured it out yet."

Raoul was quiet, choosing his next words carefully. "He is dangerous, *cariño*. Stay away from him."

She paused, staring down at him with stone cold resolve in her eyes. "Did you really think I planned to do otherwise?"

When he said nothing, she turned and left the kitchen, even more volatile than when she had entered.

Raoul buried his face in his hands and cursed whatever sick twist of fate it was that had brought Wyatt Bailey to New York.

FIVE

I never liked this damn city," Cy grumbled, gazing around with bored eyes at the elegantly dressed high society patrons who enjoyed dinner in *Cherir*. He much preferred the Hollywood crowd back in L.A., the leisure-rich with trouble free laughter and a laundry list of expensively dirty vices.

Regardless of his distaste for the atmosphere, he relaxed in the corner booth seat with his arms draped over the back rest casually. The crimson dress shirt he wore was deliberately unbuttoned at the top, the sleeves rolled up to his elbows in pure defiance of the northeastern pretentiousness of the establishment itself.

Across the table from him, Duke knocked back the rest of the Maker's Mark whiskey in his glass, just as tired of New York as his cousin was. He held the glass up impatiently to catch the eye of the waitress before setting it down with a thump on the table. "The city is the least of our problems."

Cy snickered, turning his attention from the dinner crowd and back to Duke. "So what do you suggest we do? The old-timers are getting antsy. They've been hanging out, heads together, conspiring about something most likely. Maybe they'll just kill the bitch."

Duke let out a dark laugh as the waitress dropped off more whiskey. He took another sip and sat up a bit straighter, his eyes hardening as he registered the weight behind the statement. He held up his glass and pointed a finger at his cousin decisively. "We can't make any brash decisions here. If we're going to stop her, we have to be clever about it."

"And do what?" Cy demanded, reaching for his vodka tonic and sloshing it around irritably. "Let's face it, she's steamrolled us and there's nothing we can do about it."

Duke leaned back comfortably, lifting his drink to his mouth before he spoke. "We'll see about that."

His eyes shot over his cousin's shoulder then as he watched a man in faded jeans, a black t-shirt and a black fedora stroll into the restaurant. When they made eye contact, the man froze for the briefest of seconds. Surprise registered over his face before it was quickly replaced with easy confidence.

As the man walked toward them, Duke's smile sharpened. "I'd heard you were slinking around, Wyatt. I wasn't sure the rumors were true."

Wyatt stopped before their table, hands tucked neatly into the pockets of his jeans. The gesture of a handshake with these two went radically against his conscience. As a steadfast rule, he didn't shake the hands of men he didn't trust.

"I seem to inspire many rumors," Wyatt said easily. "Then again, so do the Vassers."

Duke snorted out a laugh, though it was filled with anything but humor. "The affairs of my family are none of your business. I thought you knew that by now?"

"And here I thought you considered me part of the family," Wyatt replied dryly, turning to Cy when the other man started laughing.

"What are you even *doing* here, Bailey?" Cy asked in between laughs, shaking his head. "Are you seriously trying to get with our cousin again? I'm pretty sure that ship sailed when you left Vegas all those years ago. Though you're much better off, in my opinion."

Wyatt only continued to smile, his nonchalant attitude visibly irritating Duke—which was, of course, the plan. If he was going to talk with those bastards, he was going to have fun doing it. "You sure can read me like a book, Cy."

Cy rolled his eyes, then lifted his drink in a mock toast. "Whatever the specifics, we're all here because of that woman. She always was great at making men fall to their knees and submit."

"Lesser men pale in the shadow of greatness," Wyatt replied, his expression darkening as his eyes took on a sharper edge. He stared at both men, the easy humor fading to reveal his true loathing. It took them a moment to adjust to his swift change of mood, and he enjoyed the apprehension on their faces as he leaned closer, resting his hands on the table so he could meet their eyes evenly. "If she doesn't squash you like the bugs you are, then you can bet I will."

Duke recovered first with an arrogant smile. "You should go say hello to Raoul. He's probably back there in the kitchen right now."

Wyatt stiffened, an old hatred exploding through him. He avoided the instinctive urge to glance toward the kitchen and instead tipped his hat as he straightened, his mask of relaxed indifference sliding smoothly back into place.

"Maybe next time. See you around, gentlemen."

He turned and left, his gait languid despite the toxic exchange. He imagined the looks of hatred on their faces as he made his way through the lobby and straight into the hotel's upscale bar, *Amoureux*.

They would be wise to remember that he wasn't afraid to do what had to be done to protect the only woman he had ever loved. Unfortunately for them, he intended to stick around for awhile to keep an eye on things.

If they made a move, any sort of move, in a direction that would hurt Madison, then he would kill them.

He wandered up to the crowded bar, flagging down the bartender with an impatient wave of his hand. Around him, some kind of European rock music was playing. Its techno beat blasted through the lofty, high-ceilinged room with a heavy bass intended to up the pulse and drown patrons in liquid emotion. From the look of the women who sauntered by and eyed him, he knew its effect was in full swing.

But he could care less about any of them. Sure, he could find himself a willing female to distract himself with, but he knew it would be anything but satisfying because she wouldn't be the one woman he wanted. The one woman he had never been able to forget, who he happened to know was upstairs, working late. The temptation to go to her was choking him like a noose.

He ordered a shot of Patron and a Heineken; the shot he downed eagerly at the bar, the beer he took with him as he made his way toward the back where an empty table waited. He had barely settled into a seat when someone joined him.

"You still drinking that crap?" Linc asked with a grin, nodding at the beer Wyatt held.

Wyatt's smile was immediate and instinctive, his mood almost instantly improved. "Beats whatever you're drinking these days."

Linc glanced down at his bottle of Corona and shrugged. "Still an improvement." He held it up cheerfully in a toast that Wyatt accepted, their bottles tapping together merrily. "To the shit always managing to hit the fan right when we're standing in front of it."

Wyatt chuckled, taking a long pull from his beer before setting it down on the table, his eyes darkly amused. "Couldn't have said it better myself."

As Linc settled into his chair and relaxed, he eyed Wyatt with a mixture of curiosity and nostalgia. He noted the man was in some sort of mood and pondered over the source of it.

There had been a time, long ago, when they had been relatively close friends. They'd gambled together, shared memorable stories over a twelve-pack of beer, gone hiking and fishing in the Sierra Nevada Mountains. But even as he sat there and watched his old friend, Linc realized he had no real idea why the man was still in New York. In fact, he was still incredibly surprised that Wyatt had shown up at all.

Wyatt had always possessed a self-serving, wanderlust nature, which Linc blamed for him leaving Madison all those years before. It had been easier to assume that Wyatt had merely wanted out, and Linc wasn't the kind to hold grudges the way Grant or Madison did.

But now...well, Linc remembered distinctly what had happened the night of the fundraiser and on the day of Cyrus' funeral. Wyatt had been there, both times, undoubtedly to see Madison. Linc knew he'd have to be blind to have missed the rekindling of whatever it was that had been between his sister and his friend.

But what did it all mean? With everything else happening with the family, Linc knew this issue wasn't entirely important. Yet he couldn't beat back his desire to know what was going on. He just had to hope Wyatt would tell him the truth.

"The cops confirmed that there was PCP laced with the weed my dad had on the night he died," Linc began, hedging his bets and starting at a point he knew was common ground between them. "Jorja's been making the rounds on the talk shows, blaming me, Mads, the fucking hotel, Grant's dog..."

Wyatt laughed, his free hand snaking its way through his bronzed hair. "She's a real piece of work, isn't she?"

Linc snorted derisively, suddenly wishing for something stronger to drink. As a waitress passed by, he quickly flagged her down and ordered two double shots of tequila. When the waitress walked off, he turned back to Wyatt and sneered. "That damn actress has been the bane of my existence ever since she weaseled her way into my life."

"If I remember right, the tabloids showed you all too willingly weaseling your way under her skirt at that bar on the West Side," Wyatt mused, taking another sip of beer. "Or am I mistaken?"

Linc winced, shuddering at the memory. "What was I thinking?"

"You mean, what was your *cock* thinking?"

"That too." Linc paused as the waitress dropped off the shot glasses filled to the brim with top-shelf tequila. He nudged one at Wyatt and then lifted his own in a second toast.

This time, Wyatt chimed in before Linc could decide what to toast to. "To the gorgeous redhead you've managed to capture. Thank God she replaced that Hollywood bitch."

"Amen, brother." Linc's face lit with a bright grin as he knocked back the shot. He dropped the glass down upon the table cheerfully, already feeling much better about pretty much everything. Which led, of course, to a prompt loosening of his tongue and a swift loss of tact. "Alright, Bailey, I have to know. What's going on between you and my sister?"

To his surprise, Wyatt burst out laughing, shaking with it as he leaned over the table. When he felt the dark amusement begin to fade, he lifted his eyes to meet his friend's. "I was wondering how long it was going to take you to ask me about that."

Linc shrugged lightly. "I don't like to pry, but I'm a bit worried for you."

"Worried?"

"She's got a lot on her plate right now. I don't know if you being here is necessarily a good thing for her," Linc admitted, wanting to be honest. "With the scandal and all the death that's been going on around here...she's under a lot of pressure to keep everything together. The last thing she needs is to dwell on the past."

Wyatt's eyes narrowed, but he kept his temper in check. "I'm not here to rehash the past, Linc. I'm here to help her."

"But that's just it." Linc frowned, trying to find a way to explain it. "If you really wanted to help her, you'd leave."

"I can't do that," Wyatt asserted, leaning back in his chair now and watching his friend cagily. "I want to get her back."

Linc stared at him for a moment, acknowledging that this wasn't a surprise and yet he still found himself stunned by it. "But you left her."

"I didn't *leave* her." Eyes hardened to bitter steel, Wyatt stared down at the beer in his hands as he came to terms with the emotions roiling inside of him at that moment. The hate, the fury, the violence... the helplessness. The loss. "I saved her from something that would have destroyed her."

Linc blinked at his friend's ominous admission, unsure he'd heard him right. "Saved her from what, exactly?"

Wyatt looked up with an edgy smile. "One day, maybe I'll tell you. Today's not that day." He rose to his feet and patted Linc on the back before slinking out of the bar.

Linc stared after him in bewilderment. What in the *world* had the man meant?

WHEN HE STORMED into her office, she feigned annoyed surprise. She had to do something, anything, to counter what she felt just at the sight of him. He looked dark, dangerous, and downright mean.

"What do you want, Wyatt?" Madison asked, eyeing him imperiously.

Instead of answering her, he slammed her office door shut and approached her desk, shoving his hands into the pockets of his jeans sourly. "I want to talk to you."

"Well, I don't want to talk to you," she replied effortlessly, already reaching for the phone on her desk. "Leave before I call security."

He laughed at her—dark, cynical laughter that shivered through her bones and set off warning signals in her brain. He was in one of his moods, a mood she'd long ago known how to ride out, how to embrace, how to tame. But now, with all that stood between them, all the tension and the madness and the bitterness...what would happen to her now if she attempted to brave the flames?

"Why is it always threats between us, sweetheart?" He began to pace before her desk, filled to the brim with volatile and restless energy. His conversation with Linc just minutes before had riled him up, had released the beast within him that was eager for a fight. And he had some hefty punches to throw before he went down.

Madison stared at him, hating him for still having this hold over her. Hating herself for not being able to let go. "Must I ask you again, Wyatt? What are you doing in New York? Why won't you just leave me alone?"

He stopped and turned, those eyes that had always haunted her filled with both longing and rage. Rage over what came between them, what had destroyed the only good thing he'd ever known.

"I came to New York to help Win, but I'll be damned if I leave without making you realize that what's between us isn't over."

Madison's heart jolted and ached, and she struggled to maintain some semblance of control. Her gaze held his, intense and feral, as she said the first words that came to her mind, to her heart. "How can I trust you?"

He hesitated, the brutal storm within him simmering as he acknowledged her question, digested it, understood it. He accepted the challenge that he would have to earn back her trust, and that it may be an impossible task. It was worth every risk he faced to accomplish it.

"The night before Cyrus' funeral, when I told you that I still loved you, did you believe me?"

She bit back a curse and avoided his eyes, the memory of that moment consuming her with fiery grief. She knew she wasn't over him, had known for awhile now.

What she felt for Wyatt was, and had always been, an explosive, greedy longing that tore through her like a horrible storm. While her shattered heart demanded answers for his sudden desertion all those years ago, it was also bursting with this intense love that had never gone away. She knew it never would.

In the end, though, her natural instinct for self-preservation over-rode any other desire. Trusting him could very well be her downfall, and she put her duty to her family's business over everything else.

Saying nothing, she shook her head.

He could tell she was lying to him, could see it on her face. His admission had shaken her deeply, and knowing that fact quelled some of the restlessness plaguing his spirit.

"I can be patient," he told her, his voice oddly level and calm now. "You'll come to me, sweetheart. And when you do, we can have a real conversation and move past all of this."

Before she could find any words to say to him, he left, leaving her office door wide open. Her mouth fell open and her breath came out in a shuddering rasp as her emotions boiled over to claim her, cloaking her in spontaneous desperation. No, this time he wasn't going to get away from her. Not after that, not after ripping out her heart and shoving it back into her face, forcing her to examine her own feelings for him that had never faded, never died.

Jumping out of her chair, she swept from her office and out into the hallway, spotting him standing just outside the elevator, patiently waiting a ride up to his floor. She stalked up to him and grabbed the collar of his shirt, pulling him in aggressively and crushing his mouth

with her own. Without hesitation he responded to her, his hands sliding over her back and grasping at her hair, letting her wild emotions
rule his own.

Relief gripped his heart like a fist and then let go, releasing him.

The answering wave of passion that poured out of him should
have frightened her. Instead it only caused hers to rear up and
match his own, just as it had the many times before when they'd
come together.

She cried out as he suddenly shoved her up against the wall in
between two of the elevators, her back pressing into the buttons so
the lights illuminated behind her. Around them, the entire floor was
dimly lit and silent, the work day long over and the others all gone. It
was just them, and their urgency.

He dragged at her clothes, consumed by the madness she sparked
within him, the complete and utter loss of all control. It was a sensation he welcomed, one he reveled in and had missed with a desperation he couldn't explain. When he pulled away so he could stare into
her eyes, seeing the amber in them hot and bright with desire, he tore
down the walls of his heart and bared it to her.

"I need you to believe me, Madison," he grunted, his hands gripping her waist, his fingers digging into her flesh and sending her mind
reeling with a dark and primal need.

Her head fell back against the wall as she smiled, the movement
of her lips red-hot and sinful. Her laugh was vivid and real, deep and
untamed, as her eyes met his once again. "Convince me, Wyatt. It
better be damn good."

She kissed him again as the elevator doors to their right slid open.
She dragged him inside with her, throwing him against the back wall
as the doors shuttered closed.

SIX

Like clockwork, each day he rose before the sun. His entire life had been built upon this same structure, rising at dawn and beginning work before the first rays even crested over the city skyline.

But these days, Grant found himself lingering in bed just a little bit longer, stalling just a few more minutes so he could savor these brief moments. Moments when he could watch her sleep, tendrils of her hair falling over her face and her lips curved into a peaceful smile as she dreamed. He brushed at her hair, his fingers sliding gently over the skin of her cheek as he leaned in to kiss her. It wasn't his intent to wake her, but he couldn't help himself. When she was lying beside him like this, it took every last ounce of practicality in his bones to convince himself to get out of bed and leave her.

Quinn's smile deepened as she felt his lips over her own, her mind waking from the haze of sleep. Her eyes slowly opened and met his, the room around them lit only by the dim, early morning glow filtering in through the windows.

She leaned into the kiss, her eyes closing again as she reveled in this moment of both dreamy slumber and blissful consciousness.

He slowly moved over her, pinning her beneath his body as the heat began to flood through his system, the burning need for her he couldn't shake. His sudden urgency jolted her into awareness, startling her awake as she responded to him, matching his need with her own. Her hands grasped at his bare back, her heart beginning to race as his mouth cruised over her neck, then back to claim her lips once again.

When his cell phone alarm went off, he grunted and had the violent thought of throwing the device out the window. But Quinn gently pushed him away, her gypsy eyes warm as she grinned.

"Duty calls, Mr. Vasser," she reminded him playfully, biting her lower lip as she watched him reach over to grab his phone and turn off the alarm. The muscles beneath his long, lean torso and arms shifted with the movement, and she had to bite back the urge to keep him with her, warm and safe in his bed.

But no, his life didn't allow for that. He was needed by his family, by his hotel, and she wasn't selfish enough to keep him from them.

He tossed his phone back on the nightstand impatiently and returned to her, frustrated heat in his eyes as he immediately resumed what he had been doing before the interruption. She giggled against him and then gasped when he nipped the tender spot beneath her left ear with his teeth.

"I need to get out of bed," he groaned, tightening his hand in her hair and kissing her again, still unsatisfied.

"You do," she panted as she held him closer, enjoying the sensation of his hands cruising over her skin. "You have that meeting with Senator Shaw."

He pulled away from her with a grimace. "That is today, isn't it?"

She nodded, reaching out to smooth the frown lines from his brow as she smiled. "Linc needs you for this. It's important."

"I know." Grant sighed, resting his forehead against hers as his eyes closed. "When he showed me those text messages, I couldn't believe what I was seeing. For a sitting senator to threaten this way..."

"That's why you're going to get to the bottom of it today," Quinn said cheerily, wanting to see him smile. "I'm sure it's all just some big misunderstanding."

He opened his eyes and stared at her, humbled as always by her sunny optimism. "I hope you're right."

He kissed her one last time before he slid out of bed, imagining the cold shower he was going to have to take to cool the heat still rushing through his system.

Before he could disappear into the bathroom, she called out to him.

"I almost forgot. Linc asked me to find out the name of Senator Shaw's opponent, he thought it might be important."

Grant turned around to face her, rubbing the back of his neck. "What is it?"

"Jack Morgan. He and his father were both in the Army." She shrugged, hugging her knees to her chest beneath the blankets. "That was all I was able to find out."

MADISON OPENED THE door to Wyatt's suite as carefully as she could, praying that it not make a sound. She knew he had ears like a damn hawk, but the last thing she wanted to do was wake him.

In any event, she didn't know if she had the nerve to face him. The one thing she had promised herself, promised Raoul, wouldn't happen had at last occurred.

She knew she shouldn't be surprised. Sex was a purely healthy and natural urge to have and no man had ever attracted her the way Wyatt did. But if she had thought he was a complication just by hanging around, he was an even greater complication if she decided to continue on as his lover.

Thinking of the night before, of how his words had shattered through her steel heart and revealed the stunning, bleeding mess within, had her breath catching in her throat. Dizzying emotions whirled through her like a firestorm, whipping up every past fear and desperate longing. She paused before the cracked open door, needing to center herself, to regain some measure of control. It felt as though the world were crumbling down upon her very head.

Wyatt Bailey had done it again. He'd reopened her wounds and made her remember loving him, what it had felt like, been like. She couldn't help but despise him for it.

When she felt him come up behind her, she fought back the instantaneous desire to take a violent swipe at him.

"Can't you see I'm trying to leave?" she snarled, whirling around to face him just as he pushed the door shut behind her.

"I *can* see that." A grin twitched over his mouth as he folded his arms over his bare chest, his legs covered with jeans, lazily unbuttoned.

She rolled her eyes in an attempt to avoid looking at him. To avoid remembering the enjoyment she had gotten running her hands over his body after all these years. "I have to get home."

Instead of answering her, he pushed her up against the door and kissed her, needing to feel her yielding to him. He had to feel her give in, just as she did the night before...

"What's your hurry, sweetheart?" he asked, his voice thick with need as he ran his hands down her sides, taking her in with all of his senses.

"I have to work." Her eyes fluttered closed as she felt her knees giving out, her heart thudding with vivid hot pain and desire at his touch. She felt her anger building to match the passion and used it as she shoved him purposefully away from her. "Stop it."

He glared at her, a dark shadow haunting his face as he realized they were falling back into the same old game. It came as naturally to them as breathing did. "I'm not going away this time. You can count on that."

She stared into his eyes, wanting to believe him and yet still so wary. He was virtually a stranger to her...what did she really know of his intentions? He got off on toying with people, on manipulating and twisting circumstances to suit his own needs. She knew that because she did it herself. But when two people of that same, carelessly cruel nature came together...well, it was quite simply volatile.

And damn it all if she didn't get off on that, too.

She smiled slowly as she changed tactics, stepping toward him and reaching up to grab the back of his neck and yank his mouth down to hers. She kissed him wildly, pouring all of the dark, vivid emotions she felt into the act, knowing it would unsettle him. Knowing it was the one thing he could not overcome, could not resist.

As she broke the kiss and backed away, the light caught her eyes, disarming him and nearly knocking the very breath from his lungs.

There she was, the same girl he'd met at his blackjack table in Vegas, the vixen with those glorious honeyed eyes. The memory of it hit him like a crushing wave, and the misery it brought stifled him.

Oblivious to his pain, she smiled and patted his cheek. "It's been fun, darling."

She turned on her heel and strolled from the room, swiftly shutting the door at her back. Wyatt stared after her, his blood a furiously raging river in his veins.

Somehow, in the years since he had last seen her, she had learned how to always leave with the upper hand.

He didn't know whether to be proud or alarmed by that fact.

LINC WAS ON edge, his movements erratic and his mind clearly distracted. Grant walked beside him as they strolled down the block to the restaurant where Shaw had agreed to meet them.

Even with his brother's presence, Linc couldn't shake the uneasiness he felt. The hostility.

The man had threatened his family, after all. And potential future father-in-law or not, Linc wasn't going to let Shaw get away with words of ominous violence, even if they were just in a text message.

It had taken several phone calls to Shaw's office before the man agreed to even speak to him. Even though Linc would have been content with an explanation over the phone, Shaw objected. Apparently, whatever conversation he wanted to have with Linc was dangerous enough that it couldn't risk being overheard, even by his own staff.

Which only caused Linc to question the whole scenario even further. What was Lynette's father's angle in all of this? Was his only intention to prevent his daughter from further involvement with the Vassers for his own selfish political reasons? Or was there something more to the story?

Clearly the man knew something. Unless he made a habit of declaring that hell was coming to people's families just for the fun of it.

"You'll need to resist the urge to throw the first punch," Grant said suddenly as they came up to the broad glass doors of the restaurant.

Linc glanced up at his brother with a cynical grin. "I promise to be on my best behavior."

Grant nodded and held open the door for an elderly couple to pass through on their way out. "Good. We don't know who may be watching us."

"What, like the press?" Linc asked, keeping his voice down as they walked inside.

Grant scanned the crowded dining room for Shaw. "Maybe."

"Who else, then?"

Spotting Shaw in the back corner of the restaurant, Grant patted his brother on the shoulder. "I'm not sure. Just be careful what you say."

Linc snorted as they began to weave their way through the tables toward the back. "Why do you assume that *I'm* the one who's going to say something brash? Everyone knows you're the loud mouth of the family."

Grant shot him a wry look just as they came up to Shaw's table.

Senator Warren Shaw rose to his feet respectfully, holding out his hand. "Nice to see you again, Grant. Linc."

"You as well, Senator." Grant accepted the handshake, looking the man in the eye purposefully as he did so. The senator looked confident, headstrong and capable. Not quite what Grant had expected from a man who'd sent desperate and threatening text messages foretelling the end of the Vasser family.

Linc shook Shaw's hand next, the movement more than a little combative. "How's the Waldorf these days, Senator?"

Shaw's eyes lit with amusement as he smiled. "Just fine, Linc. I do miss the Vasser Hotel, though."

"I'm sure you do." Linc settled down into the chair beside Grant, with Shaw across from them. "I hear their concierge is a real asshole."

"I wouldn't really know. I just sleep in their beds," Shaw replied lightheartedly, taking a sip of the whiskey he'd been enjoying before they had arrived. "Get a drink, boys. This round's on me."

The waitress approached and Grant ordered a water with lemon while Linc asked for a Corona. Once they were alone again, Linc leaned back in his chair and eyed Shaw with intense distrust.

"So let's get right down to it, Senator. I want to know what you meant in that message you sent my girlfriend."

"You mean in the message I sent my *daughter*," Shaw corrected, eyes flashing with annoyance. He waved his hand in the air dismissively. "I still refuse to believe that whatever is happening between y'all is permanent."

Linc snorted out a derisive laugh, shaking his head. "Just answer the question."

Shaw's eyes shot from Linc to Grant, and he seemed to contemplate his next words carefully. "I'm afraid your family is smack-dab in the middle of a little political brawl. It's nothing personal, you see, but things are going to get a bit nasty."

"I don't understand," Grant interrupted. "If this has to do with your daughter's involvement with us, then wouldn't it be in your best interest to help us rather than hurt us? She's not going to stop seeing my brother, Senator. She's made that quite clear."

"Ah, yes I know that. She reminds me every day that she doesn't return my phone calls that she chose Linc over me," Shaw said with a resentful sigh, only to then lean over the table conspiratorially. "Understand this, boys. I'm not looking to hurt your family. The media and your own granddaddy have done that well enough already."

"Then why threaten us?" Linc charged, pausing only when the waitress dropped off their drinks. As she walked away, he took a long pull on the Corona. "I must be missing something really important here."

Shaw chuckled, his hands toying with his glass of whiskey and his eyes darting between them. "What I told my daughter was not a threat; it was a warning of what is to come."

"And what is to come?" Linc asked mockingly, despising the round-a-bout way the bastard was taking to get to the goddamn point.

"I don't know if you're aware of this, but my opponent—"

"Jack Morgan," Grant supplied, recalling the name Quinn had told him that morning.

"Why, yes. So you do know, then." Shaw looked at both of them for confirmation, but they only looked confused.

"Know what?" Linc asked, brow furrowing. "Is Morgan planning on using us against you? Does he have some attack ad that shows me and Lynette together or something? Because the public isn't going to give a shit about that."

"Oh, no. Well, he might try that, but I doubt it," Shaw corrected. "No, I suspect he'll try very hard to avoid discussing your family during campaign season. But I'm going to use every opportunity I have to bring the Vasser name into the conversation."

"Why?" Grant felt more than a little uneasy as he watched the confident way Shaw dangled this little carrot of information over their heads. It made him remember why he despised politicians.

Shaw continued, "Jack Morgan is the son of Paul Morgan, who was a part of the CID in the Army back in World War II." He paused, eyeing both men as though waiting for something to click.

Linc was only more frustrated. "That's great. What does that have to do with my family?"

"Paul Morgan has everything to do with your family, son," Shaw said slowly, his expression darkly humorous. "You see, he's the fella your grandma persuaded to cover up the murders of Cyrus' three brothers in the war. The murders Cyrus has since then admitted to doing. Before his death, of course."

For a moment, neither Grant nor Linc said anything. They glanced at each other, trying to process the weight of this new information, but it was clear that neither had expected anything like this.

"So...this Morgan guy was the one who buried the file?" Linc questioned.

"And you want to go public with this information," Grant concluded, staring pointedly at Shaw. "You want to go to the press and out Jack Morgan as the son of a liar and attempt to ruin his reputation. All the while focusing the media attention back on us and on your daughter."

"Lynette's dating life is much less damning politically than what I have on Morgan," Shaw said decidedly, smiling again. "I don't expect him to be able to recover from this."

"You really think people are gonna give a shit that his father was involved in a cover-up over sixty years ago?" Linc laughed, more disdain than humor in the sound. "I think your little dirt on your opponent is a bit dull, Senator. You really couldn't dig up a mistress or a drug problem somewhere?"

"Son, this all may seem a little silly to you. But to the voters back in the great state of South Carolina, we take government cover-ups quite seriously. This won't go over well for Morgan, I can assure you that."

"So why wait? Why haven't you come out with it already?" Linc demanded. "If this is such a big bombshell, why not use it?"

"Timing is everything in politics." Shaw shrugged off the comment carelessly, taking another sip of his drink. "I'm biding my time. Morgan knows that I know, and he's probably hoping I'll keep it under wraps because of Lynette. But he's quite mistaken."

Grant and Linc looked at each other again, clearly wondering the same thing. What was going to happen to their hotels when Shaw came out with this information—a month, three months, even a full year from then? It would surely rehash everything they were working to bury again. This would, as Shaw had so callously put it to Lynette, really bring hell to their family.

"I appreciate you meeting with us, Senator, but we really must get back to the hotel," Grant said suddenly, rising to his feet and extending his hand to Shaw. Linc got up as well, rubbing the back of his neck wearily as he watched his brother shake hands with the man who was cheerfully putting politics over their family's reputation. When Shaw reached out to shake Linc's hand in turn, Linc hesitated, meeting eyes with the man instead.

"I get what you're trying to do, Senator. I really do. And I don't blame you for trying to win your election. But I hope you think twice about what this is going to do to Lynette. She doesn't want us to be at war with each other, but if you go public with that information and consequently fuck over my family, I will consider that a declaration of war."

He accepted Shaw's hand, shaking it a bit harsher than normal.

"My daughter has decided to be in your care now, Linc. If anything happens to her, it will fall on you, not me." Shaw smiled and released Linc's hand. "It's just politics, son. Don't take it so personal."

"Enjoy the rest of your stay in the city," Grant cut in, placing his hand on Linc's shoulder in warning as he pulled his brother away from Shaw. The murderous look in Linc's eyes was not helping the situation.

As they turned and left the restaurant, Linc clenched his hands and shoved them into his pockets, his body vibrating with fury. Beside him, Grant felt more worry than anger, more apprehension than rage.

They pushed through the doors and out into the midday sunlight, neither noticing the unmarked, window-tinted van sitting across the street, the men inside carefully watching their every move.

SHE COOLED DOWN after the rehearsal, stretching her tired muscles on the smooth, wooden floor of the ballet studio. Her breathing began to slow, her heart settling back into its normal rhythm as she let her mind slip into the satisfied calm that always followed vigorous activity.

Lynette smiled to herself, her eyes closing as she began to relax. Her thoughts drifted to Linc and her heart filled beautifully.

Regardless of what was happening with her father and with the scandal Linc's family was facing, she knew without a doubt that these last few months had been the happiest of her life. At last, it seemed, she had nearly everything she had ever wanted. A rewarding career, a loving boyfriend, a new friend in Quinn...the only thing that seemed to be in chaos was her relationship with her parents. Funny how it seemed she had to give up the old things in her life in order to welcome the new and exciting. But, perhaps that was just the way it had to be.

And having Linc, the charming heir of the Vasser Hotel dynasty... well, that was enough to satisfy nearly every want, every need, every desire she had ever had.

But even he could not repair the broken pieces of her relationship with her family. In her eyes, it was easier to just ignore her father and move on, but Linc was insistent that there was something more to her father's words than she assumed.

The two had met with each other earlier that day. She had yet to hear from Linc just what her father had to say. Perhaps it had been, just as she supposed, nothing.

Contenting herself with that thought, she got to her feet and began to stretch her quad muscles.

Across the room, a few of her fellow ballerinas turned on the radio and began flipping through the stations, searching for music to listen to while they wrapped up for the night. Lynette was only half listening to them as she began to gather up her belongings, but when she heard her father's voice, she froze.

She blinked as she looked up, expecting to see him in the studio. Confused, she glanced around, only to realize that his voice was coming from the radio.

Before one of the girls could change the station again, Lynette rushed forward and silently stopped her. Her eyes widened as she listened in to what her father was saying.

"I've heard just this afternoon from a viable source within the Vasser family that it is Madison Vasser who is responsible for her father's death. Now I know some of y'all believe it to be a typical suicide, but my source tells me that the drugs Win Vasser had consumed the night of his death were altered in such a way as to make him crazy, which in turn is what killed him."

"Who is the source, Senator? And why are you getting involved?"

"My source insists on anonymity for obvious safety concerns, especially since Madison Vasser should be considered a suspect. And I was approached on this matter by the source, who had nowhere else to turn because they knew of my involvement—albeit distant—with the Vasser family."

"Your only daughter is dating Lincoln Vasser, is she not, Senator?"

"Yes, though my daughter has assured me that she has plans to leave New York City and return home soon. I don't expect the relationship to continue on after that."

As the host thanked him for coming on the show, the other girls turned and stared at Lynette with wide eyes, unsure what to make of what they had all just heard. She stood perfectly still, her lips parted in startled alarm as she stared at the radio.

How *dare* he, she thought wildly, suddenly clenching her fists at her sides as she filled with outrage. And who in the hell was this *source* he'd been talking to? And for what purpose had he gone public with such heinous lies about the Vassers?

She blinked back angry tears from her eyes, her mind reeling with disbelief at the madness of it all. After this, he'd be lucky if she ever even set foot in South Carolina again, much less to visit him. He could go straight to Hell.

Without a word to the others, she took off out of the studio, racing down the steps to the street and hailing a cab. When she was safely inside she told the driver to take her to the Vasser Hotel, then she let the tears of anger fall down her face.

The cab pulled up to the hotel several minutes later. She tossed some cash at the driver before tearing out of the car, her breath catching in her throat as she stumbled past the doorman at the entrance and made her way to the front desk.

Before she got there, a man she didn't recognize stopped her.

"Aren't you Linc's new girl?" Cy asked, visibly drunk and swaying on his feet. She eyed him with disdain and considered just pushing past him. But he stood purposely in her way, forcing her to address him.

"Yes, I am," she mumbled, knowing she looked like a train wreck with blotchy, tear stained cheeks and her hair frayed from rehearsal. "Please, I need to talk with him."

"Slow down, babe. What's your hurry?" Cy chuckled, reaching out to run his hand down her arm in a move that was decidedly flirtatious. "I'm his cousin, Cy. I run the Vasser Hotel in L.A. You ever been?"

"I hate California," she spat, irritation flavoring her tongue even though she didn't really mean the words behind it. "And don't touch me."

Instead of heeding her request, he moved in closer so he could place his hands on her waist. His breath stunk of liquor and his green eyes seemed lazy and unfocused as they met her own. "A Southern girl like you just doesn't get what L.A. is all about. You'll have to come on out and I'll show you a good time."

Before she could slip out of his grasp, Linc was throwing him off her with surprising strength, violent heat in his eyes.

"What the hell is wrong with you?" Linc roared, shoving Cy in the chest. Cy stumbled back, only to double over with hysterical laughter.

"So fucking *touchy*, slick. God, I was just talkin' with your girl. No harm, no foul," Cy said in between laughs, fighting to catch his breath.

Linc turned away from his cousin in disgust and went to Lynette, reaching up to touch her face gently. "Are you okay?"

She nodded, her body vibrating with adrenaline from the confrontation. Her voice was shaky as she spoke. "I have to talk to you."

"Okay." He leaned in to give her a quick kiss. "Just give me one moment."

He turned around and grabbed Cy by the collar of his shirt, pulling him in until they were eye to eye. "Blood or not, I'll kill you if you touch her again."

Cy waved off the threat easily, laughter still bubbling out of his throat. "Whatever, fine. I was just being friendly."

"Sure you were." Linc released him roughly, wishing they were in a more private setting so he could clock the bastard. As it was, there were already hotel guests staring curiously in their direction.

"You guys have been having all the fun up here in New York, Linc," Cy said abruptly with a markedly cagey smile. "I think it's about time you let the big boys take charge. You're a little out of your league, here."

"We've been over this. Madison is not stepping down," Linc growled, fists clenching at his sides.

Cy only continued to grin, the liquor giving his already loose tongue an even sharper bite. "After tonight, she may not have a choice."

"What the fuck is that supposed to mean?"

Lynette stepped forward, putting her hand on Linc's shoulder. "We need to talk, Linc. I know what he's talking about."

He tilted his head to look her in the eye, then turned back to his cousin. "Stay out of trouble, Cy. I mean it."

He wrapped his arm around Lynette and led her around the front desk and back to his office, where he shut the door and locked it. He motioned for her to sit down, then rested his hip against the edge of his desk.

"Alright, let's hear it."

Lynette let out a shaky breath as she nodded, only to suddenly scrunch her nose and stare around his tiny office. "Why does it smell like cigarettes in here?"

Linc snorted out a half laugh. "You don't want to know."

She frowned, but decided against pressing him on it. There were more important things to worry about at that moment. "So I was just at rehearsal, and one of the girls turned on the radio. I heard my father's voice and listened in...he was on one of the local talk shows, discussing your family."

"What did he say?"

Tears sprang into her eyes as she hesitated, unable to look at him any longer. Shame and guilt raced through her as she realized that if it hadn't been for her, her father would have never gotten involved.

"Lynette?" Worried by her silence, Linc reached out to tilt her face up to his, alarmed to see her tears. "What is it?"

"He claims that a source from within your family came to him with information...the source says that Madison is responsible for your father's death. That she tampered with the drugs he used that night. Then he said that he's spoken with me, and that I told him I plan on leaving New York."

A sob escaped her throat as she started crying, unable to help herself. Linc kneeled down before her and pulled her against him.

He absorbed her words as he listened to her cry, rage building within him like an awakened volcano.

So the man had been lying through his teeth when he'd said that he didn't intend to hurt his family, Linc thought indignantly. Clearly he intended to do whatever he could to destroy them, and in turn drive Lynette away.

The very nerve of it set his blood boiling, and it took all he had to not stand up and punch his fist right through the wall.

"It's all my fault," Lynette managed, her throat aching miserably as she buried her face in the crook of his neck, needing his comfort. "If I wasn't here, then he would have never had a reason to get involved."

"That's not true," Linc retorted heatedly, his mouth set in a grim line as he pulled her away so he could look at her. "This has nothing to do with you, Lynette."

"How is it not because of me?" She wiped at her tears, feeling embarrassed and ashamed. "I'm your only connection to him."

"Actually, you're not." Linc reached for a tissue from the holder on his desk and handed it to her before placing his hands on her knees. "When I met with your father earlier today, he told me a little secret that I probably shouldn't be sharing with you, but I feel you should know."

"What is it?"

"Your father's opponent in next year's election has a damning connection to my family," Linc began, his face tightening with both anger and dread. "His father is the man who covered up the murders my grandfather committed while overseas during World War II. He consorted with my grandmother and buried the files. Your father plans to use this information against him in the coming months."

Lynette digested what he had told her, disbelief clouding her eyes. "This is insane, Linc. What are the chances?"

"I know." He managed a tired smile as he watched her. "But it's something we'll have to deal with, as is what your father said tonight."

"But what if they arrest Madison?" Lynette asked fearfully, reaching for his hands. "Can they do that?"

"I doubt it. It's all hearsay until there's proof and, as far as I know, the cops have already deemed this a legit suicide." He sighed, leaning in to rest his forehead on their joined hands. "But I would hate to be in the room when she gets word of it. It's going to break her heart."

"I'm so sorry. I feel so helpless…"

"So do I." He pressed his lips to her fingers before rising to his feet, pulling her with him. He held her, shutting his eyes tight against the still simmering anger flooding his system. "This is war now, Lynette. Your father is my enemy."

"I know," she whispered, her throat clenching at the thought.

It appeared that, at last, hell had been delivered.

SEVEN

Her office had never been a lonely place to her until now. She found herself holed up there more often these days with nothing but her sense of duty to keep her company. Though she'd never had much more than that in the first place, a weight was currently hovering over her, a cloud of responsibility and expectation that never left her alone.

And being told that she was responsible for her father's death did not make the weight any easier to bear.

In her hands she held the transcript from the radio show that had aired the night before, though she didn't bother reading it in its entirety. She had seen the worst of it when she read Shaw's words about her and her father.

Linc and Grant had presented the transcript to her that morning, both solemn and apprehensive. Rightfully so, as even she had expected herself to scream and curse and rage. Instead, she had shut out her brothers and read the words in private, absorbing them on her own. While she did feel some measure of anger for Shaw, she also felt pity for him. The man was walking a dangerously fine line, one that could split very easily if he wasn't careful.

The few people in her life who had dared cross her had lived to seriously regret their decision. The classmate in preschool who had stolen her prized antique pocket watch, a gift from her grandfather. The professor in college who looked down his nose at her and attempted to fail her because he didn't like her family and what they stood for. The French bastard she'd caught trying to slip a roofie into her drink in a bar in Paris.

All had paid a dear price for what they had done. She had seen to it personally.

As for Shaw, his actions were decidedly more painful than those others had been. He had seen fit to blame her for a tragedy she was still grieving, one that he had no right to be involved with in the first place.

She was still left with the question of who this secret source of his was. It troubled her that the first person who came to mind was Duke. But as jealous as he was, her cousin wasn't an idiot. He would understand that something like this would only draw more attention to the scandal, which would hurt him as much as it hurt her.

So who was it? And where had they gotten the idea that somehow she, Madison, was responsible for tampering with the drugs that led to her own father's death?

Feeling sick to her stomach, Madison threw the transcript in the trash can beside her desk. She fled her office and sought a distraction, any distraction, to take her mind off Shaw and her father's death. She made her way into the kitchen of *Cherir*, deciding to work on the seasonal menu updates with Raoul. The frenzied chopping of a knife stopped her short of entering.

Raoul stood at the kitchen island and had a large butcher's knife in his hand, which he was using to furiously hack away at a tomato that was swiftly turning into bright red mush. Beside him, Quinn watched in cautious silence, her eyes darting up to meet Madison's. The alarm Madison saw in the other woman's face had her heart clenching.

"Raoul, stop it," she ordered.

He faltered, his head lifting to face her, his dark eyes wide and frantic and his lips curled in a snarl. His chest rose and fell with his labored breathing, while the hand that held the knife trembled in one quick spasm.

When she saw the shock pass over his face and weed out the violence, she walked forward and gently removed the knife from his hand. He let her take it, his mind and body dulled from the outburst.

"I'm sorry, *cariño*," he murmured, immediately turning away from her to busy himself across the kitchen.

Madison watched him brush her off, and her temper immediately flared. "Do I need to send you home?"

"No," he barked, reaching for a stainless steel pan and smashing it down upon the stove. He began to fill it with olive oil, ignoring her as she came up beside him.

"What the hell is wrong with you then?" she demanded, forgetting Quinn's presence altogether. Worry for her friend tore through her, and she couldn't shake the image of him losing control that way. She'd seen him in fits of rage before, but nothing like this. He seemed downright mad.

When he said nothing, she pulled on his arm and turned him to face her. "Damnit, answer me!"

"It is nothing." He grit his teeth and turned back to his work, struggling to ignore the distress in her eyes.

"We were listening to the radio, and they replayed what Senator Shaw said about you last night," Quinn supplied, wringing her hands together anxiously.

Madison didn't take her eyes off Raoul, a distinct coldness hardening her face. "I see. Darling, you can't let that upset you. I'm handling it."

In response, he slammed another pot down upon the stove, its echoing bang resounding like a gunshot through the kitchen. To her credit, she didn't flinch, but instead focused on him as he faced her. Their eyes met, and she detested the enraged misery she saw reflected in his.

"They tarnish your name and blame you for that fool's death," he snapped, throwing his hands up in the air dramatically. "I should kill that senator for this."

"I appreciate your conviction, but that may only make things worse." Madison attempted a smile, reaching out to him. When he backed away from her instead, she eyed him curiously. "What is it?"

For a long, haunted moment, he said nothing. When he finally spoke, his voice was dangerously low and condemning.

"You didn't listen to me, *cariño,*" he said quietly. "You think I don't have eyes watching his every move while he stays in this hotel?"

She didn't have to ask who it was he meant. It was obvious in the infuriated way he was watching her. But knowing that he knew about her and Wyatt, acknowledging his disappointment, brought her way more guilt than she realized it would.

"So I have a weakness," she confessed, her chin lifting defiantly. "I don't have to explain my actions to you."

Leaving it at that, she turned on her heel and stormed out of the kitchen, only to run directly into Kennedy just outside the stainless steel doors.

"What is your *problem*?" Kennedy cried out, glaring at Madison.

Madison's jaw clenched as she stared down at her little sister. "I have many problems, darling. None of which I would ever wish upon you."

"You know, I learned about sociopaths last year in school. I seriously think you're one of them," Kennedy charged, pointing a finger at Madison accusingly. "You feel no emotion; you're cold to the bone. You are a self-serving narcissist who will hurt anyone and do anything to get to the top. Grandpa was the same way, and both of you get a kick out of destroying everyone else's happiness. Like dad's...you just had to get rid of him, didn't you?"

Shock registered briefly over Madison's face before she controlled herself. "Excuse me?"

"You killed him!" Kennedy's face contorted with anger as her eyes filled with tears. "It all makes sense now. He got in the way and so you did something to his weed, which he only used to help the pain he was in. But you couldn't leave him be, could you? You locked him up like a criminal and then played on his weaknesses so he had no way out but to die."

Madison's heart jolted with both indignation and despair at her sister's callous words, but she couldn't help but feel she was right. She had indeed locked her father up like a bird in a cage, too embarrassed by his antics to let him loose like the free man he had been. And in doing so, she was in part responsible for his death. It was something she would have to deal with for the rest of her life.

Before she could think of what to say to her sister in return, Quinn appeared from inside the kitchen and came up beside Kennedy, resting her hand on the girl's shoulder. As Kennedy leaned into Quinn for comfort, resentment hit Madison like a steel mallet to the chest.

"What's going on?" Quinn asked, her arm wrapped around Kennedy. "Are you okay, sweetie? You're crying..."

"*I hate her!*" Kennedy snarled.

Alarmed, Quinn shot a quick look to Madison before addressing the girl. "You don't mean that, you're just upset."

"Yes I do," she declared cruelly. "She doesn't give a shit about me and never has. I wish she was dead."

She tore free of Quinn's grasp and flew out into the restaurant, leaving Madison and Quinn hovering in stunned silence.

Before Quinn could attempt to console her, Madison left. She was in no mood to deal with comforting words or pointless excuses for behavior.

Quinn watched her go as Raoul came up beside her, rubbing the back of his neck tiredly.

"She doesn't show it, but she wears many scars inflicted by that little girl," he said quietly, thoughtfully.

When he turned around to go back into the kitchen, Quinn had to rub her arms to chase away the chill that came from his words.

GRANT WAS WELCOMED home by the alluring scent of garlic, tomato sauce, and basil. It wafted out of the kitchen and greeted him as he came through the front door and discarded his briefcase and coat, his mind and body exhausted from work.

It had been, in the simplest of terms, a trying day.

The whole family was on edge because of the radio interview and Shaw's accusations, and as a result, tempers were easily provoked. Linc had almost come to blows with Cy, Madison had bickered with Kennedy, and he had gotten into an argument with his mother over what they were going to say to the press. That task was usually Linc's job, but because his brother was more than a little spiteful and unpredictable these days, Grant felt it was best if he and Madison handled it.

Only, he hadn't been able to talk with his sister all day. She had locked herself in her office, then slipped out unnoticed at some point to go home. She wasn't answering her cell, and when he had tried her at home the phone had been disconnected. Clearly, she did not want to be contacted.

He couldn't blame her, but it left him high and dry as the only Vasser capable of answering the media's questions. Other than Duke, of course, who had burst into his office earlier that day to elect himself as the new family spokesperson. Grant had not so gently repudiated his cousin's attempt to interfere, citing that it would only cause more confusion.

There were enough members of the Vasser family in the spotlight as it was.

But now that the day was over and he had done all he could, Grant was just glad to be home. Coming home from work this way, with the intoxicating scent of delicious food cooking in the kitchen, the sound of Stevie Wonder's *Signed, Sealed, Delivered* echoing throughout the town house accompanied by Quinn's own voice joyfully singing along, and the sight of her dancing with a bright red apron tied around her waist, gave him hope. It gave him a sense of relief, of contentment. One that only she could provide.

She was singing into a wooden spoon as she suddenly turned around and saw him. She jumped, only to burst into embarrassed laughter.

"Hey! I didn't know when you'd be home." She grinned, clutching the wooden spoon in her hands and feeling foolish. Realizing the music was probably too loud, she reached over to turn off the radio sitting on the counter before facing him again. "How was your day?"

Grant sighed, his smile fading as he leaned against the doorway to the kitchen and stared at the floor. "Life goes on."

Sensing the weight of the stress he carried, she set aside the spoon and went to him, wrapping her arms around him securely. "Life does go on, Grant. We will get through this."

"It's not your battle," he said softly, running a hand through her hair as the other roamed over her back.

She bit back the hurt she felt from his words, realizing he still wanted to maintain some sort of distance between them. It was as though he was afraid if he brought her in, she would be put in harm's way, in the spotlight glaring down at his family. But the truth was, there was no place she'd rather be than publicly by his side instead of secretly his lover.

"I would do anything for you," she reminded him, tilting her head back to look him in the eye. "If this is war, I'll fight beside you."

Irritation flashed over his face. "This isn't war, Quinn. It's just politics and bad press."

"It's your livelihood and your family that they're attacking. Of course it's war," Quinn argued, eyebrows raised. "Shaw and Jorja and all the others, they're trying to ruin you."

"We won't be ruined by threats and lies." He backed away from her, needing distance. The wounded look she was giving him was making him uneasy. "We're working to pull the company together, to prepare ourselves for the changes that must be made. Linc's putting together a new marketing plan, Mads is working with the lawyers, and I'm trying to keep my head on straight. This isn't as bad as you seem to think it is."

"Lynette's father went public with the news that Madison might be responsible for your father's suicide. How is that not bad?" Quinn charged, hands on her hips as she stared at him disbelievingly. "My mother is calling me every other day to confirm the slander she's hearing about you and your family in the paper, on television, online... it's gotten to the point where I've had to tell her that none of what she hears is true. But she's worried, Grant. She's worried about you, about me, about everything."

He let out a long exhale, unable to look at her. "It will take time to fix the damage that's been done. That's just the reality of it."

"I understand that. But don't push me away when I tell you I want to help." She threw up her hands, frustrated. "Even Kennedy comes to me for comfort before you do. Just earlier today she cried in my arms while she and Madison were arguing."

Grant eyed her darkly, coldly, for a long moment before he spoke. "You're just making yourself right at home, aren't you?"

The moment he said it, he regretted the words. It brought a startling flash of pain to her eyes, and he silently cursed himself for it. But the truth was, he was uncomfortable with her settling in among his family. He couldn't say exactly why that was, but something about it bothered him.

Perhaps he just wanted her all to himself. She was his, not theirs to take and use and drain dry. His family was not a friendly, easygoing group. Quinn was leagues above all of them, a better person by far than anyone else he knew.

If his family got to her and tarnished her spirit with their drama, he would never forgive himself for letting it happen.

Quinn blinked back a few angry tears that formed behind her eyes, wondering just what to say to his callous remark. Surely he wasn't *angry* that she was trying to be friendly with his sisters and with his mother, even though the latter was cruelly opposed to her. It still begged the question: did he really want her in his life at all?

"What am I supposed to do, then? Just hide in the corner, out of sight, until it suits you?" she asked, her voice cracking as her heart ached. "I told you once that I will give you everything I have, everything I am. I was under the impression that you *wanted* that of me."

"I don't know what I want," he admitted, rubbing his face with his hands jadedly before facing her again. "You make me a better person, I can't deny that. But the drama within my family, the scandal...I don't want to put you through what I've been facing each and every day."

She noticeably softened, though her eyes were still wet with unshed tears. With a heavy, burdened sigh, she reached out for one of his hands. When he accepted, she squeezed it tightly in her own and attempted a small smile.

"I love you, and you love me. That's as good a start as we can both ask for right now. The rest we'll just have to improvise as we go," she decided, eyeing him a bit defiantly. "But if you get fussy again over me taking care of your family when you're not around, I will use my mother's famous, nasty Sicilian threat on you."

"What's that?" he asked, unable to help himself.

She tilted her head up proudly. "I'll take that pan off the stove with your dinner in it and dump it all over your head, then hit you with it for good measure."

A laugh managed to escape his throat as he knelt down before her, impulsively pulling her in so he could rest his head against her stomach. She welcomed him in, her fingers winding through his dark hair, silently stunned by his surrender.

"I'll take care of you, Quinn," he told her quietly, firmly. "Just as I'll take care of my family."

Her eyes closed as she sank to her knees before him, letting him envelop her and hold her close. "Just remember that we're in this together. I'll never leave your side."

THE LETTER LAY on her black granite kitchen counter, unopened. Madison leaned against the cabinets a few feet away, sipping a glass of mellow red wine as she considered her next course of action.

She knew what it was, had known it the moment it had shown up in her stack of daily mail. A white envelope, no return address, her own name and address in plain, black font.

Within an hour of receiving it, she had tucked it inside her purse and left the hotel as discreetly as possible. Grant had been trying to reach her all day, but she just wasn't in the mood to discuss Shaw. Especially not now, not when she had a fresh threat sitting before her, eager to be read.

Part of her seriously considered tossing it in the red hot flames of her fireplace. The contents couldn't hurt her then, couldn't anger her. But her shameless curiosity and morbid nature wouldn't give her the nerve to destroy the letter. No, she was going to read it.

It was just a matter of when.

She continued to stare at it, letting the wine smooth out some of her anger and anxiety. The first letter had thus far turned into nothing, so there was no reason to believe this one would be any more destructive.

Just do it, she ordered herself, setting her wine aside and grabbing the envelope. She tore it open hastily, unearthing the paper within and unfolding it.

She shut her eyes for a brief, careful moment, then opened them to read.

> *When the Queen's courage blinds her, she does not notice the blood at her feet.*

Her breath held frozen in her lungs as she processed the words, yet again typewritten in simple, black font. The fear skittering beneath the surface of her skin annoyed her, but she couldn't avoid it. This letter was decidedly more threatening than the last had been.

Perhaps not to her, but certainly to those whose blood this person suggested would pool at her feet.

Did they mean her family? Her brothers?

The thought sickened her, a coldness settling over her entire body until she shuddered from it. Setting the letter aside, she lifted her glass of wine to her lips and attempted to quell the nausea now swimming in her stomach.

Who was this person, and just what were they trying to do? Scare her?

If they were, then she wasn't going to give them the satisfaction of a surrender. It was still a faceless, nameless threat. If this person was cowardly enough to send nothing but letters, then what danger could they really pose to her?

But the uncertainty of it terrified her. She couldn't ignore the letters anymore than she could address them. Both would be foolish acts, and both could provoke further threats, or even an attack.

For now, it would be best to keep the letters a secret and pray that they were nothing more than wasted paper.

Her cell phone suddenly began to ring.

Here comes the rain again...

She checked the caller ID out of habit, and as she did so she instinctively began to ignore the call. But something stopped her, some urgent, driving need that she couldn't shake. It had her accepting the call and numbly lifting the phone to her ear.

"Hello, darling." She tried to put some measure of confidence into her voice, but knew she failed miserably. Her fear failed her, and she could tell by his initial silence that he noticed it.

"*What's wrong?*" Wyatt asked sharply. She heard him shuffle around, probably rising from where he had been laying in bed.

"Nothing's wrong," she answered, even as her eyes automatically shot to the letter, still lying open on the counter. As she took a sip of her wine, her hand trembled once.

"*I'm coming over.*"

"Don't," she ordered, though she was suddenly overcome by an intense, conflicting desire to see him. Damn him for opening her up to this urgency again, this reliance that was ridiculously unhealthy for her sanity. She said the next words more as a confirmation for herself than for him. "I don't need you."

"*I never said you needed me, sweetheart,*" Wyatt shot back. "*I know you're more than capable of handling yourself. However, you sound upset, something I'm not used to hearing so I would really like to come over and see for myself that you are okay.*"

"I was just going to bed."

"*Liar,*" he replied, though she could hear the affection in his voice. "*I called you to see if you wanted to get dinner with me tomorrow.*"

"I'm very busy," she said without thinking, her response mechanical, without feeling. But when she heard him laugh, as though he had completely expected that answer, she inhaled deeply and tried again. "You can pick me up at eight."

Before he could reply, she hung up and held her cell phone to her lips, her eyes fluttering closed as she let out a long, troubled breath.

"I still love you, you bastard," she whispered, her heart exploding to bloody pieces within her chest as she felt tears spring into her eyes. Tossing the phone aside, she grabbed her wine and fled her kitchen.

Tomorrow was a new day.

Eight

J ack Morgan was a desperate man. He was filled with hostility, was distrustful of others, and had always been an inherent pessimist. He had a laundry list of neurotic habits, accompanied by a childish desire to win every game, and challenge every competitor. His monstrous ego fueled his every waking thought and made it impossible for him to see reason outside of his own selfish pursuits.

But only those who knew him best, those within his inner circle of advisors, saw this side of him. The rest of the world, namely his constituents, saw him as a man of supreme dignity and class. A confident, charming leader with a heart of gold.

It was an illusion he played well. While his marriage was a lie, his children hated his guts, and he had more than one enemy out there who wished him dead, he continued forward relentlessly on his path to the top.

If only the top didn't look so distant at the moment.

He sneered at the television set up in his Charleston office, disgusted by the continual dribble on the networks about the Vasser family and their sordid scandal. As if there weren't more important things to talk about, he scoffed to himself, shaking his head. Instead, America seemed enthralled, eager for more and more information on the Vassers and their illustrious hotels.

It was downright maddening.

If circumstances had been different, he couldn't have given a shit about the Vassers. In fact, he would have probably joined the front lines of those condemning the family. As a lawyer, he certainly would have found some way to profit off the scandal. Surely there was some nitwit out there ready to file some sort of lawsuit.

But, alas, he found himself an unwitting player in their pitiful fall from grace. He could only be thankful that he knew now of the connection he had to the Vassers, instead of learning of it down the road from the lips of an opponent. At least this way he could prepare himself.

Years earlier, his father had laid in his death bed, strapped to machines determined to keep his heart beating despite the heart attack that had nearly taken his life on the spot. He hadn't had much time left, and in his remaining minutes on this planet he confided in his only son the terrible misdeed he had committed decades earlier.

Jack had learned that day that his father was responsible for covering up a war crime, an action that was second only to treason in the eyes of the law. His father had knowingly pushed aside evidence proving the guilt of a killer, burying the truth.

Then his father died, his conscience clean. He could have never predicted the drastic repercussions that would arise from his actions, the ones his son was now hampered with. Never in his wildest dreams would he have imagined that something he had done so long ago would come back to haunt his only child.

Jack considered him a pathetic fool for it.

Anger tore through him as he reached for the glass of scotch on the coffee table before him, his fingers clenching until his knuckles were white. He took a sip, welcoming the burn, letting it fuel the violence in his blood.

Violence for the Vasser family, for their patriarch Cyrus who had shamelessly murdered his own brothers in combat and demanded it be covered up by the one man who could do it. The one man who could be blackmailed into action because of his own connection to the family.

His wife—Jack's mother. She had been born with the Vasser blood in her veins, and as such Jack carried it as well. It was a trait he should have used to his advantage, but instead it was to be his undoing.

At least, it would be if he let it. He had no intention of letting that bastard Shaw successfully use this scandal against him, not when this election was rightfully his. He deserved that senate seat, knew it would propel him upward and give him future prospects of a cabinet position or even the presidency. The good people of South Carolina adored him and would continue to adore him all the way to the voting booth.

His eyes narrowed with sudden annoyance at the urgent knock on his office door. He took another sip of scotch before inviting the unwelcomed visitor in.

Miles Coulter, his assistant, advisor, and all around errand-boy, entered the office looking more than a little harried. He swept a hand through his crop of dusty blonde hair and faced his boss.

"The team we sent to New York followed Shaw, just like you asked," Miles began, nervously tugging at his collar at the fierce look in Morgan's deep blue eyes.

"And...?"

"He met with two of the Vassers at a restaurant a few blocks from the hotel."

Morgan's temper sparked, dread a molten hot weight in his gut. "Which two?"

Miles chewed on his lower lip anxiously. "Grant and Linc. Shaw's daughter wasn't there. We sent a man in to sit nearby to record their conversation. Sir, Shaw told them about your father."

Morgan sipped on his drink, giving the news careful consideration. This undoubtedly changed things. If Shaw saw fit to tell the Vassers about the connection he had to their family, then he must be preparing to go public with it. And once that news got out...well, all hell was going to break loose. It could cost him everything.

It would have been easy enough to discredit Shaw in the media, proof or not. Facts didn't matter if he got to the press first.

But if the Vassers corroborated Shaw's story, if they confirmed the truth of it, then that would be much harder to combat. Not that the public trusted the Vassers, but if Shaw played his cards right that might not even matter.

What it boiled down to, Morgan realized, was that he would have to ensure that the Vassers stayed silent.

"Sir?"

His eyes shot to his assistant, clearing from the haze of thought. He scowled and took another drink. "What?"

"What is our next course of action?"

Morgan toyed with the glass in his hands. He looked back at Miles with a dangerous gleam in his eyes. "We do something about the Vassers."

"WHAT ARE WE going to do, Marshall?" Charlene asked as she stared intently at the wine glass filled with Chardonnay in her hands. She watched how the light caught in the golden liquid, sparkling beautifully. If only she felt like drinking it; it really was a waste of a fantastic vintage label.

"Well, Charlene, we're moving forward," Marshall replied, trying to put some assurance in his voice to calm her. It was his natural instinct to protect and shelter, to make things right. "The kids are doing a great job—they're so dedicated."

"Of course they are," Charlene snapped, eyebrows raised. "I would expect nothing less of them."

He only smiled and sat back in his seat, gazing around at the crowd surrounding them in *Cherir*. There were still quite a few people dining there and at the other restaurants the hotel housed, giving him some measure of hope. Some people likely just weren't paying attention and did not know of the scandal, while others probably didn't care. He liked to think that maybe there were some who came to support the Vasser family, that maybe they could sympathize with the living heirs of a killer. It wasn't as if *they* were killers, too. They were simply innocents who were caught up in a chaotic, bloody whirlwind.

And then there were those that came *because* of the scandal—the ones that fed on the drama of other's misfortunes. Regardless, he'd take their money all the same. At least it was keeping the hotel afloat while they enacted all these changes Madison was forcing upon them.

He grimaced, thinking of his brothers and how saddened they were by this whole mess. It seemed to hit them the hardest. They had been removed from Cyrus and the New York Hotel all those years, and now their legacy was being tossed right back in their faces. All of it taken away and given to a young woman. A capable young woman, but nonetheless one that none of them would have anticipated to be crowned the matriarch of the entire Vasser family.

Even he had not known just *how* close she had been to Cyrus. Her shocking admission revealing her knowledge of his grandfather's murder had been a major blow. The girl he thought he had known so well, the niece he loved and adored, had kept something as dark and heinous as *that* secret from him for all these years.

In essence, she had been working against him. He didn't believe Madison when she claimed she had no idea Cyrus would grant her the power and the position that was rightfully his. Although Marshall tried his best to maintain their relationship, he still knew he could never trust her again.

"I assume Clark and Doc have left. I haven't seen them around," Charlene said suddenly, insult evident in the tone of her voice. "No one sees fit to tell me anything anymore."

Marshall chuckled. "They flew home this morning. You are not that late in learning the news of their departure."

"But their sons are staying? Why is that?"

"Duke and Cy will stay on for a bit longer to help out with the changes being made to the company." Marshall reached for his glass of red wine, swirling it gently before lifting it for a slow sip. When he set it aside, he met her eyes. "They are good boys. They only want what's best for the family."

"They are jealous of my daughter," she huffed, her eyes narrowing. "I don't trust them."

Marshall started laughing, his smile wide beneath his full moustache. "Correct me if I'm wrong, Charlene, but even *you* have been known to be jealous of our Maddie from time to time."

She carelessly waved the thought away. "She gets under my skin. But I am still her mother. I want to see her get what's rightfully hers. I didn't marry into your goddamn family to have unsuccessful children."

His face notably tightened, as it usually did when he was confronted yet again with her more callous, calculating nature. For all Win's faults, his brother had at one time loved this woman. Although Marshall wasn't sure if Charlene had ever loved Win in return. "Speaking of you marrying into my family...tell me you don't believe Madison is responsible for tampering with the drugs Win took?"

Charlene tensed and sipped at her wine. "No, I don't believe she is."

"I think it was that Jorja Hale," Marshall growled. "She always was a poison to this family."

"That is a possibility," Charlene replied, avoiding his eyes. "It could be any number of people. All one would have to do is buy off the dealer."

Marshall frowned, mulling over the thought. "I wouldn't even know where to buy drugs. Never touched the crap myself."

"Well, these young people, they know where to look," Charlene began, pursing her lips. "And I would not be at all surprised if that little tart secretary of Grant's knew where to get them."

"Quinn?" Marshall managed, laughter bubbling in his throat. "She's as straight and narrow as they come, Charlene. Has the best smile I've ever seen on a woman."

"We know nothing of where she comes from, nothing of her schooling or pedigree. If I thought I could convince him, I'd order Grant to get rid of her immediately."

Irritation flooded over him as he glared at her. "Damn right you won't convince him. He knows what he wants and doesn't need you meddling in his life. Same goes for Linc and Maddie as well."

For a long, haunted moment she said nothing, her thoughts drifting to Wyatt. When she spoke, rage flavored her words. "That bastard from Las Vegas has been staying in our hotel. When I saw him at the fundraiser, I couldn't believe my eyes."

"I know." Marshall sighed, reaching out for her hand in a comforting gesture. They both knew the horrendous pain Wyatt had put Madison through, and neither desired to see it happen again. "Only our girl can make him leave. And if she sees fit to let him stay, then there is nothing more we can do."

Saying nothing, Charlene removed her hand from his and drank more of her wine. She refused to accept his casual solution. There was always more that could be done.

"I'm expecting a copy of the Army's file on my father to arrive in the mail any day now," Marshall said then, leaning back in his seat.

Charlene stared at him, wide-eyed. "How did you manage to get it?"

"I have a connection that finagled a copy of it for me. This way we can find out once and for all who it was who covered up the murders."

"Why does it even matter, Marshall? It's old news."

"I don't expect you to understand," he muttered, finishing the last sip of wine in his glass and sliding from the seat. He stared down at her, a haunted sadness in his expression. "This isn't your blood, Charlene. But it is mine. I need to know the whole story."

She stayed where she was as he walked away, watching after him as she thought of her children. *They* were her blood, her one claim to the Vasser empire. She would not stand by and let them be threatened.

WYATT SLIPPED INTO his Porsche and turned the classic rock on full blast. With the windows rolled down to let in the chilled April night air, he took off down Park Avenue and cruised the streets of New York in an attempt to clear his head before his date with Madison.

He toyed with the idea of cancelling and making a run to Atlantic City, craving now more than ever the bright lights, easy money and casual conversation. It would please him to be back in his element, away from the lavish, ostentatious world Madison lived in.

These days, it seemed as though the very city itself was beginning to strangle him.

He had never understood what it was about New York that drove so many people to its streets, to its monuments. While he could appreciate the history of the place, he could not understand the driving need people all over the world felt to come to this bustling metropolis.

Then again, perhaps many of them came for the same reasons he had. Retribution, guilt, friendship, even love. The guilt and the friendship he had seen to with his attempt to help Win. Granted, the whole thing had, in essence, backfired in his face. But how could he have predicted that Win would kill himself?

That left retribution and love. He hadn't really intended on exploring those two when he'd come to the city, but now it seemed he had no choice. The men who had ruined his life surrounded him, as well as the woman he had been forced to give up. How could he turn his back on her now, when she so clearly needed someone on her side? Someone other than her brothers, who were so wrapped up in their own agendas and issues it was amazing they even noticed Madison anymore.

Then again, maybe his hanging around was only distracting her from her true purpose, her destiny. Maybe, just as he had wondered all those years ago, his need for her was something she should avoid for her own well-being. It had occurred to him many times over the years that his presence in her life had hurt her more than helped her. And as much as he wanted to deny it, he couldn't.

Look at her now, he thought proudly. Queen of her family's empire, brilliant and stunning and a true success. More capable and clever than she had been at nineteen and as ambitious and ruthless as Cyrus had been.

In the years he had been away from her, she had risen from the ashes of destruction as a goddess of a woman, glorious and strong.

Then he'd slithered back into her life, just as her entire world was crumbling all around her. He was confident that she could hold her own without him, but he'd be damned if he'd leave her again. Not when his own selfish needs were churning within him, blinding him to what was best and instead urging him toward what he wanted. What he had to believe *she* wanted as well.

Madison loved him still, he could see it in her eyes. While she may hate him more than love him, he was willing to gamble that in time he could earn back her trust and find his place in her life once again.

He thought of his business back in Maine, his home in the seaboard town of his childhood. He missed it, craved it, but he could not go back there. Not yet.

Linc had been generous enough to wave the cost of the hotel room for him, but Wyatt still insisted on paying his way. He had enough stored up in his savings to at least last him another few weeks, so he had time.

Once that time was up, he would have to make a decision. Give up his life in Maine and stay with Madison in New York, or give up on her yet again.

He fumed at the thought, wondering what would have become of them had the dice been rolled differently, had the cards been played in his favor...

Would she have stayed in Las Vegas? Or would she have dragged him here, to the city he despised to be her lapdog? Showered with expensive clothes, cars, and anything else she could force on him.

That's what she had done then, so what was to stop her from doing it now?

They were both different people this time, he realized. Back in those days, he'd been helpless to refuse her. Obsessed was too light a word to describe what he had felt.

And she...well, she had been as all young women are when they first discover the power females wield over men. She had used it, abused it, and tortured him with it until he'd been all but helpless in a puddle at her feet. Until he'd had no choice but to fight, or else lose himself to her.

Those had been the rougher times in their year-long affair. Perhaps they had been what led up to his ultimate decision to leave. Not that he'd been given much of a choice, but the decision had been presented to him regardless.

If he had refused, she would have been ruined, and he along with her.

No, the best course of action had been to leave without a trace, giving her time to become who she had to be for her family, and giving him time to shake loose the wanderlust and wildness from his nature.

But it all came back to now. He was committed to seeing it through and giving her his support as she pushed forward.

She was beginning to come around to the idea that she loved him. Once she accepted it, then he could tell her the truth about why he had left her. Until then, he wasn't sure if she could handle it. Especially not while she was burdened with so much deception and distrust within her own family. The truth he had to tell her would without a doubt shatter many of her illusions, and while it would serve his purpose, it would only harm her.

Surprisingly, Madison's loyal companion Raoul had yet to show his face, but Wyatt was willing to bet that the Spaniard was stewing with both rage and suspicion.

He remembered the look on Raoul's face when he discovered Madison and him together, making out in a dimly lit hallway near the maid's station in the casino in Vegas. Raoul had flushed an angry red at the sight of his boss wrapped up tight with the dealer he had never much liked to begin with.

At the time, Madison had brushed it off with a laugh. But clearly she had not noticed the fury in the man's eyes the way Wyatt had.

It was a moment he wasn't likely to forget anytime soon.

Wyatt whipped his car around and headed toward Madison's town house, having done enough driving. He was ready to face his demons and bring them the fight that had been coming for a very long time.

NINE

J ust three days after the accusation leaked that she had killed her father, Madison faced yet another hailstorm in the press. Only this time, instead of being hit with grief and outrage, she found herself somewhat amused.

VASSER HEIRESS IN DANGER-OUS ADDICTION SPIRAL

Inside source unveils disastrous state of the young woman now running the last of America's great hotel empires.

"So..." Linc began, eyebrows lifted apprehensively as he watched his sister. He didn't like the odd smile quirking her lips, or her silence. "I would normally say we should ignore this, but it's not a tabloid. It's the *New York* Fucking *Times*."

Beside him, Grant let out an irritated huff of breath and lifted the newspaper from his sister's grasp, causing her to look up and meet his gaze.

"I'm going to put in a call to the paper and request that they rescind the article on the basis that there are no facts to this," he said evenly, gauging her reaction. "We don't have the time right now to waste on personal attacks. We need to continue moving forward."

Madison laughed, though there was a blatant tartness to her voice as she spoke.

"I find it interesting that I am the focus of all of these attacks," she said, eyes darting back and forth between them. "It's as if someone has it out for me."

"It's probably just Jorja, trying a different angle," Linc ventured. "She's still out for vengeance over what happened to dad, even though I'm still not convinced this isn't just some big publicity stunt she created to get her name back in the papers."

"You think she tampered with the drugs to kill our father and subsequently has manufactured all this drama just to get people talking about her again?" Madison asked, one eyebrow raised in doubtful amusement.

"It's working, isn't it?" Linc grunted. "I looked it up. DVD sales on her past flicks have practically doubled. People are writing op-eds hailing her as some kind of hero, out to expose the big, bad, evil, hotel family that destroyed her happiness. It's pathetic, but it's working to her advantage."

"That doesn't mean she's the one behind this," Grant reasoned, rolling the paper up in his hands. "She is still the most likely suspect, but we can't go around accusing her without proof."

Madison sighed and leaned back in her chair, chewing on her lower lip as she gave the issue some thought. Her brothers were right; Jorja was most likely the "family insider" that had been feeding false accusations to the press. She did have a motive and a known hatred for the family.

But if Jorja was responsible for these public, blatant attacks on the family, then was she also the one behind the threatening letters Madison had received? Somehow, she just didn't peg Jorja Hale as being the type to send menacing letters.

The woman's style was flashy and obvious, such as her repeated appearances on talk shows to discuss her troubles with the Vasser family. It wouldn't be unreasonable to assume that she had now stepped up her game and was tipping off the press as a "secret" inside source to the family. And the press probably ate it all up because they knew Jorja had been involved, on and off, with the family for so many years that she must be privy to their habits and intentions.

But while that narrowed down the case on who was leaking lies to the press, that still didn't answer the question of who had sent the letters.

The letters that remained Madison's dirty little secret.

"Linc, I want you to draft up our formal response, keeping it as simple and concise as you can make it. Tell them that this accusation is false and that we hope a paper as prestigious as the *Times* would come up with more facts before publishing slander." She turned to Grant, a spark of heat flashing in her eyes. "When you speak with the asshole that wrote this, tell him—"

Carrie's voice suddenly floated through the intercom, causing the three of them to stare pointedly at the phone. "*Jorja Hale on line one for you, Ms. Vasser.*"

"You've *got* to be kidding me," Linc muttered. "Calling to gloat, most likely."

"Do you want me to talk to her?" Grant offered.

Madison merely waved him off and grabbed the phone herself. "This is Madison Vasser."

"*My, my, how the mighty have fallen,*" Jorja gushed, laughter in her voice. "*You catch that juicy little article about you in the* Times *today?*"

"Very clever, Jorja. But lying to the press will only get you hit with a lawsuit."

"*Oh, I had nothing to do with this, honey. Wish I had, though,*" Jorja preened, giggling again. "*Eddie was telling me all about your little Vicodin habit. Guess someone else found out about it and decided to blab.*"

"What are you talking about?" Madison demanded, but Jorja only continued to ramble on.

"*With all that pressure you must be under, I can't blame you. But hey, we reap what we sow and all that jazz, and karma's coming back to bite you for what you did to poor Win. I'm just thrilled I get to see it all go down.*"

"So if you didn't go to the press with this, then who did?"

"*Beats me. Looks like you've made yourself a few more enemies,*" Jorja laughed. "*Be sure to tell Linc I said hello. Looks like his little girl-friend's daddy doesn't approve. How sad. Let him know I'll be waiting when he gets lonely. Ta-ta for now, Queen Bitch.*"

She continued to laugh as she hung up, leaving Madison clutching the receiver and staring at her desk, her face carefully void of emotion. As calmly as she could, she replaced the receiver.

"Well, what did she say?" Linc barked, his hands clenching into fists. "I take it she said she didn't do it."

"She claims it wasn't her," Madison said evenly, gazing up at him. "With the obvious glee she had about the whole thing, I find it hard to believe she wouldn't take the credit if she could."

"So what then, is Shaw behind this just like the accusation about you and dad?" Linc thundered, the very thought infuriating him.

"Why would he keep his name out of it this time if he had no problem revealing himself the first time around?" Grant put in, trying to maintain reason. "It doesn't make any sense."

"I don't know, because he's playing some kind of fucking game with us and he probably just wants to make it look like we have threats coming from all sides when in fact it's just him and Jorja." Linc reached into his jean's pocket for his cell phone, immediately dialing Lynette's number.

Grant shot him a warning look. "Don't be brash, Linc."

Linc ignored him, only to hang up the phone moments later when Lynette didn't answer. He turned to his siblings, frustrated. "It's Shaw. Who else could it be?" When they said nothing, he nodded with a dark laugh. "Right. Well, while you guys think it over, I'm gonna take action and go get some real answers. I'll be in touch."

He swung out of Madison's office, shutting the door promptly behind him.

Grant sighed and looked back to his sister, shaking his head. "Well, what do you think?"

Madison rubbed a suddenly aching spot on her right temple, closing her eyes for a brief moment as she gave it some thought. She had to wonder if Linc was on to something, that perhaps Shaw was just trying to make it look like the family had threats coming in from all sides. That could explain the mysterious letters, his public interview with the press, the anonymous leak to the *New York Times*. He could be staging all of this, piece by piece.

But what was his motive in doing so? Why would a sitting senator, up for re-election in just one year's time, risk his reputation by going on an all out rampage against the Vasser family?

It just didn't add up. Either she was missing some crucial piece of information that would justify Shaw's actions, or it simply wasn't him.

And yet, if it wasn't him, and it wasn't Jorja, then who could it be?

"I feel as though I'm missing something here, Grant," she said quietly, lifting her eyes to his. "Why is Linc convinced that Shaw is behind this? Other than that one radio interview and those text messages, both of which I'm assuming were attempts to scare his daughter away from Linc, what motive does he have to personally attack me this way?"

Grant walked to the window behind her, his hands clasped behind his back as he stared out at the city. He hadn't planned on telling Madison about what Shaw had told him and Linc a few days earlier, at least not until it became necessary for her to know. Now, it appeared, the necessity had arrived.

"Linc and I met with Shaw the day he did that radio interview," he began, his jaw clenching at the memory. "We asked him why he had sent those text messages to Lynette. He proceeded to tell us something that we weren't prepared to hear."

"What did he say?" Madison asked coolly, masking the spark of temper she felt at being kept in the dark.

"The man who plans to run against him in next year's election, a man by the name of Jack Morgan, is the son of the man who covered up our grandfather's crimes."

Madison blinked once as his words sank in, and she let out a slow, measured exhale. "I see."

"No one else knows of the connection Morgan has to us, just Shaw. He plans on using it against him. Using *us* against him."

"So he's doing all he can to trash our reputation further, trash *my* reputation, all so that he can land this blow against Morgan and really make it count."

Grant nodded silently, turning back to his sister. She could sense his anger, could see it in his eyes as he stared right at her. He hated this as much as if not more than she did. But that didn't make it any less their reality.

"Alright, so based on what you just told me, Shaw is enemy number one," she said smoothly, rising to her feet to face her brother. She planted both hands on his shoulders, unwavering resolve in her eyes. "While it bothers me that you didn't tell me about Shaw in the first place, I forgive you. I know you were just trying to shield me from it."

"Mads, I—"

"Don't," she murmured, attempting a smile as she reached up to touch his face. "Just be my strength and my reason, darling. I need your composure now more than ever."

He nodded and pulled her close, wrapping his arms around her.

While she held on to him and gave him the assurance he needed that she would be alright, the wheels in her mind were turning over how she was going to make Shaw pay for what he had done.

Especially for those damn letters.

WHEN LYNETTE ARRIVED home from rehearsal, Linc was waiting, furiously pacing back and forth in her kitchen. She froze, her keys dangling from her hand as her eyes widened with alarm.

"What's wrong?" she asked, immediately dropping her duffle bag and keys to the floor as she rushed to him. "Did something else happen? What is it?"

Linc stopped pacing and tossed that day's edition of the *New York Times* down on the kitchen island counter before her, opened to the article about Madison.

Lynette hesitated, brow furrowing as she read the headline. Her hand lifted to her lips in shock. "Goodness, not again."

"Exactly," Linc snapped, slamming his fist down upon the counter to emphasize the word. When she edged away from him, caution in her eyes, he tried the best he could to control his temper. He didn't want to blame Lynette, couldn't find the reason in it, and yet there she was. The daughter of his greatest enemy. "Just answer me one question, Lynette. Did your father do this?"

She gaped at him, her head shaking automatically. "I don't think so. Why would he?"

"Don't react, think. Could he be responsible for this?" Linc planted both hands upon the counter and leveled his gaze with hers.

"No," she asserted, crossing her arms. It was as much a defensive gesture as it was a divisive one. "He has no reason to make up lies."

"You mean like he did the other night on that radio show?" Linc rolled his eyes. "Remember what I told you about Morgan. Your dad has a motive to destroy my family so that when he reveals Morgan's connection to us, it makes Morgan look just that much worse."

"Yes, but he wouldn't out and out lie, Linc," she argued, a shiver running down her spine at the thought. "There's too much at stake for him."

"So you think that what he said about my sister being responsible for my dad's death is true? Because despite how upset you were about your father the other night, now you're telling me that he wouldn't lie."

She bit her lip uncertainly as she tried to think of what to say to him. "Linc, I—"

"Just answer me," he ordered, hostility flavoring the words.

It took all she had not to rush from the room to avoid the conflict. It was driving her mad to be wedged between two such violent forces, pushing and pulling her in every direction. All she wanted to do was crawl into the shadows and disappear.

But she couldn't do that. Instead, she let her own resentment and anger over the situation flood her system, and darken her tone. "Maybe it is Madison's fault your father is dead. She did lock him up for days on end, and we have no proof that she *didn't* tamper with the drugs. It's entirely possible that my father wasn't lying."

Linc's face flushed with indignation. "How can you *say* that? She's my sister!"

"And he's my father!" Lynette shot back, angry tears filling her eyes. "None of this changes that."

"Why do you keep defending him like this? You know he's behind this just as well as I do!"

"Oh, just like how you know Madison didn't do all she could to take your dad out of the picture?"

Linc let out a strained laugh, and he had to turn away from her or else risk doing something he'd regret later. He rubbed at the stubble on his chin angrily, yet again suffering under Lynette's defense of her father. God, was it ever going to end? Or would he always have to compete with the bastard for her loyalty?

Realizing that if he stayed and talked with her any longer, the situation was only going to get worse, Linc made the instant decision to leave. He whirled around to face her, but kept his distance.

"Don't come around the hotel anymore and don't call me," he stated flatly, derision in his voice. "If and when I feel like seeing you, I'll be in contact."

He left before she could respond, slamming the door shut behind him. Lynette's breath shuddered out of her chest as she crumbled onto her sofa, struggling to wrap her mind around what had just happened.

Had he just left her?

Tears formed in her eyes as she pulled her knees up against her chest and buried her face in her arms, her heart cracking in two.

She cursed her own carelessness, her father's arrogance, and most of all, she cursed the Vasser family for coming between what should have been a perfect romance.

"WELCOME HOME, PUMPKIN," Senator Shaw beamed, his arms spread wide as Lynette walked up the wooden steps to her childhood home.

She didn't return his smile, but followed through with the embrace all the same. She breathed in the familiar scent of her father's cologne and released a heavy sigh. "Hi, daddy," she murmured, her throat tightening as she pulled away.

"I have to admit I'm surprised to see you here," he admitted, gesturing for her to sit down on one of the cozy armchairs gracing the wide porch of their plantation style home. "When your mother said you called and were coming home, I wasn't sure what to make of it."

"I know, I've been avoiding the both of you," Lynette said tiredly as she sat down, her hands interlacing in her lap. She stared down at them, unable to meet his eyes. "I needed some time away from New York. Just for the weekend, then I need to go back."

"What for, honey? You having troubles at the studio?" he asked, sitting back in his chair casually. Behind them, birds darted through the trees in the garden, cheerful at the warmth of spring. It was a sound that normally made her happy, but today it just added to her misery.

She looked up at her father, fighting to keep the emotion from her face. Despite her attempts, her sadness shone through in her lake blue eyes. "What you said about Linc's sister was nothing short of deplorable. And he told me what you said about Morgan, about how you plan on going public with the connection between Morgan's father and the Vasser family. Why are you involving yourself like this? It's only making you look petty and desperate."

Shaw sighed, then looked at his daughter with pity. "I went public with the information on Madison Vasser because it *is* the truth, pumpkin. The source was able to confirm it with the dealer who provided the drugs to Win. And when they came to me with the truth, too afraid to go public with it for fear of repercussions, I knew I had to act. It has nothing to do with Morgan. I was just doing my duty as a public servant."

Lynette paled, unsure if she believed him. "How can you be sure the source was telling the truth? Who was it? Someone within the family?"

"Now, honey, you know I can't tell you that," Shaw chuckled, reaching out to pat her hands sympathetically. "You'll just run on back and tell your little boyfriend. I can't risk my source's confidence that way."

"So then what about the article in the *New York Times* yesterday, the one claiming Madison is addicted to painkillers. Was that your doing as well?"

Surprise flashed over his face. "I hadn't heard about that."

"So it wasn't you?" Lynette shook her head, hoping to God he was telling her the truth. She wanted to believe that he wouldn't lower himself to something so petty...

"No, no it wasn't," Shaw mumbled, thoughtfully leaning back in his chair again.

"Could it have been your source? Maybe they decided to go to the press on their own this time?"

"I don't think so. My source was adamant about not wanting to be tied to the drug accusation. It's important for my source's safety that the dealer remains unknown." Shaw frowned, scratching his chin. "No, I'd say it's someone else entirely who went to the paper with that information."

Lynette buried her face in her hands, feeling lost. She believed her father, though she was still angry with him for what he had done. But knowing he wasn't behind the most recent attack gave her some measure of comfort while at the same time raised even more questions in her mind.

"My intention is not to hurt the Vasser family or Linc, Lynette," Shaw said then, watching her closely until she looked at him. She saw the honesty in his expression, and his eyes softened the way they always did when he felt sorry or hurt. "Listen to me when I tell you this. I spoke out about the suspected connection between Madison Vasser and her father's suicide because I felt the need to protect you. If she really is as dangerous as I assume she is, then I needed you to know. And since you won't return my phone calls, this was the only way I could get your attention."

Lynette's throat tightened as he continued, "I told you before that hell is coming to the Vassers. It was my colorful way of reminding you of the hell storm they've gotten themselves mixed up in. I wish you would distance yourself from it, but I know you won't. You're as stubborn as your old man."

A laugh managed to find its way out of her, though she felt so ashamed. She had been so brash to side against him, though her conscience had told her time and time again that he wasn't this evil man she had come to see him as. He was her father and always would be.

"And in regards to Jack Morgan...well, I'm only out to expose what he's so eager to bury," Shaw reasoned, reaching for her hand again. "The public has a right to know about his father."

"What about the Vassers?" Lynette asked.

"With the way things are going, I doubt this news is their biggest worry right now, Lynette."

She nodded, acknowledging he was probably right. "Linc wants me to marry him, daddy."

Shaw froze, stunned by her words. "Isn't it a bit soon to be talking marriage?"

"I love him," she told him, trying to hide the tears that suddenly leaked from her eyes. She welcomed his arms when he reached out to hold her.

"Then why are you crying?"

Lynette choked back a sob, leaning against her father's chest. "He left me. That's the main reason I'm here. I couldn't stand being in the city anymore."

"Maybe this is for the best, pumpkin," he began, rubbing his hand over her back. "He needs to focus on his family right now, and you have your dancing. I think you should stay for the week and take some time to clear your head in the Carolina sunshine."

She stayed silent, knowing in her heart what he was trying to do. He still did not want her to be with Linc, and while he wouldn't come outright and say it, the truth was evident in his voice.

But she wasn't going to give up so easily. In two days time, she'd go back to New York and find some way to contact Linc. She'd apologize, tell him what she had learned from her father, and then they could move on. She would not lose this battle, not when she still had enough vigor left in her for a fight.

TEN

Raoul left work like he always did, slipping out of the employee entrance on the east side of the building. He flipped up the collar of his black leather jacket in an attempt to keep out the chilly night air, grumbling under his breath in Spanish as he did so.

Nearly a decade of living in the city and he still wasn't accustomed to the lingering winter frost that held on long after the last snow fell. Some years mother nature was kind to the city and blessed her with warm, Atlantic air. Other times, nature turned a vindictive eye on the Big Apple and shut her down with a coldness that rattled the bones.

Already a proud pessimist, Raoul made no secret of his distaste of the weather. Even when there was no one around to hear it, he still griped and complained simply for the sake of venting his ever erupting volcano of frustration.

It was a habit that chased away most people, leaving him with few friends and little family that wanted anything to do with him. But, as with most people of a more prickly nature, less was more when it came to social obligations and the situation suited him just fine.

All he needed in his life was food. It was his passion, his craft, his *soul*. As long as he had a kitchen to work in and people to feed, he was content. If the world came crashing down around him, he would be the first to proclaim *Let it burn!* as long as they still came to eat.

Perhaps it was ironic then, that the world *did* appear to be crashing down around him, and he was not able to handle the disaster as well as he had hoped.

Madison was suffering, and it pained him to see it. He despised almost every member of that family, and seeing the way they used and abused her was driving him mad. Did they not see how capable she was? Could they not put aside their own agendas and understand her genius, her creativity, her ambition?

It appeared the only Vasser who *had* known of her true value and worth was Cyrus, the murderous son of a bitch. Now he was dead, and all he had done was leave Madison and the others with a scandal that would very likely ruin them before it was over.

He grunted bitterly as he shoved his hands into his jacket pockets, the stress and indignation of it all mauling him like a rabid dog. Around him, the dark alleyway glistened with rain that had fallen hours earlier, and he grimaced at the musty smell it left hanging in the air.

Madison wasn't listening to him and hadn't been for awhile now. Instead, she was letting herself fall into a trap, not only with the press and her family, but with Wyatt Bailey. As far as Raoul was concerned, there was no one left on her side except himself. No one else cared about her well-being like he did, and clearly no one saw the danger she was in.

Not only to her reputation, but to her life.

His attempts to help her had failed. Although he didn't want to, it appeared he may have to step up his efforts.

He continued down the alley, only to spot a dark figure approaching him from the busy street ahead. The man headed straight for him, and when the dim, orange light of a nearby security lamp exposed the man's face, Raoul's scowl deepened.

"The snake rises from the grass at last..." He sneered, his dark eyes taking in the trim and tidy business suit of Madison's cousin, also his former boss.

Duke managed a tight smile. "I love the colorful way you describe things, Raoul. It's very...European of you."

Raoul crossed his arms, saying nothing.

Duke chuckled before speaking again. "Has Mr. Bailey come by to talk with you yet?"

"That son of a bitch knows if he comes sniffing around my kitchen that he will not leave with his head," Raoul snapped, murder flashing in his eyes.

"Such violence..." Duke mused, eyebrows raised. "It appears he intends to stay for awhile...I suspect he's fucking my cousin again."

Raoul's hands clenched over his forearms, disgust and disapproval flashing over his face. "I have tried to warn her, to keep her away from him. She doesn't listen."

"I told you before, if he decides to go all noble and tell her about what happened in Vegas, we will find ourselves in one hell of a predicament," Duke reminded him. "But since he has not told her the truth yet, I doubt he ever will."

"He's afraid she won't believe him." Raoul managed a dark grin, the dim light shadowing the lines of his face. "She still loves him, but her hatred and distrust is stronger."

Duke nodded, suddenly thoughtful. "It surprises me that you followed her here to New York, and yet you didn't take her. All these years, and yet you still serve her like an obedient puppy."

Raoul's temper simmered dangerously. "I only want to protect her. She is my family."

"No, she's *my* family." Duke's smile turned into a grimace. "But given the circumstances, I'd gladly get rid of her."

"Giving up is not an option. She will fight you to the death," Raoul said with full confidence, stuffing his hands back into his pockets and pushing past Duke to make his way to the street. He mumbled curses under his breath as he went, only to freeze as Duke called out to him.

"In the end, she will have no choice."

Raoul grit his teeth and shut his eyes, fighting back the urge to beat the man to a bloody pulp for everything he was, everything he stood for. He restrained himself and continued to walk, disappearing into the crowd that walked the streets.

"I'M SO SORRY to bother you like this." Lynette stepped into Quinn's quaint apartment awkwardly. "I just didn't know where else to go."

"Hey, it's okay. That's what friends are for." Quinn smiled good naturedly, motioning toward her hand-me-down plaid sofa in shades of chocolate and burnt orange. It was one of the few pieces of furniture in the tiny living room, accompanied only by a stained, oak coffee table and a T.V. stand with no T.V. on it. Quinn had instead placed a bouquet of silk sunflowers, bright and sunny, in its place.

Lynette sat down on the couch and sank into the cushions, embarrassed that she could find no way to sit that didn't cause her to slouch. Her mother's voice rang out in her head, reminding her to sit straight, but Lynette pushed the thought aside and sat comfortably anyway.

Quinn quickly gathered some mugs with hot coffee and a tray of freshly baked cookies from the kitchen, setting them on the coffee table before settling onto the sofa herself. She cupped her mug in her hands, warming them as she eyed Lynette curiously.

"So you spoke to your dad?" she asked. "Grant told me all about Morgan and what your dad is planning to reveal to the press."

Lynette nodded slowly, sipping her own coffee as she tried to figure out where to begin. "He feels that the public has a right to know what Morgan's hiding. He doesn't think it will hurt the Vassers more than they've already been hurt."

"But it certainly won't help them, either," Quinn replied, her protective nature kicking in. "Isn't there some way you can convince him to let this go?"

Lynette let out a weary laugh, shaking her head. "He's stubborn. Once he's convinced himself that what he's doing is right, he doesn't change his mind."

Quinn frowned, though she understood. Wasn't she the very same way? Stubborn as an ox, pursuer of truth. "Well, then we need to soften the blow somehow when it does finally hit. What about the other leaks to the press? How does he explain that?"

"He claims that his source knows the drug dealer who supplied Linc's and Grant's dad with the drugs...apparently the drug dealer said that Madison told him to tamper with them."

Quinn blinked once in instant disbelief. "That's ridiculous."

"I thought so, too..." Lynette admitted, chewing on her lower lip restlessly. "But when I gave it more thought, I realized that I just don't really know Madison or her motives. I know Linc loves her, but love is often blind."

"Yes, but we don't know this source, either. They could be lying," Quinn charged, anger in her eyes now. "Hell, for all we know, Jorja Hale is this mysterious source and she's just trying to cover her own tracks by placing the blame on Madison."

"I contemplated that as well," Lynette said, her hands clenched together in her lap. "Except it doesn't make sense. If Jorja tampered with the drugs with the intent of coaxing Win to kill himself, why would she insist it wasn't merely a suicide? Why make a huge fuss if she's responsible? It only increases her risk of being caught."

Quinn frowned, realizing Lynette was right. It just didn't add up. "So then it's possible Madison did this. And it's also likely Jorja is the source *and* the one who's been leaking information to the press about Madison in an attempt to expose what really happened."

Lynette nodded, at a loss for words. Dread and fear coursed through her, and she buried her face in her hands as a sob built in her throat.

Quinn immediately wrapped her arm over Lynette's shoulders and pulled her close, fighting back her own dulled shock and alarm. "It'll be okay, we'll figure out what to do. Why don't I call Grant and we can meet him and Linc over at his place, and—"

"Linc doesn't want to see me," Lynette interrupted, looking at Quinn. "We had a fight about my father...that's why I went down to South Carolina for the weekend."

"Oh." Quinn faltered, pity flashing in her eyes before she replaced it with sunny optimism. "He'll get over it. He doesn't hold grudges, Lynette, you know that. He's just stressed out right now, we all are. Grant and I had a fight the other day, too."

"About what?" Lynette asked, trying to let Quinn's easy faith lift her spirits.

"Apparently he was irritated that I've been getting so involved. He doesn't want me to get hurt by all of this."

"How would you get hurt?" Lynette shook her head. "All you want to do is be there for him."

"I know, that's what I said." Quinn sighed, rubbing her friend's back consolingly. "But after I threatened to bop him over the head with my frying pan, he got over it."

"Smart man." Lynette's smile faded as the sinking feeling returned, and her eyes sobered as she watched Quinn. "How do you think they'll react to all of this?"

Quinn thought it over for a long moment, weighing the pros and cons in her head. Though it didn't sit right with her, she realized there was only one course of action they could take. "I wonder if maybe it's best for us to keep this to ourselves for now. I don't like lying to Grant, but until we know for sure that Madison did what we think she did, I think it's best for us not to say anything. The last thing the family needs is to be even more divided than they already are."

Lynette nodded. "You're probably right."

Just then, her cell phone went off in her pocket, and she pulled it out curiously. She shot a worried glance at Quinn. "It's Linc."

"Answer it!" Quinn grinned, pleased to see the excitement return to her friend's eyes. She prayed that it was Linc calling to apologize and not to sever ties even further.

Lynette lifted the phone to her ear, her hand shaking. She put all the cool reserve and confidence she could into her voice as she spoke. "Hello?"

"*It's me.*"

"I know," she replied flatly, even though her heart raced.

She heard Linc sigh audibly and could picture him running his hand through his hair. It was something he always did when he was agitated.

"Is something wrong?" she asked.

"*I'm ready to forgive you if you're ready to apologize.*"

She blinked in surprise and spoke without a moment's hesitation. "I'm sorry."

He was silent for a brief moment before speaking again.

"Alright, good enough. I'm sick of being mad at you. I miss you."

"I miss you, too." Lynette smiled in relief as she eyed Quinn, who was silently clapping her hands.

"Where are you? I went by your apartment but you haven't been there."

"I'm at Quinn's." Lynette could hear the television on in the background and assumed he was at his own place. "I'll head home right now if you want to meet me there."

"Yeah, that sounds go—" He cut off mid-sentence, but Lynette could still hear the television.

"Linc?"

"You've got to be fucking kidding me," he growled.

"What is it?"

He was silent for a moment longer, apparently listening to the newscast, and when he spoke again there was a definite fury in his voice. *"Things just got a lot more interesting."*

MADISON SAT IN her office, watching the newscast on the small television she'd had brought in. She took in the image of herself, a candid shot of her exiting the hotel that the paparazzi had managed to capture just days earlier.

It bothered her to see the exhaustion lining her face, the temper she normally kept so viciously in check visible in her eyes. This was how the public now saw her, as some harried, likely guilty woman clinging to her throne as her empire crashed and burned around her.

The gleeful reporter was rambling on about how they had been exclusively informed by an inside source with the family that Madison had known for years about her grandfather's horrific crimes. And that, despite her knowledge, she had kept the information a secret.

It was likely to ruin any chances the company had of going public and corporatizing, unless Madison stepped down. Or so the reporter claimed.

Madison only continued to watch and let the realization sink in that she had been betrayed. Not by Shaw or by Jorja Hale, not by some mysterious letter-sender.

She had been betrayed by her own family.

The only people who knew about her knowledge of what Cyrus had done had been sitting in the conference room with her that day when she had confessed of it. Whether or not they had blabbed about the secret to their wives, girlfriends, or friends, she couldn't know. But the truth was that one of them had seen fit to exploit the information and in turn put the entire family at risk.

One of them had gone to the press, their intention clearly to put her in the spotlight and have her shamed into resignation.

But who had done it?

She remembered the way Cy had practically leapt over the table in his angry attempt to attack her, and the cold and callous way Duke had berated and questioned her. She recalled the stunned disbelief on her three uncles' faces and the mortified disgust that had followed. The idea of any of them turning on her was not a far-fetched one.

Or even her own brothers, who she wanted to believe would never hurt her. Grant had yet to bring it up again, which meant he was still stewing over it, and Linc had only half-forgiven her. It was clear that their trust in her had wavered and, as a result, she had to wonder if they would view this as an opportunity to force her to back down.

She shivered and had to steel herself against the sharp, piercing cold pain of it all, wrapping her arms over her torso as a means of defense. Her eyes closed tight as she tried to sort through all of it in her head, the players and the events and the threats. How was she supposed to save her family's company when everyone was against her? How could she move forward when every step she took only forced her two steps back?

Disillusioned and aching, she fought back the useless and help-less tears and tried to think of her grandfather. What would Cyrus do in this situation?

She stared down at the tattoo on her wrist, running her thumb over it, trying to find some bit of strength to pull from.

"What do I do, *pépère*?" she whispered, her throat tightened as if clamped shut by a vice. "I can trust no one, now."

She wondered if he spoke the thought that suddenly flew through her mind, only because such a revelation could only have come from the depths of Hell itself. Surely it was foolish, and she'd be damned if she didn't see the irony of it...and yet it was so perfect.

The only person who knew nothing of her secret also happened to be the person who had held the same knowledge for years, long before her father had gone to the press and made headlines with the news that Cyrus had killed Winston.

The only man her father had ever trusted, and consequently the only man to have ever broken her heart, was now the one person she could guarantee had not betrayed her on this.

It amused her to understand then that, despite everything between them, he was now going to be her salvation.

It was an irony Cyrus would have appreciated.

She shot immediately to her feet and left her office, making her way upstairs to his room. When she got there, she rapped impatiently on the door.

The second Wyatt opened it, she pushed him back inside and assaulted him, her mouth eagerly finding his. The door slammed shut and the sound of it thundered through her as she emptied everything she had into this one, frantic act.

She didn't want to need him, didn't want to even be there with him. But sometimes wants are overshadowed by a pure and primal need, and hers at that moment drove her to him.

Wyatt held her, stunned by her urgency and concerned by her desperation. This was no longer the cool, reserved, and controlled woman he loved. This was a woman with her chest torn open and her heart exposed, with all her insecurities laid out for him to see.

She was on the edge of ruin, and she sought something he had been trying to give her all along.

Strength. Comfort. Love.

Madison raked her nails over his back as she broke the kiss and buried her face in his neck, knowing there were tears in her eyes and not wanting him to see. She didn't know what he would do, what he would say, if he saw them.

Then again, she'd come to him in a moment of weakness. As much as she despised crying, this time she let herself embrace it. She let the tears overflow and spill down her cheeks, the warmth in its own sorrowful way bringing her comfort. Giving her release.

Without words, Wyatt lifted her off her feet and took her to the bed. He put her down and then laid beside her, pulling her to his chest and holding her tight against him.

She let out a long breath that caught in her throat, shutting her eyes and resting her head in the crook of his neck. Her hand trailed over his chest, and she let herself be comforted by the feel of him beside her.

Wyatt ran his hand idly through her hair, giving her time to pull her thoughts together. He knew she would appreciate having the first word. She hated being pestered when she was upset, and the fact that she had come to him meant she had something to say. He had to fight back his own shock and panic over her outburst and accept that soon she would explain herself to him.

When she finally spoke, he carefully noted that there was more sorrow in her voice than anger. That was never a good sign.

"I have no one to trust now," she murmured, her eyes glassy as she stared unseeingly at the wall. "And of all the people I ever thought I'd come to in a crisis like this, I never expected it would be you. And yet here I am."

For a moment he said nothing, he only absorbed her words and carefully dissected them.

"Tell me what happened."

She felt a fresh wave of pain wash over her and bit it back as she continued. "You knew all these years that my grandfather had killed Winston. You kept it secret, because you respected my father's wishes."

When he remained silent, she pulled away so she could look into his eyes. He stared back, and the quiet concern she saw steadied her. He had always been cool under pressure, level-headed despite mounting chaos. They were the very traits she normally possessed herself, except this time the turmoil was overwhelming her.

But with his help, she wouldn't be overwhelmed for long.

"I knew it, too," she admitted, her face open to the righteousness she felt, the vindication. "I've known since I was nine years old."

Wyatt studied her, not at all surprised by her admission. He knew how close she had been to Cyrus, how much she had trusted the man and admired him. While Wyatt had stood on the opposite side in support of Win, he could still understand why Madison had looked up to her grandfather.

"Did you know about the other murders?" he asked, though he knew the answer. Madison would have never supported the greedy slaughter of one's own brothers.

"No." She rested her head in her hands over his chest, keeping her eyes on his. "He trusted me with many of his secrets, but not that one."

He nodded slowly, reaching out to brush a strand of dark hair from her forehead. "Tell me the rest, sweetheart."

A fresh tear slipped down her cheek. "Someone let it leak to the press that I knew about the murder. The only people who knew were my family."

His eyes hardened to cold steel as he processed the news. "Someone inside the family did this?"

"It appears so," she said quietly. "And I don't know who."

Wyatt kept his suspicions to himself. He wouldn't be able to explain them to her without telling her the truth about Las Vegas, and he knew right now was not the time to reveal that horrid truth. Not when she was already suffering over her family's betrayal.

"The public now views me as the architect of a murder cover-up who coaxed my own father into suicide. Oh, and I'm also apparently a Vicodin addict," she said then, a dark laugh escaping her throat at the absurdity of it all. She laid her forehead against her hands as she continued to laugh, more tears falling from her eyes as she did so.

Wyatt only lifted her face, forcing her to look at him. He was remarkably steady as he spoke, and his words shook the dark amusement and fear right out of her.

"You're a fighter, Madison. You always have been." The confidence in his eyes shattered her, and she clung to it like it was her lifeline and she was perilously close to plummeting to her death. "You're going to turn all of this to your advantage."

"How?" she asked, though her eyes widened with hope at the thought. Her own mind began turning as he continued.

"Stage a press conference, go directly to the public and give them the truth. Knock out all the wagging tongues by calling them on their bluff." He cupped her face in his hand as his lips curved into that trickster's grin she had always loved. "Make headlines, baby. Show them what you're made of. What the Vasser *legacy* is made of."

Inspired, she smiled and shifted forward, kissing him hard and fast on the mouth. She stared down at him, pleased to see the heat come into his eyes as his hands cruised over her body. "Just what am I made of, exactly?"

He grinned again, tightening his hand in her hair and pulling her in until her lips brushed over his. Their eyes held, close and direct, and she nearly shivered from the intensity she saw in his.

"The very best of Heaven and Hell," he declared, abruptly flipping her so she was beneath him, already arching as he pressed seductively against her. A moan escaped her lips as her head fell back, her heart flooding with fire and dark, dark need. It beat hot and true with her love for him, and she let it fuel her as she kissed him again.

"I don't know why, I don't know how, but I still love you, Wyatt."

His hands tightened their hold on her waist as he grinded against her, his breath catching in his throat at her words. He found he had to rest his head against her forehead to steady himself, as the violent surge of emotion, flames of both relief and desire, consumed him.

"Say it again," he demanded, eyes flying open to bore into her own. He tore at the blouse she wore, exposing her as she smiled breathlessly and her nails bit into the flesh of his back.

"I love you."

It was all he had been waiting to hear.

ELEVEN

Though it went against convention, she dressed in red for the press conference.

It was a scarlet dress that hugged her curves and had a modest, straight lined collar. The sleeves ran long to her elbows and the skirt rested comfortably at her knees. She'd paired it with her grandmother's engraved gold locket, which rested between her breasts as a glaring symbol of her heritage and her bloodline.

Madison had left her hair to hang loose to her shoulders, and the light caught the gold in the coffee brown of it as she stood at the podium, her eyes scanning the crowd that stood before her in the ballroom of the hotel. Chairs had been arranged to seat the dozens of people that had shown up, while the camera crews hovered in the sidelines, ready and waiting.

Off to the left of the low level stage, her brothers stood anxiously side by side. Both had advised her against this little spectacle, but she brushed their concerns away. She had a lot to say, and she needed the world to hear it.

Press from all the networks hovered in silence as they waited for her to begin. Cameras flashed off every few seconds, and she made sure to reveal her inner strength of will in each and every shot.

They would not know of her meltdown the night before. Instead, they would see her as she was now, filled with purpose and dedication. She was a beacon of strength, an embodiment of everything good her grandfather had been.

As for his sins...well, she was ready to prove she wasn't guilty of the same ones.

"Thank you all for coming to our beautiful hotel today," she began, her smile somber yet graceful. She couldn't let her true derision of the press to show through; they were going to be her only means of saving herself and her company. "It is my intention to set the record straight on some matters involving myself and the Vasser Hotels that have been circling the gossip mill these last several days.

"I want to begin by stating that, as my grandfather's successor, I fully intend to restore my family's good name and reputation in this great country of ours and across the world. We have been a standing testament to the power of the American dream as well as a leader in luxury hotel innovations for over a century, and we intend to stay that way. I have a solid plan that will restore America's faith in us, all the while giving us the opportunity to prove ourselves worthy of her trust and business."

She paused, carefully watching the faces of those before her, pleased to see she had their full attention. Her voice took on a hint of anger as she continued, and she made sure to convey the power she felt in every syllable.

"Lately, there have been some allegations made against me that I feel the need to address. I have no intention of allowing myself or my family to be bullied and harassed without countering these claims with facts.

"Firstly, I played no role in my father's suicide. I guarded him from the public in an attempt to protect him, keeping him housed safely inside the hotel. We will never know if that played a part in his despair, but my best guess and the opinion held by the local police department is that the drugs were the leading factor. Senator Shaw has claimed that I conspired with the dealer and tampered with the drugs, but that accusation is entirely false. Despite what the senator and others would have you believe, I will not resort to killing off members of my own family in order to get what I want. In that way, I am not my grandfather.

"Secondly, I have been accused of being addicted to painkillers." She held up a piece of paper, lifting it so the crowd could see it. A bunch of pictures snapped off as she did so. "This morning I went to the hospital and had a drug test performed. The results are negative. I hope this puts the matter to rest."

There was a slow rumble of voices as the crowd murmured to each other, clearly startled at her bold display of confidence. She only smiled to herself as she set the paper down and addressed the crowd once more.

"And lastly, I have been accused of being aware of my grandfather's role in the death of my great-grandfather since I was a child. I will not deny this claim. In fact, I will elaborate on it."

The crowd burst into another wave of conversation as reporters suddenly began shouting out questions to her, unable to hold their silence any longer.

"Ms. Vasser, if you knew about the murder, why did you not go to the police?"

"What do you have to say to the rest of your family?"

"How can you expect America to trust you when you kept something like this a secret?"

She only smiled again, remaining cool and composed despite the attack. Perhaps it was her disarming expression that had the reporters backing down, their questions unanswered, as they all anxiously awaited her response.

"As I'm sure you are all well aware, legally I was not obligated to say anything," she began, her voice steady and self-assured. "I was a child when I learned of the murder, and as such was manipulated into believing it was what was right for the future of my family. I lived my life up until the last few months believing that to be true.

"I loved my grandfather more than any other person on the face of this earth. While all of you make a scandal out of the sins of his life, you easily forget the long list of remarkable feats he accomplished, the jobs he helped create and the strength of character he exhibited on a daily basis while none of you were watching. But I was. I was there, by his side nearly my entire life, waiting patiently in his shadow for the day I could prove myself worthy of his pride.”

She inhaled slowly, her teeth flashing in a smile as she reveled in her good memories of him and let them cloak her. “That day has arrived. I am now the face of the Vasser family. As we enter this new era and break free of some old traditions while carving out our own, my brothers and I, and the rest of my family, will remain united and strong. We *are* America, proof that a man can start with nothing and build an empire, a business that employs thousands of people across the world. And as we move forward with our plan to restructure our company, we will be employing many more and welcoming more to our doors for a comfortable, reliably luxurious hotel stay. I hope you will join us. Thank you.”

She turned to leave the podium just as the crowd erupted. Some of them just watched, stunned speechless. Others scrambled after her, cameramen in tow, as they continued to ask her questions.

She only smiled and politely excused herself, Grant and Linc flanking her protectively and leading her from the ballroom and into a side room away from the crowd. More pictures flashed behind them as Grant shut the door, enclosing them in a small office. He locked the door and then folded his arms.

Linc stared at his sister, who met his gaze determinedly and didn’t let go. For a few moments, neither said anything as they absorbed the weight of what just happened.

Suddenly, he reached out and pulled her into a tight hug, a disbelieving laugh bubbling from his throat.

“You kicked major ass out there, Mads,” he told her as he stepped back, holding her at arm’s length. His lips were spread in a wide grin as he shook his head. “I wasn’t sure how this was going to go, but you really nailed it.”

She released the breath she had been holding, a smile blooming over her face. “Yes, yes I did.”

Grant approached her and gathered her close, shutting his eyes tight as his heart finally settled down. He’d been so afraid for her, so utterly convinced this would backfire. Time would ultimately tell if it was going to help or hurt the family, but from the looks on the reporters' faces, he had a feeling Madison had just done the best thing possible.

"You were excellent," he said as he pulled back, turning then to Linc as his brother piped in.

"Yeah, we should have trusted you. I promise to do so from now on, scout's honor." He held his hand up to his forehead in a salute and grinned again.

She couldn't help but smile in return. He was her charming, loyal-to-the-bone brother, her ray of sunshine in her darkest days. He wouldn't betray her...and Grant, well, he didn't have a manipulative bone in his body. He was too direct and blunt for that.

Realizing she had done herself a major disservice for even doubting her brothers for one second, she kissed both of their cheeks in turn.

"No matter what happens, the three of us stick together," she said, eyeing them earnestly. "I need you, both of you."

They blinked in surprise, not used to hearing her speak that way. They looked at each other before turning back to her.

Linc reached out to pat her on the shoulder. "We're family, Mads. We'll always stay together."

IN THE WEEK that followed, Madison Vasser was the topic of nearly every news outlet. There were a fair share of critics and naysayers, but there were far more supporters. More, in fact, than any of them could have imagined possible just weeks before.

"She's practically a celebrity," Quinn grinned, curling up to Grant as they lay in his bed, watching Madison on television as she chatted casually with Jay Leno. "People are fascinated by her. They can't get enough."

Grant grunted in agreement, his eyes glued to his sister and his heart feeling lighter than it had in days. It appeared that the press conference had, for reasons he couldn't quite figure out, completely changed public sentiment about the Vassers. For now, at least, the public was having its love affair with Madison.

And he had to admit, she was nothing if not impressive.

"Look at how she smiles, how she laughs," Quinn pointed out. "So much control and yet, she seems so at ease, so relatable. I don't get how she does it."

"She's always been good at showing people the face she wants them to see," Grant told her with a heavy sigh. "I've always considered it manipulation, and yet here she is, using it to her advantage in a way I could never do."

"Every man in that room wants her, and every girl wants to be her." Quinn laughed, tilting her head and kissing Grant's cheek. "You should be proud of her."

"I am," he confirmed, his eyes still on his sister as she related a story of her childhood to Leno. "But with every rise, there is an inevitable fall."

Quinn's smile wavered, and she thought, yet again, about telling him what Lynette's father had said about the drug dealer. It was difficult to not share it with him, just to see what he would say. Even though she was beginning to have doubts about the validity of the claim herself.

"Such a pessimist," she joked, trying to hide her uncertainty behind a sunny smile. "We just have to make the inevitable fall a graceful one."

He frowned at the television, eyes narrowing as he watched a popular singer who had started her own production company walk on stage to sit beside Madison. The woman visibly gushed as she shook his sister's hand. "Women seem to have a particular fascination with my sister."

"She's earned their respect by standing up for herself," Quinn replied easily. "She's running a company formerly run by nothing but men, and she's taking charge of her own destiny. As a fellow woman, I can see a lot to admire in that. We can all learn something from her."

Grant looked at her, his lips upturning slightly at the corners. "You know, Madison could learn a lot from you, as well."

She rolled her eyes and grinned. "Please. I'm just me. I talk too much, am way too stubborn, quote my mother to an embarrassing degree, and eat peanut butter out of the jar with a spoon."

"You're incredible," he corrected, tilting her face up so he could kiss her. Her answering laugh was cut off by his mouth claiming hers, and she melted into him, her heart fluttering at his words. He used them so sparingly, and yet when he did it was like magic.

"You know what my mother would say at a time like this?" Quinn said, breaking the kiss and sitting up with wink.

"What?"

"Let's break out the Cabernet, put on some Dean Martin, and see where the night takes us." She beamed at him, her eyes glowing with warmth. "Whaddya say?"

He smiled. "Lucky for you, my Martin collection is impeccable."

IN THE WEEK since the press conference, Madison's schedule went from busy to crowded to hectically on overdrive. Carrie was no longer merely an assistant, but now wore various hats, including agent, promoter, time manager, and stylist.

The hotel experienced a boost in reservations, which put a smile on Grant's face. The press was, for once, printing positive pieces about the family, which gave Linc a reason to live again. And for the first time since Cyrus' death, Madison felt as though the rest of her family was actually on her side. At least, they were pretending to be.

She still had yet to determine who had leaked her secret to the press, but with all of the interviews, appointments, lunches, functions, and overall busy romance with the public, she was too tired to think about it. She kept the thought at the back of her mind, to be re-visited the second she could catch her breath.

As it was, she only planned to engage in this revelry for one more week. She was running up against the deadline she had set for the company to take its first steps toward corporatizing, and she couldn't let anything get in the way of that.

And, if she was being honest with herself, she was already sick of it. While she played the part of the admired, relatable, and brazen hotel heiress well, she still had a job to do. Her family was counting on her to get the company back on track and she had no intention of failing.

With the added boost in popularity, hopefully things would run much smoother from here on out. The "inside source" that Shaw and the papers had credited for the previous accusations had gone mysteriously silent, which meant either they had no further tricks up their sleeves or they were biding their time for something even more detrimental.

What that could be, she had no idea. But if and when it happened, she vowed to be ready for it.

Now that her face and name were gaining notoriety, people began to take a fascination with her love life. The simple fact that they called what she had a "love life" amused the hell out of her.

She preferred to call it a dangerous, slippery jaunt through a field of prickly roses, both beautiful and deadly, with plenty of razor sharp thorns along the way. It was an experiment in madness, and she was well aware that she was going against every ounce of common sense she had to pursue it.

But, as with most things of a darker, more sinful nature, the pleasure she received was well worth the risks.

She stared at a picture of herself with Wyatt in one of the tabloids, exiting the hotel on their way to dinner two nights earlier. The slim, gold dress she wore caught the light of the flashing cameras, and a seductive half smile softened her face. Beside her, dressed in a casual black suit paired with his fedora, was Wyatt. The hat shielded his eyes as he tipped his head down, but the light stubble that graced his jawline and the subtle, arrogant curve of his mouth spoke of the kind of man he was.

The worst kind of bastard. The one you can't help but love.

"What a headline," Wyatt murmured from behind her, his hands expertly kneading her shoulders. "*The Inside Scoop on the Man Behind the Brazen Vasser Hotel Heiress.*"

"I think they love you more than me," Madison mused, flipping through the magazine to find the article. When she did, her eyes scanned the words and images, amused by the other shots of both her and Wyatt together. There was the usual wedding speculation, including date, location, and honeymoon spot. Why anyone gave a damn if and when she got married she didn't understand, but then again, such was life in the public eye.

She read over the short biography put together on Wyatt and paused when she saw the word Kansas, along with the name of the high school he attended. Her eyes narrowed as she tilted her head back to look at him. "You didn't live in Kansas."

He smiled cagily, squeezing her shoulders once before lifting the magazine from her hands. He read the piece himself, then tossed it back on her desk with a shrug. "After my mom died, I left Maine and lived with my aunt for a couple years in Kansas. The second I hit eighteen, I was gone."

"Why didn't you tell me that before?"

"You never asked." He brushed it off, not wanting to talk about his past with her. It wasn't something he was exactly proud of. "What does it matter?"

She only watched him quietly, assessing his discomfort. He'd closed up on her like a steel trap, guarding some dragon he didn't want her to see. It reminded her, yet again, that he was just as much a man of secrets now as he had been all those years before.

"How am I supposed to trust you when I don't even know you?" she asked heatedly, rising to her feet to get in his face. She tilted her head to the side as she looked up at him, fire in her eyes. "You might as well be a stranger to me, Wyatt. You keep more secrets from me than you share."

"Don't act like you don't have secrets you keep from me, sweetheart," he shot back with a cold grin. On impulse, he grabbed her wrist, lifting it so he could look at the tattoo that marred her skin. "Like this one. You've never told me what it means."

She let out a long, slow exhale, her blood quickening beneath her skin as her eyes met his and held. She hated knowing he was right.

"It symbolizes the age I was when my grandfather entrusted me with his secrets," she told him, her voice flavored with both heartache and temper. "And you never asked."

Dark humor flashed over his face as he pulled her tight against him, his mouth teasing hers. He smiled, his teeth nipping at her lower lip. "We always were two of a kind."

"God, we're vain," she moaned, her hands reaching up to take hold of his length of bronze hair.

"Not vain...we're infamous," Wyatt growled, lifting her roughly by her hips onto the desk and crushing her mouth with his. Before he could tear her clothes off, there was a quick, rapping knock on the door before it was shoved open.

"Hey, Mads, I—" Linc waltzed in, a bottle of champagne in his hand and Lynette close behind him. He froze, then covered his eyes with a groan. "Really, guys?"

Lynette burst into giggles behind him and had to cover her mouth while Carrie peered in from her desk curiously. Wyatt only grinned and backed away from Madison, holding his hand out to help her back onto her feet. He then walked over to Linc and patted him cheerfully on the back.

"Afternoon delight is not just a song, man." He winked, then turned to Lynette. He bowed his head, tipped his non-existent hat graciously, and smiled at her. "*Mademoiselle.*"

She bit back a laugh and lifted her chin regally, extending her hand to him. "Mr. Bailey."

He accepted her hand and leaned in to press his lips to her skin, eyes shifting to Linc as he straightened. "Is that champagne for sharing or did you just come here to bother us?"

Linc gave him a sidelong look. "Believe me, if I thought I'd be interrupting something, I would have taken this party elsewhere."

Madison straightened her dress, eyebrows raised as she looked at her brother. "What are we celebrating?"

"A changing of the tide," Linc announced, tearing open the wrapping on the bottle and happily popping the cork. Lynette was at his side in an instant, plastic champagne flutes at the ready. He poured the champagne as he continued, "Not only have I put the final touches on our remarketing campaign, thanks to all the free time I've had this week *not* having to worry about the press," he winked at Madison and handed her the first glass. "But I also just got off the phone with the CEO of McAllister Hotels...he wants to go in with us on our expansion and take on our brand name. We could have a full line of classy yet affordable three-star hotels bearing the Vasser name within three years."

Madison's lips parted as surprise flashed over her face. "That's... incredible."

Just then, Grant and Quinn walked in.

"Did you tell her?" Quinn asked, teeth flashing in a bright grin.

"I'd say by the look of shock on her face, she knows," Grant put in dryly, though he met his sister's eyes and smiled. "What do you think, Mads? Should we accept his offer?"

Her gaze shifted between her brothers as she gave it some thought, trying to quickly work out all the angles of this new opportunity. It would definitely be a head start on her plans...

"Arrange a meeting and we'll make this happen." She lifted her glass in a toast, smiling as Grant and Quinn were poured glasses and joined in with the others. Her eyes flickered to each face, from her lover at her side, to her brothers across from her, to the women they loved who were becoming something of friends to her. It humbled her deeply to have them all there, taking part in this monumental turning point in the Vasser legacy. "To our empire. Though it has fallen, witness now as it rises from the ashes to begin anew."

"Amen to that," Wyatt added, clicking his glass to the others and turning to Madison before sipping. While the others began talking, he leaned in to kiss her cheek, then hovered beside her ear. "Don't forget that with every success comes those who want to take it away from you."

She met his eyes as he pulled away, her gaze fierce and her smile wicked around the edges.

"I dare them to try."

DUSK CLAIMED THE sky as her sneakers hit the pavement. She jogged swiftly, expertly, her body well tuned to the rhythm of the hip hop that blasted through her headphones.

Kennedy avoided pedestrians on the sidewalk, darted between parked cars and kept her eyes open for bicyclists. It was like an obstacle course, but it was one she loved.

Out here, she wasn't Kennedy Vasser, useless kid sister to the glorious Madison Vasser. No, she was just a girl enjoying a run, comfortable in her own skin.

Angry tears clouded her vision as flashes of Madison all over the television and magazines plagued her, her sister's notoriety the talk of the town. Everyone suddenly loved her, for some stupid reason, and her brothers were getting a fair share of the attention, too. Suddenly her family was all the rage, victims of bullies but ready to rise above the demons of their past.

It made her sick to her stomach.

She was still a nobody. It seemed the press couldn't be bothered to print anything about her. She just wasn't important enough, apparently. No one cared about *her* opinions, or *her* accomplishments. No, all they cared about was how Madison had stood up for herself against the people she claimed lied about her.

But Kennedy didn't believe a word of it. As far as she was concerned, Madison was still responsible for their father's death. Even if she didn't have anything to do with the drugs, she had still hated him and wanted him out of the way. That was enough to make any father kill himself.

And the fact that she'd known about their great-grandfather's murder for all these years was unforgivable. How could she even *live* with herself?

Her fingernails dug into the palms of her hands as she picked up her pace, letting her anger fuel her. At some point, karma was going to come back and hurt Madison for her actions. She didn't know when, she didn't know how, but she knew it would be one hell of a doozy when it hit.

She sincerely hoped she had some part to play in it when it happened.

The van slowed and pulled to the curb behind her, but she didn't notice it. All she could hear was Jay-Z's voice rapping adoringly about the concrete jungle they both called home.

A startled gasp escaped her lips as an arm suddenly wrapped around her torso, her sneakers skidding as she jolted to a stop. Before she could register what was happening, she was dragged into the van and gagged, a black cover pulled over her head as the door shut with a loud slam.

The music continued to blast in her ears as her hands were tied. In her panic, she barely felt the needle that slipped into her arm, the drug coaxing her almost instantly to sleep.

TWELVE

Charlene sat at the oversized, cherrywood dining table in her town house, the phone held impatiently against her ear. She rapped her fingers against the table, her nails clicking over the wood as the phone continued to ring. When Kennedy's voicemail picked up, yet again, she hung up the phone and slammed it down impatiently.

She stared at the table, graced with heirloom china, spotless ivory lace placemats, and fresh pink orchids. Roasted chicken with sprigs of asparagus sat uneaten on a plate before her, another full plate across the table. She glared at the food, now going cold, trying to beat back the worry that slithered horribly into her gut.

Kennedy was always home from her run by seven o'clock. It was already nearing nine. Charlene grabbed the phone once more and dialed her daughter's cell, a furious scolding on her tongue as she waited with bated breath for an answer.

Nothing. She quickly dialed Linc's number, the idea suddenly occurring to her that Kennedy could be at the hotel visiting him. Though it had been weeks since she had wanted to go to there…

"*What's up, mom?*" Linc answered, the sound of a ballgame on in the background.

"Is Kennedy with you?" Charlene demanded, irritated that her voice shook.

"*No, why?*" The sounds of baseball died out as he muted the television, his voice hardening. "*What's going on? Is everything okay?*"

"She hasn't come home yet." Charlene frowned, rubbing at her temple wearily. "I've tried calling her dozens of times. She won't answer."

"*Maybe she's out with friends. She's nineteen, mom. She's allowed to have a social life outside of you.*"

Charlene bristled. "She knows better than to not call me."

Linc sighed audibly on the other line. "*I'm sure she's fine. Don't stress out, and just think of the ass-whooping you get to give her the second she slinks back into the house. God knows you gave me more than one.*"

Despite the circumstances, she smiled. "Goodnight, Linc."

She hung up the phone and cut into her chicken breast, attempting to eat. She managed to swallow a few bites before the deafening silence of the house got to her.

Damnit, she was used to that obnoxious music Kennedy listened to, blasting down from her room upstairs. The house suddenly seemed so empty without it.

She sipped at her glass of wine and tried desperately hard not to imagine her daughter lying dead in a gutter somewhere.

Things like that didn't happen in this neighborhood, she reminded herself. No reason to panic.

HIS DREAMS TOOK him deep into the past.

Marshall saw his mother as she had been in his youth, vibrant and full of life. Her blonde hair glowed golden in the sun as she stood beside him outside of the hotel, her lips painted a brilliant red that contrasted with the radiance of her smile. Eyes of the richest blue stared down at him, always clever and a little bit mysterious. He was a child again and her hand held his tiny one, close and secure.

His mother Stella had been the only woman he had ever truly loved. Although he had lost her long ago, his memories of her were still extraordinarily vivid. Her laugh, her smile, her quick wit and sharp tongue. She had been, in his opinion, the most amazing woman to have ever lived. His father had been a lucky man to have convinced her to marry him.

She often walked beside him in his dreams, taking him back to his childhood and the times he missed the most. Life had been easier then, happier and filled with prosperity. The family business grew after the war and, as with most Americans, the Vasser family thrived.

Perhaps that was why his dreams took him to those years more often than not. The years before *it* happened.

Before the suicide that had rocked his family to its very core.

Well, suspected suicide. But none of them had been any the wiser to that fact at the time.

Marshall tossed and turned restlessly in his sleep, the image of his mother sharpening into clearer focus as she suddenly let go of his hand. He let his arm drop to his side as he watched her walk away from him, her legs carrying her out into the street. Cars drove by, old Fords and Buicks that gleamed in the sunlight, but they didn't seem to notice her.

He started to rush forward to stop her, but his feet wouldn't move. He seemed glued to the concrete, his body frozen and useless. Panicked, he called out to her, but she wasn't listening. Instead she continued ahead until she was standing in the middle of one of the lanes. She paused, then turned around slowly to face him.

He barely recognized her sultry yet vindictive expression. She wore red now, her body draped in a dress that reminded him of blood. As she stared at him, those blue eyes he'd loved suddenly burned with ice cold fury, and his own widened as a jolt of fear shot through him.

Suddenly, a car drove past her at a rapid speed, blocking her momentarily from his view. He jumped in his own skin, his heart galloping wildly within his chest. In that heartbeat of a second, fear choked off his breath and trembled through his child's frame.

The car passed, and his mother was gone. In her place stood Madison, wearing the same dress and cruel facial expression. He swallowed the lump that filled his throat, unable to comprehend what he was witnessing. Before he could do more than blink, his niece's face twisted in an expression of absolute horror, just before the car struck her and the world went black.

He jolted awake, his eyes flying open and sweat beading on his forehead. His breath came out in rasping coughs as he stared frantically around his darkened bedroom, as though expecting to see the women there.

After a few moments, he managed to calm himself down. His heart was still beating furiously fast, but at least it had been just a dream.

A mortifying dream, but still nothing more than his imagination.

He tumbled out of bed, noting the clock read just past two o'clock in the morning. Rubbing his forehead tiredly, he made his way into the kitchen and poured himself a strong drink. He took it with him into his office and collapsed in his favorite armchair.

The image of Madison's face blurred with that of his mother in his mind, replaying over and over again as though hell bent on burning into his very skull. He fought to keep his eyes open as he sipped the bourbon, attempting to ward off the image.

Despite his efforts to be rid of them, the two most important women in his life continued to haunt him.

He had often compared the two of them, acknowledging the similarities that came from the bloodline. Madison possessed the same elegance, clever mind, and determined nature that his mother had. So it was no surprise that he should dream of them together, their faces meshing into one, stunning creature.

A creature of death.

He shuddered as he polished off the rest of his drink, his face strained and contorted with grief and disgust. The information he had learned earlier that day had changed everything he knew about the love of his life—his mother. His denial had been immediate, but there was no getting past the cold hard facts of what had been laid out before him. He couldn't escape it, couldn't rationalize it, and couldn't accept it.

His mother had helped cover up what his father had done. Because of it, she was just as guilty of murder as Cyrus had been. Just as guilty as Madison was.

Marshall grit his teeth as anger surged into him, causing his hands to shake as he seriously considered hurling the glass he held into the wall just to have the satisfaction of destroying something. Had he been twenty years younger, he might have. Now he just didn't have the strength left to do something so violent.

So instead he set the glass on the little table beside his chair and reached for the Army file he had received that morning. He opened it up again, scanning the documents inside.

This Paul Morgan had done a good job of covering for the murders. He had systematically stamped each of the eyewitness accounts as inconclusive, citing the confusion and terror of wartime. The report listing the evidence of rope around the bodies was also stamped as inconclusive, disproved by a follow up report confirming the presence of rope in that vicinity used for securing cargo on the trucks.

Every supporting piece of evidence that should have placed the blame on Cyrus Vasser was quietly buried under Morgan's discrediting stamp.

But what he hadn't thought to hide was the note, likely by his secretary, documenting the visit of Stella Vasser on October 2nd, 1944. Naturally, one would expect that he had scheduled the meeting with the wife of the accused soldier in order to explain to her his final ruling on the case and the actions to be taken against her husband.

Except that the date his secretary had stamped on the file was October 5th, 1944. Which could only mean that Stella had visited with Morgan and convinced him to initiate the cover-up. There was no other explanation; Morgan would not have covered up the crimes on his own, and Cyrus was overseas in France at that time, trying to get back to the States. The only person within the Vasser family who met with Morgan was Stella.

Which meant that Stella had known of the murders, accepted them, and assisted Cyrus in covering them up.

The very thought of it made Marshall sick to his stomach.

But what was almost worse than discovering the true nature of the mother he had worshiped his entire life, was finding out the incredible connection that Paul Morgan had, not only to his own family, but to the greatest enemy facing the Vassers. His contact had unearthed the information and written a note to him enclosed with the file.

The note had disturbed him more than the file itself.

Morgan's wife had been of Vasser lineage, which explained how Stella was able to blackmail him. If the Vasser family had been torn to shreds by murder, then he and his wife likely would have suffered as a result of the association.

And Morgan's son, Jack Morgan, was now running for a senate seat in South Carolina.

He was going up against the incumbent, none other than Senator Warren Shaw.

Marshall shut the file and tossed it aside, apprehensive and fearful for his family. He had no way of knowing if Shaw knew of this connection, but if the man ever found out, he'd surely use it against his opponent. Who wouldn't? It was incredibly damning.

If Shaw did go public with it, what would this Jack Morgan do to soften the blow? Would he throw the Vasser family under the bus to save his own hide? Or would he join with them in combating the truth?

Only time would tell. But the whole mess left a bad taste in Marshall's mouth and a feeling of dread in his gut.

For the very first time, he felt his age. Burdened by life and jaded by its cruelty.

He was helpless to do anything now. It was up to the young ones to protect the family. He didn't have the strength left to fight.

GRANT SIFTED THROUGH the paperwork on his desk, pleased by what he saw.

Even though the press had begun to move on to other topics, Madison had left an impression. The New York Hotel had seen a healthy rise in reservations, and the deal that had been struck with the CEO of the McAllister Hotels had been publicly announced and well-received. The concept of Vasser luxury tied with McAllister convenience and affordability was a home run, and suddenly the cloudy future for his family's company appeared lined with silver.

But being a born and bred cynic had him doubting the glowing, bright stars appearing on their horizon. Surely something was bound to happen that would put a wrench in their plans. That was what always happened, and he'd rather be prepared for the inevitable instead of starry eyed like his brother was. Even Madison seemed more optimistic, her ambitious spirit in full gear and her determination unstoppable.

The deadline for enacting the changes Madison had planned for the family was looming closer, just under a week away. Grant was surprised to see that both Cy and Duke seemed to be more accepting of this inevitability as it got closer. It was as if their eyes had suddenly opened to the possibilities. Or they had just lost steam in their battle against it.

Regardless, he was happy to see his family getting along better these days.

Shaw had quieted down since Lynette had gone to see him, which unnerved Grant. He didn't believe that the man had ceased his efforts, only that he was biding his time. It was highly possible he was waiting for the good press to fade, in order to yet again dredge up the past as it related to his opponent.

Jorja had continued with her outspoken disgust with the Vassers, vainly attempting to keep the subject of Win's suicide in the public eye. But people seemed to have moved on and less and less talk shows and publications were willing to humor her now.

He wondered if being brushed off like this would make her slink away, shamed, or if it would only encourage her to double her efforts.

The woman had always been a wild card.

His office door opened suddenly and Duke strolled in, looking oddly pleased with himself. There was a gleam in his eyes that Grant couldn't interpret, but he decided the man was probably just in better spirits.

"Good morning," Duke greeted, shutting the door behind him before taking a seat across from his cousin. "I assume that Madison is happy."

Grant's eyes narrowed. "Why is that?"

Duke grinned, his hands tapping against the arms of his chair. "She's putting her little plan in motion a week early, and it's proving to be successful already."

"The opportunity presented itself; we would have been foolish not to accept."

"Right." Duke nodded, pursing his lips thoughtfully. "I suppose it is a smart move. Not one I would have made, of course. But then again, I'm not the one in charge."

He laughed, which made Grant a bit uneasy. "No. But your input is valued, Duke."

"Right. Anyway, I wanted to come by and let you know that I've talked with my father. He says the reservation numbers are up at the casino, and that the protesters have left."

"There were people protesting outside the casino?" Grant asked sharply.

Duke nodded. "The Hollywood types are all on Jorja Hale's side. They have been protesting in front of the L.A. hotel and the casino for a few weeks now. But since Madison's little display of arrogance, they've dwindled in numbers. Today, they didn't show up at all."

Grant let out a slow sigh, irritated that his cousin had not shared this information with him sooner. Then again, they were all so busy with their own obligations these days...

Before he could respond, Quinn knocked politely on the door to his office and poked her head in.

"Grant, the mail just arrived for you." She lifted the stack of envelopes she held. "Would you like me to go through it or do you want to?"

"The man can open his own mail," Duke asserted, gesturing for Quinn to come inside before shooting a look at his cousin. "Let the poor girl get back to more important things."

"Oh, well, I don't mind." Quinn paused in the doorway, a brief flash of annoyance in her eyes as she stared at Duke. When she turned to Grant, she asked again. "Would you like me to deal with it?"

Grant shook his head, fighting back his annoyance with Duke. "No, I'll handle it."

One of her eyebrows arched curiously but she nodded, bringing the stack over. She stumbled over something and a few of the envelopes fell from her hands, landing on the floor at her feet.

"Oops." She laughed at herself, kneeling down to gather up the mail. "I swear, I'm the only person alive who can walk over a perfectly smooth surface and still manage to trip."

A smile tugged at Grant's lips as he rose to his feet to help her, while Duke stayed where he was, watching her gather up the mail silently.

As Grant picked up one of the stray envelopes, his gaze focused on Quinn. "Should I buy you a helmet?"

"Ha, ha, very funny."

He smiled and accepted the stack of mail from her. He glanced down at the envelope he had picked up, and as he did so his smile faded.

The envelope had no return address. His name and the hotel's address were typewritten in plain, black ink on the front. He started to open it, only to be interrupted by the phone.

"Oh, crap," Quinn muttered under her breath and ran out to her desk to answer the phone. Seconds later, she called out to Grant. "It's your mother. It's urgent."

He let out an impatient sigh as he answered the phone. "Good morning."

"*Kennedy didn't come home last night,*" Charlene cried, her voice ragged and frightened.

"What?" Grant gripped the phone tighter in his hand. "Calm down. What's going on?"

"*I don't know what to do, she won't answer her phone. Something's wrong.*"

"Have you called the police?"

"*No, not yet. I didn't know what to do. If she's doing this on purpose just to mess with me...*"

On instinct, Grant lifted the curious letter and tore it open while his mother continued to ramble on. What he saw inside sent a shiver of dread down his spine.

"Call them immediately. We've just received a ransom note."

ABOUT AN HOUR later, Grant stood looking out his office window, focused on nothing in particular. Duke and Charlene had both contacted the police, leaving him to stew in his own fear, guilt, and grief.

He heard Quinn come in behind him and let out a long, strained breath as she ran her left hand up his back. She wrapped her arms around him and held on silently, having no words to say.

What could be said? Grant's little sister had been kidnapped. Everything that had been happening to the family had just gotten a lot more real and dangerous.

"I barely even know her," Grant murmured, dark grief thickening his voice. He gripped Quinn tighter, shutting his eyes against the fear licking at his insides. "My own sister, and she's a stranger to me."

"They will find her," Quinn stated as confidently as she could, looking up at him. "Once she's home safe, you can start fresh and be a bigger part of her life."

"I should have protected her. She needed me, and I failed her."

"Don't blame yourself, Grant." Her face was strained as she shook her head. "That won't help her. You have to stay positive that the police will find her."

"And if these people kill her?" he managed, his eyes filled with darkness and his voice cynical and cold. "How will I live with myself?"

"Stop it," Quinn demanded, glaring at him. "You're better than this. Take charge, take action, do whatever you have to do to get her back safely. Stop wallowing and do something, damnit."

He stared at her for a long, haunted moment, his face unreadable. She wondered if she had crossed the line with him, but she didn't care. She wasn't going to let his guilt swallow him whole. He was capable of so much more than that, and she would risk whatever she had to in order to remind him of it.

She watched as the coldness in his gaze warmed and intensified, and before she could do more than blink, he leaned in and captured her mouth with his. He kissed her fiercely, possessively, until her knees felt weak and her mind blurred the lines of reason. Unable to do more, she grabbed his coat and held on for dear life while his bottled up emotions exploded out of him.

When he broke the kiss, her eyes flew open to stare at him. He met her gaze, filled with renewed vigor and purpose.

"Thank you," he said simply, releasing her and stalking back to his desk to grab the phone.

She stared after him, stunned. "What are you doing?"

"Calling the family in for a meeting. We're going to find her."

Thirteen

S he's playing a silly, little prank on us," Madison said disparagingly as she handed the ransom letter back to Grant. "She's been feeling left out lately and she's just trying to get our attention."

Grant's face hardened considerably at her callousness. "You're suggesting that she staged her own kidnapping?"

"Yes," Madison snapped, frustrated. She rose from the head chair of the conference table and walked to the wide windows, her arms crossed defiantly. "Isn't it obvious by the foolish request written in the letter? That isn't a real threat; it's child's play. She's probably staying at a friend's house, enjoying distracting us."

Linc grabbed the letter from Grant and read the words out loud, "*The girl will be released only when Madison Vasser resigns and is charged with aiding and abetting a criminal. She deserves to be punished for her crimes. No one is above the law.*" He paused, sneering instinctually. "I don't know, Mads. I don't see Kennedy going this far."

"You didn't see her the other day," Madison replied coldly, bristling at her brothers' refusal to understand. "She hates me. She wants me dead for what I've done. Both to our father and for our grandfather."

"She's just a kid," Linc began, frowning as Madison whirled around, heat flaring in her eyes.

"She *hates* me. Don't you get that?" she snarled, losing her composure as the anger and uncertainty consumed her. She wanted to believe her own reasoning, and yet somehow there was a nagging possibility at the back of her mind that she could be dead wrong. And if she was...

Linc's own temper rose up to combat her own. "This isn't about you right now. This is about Kennedy and making sure she's safe."

"Of course it's about *me*," Madison fired back. "*All* of this has been about me. Don't you see that? The people targeting us are after me, not either of you, not the rest of the family."

"Shaw's plans have nothing to do with you," Grant put in coolly.

She shot him a dark look. "Maybe not, but he still used me to do his dirty work."

"Kennedy could be dead right now and you just don't give a shit, do you?" Linc shouted, rising to his feet to stare at her accusingly. "Even if she *did* stage this, which I don't believe for one goddamn minute, we still need to get her back. She's family, Mads. As much as you two may not get along, she's blood. Your blood, my blood, *our* blood. We don't leave Vassers out to die in the battlefield. We go and we get them."

Madison sucked in a deep breath, fighting back her anger and her stubborn pride. She knew it was foolish, knew it wasn't helping. Linc was right, even *if* Kennedy was playing them for fools, it was better to figure it out just in case she wasn't.

The clock was ticking, after all, and she had been missing for fifteen hours.

Marshall and Charlene burst into the conference room, Duke and Cy trailing in behind them. Cy shut the door as the others all took seats.

Charlene's face was red and puffy from crying, which she had tried unsuccessfully to cover with makeup. Her steely composure wavered as she stared at her other three children, unable to help thinking of the one who was missing.

Marshall sat beside her and carefully wrapped an arm over her shoulders in an attempt to comfort. He was still in shock over the news, in disbelief of this new horror to strike his family.

Though, he had a pretty good idea of who may be responsible.

Linc sat back down, still vibrating with anger, while Madison remained standing. She stayed by the window, arms crossed and her expression coolly distant.

Deciding no one else was going to speak first, Grant chose to begin. "The police are assigning a detective to the case. Given the publicity our family has experienced lately, they're taking all precautions and wasting no time."

He paused, shooting a glance at his sister. Her expression was cold and impossible to read.

Irritated with her, he continued. "We must consider the possibility that Kennedy is doing this as a prank, however unlikely that may seem."

"I have a theory, Grant," Marshall interrupted. All eyes turned to him. "I received the case file from my contact in the Army and reviewed it. While there were a number of things that disturbed me about the file, there was one bit of information included that I think pertains to our current situation.

"The man who covered up my father's crimes was a man by the name of Paul Morgan. His wife was of Vasser lineage, and therefore he was blackmailed into hiding the truth. His son is now running in the senate race against Shaw. It is my belief that Shaw wants to use this information to hurt Morgan's chances, and in preparation for that he may be doing all he can to dirty our name."

Grant and Linc shot each other knowing looks before looking back to Marshall.

"We knew that already," Linc began, watching as doubt and surprise contorted his uncle's face. "Grant and I met with Shaw several days ago and he warned us about his plans to go public with that information."

"Why would he warn you?" Cy asked, laughing at the thought. "That seems like a stupid move."

"Because he thought he was doing the noble thing by letting us know beforehand. That way maybe we could prepare for the backlash likely to come from it," Linc replied. "Either way, if we're going to start assuming here that *he* kidnapped Kennedy, then I think we're kidding ourselves."

"He's a sitting senator, this would ruin him," Grant added, staring around the room. "I for one think this goes deeper than all of that."

Madison immediately thought of the secret letters she had received and felt sick to her stomach. She turned toward the window to hide the startled realization on her face.

This was it. This was her courage blinding her to the blood at her feet. It *was* going to be her family's blood. Kennedy's blood.

She didn't hear what else was said by her family as they continued to theorize behind her. Instead, she stared out the window at the city, the buildings shadowed by clouds that slowly blocked out the sun. Guilt crept into her heart, punching her viciously until her chest tightened with misery.

Someone out there wanted her gone.

If she held firm and refused to back down, her sister may die. If she gave in and relinquished her position, her family may crash and burn.

Her eyes shot to the sky, narrowing with fury. If this was God's plan for her, then He clearly had a sick and twisted sense of humor.

DETECTIVE TINA CRAWFORD sat patiently in the alcove outside Grant's office hours later, her hands folded over her notepad and her eyes curiously taking in her surroundings.

Her light hair and eyes spoke of her Swedish heritage, while her short stature and slim build had made her early years on the force a never-ending fight. She was composed, quietly serious, and stronger than she looked. When she'd been offered the promotion to detective five years earlier, her entire life had clicked happily into place.

She enjoyed puzzles and had a particularly good sense of other people and their motives. It was this skill that she used now as she analyzed the Vasser Hotel.

She'd never been inside before, but found it to be everything they said it would be. Luxurious, sophisticated, metropolitan...it perfectly suited the block of the city it resided in. People didn't come to the Upper East Side for a cheap motel. They came for extravagance.

Despite the lavishness of the lobby and restaurants, she found the offices upstairs to be practical and sensible. The furnishings were quietly expensive, the walls painted in welcoming earth tones. It presented a much different side of the Vasser family than what she had been expecting.

She had done her research and knew about the young heirs that ran the hotel. She also knew the oldest sister had recently been in the headlines and was now running the company. It painted a peculiar picture of a family whose legacy was infamous, their role in the hotel industry unprecedented, and the murders that plagued their past nothing short of notorious.

But what was it about Madison Vasser that had spawned the kidnapping of her own sister?

"Do you want coffee, Detective?" Quinn offered with a polite smile, rising from her desk.

Tina shook her head, studying the other woman carefully. "No, thanks."

Quinn took her seat again, chewing on her bottom lip anxiously. Tina noted this, filing the information away for later. It was her job to analyze any and all components of an investigation, and that included all of the people involved or related to those involved.

When the door to Grant's office opened and he stepped out, Tina observed the way he looked at his secretary and the quiet affection that passed between them. Though it was unspoken, she could see the dedication in the other woman's eyes and the fondness in his.

She filed this information away, as well.

"Mr. Vasser," Tina greeted as she rose to her feet, her hand extended.

He accepted it politely, briefly, then nodded for her to join him in his office. He took a seat behind his desk and watched her closely as she sat across from him. "What information can you give me, detective?"

"We've sent out an APB for your sister to all surrounding areas within a fifty mile radius. We have units currently canvassing the area where we believe she was jogging when she went missing. They'll be knocking on doors and seeing if anyone saw anything that night, as well as checking traffic cams of nearby intersections to see if we can get a shot of her in the area."

"Is there anything I can do?"

The detective attempted a smile as she shook her head. "Other than tell me any and all information you think may pertain to your sister's disappearance. I'll also need a list of the members of your family, as well as their contact information. I will be confirming everyone's whereabouts that night."

Grant nodded slowly. "You think someone within the family may have done this?"

"In situations like this, that's usually the case. And since the ransom is not for money, but for justice, I am forced to conclude that the person responsible has their sights set on your other sister. This person has probably set out to ruin her and possibly the family business as a whole." She hesitated, jotting down a quick note in her pad before glancing up at him again. "Are there any other people who may be out to hurt the family, Mr. Vasser?"

Grant let out a dark laugh, though he was anything but amused. "The list is getting longer by the day, Detective."

"Names, please."

He sighed, rubbing at the ache in his left temple. "Jorja Hale has made her vendetta against us known for weeks now, so you may want to check in on her. Senator Warren Shaw has also publicly criticized us, though his involvement is unlikely. And I suspect there are others, though I don't know who yet."

Tina jotted down the names and noted his assumption of other, as of yet unknown, threats.

"One last thing." She underlined the words 'threat within the family?' before she looked up and met his gaze assertively. "Where were you last night?"

Grant stared right back at her, unflinching. "I was with my girl-friend at my home."

"Can she corroborate your alibi?"

"Why don't you go ask her?" Grant gestured to the door of his office frostily. "She's right outside."

Tina paused, keeping her gaze level with his as she assessed his statement. Deciding he probably wasn't lying, she jotted down a few more notes and then rose to her feet.

"Thank you, Mr. Vasser. I'll be in touch."

She held out her hand, which he took in his own as he stood. "Detective, I think it may be prudent for you to consider during your search for my sister that the person involved may not be out to destroy my family."

"Then what are they out to do?" Tina released his hand, eyeing him curiously.

Grant's expression stiffened with both anger and anxiety. "They want to *control* my family. This person does not want Madison in charge."

She nodded, acknowledging his point. The definitive way he said it was also filed away.

"I'll keep that in mind."

SHE PACED IN front of her fireplace, the glow of the raging flames within silhouetting her figure. Wyatt had shoved a glass of red wine into her hands moments before, but she had yet to drink it. Instead, she gripped it tight in her fingers as she prowled around restlessly.

It had now been over twenty-four hours since Kennedy had gone missing. Madison absorbed this fact, letting the reality of it sink in and fester in her gut. She tried not to imagine how frightened her sister must be, or how hopeful she probably was that her family would find her.

Then again, the thought occurred to her that Kennedy might be thinking there would be no help for her, that Madison would let her die. If Kennedy believed that Madison wouldn't resign because of this, then she would be correct.

She didn't have any intention of stepping down. Not for anyone or anything.

While she stood strong and ruthless on her conviction, the guilt still crept in to haunt her.

Wyatt came out of the kitchen, two plates filled with chicken and pasta in his hands. He sat down on her sofa and laid the plates on the coffee table, his eyes flicking up to meet hers.

"Come eat," he ordered, no room for objection in his tone.

She rolled her shoulders and continued to pace. "I'm not hungry."

"You haven't eaten all day," he protested, glaring at her. "Punishing yourself by not eating is not going to help get your sister back."

"Who says I'm punishing myself?" Madison shot back, eyebrows raised. "That would mean I blame myself for what's happened. And I don't."

He watched her silently for a long moment, his face unreadable. His words were heated as he spoke again. "You shouldn't blame yourself. You did nothing wrong except fight for what you believe in. But don't look me in the eye and lie to me about not feeling at least some ounce of guilt."

She sneered. "Of course I feel guilty. The last words I had with my sister were ones of hate. If she dies because of this, I'll never have the chance to make this right." Her voice cracked, and she clutched at her throat in alarm as it tightened. She turned away from him, her eyes shutting tight against the anguish she felt. When she felt she could speak again, her tone was dangerously soft. "I'm going to find out who the bastard is who took her, and I'm going to kill him."

"Even if it's someone in the family? Someone you love and trust?" Wyatt asked, rising to his feet to stand behind her. His hands rested on her shoulders and trailed down her arms. "You need to prepare yourself for that outcome, sweetheart."

She shivered under his touch and from the weight of his words, knowing he was right. That possibility was one she had to consider.

Turning to face him, she met his eyes boldly and without fear. "In the event that this is an inside job, then the bastard better pray the police find him before I do."

Wyatt's mouth quirked up at the corners, dark humor in his eyes. "That's my girl."

He pulled her in close, breathing in the familiar scent of her as he sighed. He needed her to remain strong, to retain her vigor and courage.

She curved into him, accepting the comfort he offered. "I won't resign because of this terrorist," she declared, her hands fisting in the material of his shirt as she tilted her head back to look him in the eye. "They'll have to haul me out, kicking and screaming, biting and clawing my way from what's rightfully mine."

"That's why they fear you, *ma belle*," he murmured, running his hands through her dark hair with an indulgent grin. "The fall of Cyrus Vasser should have meant the end of the empire. But no one counted on you."

Her lips curved even as her eyes darkened with power. "What a shame."

"A damn shame," he muttered as he kissed her possessively, enraptured by the heat of her eyes and the unbendable, unbreakable steel of her spine. No woman alive compared to her, and those who had chosen to pick a fight with her were in for a world of hurt.

He looked forward to the day he could watch her squash them under the sharp point of her stiletto heel. Until then, he'd do all he could to keep her in tune with the right kind of emotions she needed to get the job done.

While her own revenge would be sated, his was, if he was correct in his assumptions, going to be carried out as well.

Vindication had never tasted so sweet.

FOURTEEN

T he lighting was dimmed seductively low at the Peacock Alley Bar in the Waldorf Astoria Hotel. Smooth jazz drifted through the room, the saxophone rich and poignant, creating an atmosphere that was both romantic and arousing.

Too bad he wasn't there to enjoy either of those feelings.

Shaw sipped at the glass of fine red wine delicately, savoring the flavor of it while he waited. He may as well enjoy *some* part of the evening, as inconsequential as a good wine was given the circumstances. His plans had taken a perilous turn, one he had not foreseen.

Who knew that the Vasser family had so many goddamn enemies?

What he had set out to do from the very beginning now seemed like child's play compared to what was being done to that family. A kidnapping, for God's sake...

He chewed on the thought worriedly, wondering if and when the Vassers would point their fingers at him. Lynette had not yet contacted him, nor had Linc. He had to hope that meant they were not sniffing in his direction.

Even the mere mention of the crime with his name in the same sentence could be damaging to his career. Politics was a dirty, hazardous business. At any moment, one slip-up or wrong move could be the end. As it was, he thought he had been playing the game safely.

Apparently he was wrong.

His double agent working to get dirt on Jack Morgan had come to him with some alarming news. Morgan knew about the meeting with Grant and Linc, and apparently he'd had someone nearby recording the conversation.

It was maddening to realize that despite the precautions he had taken to keep his intentions unknown to Morgan, the man had managed to weasel his way in regardless. And he had to wonder just what Morgan intended to do with the information now that he had it.

Morgan now knew that the Vassers were aware of his connection to them. What lengths would he go to, to keep them from exploiting it?

Would he resort to kidnapping?

A shudder ran through Shaw at the thought, despite how extraordinarily implausible he wanted to believe it was. This was a felony, not some backroom deal or greasing of a palm. No, this was a dangerous twist in the already complicated turn of events plaguing the family. And if Morgan *was* involved, then somehow Shaw couldn't help but feel the blame fell on him.

After all, Morgan would have no reason to target the family if it weren't for the very knowledge Shaw intended to go public with.

He shook his head wearily, resting his forehead in his hands with a heavy sigh. Never had he felt so worn out, so exhausted, from the business of politics. It was a game he knew well, one he'd played for longer than he could remember. Yet it had never, ever, taken on a sharp, jagged edge the way that it had this time.

The girl could die. Hell, she could already be dead. If she was, the Vassers, notably Madison Vasser, would be out for blood.

He had to hope he wouldn't be first on their list.

Just then, his date strolled in, looking like a fox that missed the rabbit by the tuft of its fluffy tail. Her eyes were heavily painted and her lips were fixed in a pout that should have been sexy, and yet, because he knew her mood was sour, was anything but. The black leather dress she wore hugged her body, cutting off high enough on her thighs to leave little to the imagination.

When she slid none too gracefully into the seat across from him, he could barely muster up the feeling for a smile.

"Miss Hale," Shaw greeted, lifting his glass to her in mock frivolity. "You look well."

"Shove it, Shaw," Jorja spat, tossing her purse on the table and scowling at him. "I need a drink."

Shaw idly held up his hand to flag down the waiter while Jorja thumbed through the menu dispassionately.

After she had ordered, Shaw settled back in his seat and watched her closely. "We've been of great service to each other, wouldn't you say?"

"I guess," she mumbled, sending him a hostile look under heavy lashes. "You seem to have gotten what you were looking for, but I still don't have mine."

"I put my weight behind the drug claim, honey, just like you asked me to," Shaw reasoned, sipping at his wine. "But without the dealer's name, that claim doesn't mean much."

"If I point the police at Eddie, then he'll blab that I was the one who bought the drugs from him. Then the cops will know I lied to them about it and I'll be screwed."

"You shouldn't have lied in the first place."

"Oh, that's rich coming from a politician." Jorja let out a dark laugh, rolling her eyes. "You play your little games, scheming and bribing and cheating."

"I have done no such thing," Shaw bristled, an angry flush blooming over his face. "I am only out to expose the truth."

Jorja snorted. "Sure. Anyway, it looks like nothing's gonna scare your little daughter away from the Vassers. You'd think she'd go running after a kidnapping."

Shaw grimaced, considering the thought as the waiter dropped off Jorja's drink. She sipped at the martini, bored.

"I have to hope that Linc will protect her," he said finally, ignoring Jorja's cynical laugh.

"Good luck with that," she scoffed before biting an olive off the toothpick that came with her drink. "This whole kidnapping thing makes ya wonder, though. Same thing with the secret Madison was hiding about her knowledge of that murder Win witnessed. Who has it out for the Vassers more than we do?"

Shaw met her eyes intently. "I don't know."

Jorja sighed. "I mean, it could just be some psychopath who's taken an unhealthy interest in the family now that they've become famous or whatever. God knows I have plenty of creepy stalkers, maybe Queen Bitch has gotten herself one. He thinks that by kidnapping her kid sister he can somehow get closer to her."

"That's certainly plausible," Shaw agreed, toying with his wine glass in his hands absently. "Either way, we can still twist this to our advantage."

"How so?" Jorja asked doubtfully. "And what is your stake in this, anyway? When you came to me in the first place, you said it was about your daughter. But if your brat kid still won't leave Linc after this, then I think you're out of luck."

Shaw managed a small smile. "First off, Miss Hale, anything that keeps the Vasser name in the headlines works to our advantage. Secondly, my daughter is not my motive."

"Oh, what is?" Eyebrows raised, Jorja leaned over the table toward him. He saw the unmistakable glitter in her eyes, exposing her darker nature. There was little information he could give her in good faith that it wouldn't be used against him at some point. She was never one to trust, after all. Just someone to be used.

But if he could keep her interested and on his side, committed to his purpose, then perhaps by the time he was ready to expose Morgan's messy past, everything would be in place.

"Let's just say that my opponent in next year's election has a damning connection to the Vassers that I hope to expose," Shaw told her, his expression carefully composed. "I'll need your help when the time comes to unveil the truth."

She smiled wickedly. "Only if we can nail the bitch for Win's death at the same time. That's my price."

He nodded, then ordered a second round of drinks for the both of them. When the waiter walked away, Shaw eyed Jorja thoughtfully.

"We will see what becomes of this kidnapping. Whoever the culprit is, they're a fool for trying something so brash."

"Unless brash is exactly what they want to be," Jorja theorized, grinning again as she accepted a fresh martini from the waiter.

Shaw lifted his second glass of wine and contemplated her statement as he sipped.

If she was right, and if he was correct in his assumption that Morgan may be involved, then things were about to get a whole lot more interesting, and fast.

"I DON'T WANT to get into this again with you," Lynette said despairingly. "He's not involved."

"I know that, Lynette, but you should at least talk with him," Linc argued.

"If you talk to your father then at least we could officially rule him out," Quinn called out from Lynette's kitchen, where she was busy plating some cheese and crackers.

Grant nodded to Lynette. "She's right. We have to exhaust all options. The police are doing all they can, but we have to do our part."

Lynette quieted, beaten down by three much louder voices than her own. She understood their points, and yet she knew it was useless. Her father did not kidnap Kennedy. He wasn't that stupid.

Then again, it wouldn't hurt to talk with him about it and see what he had to say.

"Fine, I'll call him tomorrow." She crossed her arms, sinking back into the cushions of her sofa. Beside her, Linc leaned in to kiss her forehead.

He then turned to his brother. "It's been forty-eight hours now that she's been missing. What have the police been doing to find her?"

Grant ran his hands over his face. "Very little, it seems. No witnesses have turned up yet. They're still canvassing."

"And the ransom note? There weren't any prints on it or fibers or anything?"

Grant only shook his head.

Quinn wandered out of the kitchen and set a plate of food down upon the coffee table. She took her seat beside Grant and reached for his hand, squeezing it in her own.

When he met her eyes, she attempted a smile. "We're going to find her."

He nodded, desperately wanting to believe her. If only this sick, twisted feeling would leave his stomach and let him think.

"The police will likely talk with both Jorja and Shaw," Grant said quietly, to no one in particular. "They also want to know our whereabouts the night she was taken."

"They think one of us did this?" Linc demanded, his already testy temper rising up to scorch him. "Who would be *that* stupid?"

"They're covering all the bases, Linc," Grant reminded him. "Given the demands in the ransom letter—"

"Which don't tell us squat," Linc fired back, looking frustrated. "For all we know, some lunatic out there has decided it's his life's purpose to serve justice to Mads for what she's done. It could be anybody."

"But it probably isn't." Grant frowned, mulling over the thought. "These things are usually closer to home than that."

"Says who? The cops?" Linc shot to his feet and began to pace, running his hands through his hair agitatedly. "Whatever it is, we should be out there looking. I should be walking every goddamn street in this city trying to find her."

Quinn interrupted before Grant could. "I think we need to be asking ourselves a more important question here..." When they all turned to face her, she continued, "So far, someone has gone after both Madison and Kennedy. What's to say that they won't go after either of you guys next?"

Both men froze, unsure how to answer that question. Neither really believed it was a possibility, yet they had been wrong on so many levels already...

Lynette suddenly looked very worried as she glanced over at Linc. "She's right. You should be more careful."

Linc snorted, brushing off the thought. "I'll be fine. Grant and I are big boys, we can take care of ourselves."

Before Grant could add anything, his cell phone began to ring. He pulled it from his pocket and glanced at the caller ID before answering it.

"Hello?"

"*Hey, buddy. It's Cy.*"

Grant frowned and eyed Linc warily. "What can I do for you, Cy?"

"*I need to talk to you and Linc. Meet me at Amoureux in ten minutes.*"

"Can't this wait till tomorrow? It's late."

"*No. Gotta be tonight. I'll be waiting, see you soon.*"

His cousin hung up, leaving Grant staring down at his phone in irritation.

"Well, what'd he want?" Linc asked, stuffing his hands in his pockets restlessly.

Grant looked at his brother skeptically. "He wants us to meet him at the hotel in ten minutes. Apparently he has something important to tell us."

"He might know something about Kennedy," Linc realized. "Let's go."

Grant sighed and rose to his feet, staring down at Quinn. "I'll have my driver take you home. I don't want you walking around or taking a cab."

She began to call him a hypocrite for fearing for her safety all the while neglecting his own, but decided against it. He had enough to deal with without her picking pointless fights with him.

"Alright." She stood up and kissed him, cupping his face in her hand tenderly. "Don't be too late."

"I won't." He kissed her again, then left with Linc to take his brother's car to the hotel.

WHEN THEY ARRIVED, they found Cy sitting alone in the back corner, three shot glasses and a couple of beer bottles on the table before him. He burped and attempted a lazy smile as he held out his hand to shake theirs.

"Thanks for coming by," Cy told them as they sat down. He gulped down the rest of his beer and then obnoxiously waved the waitress over for another one. "You guys want a beer?"

"Just tell us what this is about, Cy," Linc grunted, annoyed to see that his cousin was piss-drunk. Hopefully whatever he was about to tell them was worth hearing.

"Okay, okay," Cy conceded, his hands tapping nervously on the table as he glanced back and forth at both men. "I think something's up with Duke."

Grant stiffened. "What do you mean?"

"I mean he's been taking this whole Madison thing a bit too seriously. He's letting it make him crazy," Cy told them, pausing as the waitress dropped off a fresh beer. He took a hasty sip before continuing. "Look, when we first got to New York, we were trying to think of ways to get Madison to back off. It isn't right the way she played us and took control this way. I mean, I was fucking pissed about it."

"Tell me something I don't know," Linc snapped.

"Stop being a jackass, I'm trying to help you," Cy shot back angrily, the booze slurring his words and adding to his foul mood. "I don't have to say anything. I could just go home right now and get back to my life. God knows I'm fucking sick of this city."

Linc laughed. "Then why are you hanging around? It's not like you contribute anything."

Grant watched the indignant flush creep over Cy's face as he turned to him instead of Linc. "Look, I'm not accusing Duke of anything. All I'm saying is he's letting his beef with Madison go to his head."

"Do you think he took Kennedy?" Grant asked, eyes sharpening dangerously.

Cy shrugged. "How the hell should I know?"

Grant shot a dark look at his brother, unsure what to think.

"Since Madison's press conference, he's been nothing but supportive," Grant reasoned, turning back to Cy.

"That's how he acts around *you* guys," Cy informed him, waving his beer restlessly. "But when it's just me, he can't stop talking about her. He's pretty much obsessed."

"Obsessed how?" Linc asked doubtfully, eyes narrowed.

Cy let out a long, unsteady sigh. "The way he's been talking, it's like he's got it out for her. He wants her gone."

An uneasy lump formed in Grant's throat as he remembered his words to the detective.

This person does not want Madison in charge.

"YOU SURE YOU don't want me to sit up front? I can keep you company," Quinn said with a cheerful smile to the driver of Grant's car.

The driver laughed. "That's alright, Miss Taylor. I'll put on some good music for us and we can rock out."

"Sweet." She winked at him as she slid into the backseat of the town car. The driver shut the door as she buckled her seatbelt.

He started up the car and switched on her favorite Motown station. She immediately started singing along with the Temptations as the car pulled away from the curb.

It was late in the evening, so the traffic was light and the streets were damp from the rain that had been falling most of the day. Quinn stared out the window, admiring the bright lights of the city as she made her way home.

She wondered what Grant's cousin had to say that was so important. If he knew where Kennedy was, then hopefully the ordeal would soon be over. Knowing Grant was suffering under the weight of both guilt and anxiety made her feel helpless, useless to do anything to help ease his mind. Other than remaining positive. That was really all she could do.

Until his sister was home safe, their world would remain completely upside down.

"Hey, Sam, you wanna stop and get some ice cream?" Quinn asked suddenly, leaning forward in her seat. "My treat."

He smiled at her in the rearview mirror, brown eyes dancing. "My wife's got me on a diet. But we can stop for you if you'd like?"

She pouted, though her voice was playful. "It's not fun to eat dessert alone."

Before he could respond, they approached an intersection with a red light. She heard a thud as his foot drove the brake right into the floor. He tried to brake again, but the car kept moving into the intersection at full speed.

There was only a fleeting moment to panic before the town car ran the light. Quinn stared out the side window just in time to see the headlights coming straight for her, oddly slow and surreal. Her mind had a split second to process the situation, and her eyes widened as she lifted her arms to shield her face.

The crash hit with the horrendous sound of squealing tires and scraping metal. In a flash, the world collapsed into darkness.

FIFTEEN

S o, let me get this straight," Linc began, his hands clenching into fists as he glared at his cousin. "Duke's been bitching about Mads lately, and you jump to the conclusion that he's purposely hurting the family in order to get back at her?"

"I don't fucking know," Cy groaned, rubbing his face in his hands wearily. "I just wanted to do the right thing and tell you to keep an eye on him. I don't want this on my shoulders anymore."

"So how do we know that you're not just leading us to Duke in order to cover your own tracks?" Linc accused. "Because I'm more likely to believe you're capable of this shit than Duke is. He's just not that stupid."

Cy shook his head with a tired laugh. "Fine, don't believe me. I don't give a shit." He stared down at the beer in his hands miserably, his vision hazed and his mouth set in a drunken scowl.

Grant shot Linc a warning look before eyeing his cousin. "Do you know where Kennedy is, Cy?"

Cy's head shot up and his face contorted furiously. "No! And I don't know who took her, either."

Linc sighed. "Right. Well, I'm going to go home now. This has been a waste of time." He got to his feet unceremoniously, nodding to his brother. "C'mon, Grant."

Grant's eyes remained on his cousin, his mind turning over all the angles of what Cy had told them. While his brother couldn't wrap his mind around the idea that a family member could do what had been done, Grant held no such delusions. Even if Cy was lying or was wrong in his assumptions, Grant wouldn't take the chance.

Because while some of the press leaks and accusations could be linked back to Shaw and Jorja, there were still others that had no suspect, including Kennedy's disappearance.

Was Duke responsible?

He nodded to Cy as he got to his feet and followed Linc out of the bar, grateful to get out into the quiet lobby where he could hear himself think.

Before they got very far, his cell phone went off. He didn't recognize the caller ID as he answered it.

"This is Grant Vasser."

Linc stopped short and grunted, irritated and moody. He wanted nothing more than to get out and find his sister and stop wasting so much goddamn time theorizing. He needed to act, to do something—anything—to help find her.

He was about to bark at Grant to get off the phone so they could get going, but when he saw his brother's face go ghostly white, he froze.

The panic in his brother's eyes at that moment would haunt him for the rest of his life.

"What's wrong?" he demanded as Grant hung up the phone.

Grant shook his head and started running for the door, out to where Linc's car was waiting in the valet area.

"Quinn. Car accident. Hospital. Now." He ripped open the passenger door of the car and hurled himself inside.

Linc got into the driver's seat, buckling in. "Alright. Hold on."

He gunned the engine and raced out onto the street, nearly clipping a passing sedan as he went. But he didn't slow down, weaving around other cars and hurtling toward the nearest hospital. His blood froze with an icy chill as he fought to keep his fear low and his urgency high.

He shot a look over at Grant, and the instant pity he felt put a bitter taste in his mouth. Never in his entire life had he seen his brother look so terrified.

Grant's face was strained, his eyes set forward in an unseeing stare. His hands clenched over his knees, the knuckles of his fingers white from the pressure.

Though Linc had a million questions, he kept them to himself and focused on driving. At that moment, all that mattered was getting his brother to Quinn as soon as possible.

When they reached the hospital, Grant leapt from the car almost before Linc had parked it, taking off into the check-in area frantically.

He launched himself at the nearest hospital employee sitting behind the counter, his eyes dark and mad with distress.

"Quinn Taylor," he stammered, unable to think of anything else to say. He watched as the nurse nodded politely at him and typed the name into the computer.

"She's in room 208. They're still assessing her injuries."

Without waiting to hear if he could see her, he took off down the hallway with no clue where the room was. He tore through the halls and up the stairs, plowing down anyone in his way. At last, he stumbled across 208, cursing under his breath as he shoved open the door.

When he charged inside, he spotted her laying in a hospital bed, a nurse tending to a cut on her forehead.

Both the nurse and Quinn glanced up at him.

"Hey, you got here fast." Quinn smiled, her voice shaky but still cheerfully bright.

Grant stared at her in silence, relief at seeing her alive and whole shuddering through him. He blinked, then turned to the nurse.

"How bad is she hurt?" he asked sternly, stepping into the room and shutting the door behind him. He moved to the bed, but kept his distance from Quinn.

The nurse looked from him to Quinn, then back again. "Considering the extent of the accident, she's very lucky. A couple of cracked ribs, a mild concussion, no internal bleeding that we can see so far. Her ankle is sprained from being pinned inside the car. We're lucky it's not broken."

Grant nodded solemnly, fighting to keep his composure as he processed the information. "And my driver, Sam?"

"He's in critical condition, but the doctors expect him to survive," the nurse said as she rose to her feet. She smiled down at Quinn courteously. "I'll just give you two a moment alone."

She left the room, closing the door behind her.

Quinn watched Grant, confused by his coldness and his distance. Chewing on her bottom lip, she stared down at her hands and fussed with the blue hospital blankets.

"They're saying I can leave in a few days," she began, her hands still trembling from the shock of the accident. She wondered if it would ever go away. "But I feel okay; I'll get back to work before then. I don't want you to be understaffed when things are so hectic—"

"I don't care about that," Grant interrupted brusquely, his hands clenching at his sides.

She looked up at him and the anguish she saw in his eyes staggered her.

It was then that it dawned on her. His fiancé years before had died in a car accident. He must have been reliving all of the same horror, the same pain, the same grief, at that moment.

Understanding had guilt racing through her as she tried to sit up. "Really, Grant, I'm fine. The accident wasn't that bad."

But he shook his head, taking in the bandage on her forehead and the way she winced in pain as she tried to move. He couldn't help but feel this was somehow his fault. If he hadn't sent her home in his car...

His heart thudded, hot and heavy with remorse, as he knelt down by her bedside and reached for her hands. She stared at him, troubled, as he pressed his lips to her fingers.

"I can't lose you, too," he whispered, his eyes closing tight against the fear and the pain. He buried his face in her hands and struggled against the sob that wracked his throat and smoldered in his chest. Once again, he had been so close to losing everything.

Tears ran down Quinn's cheeks as she watched him, her heart aching. "I'm still here," she said, squeezing his hand. "I'm not going anywhere."

He lifted his head to look at her, and the open display of emotion on his face had her breath hitching in her throat.

"Life is so short, Quinn," he said softly, head shaking. "On the drive over all I could think about was all the time I've wasted in my life, with the business—"

"You love the business," she protested.

He sighed. "I do. But I love you more."

She frowned. "It's a different kind of love. There's no reason to feel guilty over dedicating your time and energy to your family's company; it's what you were born to do. And I won't let you talk down about yourself just because of a silly car accident. You are way too important and strong to—"

"Will you shut up for a second? Christ, woman, I'm trying to ask you to marry me."

Quinn's mouth snapped shut and then fell open again in stunned surprise. She blinked, then lifted a hand to her forehead. "Are these drugs making me loopy, or did you just say what I think you just said?"

His mouth twitched. "Was it something you wanted to hear?"

She considered his question, playfully drawing out the suspense while he stared at her anxiously. Seconds later, she titled her chin up and grinned.

"Yes, and I accept."

Having no words, he rose and leaned toward her, his hand gently cupping around her tear stained cheek. She sighed when he kissed her softly, slowly.

"Ma is going to *flip*," she said, beaming at him as he pulled away.

"I still haven't met your family," he realized nervously.

Quinn giggled. "Trust me, they'll love you."

There was a polite knock on the door. Linc poked his head in, Lynette at his side.

"How's everything go—"

"We're getting married!" Quinn shouted happily, clapping her hands together. She winced as the pain in her ribs hit her again, but she continued to smile anyway.

Linc's mouth spread in a wide grin as he turned to his brother. "Well, shit. Congratulations."

He gave Grant a bear hug and patted him on the back, while Lynette sailed in to kneel beside Quinn.

"So I take it you're okay?" Lynette asked, excitement chasing the worry from her eyes.

Quinn reached for her friend's hand. "I am now."

A COUPLE OF hours later, Grant sat in a chair by Quinn's bedside as she slept. The lights were dimmed, and the hospital was surprisingly quiet beyond the closed door to the room.

He kept his hand tucked in hers, watching her sleep with a growing sense of quiet contentment. It amused him that when he'd woken up that morning, he had no idea he would ask her to marry him. Spontaneity had never been his forte, and yet somehow, the act had seemed so right.

Nearly losing her and succumbing to the horror of it had awakened something inside of him. He needed to know she was safe and secure, and the only way to ensure that was to make her his wife. Plus, he'd have the added benefit of waking beside her each morning and coming home to her each night. It was a habit he was getting used to, and one he never realized he could crave with such ferocity.

But he did. Lord, he did.

The nurses had encouraged him to go home and get some rest, but he'd ushered them out with a cool stare and shut the door with finality. She was his, and no one could persuade him to leave her side. After all, she needed him. Given her tireless dedication to him in the past, it was clear that he owed her the same in return.

So he stayed, even though he worried for Kennedy, stressed over Cy's comments about Duke, and wondered just when the madness was all going to end. It seemed one bad thing happened right after another, and just when they saw a few glimmering stars of hope, the clouds rolled in yet again to pour down rain.

Of course, he had expected as much. Such was the benefit of being a cynic. Few bad things could occur with complete surprise.

Though he had to admit, this accident had shaken him to his very bones. The reality of just how fragile life could be was something he had learned years before. Somehow, it seemed he had forgotten it. But this gave him a renewed appreciation for the small things.

And only increased his concern for Kennedy.

Where was she now? Was she hurt, lost, or worse...was she dead? He tried not to dwell on this last thought, but found he couldn't help himself. In the back of his mind, he knew he needed to prepare himself for the possibility that he would never see her alive again. Whoever had taken her had clearly done a good enough job of covering their tracks, and until the police had a lead or until this kidnapper contacted them again, nothing could be done.

Even searching the streets like Linc wanted to do seemed so fruitless, though Grant understood Linc's desire for action perfectly. He had to keep moving, keep looking, keep trying. That was who he was.

As for himself, he'd let the police do what they did best. Quinn needed him now.

He felt her hand twitch beneath his and looked down at her. Her face was strained and her brow creased as she whimpered, and he realized she was having a bad dream.

He caressed her hand softly, unsure if he should wake her. She looked like she was in so much pain...

The door behind him suddenly opened, and he turned to glare at the unwanted visitor.

It was Detective Crawford, looking solemn and wide-awake despite the late hour.

She nodded silently, acknowledging that Quinn was asleep. Then she motioned with her hand for him to join her in the hallway.

He glanced back to Quinn, not wanting to leave her side. But she seemed calmer after his attempts to comfort her, so he slowly let go of her hand and left the room.

The door shut with a quiet click at his back as he met eyes with the detective.

"What are you doing here?" he asked, none-too-politely.

It was clear he didn't want to see her, and that he felt he had more important things to do. Tina figured she couldn't blame him. Though he was going to be very interested in what she had to tell him.

"I heard about the accident, and the officers that were on scene forwarded the information to me. I thought you should know what they found."

Grant stared at her in confusion. "I don't understand. Was the other driver drunk?"

"No, nothing like that," Tina replied, reaching into the file folder she held and pulling out a photograph. It showed the undercarriage of his town car, a close up on the brake lines. "They're still investigating the crash, but when the officers noticed this they contacted me right away. They weren't sure if it was somehow related to your sister's disappearance."

Grant accepted the photograph from her, eyes narrowing as he inspected it. "Were the brakes tampered with?"

"The line appears to be broken. It may not be intentional, but it is still cause for concern." She watched him closely as he stared at the image of his car, his expression carefully blank.

"So you think someone did this on purpose. They wanted to cause the accident," Grant said dully, handing her back the photograph.

Tina nodded. "It is a possibility. We can't know for sure until the investigation on the crash is complete. However, I did speak with your driver a few moments ago and he confirmed that the brakes seemed fine when he left the hotel, but when he needed them to stop the car at the light, they failed. In a car such as this, the likelihood of that occurring without being tampered with is small."

Grant's jaw clenched as he processed the information. "You're suggesting that the person who did this may be the same one who kidnapped my sister."

"Nothing is certain, as of yet," she reminded him. "We will know more in the next few days. Until then, we will continue the search for your sister."

"Detective," Grant said sternly, his eyes intense as he stared at her. "It's clear that I was the target. Quinn never rides in my car without me in it. Whoever did this, they wanted me dead, not her."

Tina nodded, quickly jotting down his statement in her notepad. "I'll keep that in mind, Mr. Vasser. Have a good evening."

She started to leave before he stopped her. "There's something else you should know."

She turned and faced him, eyebrows raised. "Yes?"

He hoped he was doing the right thing in telling her what he hoped to God wasn't true... "I want you to look into my cousin, Duke. He may be involved."

Her face remained stonily composed as she nodded. "Any particular reason why you think this?"

"No. Just look into it and let me know," Grant replied curtly, heading back into Quinn's room and shutting the door in the detective's face.

She made a note of it in her pad and whistled as she walked away.

THE NEXT MORNING, Linc and Lynette dropped by again with flowers for Quinn. When they entered the hospital room, they found Grant sitting beside her, holding her hand.

"Morning sunshines!" Linc greeted, slapping Grant on the back cheerfully. "You stay here all night?"

Grant didn't even spare his brother a glance as he continued to watch Quinn. "Of course I did."

Quinn grinned and then winked at Linc. "He's such a stubborn ass. I told him to go home but he won't budge."

Linc understood the feeling perfectly. "I don't blame him."

Lynette set the vase with sunny yellow flowers on the table beside the bed, clutching her hands together awkwardly as she looked down at Quinn.

"How are you feeling?"

"I'll live. You didn't have to bring me those," Quinn chided. She tried to sit up further, only to curse under her breath at the sharp, stabbing pain that pierced her side. Her breath caught and she waved Grant off when he tried to help her. "I'm fine...just the pain meds wearing off a bit. God, cracked ribs suck."

"Do you need anything?" Lynette asked immediately. "Water? A magazine? Chocolate?"

Quinn managed a strained smile. "If there's Vicodin in that chocolate, I'll take it."

Grant looked up at his brother, concern darkening his eyes. "I need to speak with you, if you have a minute."

"Yeah. Sure. What's up?" Linc asked, watching as Grant squeezed Quinn's hand and rose to his feet.

Grant said nothing as they left the room, shutting the door behind them in the hallway. He led Linc a few feet away, glancing around nervously to be sure no one was listening.

Linc's eyebrows rose as he let out a light laugh.

"What're you worried the Feds are spying on you or something?" he joked.

Grant eyed him disdainfully. "No. But what I'm about to tell you is incredibly troubling."

Linc frowned. "Okay. Hit me."

"The detective investigating the kidnapping came by here last night and told me something I was not prepared to hear."

"Does she have a lead?"

Grant shook his head. "No. But she has reason to believe that the accident last night was no accident."

"What the hell does that mean?"

"It means there's evidence that the brake lines were intentionally tampered with," Grant informed him, his anger a sinister, rooted thing deep within. "The detective thinks that whoever took Kennedy may have targeted me by messing with my car."

Linc blinked in stunned surprise. "But instead Quinn was in the car."

Grant nodded, guilt in his eyes. "She's lying in that hospital bed right now because of me."

"This isn't your fault." Linc patted him on the shoulder, though a range of fierce emotions stormed over his face. "But it is fucking scary."

"It is," Grant agreed, releasing a heavy breath. "This whole mess is getting out of hand. It's exhausting to try and keep up with it all."

"I know what you mean." Linc scowled, crossing his arms as he chewed over this new information. "Why the hell would anyone try and get you killed?"

"The only thing I can come up with is that this was an attempt to hurt Madison. Whoever is doing this is picking off the people she cares about."

Linc's eyes narrowed. "So by that logic, I should be next."

"I'm afraid that none of us are safe until this person is arrested." Grant's gaze hardened as his temper smoldered. "Our family is being threatened in a much more dangerous way, now. This goes beyond petty accusations and lies. This is life and death."

"And Kennedy is still out there somewhere," Linc said, his hands diving into his hair restlessly. "Damnit, what the hell are we going to do?"

"Take every precaution," Grant suggested, stiffening. "We do what we have to do to protect what's ours."

Linc nodded as he considered all the angles. "Lynette's at risk, too. I have to protect her."

"In all likelihood, she's not a target," Grant began, only to be cut off as Linc rounded on him.

"Doesn't matter. Don't lie to me and say you're not worried for Quinn's safety after this. Everyone close to us is at risk."

Grant's face tensed, grief flashing in his eyes. "Then do whatever you have to do. In the meantime, I have to tell Mads."

"What about what Cy said last night? Are you going to tell her about that, too?" Linc asked. "As much as I don't want to believe the jackass, at this point I don't want to take any chances, either."

"I'm going to let the police talk with Duke first. I don't know how Mads will react if she gets it in her head that he's responsible." Grant rubbed at the bridge of his nose tiredly. "I don't even want to think about what she'll say when she hears about the car."

Lynette stepped out of Quinn's room and walked toward Linc with a polite smile. "I have to get to rehearsal. You ready to go?"

Linc's face twisted with a multitude of emotions as he yanked her against him, holding her close. She clung to him, sending a startled look to Grant over Linc's shoulder.

"Is something wrong?" she stammered, eyes wide as Linc pulled away.

"We're moving in together. Your place or mine?" he asked suddenly.

She blinked, brows furrowing. "Um. Do we have to talk about this right now?"

"You're in danger. I'm in danger. We're all in fucking danger. You're not leaving my side and that's that," Linc decided, his hands on her shoulders. "I'll repeat my question. Your place or mine?"

She chewed nervously on her bottom lip, indecision and confusion sweeping over her. "I guess my place..."

"Good. After I drop you off at rehearsal, I'll bring over my things." Linc turned to his brother, eyes dark and intense. "Take care of yourself, buddy."

Grant nodded as Linc led Lynette away, explaining the car situation to her as they went. When they disappeared around the corner, Grant exhaled slowly, fighting to regain his composure. He hadn't yet told Quinn about the brakes, but knew she'd be extremely unhappy if he kept it from her much longer.

As much as he didn't want to frighten her, she had a right to know the truth.

Deciding he was going to tell her, he started to head back into the room. He paused as he heard loud voices coming from down the hall, where Linc and Lynette had just disappeared. His eyes narrowed as the voices got closer, then widened when he saw the big crowd of dark haired people round the corner, all chatting and arguing and laughing together.

Before he could find a place to hide, the older woman leading the pack spotted him.

"Oh my God, that's *him*." She gasped, a smile identical to Quinn's bursting over her face. She was a short, curvy woman, her body draped in a dress the color of sage to set off the hazel of her eyes. Her wild curls of ebony hair framed her face, the mass of it clipped back behind her head.

The others all froze, their eyes on him as he stood there awkwardly, unsure what to do. He had barely managed to blink before the crowd was upon him, shaking his hand and hugging him and patting him on the back. They were all much shorter than he was, so he towered over all of them like a giant among little people.

"You look just like the pictures in the papers," Quinn's mother was saying, beaming up at him fondly. "I can't believe I'm finally meeting you. My name is Clara."

"Do you really have a stick up your butt?" a young boy of about ten asked loudly, earning a fierce glare from his mother.

"Nico! What did I say about repeating your sister's words?"

Grant frowned. "Quinn said that?"

"You look like you don't eat enough, *mio caro*," the man Grant assumed to be Quinn's father griped, eyeing him with one sculpted eyebrow cocked disapprovingly. He was a slender man with a sharply honed face, high cheekbones and rough, olive skin. Dark beady eyes stared up at Grant from under heavy brows, and he watched curiously as the man's animated mouth twisted into a smile. "My daughter couldn't like you all that much if she's not feeding you."

Before Grant could think of a response, Quinn's mother jumped in. "David, don't be sassy. We didn't come all this way so you could be rude."

"I wasn't rude," the man corrected her sharply, though there was obvious affection in his tone as he continued to watch Grant closely. "I was simply making an observation about the man who's been courting my baby."

"Is it true that you own all the hotels in the whole wide world?" another little boy asked, pulling impatiently at Grant's sleeve.

Grant looked down at him, taken aback. Unsure what to say, he settled with a simple, "No."

Suddenly, the door to their left opened and Quinn appeared, standing in her light blue nightgown with a bright grin on her face.

"I should have known it was *my* family making all the ruckus in the hallway." She laughed, winking at Grant. "And there's my poor boyfriend, being assaulted by the clucking hens."

"Fiancé," Grant corrected her, only to realize what he had done the moment her entire family went silent.

Quinn blushed and covered her mouth with her hands, her eyes twinkling as she watched his words register in her mother's eyes. When Clara turned to face her, there were tears in them.

"*Dio*," she whispered, suddenly launching herself on her daughter and hugging her tightly.

Quinn winced from the sharp pain. "Ah, Ma, my ribs..."

"Oh, sorry, sorry." Clara backed away, her hands fluttering over Quinn's face as a tear fell down her cheek. "My baby...getting married."

Quinn's father shot a look up at Grant, silently assessing the situation. Grant winced, realizing he hadn't even thought to get her father's approval. Then again, there hadn't been much thought to his proposal in the first place.

Clara noticed her husband's face and turned on him. "David, be happy for your daughter. A good man wants to marry her, a man with a good job and money and the means to provide for her."

He nodded slowly, his eyes still on Grant.

"Daddy..." Quinn's eyes were shining as she stepped past her mother to her father, extending her arms to him. "It was all very sudden; I don't even have a ring yet."

"No *ring*?" one of Quinn's sisters cried, causing lots of feminine glares of suspicion to be sent Grant's way. He debated backing away, feeling more than a little outnumbered.

Quinn shot a disparaging look at her sisters before turning back to her father. "You should be happy to get me out of your hair once and for all," she joked, smiling at him.

His lips quirked up at her statement, and his eyes warmed. "You are always welcome in my hair." He hugged her close, then held his hand out to Grant. "Welcome to the family, Grant Vasser. I hope we don't scare you away."

Grant managed a half smile as he accepted the handshake. "I should say the same to you."

"Yes, we've heard all about your family," David replied, eyebrows raised. "I expect you to do all that you can to see that this filth does not touch my daughter."

Grant immediately thought of the brakes of his car, and the guilt crept back into his system like a slithering black snake. His head dipped in a respectful nod. "Yes, sir."

"Alright, my ankle hurts," Quinn announced, eyeing her family with a knowing look. "Anyone wants to talk to me, I'll be in bed."

The entire family burst into conversation once again and shuffled into the room, leaving Grant standing in the hallway, burdened with dark shame.

Sixteen

Returning to the hospital for the first time since her grandfather's suicide was like shoving a knife into her chest and tearing out her bleeding heart, then tossing it onto gravel and stepping on it with the spike of her favorite red stilettos.

It hurt more than she cared to admit or even acknowledge. This place held memories for her, of times long past when she had come to him for guidance, for strength. It was in this haunted, disturbing place that he had left his final words to her: a letter of goodbye, and one of commands.

But it seemed so long ago to her now, so out of reach and surreal. She still possessed the letter, still intended to follow through on the commands. Yet each step she took seemed to send her further and further into this hell that was now becoming her reality, its depths violently perilous and destructive.

Her choices had gotten her sister taken. Her pride had gotten her brother's lover nearly killed.

Since when had doing business in this world become so treacherous?

When Grant had told her that afternoon about the sabotage of his car, her immediate reaction had been acceptance. Not denial, not disbelief, not even outrage. No, she had understood at that moment that she should have expected something like this. In fact, perhaps she had.

She had just been expecting it to happen to her, not her family.

Soon after the acceptance had come the fury. The fear. The anguish. Nothing Grant said would convince her that this wasn't about her, that this wasn't her fault. Whoever had kidnapped their little sister had done so because of her. What made this situation any different?

Perhaps what hurt her the most was the realization that the hit had been meant for Grant. If the circumstances had been any different, the outcome very likely could have been the death of her brother. The very thought tore through her ravaged heart and exploded, weakening her.

More blood to pool at her feet. Blood that spilled because of her pride. The letter had said this would happen, and she had chosen not to listen. Now her family was paying the price.

Fighting back the urge to scream, Madison strolled up to room 208 and balanced the vase of elegant, white flowers she carried on one arm as she knocked.

When she stepped inside, she spotted Quinn sitting up in bed, eating a bowl of soup with Grant at her side, reading the paper. When Quinn glanced up at her and grinned, she attempted a smile in return.

"I heard through the grapevine today that my brother's getting married," Madison said, her eyes warming as she approached Quinn's bedside and set the vase down on the table.

"Yep." Quinn held out her hand, reaching for Madison's. "I've always said that when something bad happens in life, there's usually something good right around the corner to balance it out."

"Well, this is certainly good news," Madison agreed, her eyes flicking to her brother as she held onto Quinn's hand. "I would say welcome to the family, Quinn, but I'm afraid our family is not a very welcome place to be right now."

Grant's eyes flashed in warning as he shook his head ever so slightly. He still had not told Quinn about the cause of the accident, given that her family had interrupted his plans to do so. He couldn't bear to worry her when she was so happy to see her parents and siblings again.

Quinn didn't notice, but continued to watch Madison as her eyes softened with sympathy. "I'm sorry, I'm pulling you both away from trying to find Kennedy. You both should go. I'll be fine. I should be able to check out of here tomorrow, and then I can help you."

Madison eyed Quinn curiously, annoyed that her heart warmed at the compassion in the other woman's voice, the effortless faith. They were concepts that Madison had never really understood. "There's little we can do except assist the police."

"We'll find her," Quinn asserted, squeezing Madison's hand tightly. "Burned bridges can be repaired, you know. Even ones that seem hopelessly damaged."

Madison's heart stalled, the old ache of sorrow and guilt over her little sister choking her. She despised the pain, hated it with all her being. Yet, she couldn't make it disappear.

She pulled her hand from Quinn's and turned, walking to stare out of the window. It was much like the view from her grandfather's room had been—all of the towering buildings just lighting up for the inevitable darkness of night.

In the glass, she could see her own reflection. She stared at her face, noting the lack of emotion her careful mask provided. It had long been her shield, her protection against any and all who would think to harm her. Now she wondered if it was keeping her from befriending someone who so clearly deserved her trust.

She watched as Grant reached for Quinn's hand, and the way his face lit with quiet contentment as he looked at her. When he leaned in to kiss her, tender and sweet, Madison felt sorry for ever being cruel to the woman.

There was a sudden movement behind them as the door opened. She watched Wyatt step in, and their eyes immediately met and held in the reflection of the glass.

She let out a slow, even breath and turned around. "I'm surprised to see you here."

He shot her an amused glance before going straight to Quinn. "I don't know why, sweetheart. I'm just as concerned for our girl's safety as you are."

Quinn laughed as he reached for her hand and pressed a kiss to her skin gallantly. "Great, now another person gets to see me without any makeup on."

"Want me take a picture?" Wyatt asked with a wink, pulling back and turning to face Grant. He held out his hand graciously. "Grant."

Grant accepted the man's hand, though it still lacked the warmth of friendship. "Wyatt."

"Why don't you two leave us ladies alone for a few minutes. Go talk about manly stuff. You know, like cars." Madison eyed Grant knowingly, and he nodded.

Wyatt looked at Madison curiously but followed Grant outside when he led the way. After the door shut behind them, Madison sat down beside Quinn and reached for her hands again.

"I want to apologize to you," she said evenly, letting her remorse show.

"What for?" Quinn asked.

"For keeping my distance from you," Madison replied with a sad smile. "You didn't deserve the attitude I gave you. And you're right about the bridges. I hope to mend the bridge between us that's been smoldering for some time now."

"Oh." Quinn blinked, surprised at Madison's words. "Well, thank you. I guess. I mean, I'm so happy you want to be friends. I've been telling Grant for weeks now that you could use someone on your side, someone other than the usual suspects. I hope I can be that for you."

"You can. And are." Madison squeezed her hand gently. "With everything that's been happening lately, it's occurred to me that I have been pushing people away who do not deserve to be pushed. Humility and faith are not easy skills to learn."

Quinn nodded, understanding. "I'm here for you. And not because I'm marrying your brother, but because I respect you. I don't always know what your intentions are or what you're about to do, but to see the way you've dealt with all of this…it's been inspiring."

"It's a good thing to keep others guessing," Madison said with a half smile, the edges a little wicked. "Wouldn't want to be too predictable. That's boring."

"Yeah, it is." Quinn let out a quiet sigh, tears suddenly in her eyes. She leaned forward, biting back a curse from the pain as she wrapped her arms around Madison. Madison hugged her in return, her eyes closing as she let herself enjoy the comfort it gave her. "You're going to save this family, Madison. And we're all going to help you. You are never, ever alone."

Madison knew it was a simple statement, one meant to soothe the aches and fears away. And it did help, more than she wanted it to. But it still didn't change anything.

Words never changed events. Actions did. And Quinn had given her that little extra boost she needed to keep her head above the waters of despair.

So help her God, her family was going to make it through this.

"I DON'T WANT you driving that car of yours," Lynette said firmly, folding her arms over her chest with finality.

Linc stared up at her from her sofa, heat in his eyes. "This asshole isn't going to try the same thing again. That's not how it works."

"How do you know?" Lynette charged. She flung her arms out desperately and fought so hard not to give in to the fear. Her fear for him, for his life. "Good Lord, Linc, someone tried to *kill* your brother! And your sister has been kidnapped! Don't you think you should be more careful?"

"I know what's happened to my family, Lynette. You don't need to remind me." He glowered at the television, eyes unseeing. He didn't want to fight with her, but she was being ridiculous. When she stalked over to him and blocked his view of the television, he glared up at her. "Really? This is cute."

"How the hell are we supposed to get married if you die?" She crossed her arms again, her chin cocking up in challenge.

"I can take care of myself, and if—" He paused, realizing then what she had just said. His mouth fell open stupidly as he gaped at her. "Wait, what?"

"You heard me, you damn Yankee," she shot back haughtily, pleased to see the stunned look on his face. "I won't let you die on me, not now. Not when I need you so badly."

When he managed to get his senses back, he couldn't hide the grin that lit up his face. "This is because Quinn is getting married, isn't it? One of those twisted girl things where if one of their friends gets engaged, they suddenly gotta get hitched too."

Lynette rolled her eyes dramatically. "That skull of yours is remarkably thick."

He rose to his feet, his smile widening. "I'm just trying to make some sense of why women do the things they do."

He reached out and grabbed her by the back of the neck, pulling her in for a hard and fast kiss that left her weak in the knees. She stared at him when he released her, one eyebrow raised.

"So I take it you're no longer angry with me for ordering you not to drive your car," she mused.

"Nope. I wasn't planning on listening to you, anyway," he told her, leaning in for another kiss.

She backed away, worry chasing away her humor. "I'm serious, Linc. I'm scared."

He softened, hating to see that look she got when she was troubled. It broke his heart. "I'll be fine. If this guy tries to come after me, I'll kick his ass."

"What if it's not as easy as that?" she asked, her hands cupping around his face tenderly. Her eyes searched his, the thought of losing him hitting her like a bullet square in the chest, brutal and destructive. "I know you think you're invincible, but that alone won't save you."

Humbled by her words, he pulled her close and breathed in the scent of her hair, his arms holding her tight against him.

"I'm more worried about you," he admitted, his hands trailing up her back possessively. "Seeing the fear on Grant's face when he found out about Quinn..."

"Stop it," she whispered, burying her face in his shoulder to hide her tears. "That's why we're here together, remember? I'm not leaving your side."

"Good." He suddenly lifted her into his arms, pressing his mouth to hers. "I'm eager to spend the night in my new bed in my new home."

She let out a shaky laugh as he carried her to the bedroom, her arms winding around his neck. "I hope it meets your expectations."

WYATT REFUSED TO let her go home that night. Instead, he brought her back to her family's hotel and ordered her to rest. After hearing from Grant about the brakes, he was determined to not let Madison out of his sight.

She had to get her laptop from her office first, and he followed her to the darkened executive floor of the hotel. His arms circled her waist as they walked off the elevator, his teeth nipping at her ear.

"Remember that one night, sweetheart? I thought you were going to devour me in one bite with that sexy, little mouth of yours," he groaned, his fingers digging into her flesh compulsively at the memory of it.

She let out a shiver of breath, smiling as she unlocked the door to her office. "You know, you've yet to take me in this room. Remember when we used to fuck like rabbits wherever we could?"

He grinned and spun her around, his mouth claiming hers with a rough abandon that shot through her like a vivid hot dart.

"The good ol' days," he murmured, his lips trailing down her cheek and over the soft skin of her throat. She grasped at his bronzed hair and arched against him eagerly.

"We can have them again," she panted. "And so much more."

With her heeled foot, she kicked the door closed and bit back a laugh as he lifted her by her hips onto her desk, shoving aside the items gracing its surface. His hands roamed over her body and she tilted her head back, welcoming his touch as her nails raked over his shirt.

He froze suddenly, leaving her ears ringing with a steady hum of arousal as she lowered her head to stare at him. "What? What is it?"

He reached for a white envelope that sat on top of her stack of mail, only her name and address on its surface, and held it up for her to see. "What's this?"

She paled, going from lust to icy anger in one fell swoop. She snatched the envelope out of his hand. "None of your business."

"Is it another ransom letter? Why don't you open it?" he asked, eyes narrowing. She hesitated, and that was all he had to see. "So you know what it is, then."

Her hand shook as she clutched the envelope tightly, anxiety ripping through her as she realized she had to open it. Her sister's life could depend on it.

Without a word, she reached for her letter opener and tore open the envelope. She lifted out the paper inside and read the simple, black text:

> *The Queen who fails to listen and forgets how the game is played loses everything she loves by the smooth kiss of a blade.*

Madison's heart shuddered with fear deep within her chest. When Wyatt took the letter from her hands, she let it go weakly, unable to fight for it. What did it matter now? It was quite possible that her sister was already dead.

He read the words, then tossed the letter aside and shook her by her shoulders. "What is this about? Have you gotten letters like this before?"

She bit back a curse, closing her eyes. Instead of responding, she reached for her keys and slid from the desk. She went to her top drawer and unlocked it, unearthing the other two letters from within.

She tossed them on the table, then watched the emotions rage over his face as he read them.

"Jesus Christ, Madison," he muttered, completely taken aback by what he was seeing. Anger hit him first, and he rode on it as he rounded on her, shaking the letters in her face. "Why didn't you tell me about these?"

"They were my burden to bear," she said quietly, knowing it was a pathetic excuse. It was her attempt at being noble, but clearly that had gotten her nowhere. Instead, it may have gotten her sister killed.

"Damnit." He tossed the letters on the desk, grabbed his head and spun around, fighting back the urge to shake her senseless over hiding something so crucial, so damning. He turned back to face her, his expression impossible to read. "Just what were you planning on doing about these letters? Were you just going to ignore them and let them pile up? Or were you waiting for something bad to happen? Like your sister getting taken or your brother almost getting killed?"

She snarled at him. "You don't have to tell me, Wyatt. I know exactly what my inaction has caused."

"Then what are you going to do now?" he demanded, pointing at the latest letter. "Clearly the person who took Kennedy is sick of waiting around for you to take a stand."

"She's probably dead," she spat, pain hitting her violently at the words. "It's too late."

"You don't know that," he growled. "You have to take these to the police."

She snorted. "What the hell are they going to do?"

"More than you've been doing," he pointed out cruelly. "You're letting this bastard win by not using his taunts against him."

"So what, take the letters to the press? Clearly the public's sympathy has not helped me so far. All it's done is make things worse," she reasoned.

"Getting the public on your side helped you with Shaw and that actress, but it won't help you with threats like these," Wyatt told her, his voice darkening as he continued to watch her. "Are you sure this person is the same one who sent the other ransom note?"

"Yes," she replied coolly, her knees aching beneath her. She sat down as gracefully as she could in her desk chair, her expression void of emotion. "The first two letters were warnings of what was coming. The ransom note was confirmation. This letter is supposed to be the nail in the coffin on my ambitions, my plans."

"We need to ask ourselves why the ransom note was sent to Grant and not you, and why it was written differently, styled differently. It looks and sounds nothing like these letters." Wyatt looked down at the papers again, his brow creasing as he considered them. "If you ask me, they were not written by the same person."

"I believe the ransom note was sent to Grant because I didn't listen to the other letters," Madison said numbly, her eyes staring unseeingly out the window of her office as she sat back in her chair. "Whoever this is was getting tired of my disregard for his wishes."

"So they reached out to Grant instead." Wyatt sighed, running a hand through his hair. "That may be the case."

"Of course it is," she muttered, her hands clenching over the arms of her chair. "I'll take the letters to the detective tomorrow."

Wyatt watched her silently as tears began to spill from her eyes, though her face remained hard as stone. There was something hauntingly beautiful about the sight of her crying, yet it disturbed him more than anything he had ever witnessed.

Tears of rage or passion were one thing, those he had seen on her a thousand times. But the tears she shed now were tears of pure, unadulterated pain. She had been beaten down, bullied, attacked, and then built up again, only to be hit with an awful tragedy. First her sister, then her brother. She must be wondering to herself what the next big disaster was going to be.

His helplessness to do anything about it strangled him like a rope infused with barbed wire. Other than stand by her side, he could do nothing. Other than kiss away her tears and rock her to sleep at night, he was useless.

He had his own theories about who was responsible for some of the press leaks that had occurred, but the kidnapping, the brake tampering...that was something else entirely.

There was an enemy out there, a dangerous one. Wyatt had faced plenty of violent men in his day, men who had nothing to live for and didn't fear consequences or death. But there was something about a person who would kidnap a teenage girl, sabotage a man's brakes, and send threatening letters that just didn't seem all that sane.

Clearly they were dealing with a sociopathic monster. The only question at this point was if the man, or woman, was a complete stranger or of Vasser blood.

With a burdened sigh, he stepped toward Madison and knelt down before her, his hands cupping her face and forcing her to look at him. He brushed at the tears on her cheeks as their eyes met.

"It's okay to be weak sometimes, sweetheart," he murmured with a slow smile. "As extraordinary as you may be, you are only human."

Pain flashed over her face then, dramatic and real, and her heart burst at the seams from it. More tears fell from her eyes as she let her head fall forward onto his shoulder and she gave in to the misery.

He held her tightly, his hands brushing over her hair as she cried, the sounds she made beautifully horrific. She had needed this; just as he had needed to comfort her, to feel like he was capable of helping in some small way.

Because he wasn't leaving her side from this moment on, not with the mounting danger and the building pressure she was under. There was no going back to Maine—there was no resuming his previous life. The past be damned; he wasn't going to let her push him away, wasn't going to allow the men who had ruined his life do the same again this time.

He was going to expose them and soon. Though the truth would undoubtedly hurt her, it would destroy those he had a very good hunch were responsible for at least some of what was happening to her.

He was going to thoroughly enjoy delivering a well deserved dose of bad karma.

HER BACK WAS stiffer than a board and her arms were tied behind her, numb and useless. It had been days since she had been taken, or so she thought. She had no real grasp on how much time had passed, or if it was even night or day outside. Her world had become this impenetrable darkness, and her initial fear had turned into a numb acceptance.

Kennedy had no hope of ever going home. In fact, part of her wondered if her family had even reported her missing. Her captor had certainly left her in the dark about what was going on and why she was taken. Instead, all they had done was bring her an occasional cold hamburger or bottle of water, always silent despite her questions and pleas.

She had to assume that because they fed her, they wanted her alive for some reason, for money or for fame, she didn't know. But with Madison in charge, she sincerely doubted if their demands would be met.

Her sister was a ruthless bitch. And her mother and brothers were all preoccupied with their own shitty lives; they didn't care about her anymore. In all likelihood, they probably assumed she ran away to escape all the drama, and they couldn't care less if she returned home.

The very thought of it brought angry tears to her eyes, which only bled onto the blindfold she wore. Her mouth twisted around the gag in her mouth, a sob wracking her throat.

She didn't want to be here. She just wanted to go home...

Though she could see nothing, she knew she was in some sort of chamber or metal room, given the way any and all sounds she made echoed hollowly off the walls. She heard the door to the chamber rattle as the lock was opened and quieted her sobs as whoever was there stepped into the room.

She whimpered, as always fearing they had finally come to kill her. Though her limbs were too weak and numb to move, she still strained away from the direction of the intruder, tilting her head to the side as she trembled.

When she heard the voice, her heart galloped wildly with terror. All she could think of was that she was living inside a horror movie.

"This should have been simple," the voice said, guttural and disturbingly warped. It occurred to her that whoever it was, they were using some kind of voice changer like she'd seen in the movies. Either that or it was a demon straight from Hell.

She felt the person approaching, but kept her silence. Fear prevented her from making any noise.

"Your sister is quite the stubborn bitch," the voice continued, violent anger lacing the words. "She clearly would prefer to see your death than relinquish her high and mighty throne."

Kennedy's jaw clenched, her teeth biting into the gag as she forced back another sob. So it was true. Madison was doing nothing to help save her.

She really was doomed.

"Drastic measures will have to be taken."

She heard footsteps approaching her from the left, then squirmed as she felt a hand slide over her throat. Fingers clamped over her skin and forced her face upward, though she was still blind to what she was looking at. Her body shook uncontrollably as she imagined a man lifting a knife, its razor sharp blade glinting in the light.

If there even was any light.

Instead, his next words brought about a far darker, more ominous terror within her.

"I'm going to use you the way I should have in the first place."

He released her face and left, leaving her sobbing hysterically in the darkness.

SEVENTEEN

Nightfall claimed the city as she slid from her town car and stared instinctively up at the sky. It was an oddly clear and quiet evening, the world around her eerily calm. Traffic was light, few people walked the streets, and the usual drone of sirens and honking horns was absent.

Part of her wondered if it was just her perception of things that had changed, or if the world really was darkening under the weight of some impending gloom. Surely it seemed that her world was darker these days.

Her sister had been missing for four long, miserable days. The police seemed less confident now in their search, and the detective was all but useless. In the conversations she'd had with the woman, especially after giving her the letters, she had felt more like a suspect than a victim. If the police wanted to paint her and her brothers as the criminals here, then the search was going to go nowhere.

The real suspect was still out there, and she had to pray they still had her sister alive. The most recent letter had hinted otherwise, but she was determined now not to lose faith.

In the end, her faith and her vindication would be all that would save her and her family from this nightmare.

She spotted Raoul off to the side of the building, leaning against the stone wall with a lit cigarette in his mouth. A somewhat grateful smile lifted her lips at the sight of him, realizing just how long it had been, or so it seemed, since they had talked.

With everything that had been happening around her, she had lost so much of what she had once considered routine. Her life had been turned upside down and over again more times than she could count, yet Raoul had always been there.

Unlike most of the people she knew, he had never once left her side.

"You haven't smoked in years," she stated humorously as she walked up to him, the amber of her eyes glinting in the outdoor lights of the hotel.

He snorted derisively and savored a long drag on the cigarette, his eyes meeting hers. After he blew out the smoke politely away from her, his mouth formed an edgy smile. "Stress is a killer, *cariño*. I do what I can to survive."

"Well, then you better pass some of that remedy my way." She joined him against the wall, the cool stone soothing against her back through her light coat. He reached into his pocket and pulled out the pack of cigarettes, holding it out for her to take one. As she did, he tucked the pack away and held out his lighter, his own cigarette hanging loosely from his lips as he lit hers.

She let the smoke fill her system and released a heavy sigh, watching it drift out into the night air. Her head fell back against the wall as her eyes closed, and she reveled in this simple moment of peace.

"I'm sorry I've been such a stranger, darling," she told him quietly, turning her head to look at him.

He avoided her eyes as he continued to smoke. "Life goes on."

"Does it?" she mused, shaking her head as she took another slow drag on her cigarette. "Sometimes I wonder if I'm caught in this never ending cycle, up and down, back and forth. It's been several weeks since my grandfather's death, and I *still* have yet to do what he needed me to do. I keep being held back, either by my own choices or by the hatred of others."

"Maybe it's a sign from God that this is not meant to be," he grunted, running a hand over the back of his neck. "The world is telling you to stop what you are doing."

Anger flashed in her eyes. "I won't, Raoul. I can't. You know that."

He shook his head sadly, taking one last puff on his cigarette before dropping it to the concrete and snuffing it out with his foot. He turned to face her, emotions raging over his face. "You are too stubborn to see the danger you are in, *cariño*. Too blind to see what you are up against."

She sniffed bitterly, blowing smoke into the air. "Oh, I see the danger, darling. What I don't see is the reason for it."

"It exists to ruin you." He scowled, his temper and desperation warring within him.

"Yes, I know that. It doesn't change anything," she declared, shooting him a fierce look. "My sister could be dead, my brother's fiancé almost died, and I've been receiving threatening letters and accusations from what seems like numerous sources, including within my own family."

"You should heed those warnings," he replied gravely, his face tightening with dread. "There is only so much I can do to help you."

Before she could respond, he stalked off down the street. She watched him go, startled by his mood and troubled by the fear in his eyes.

What did he know that she didn't?

WITH QUINN STILL in the hospital, Grant was left to answer his own phone and file his own paperwork.

Not that he minded. It wasn't like his phone was the one ringing off the hook these days. It seemed Madison was the one to talk to when it came to the family business. He was simply a manager, attempting to maintain some semblance of normalcy at the hotel.

The kidnapping was all over the papers now. The police had at last decided to release at least some of the information to the press, though they purposely left out the demands made in the ransom letter. The last thing the family needed was the drama that would come from it.

If the public believed that Madison's voluntary resignation and arrest would bring Kennedy home safe, then their outrage would ruin the family. All of the work Madison had put into perfecting her public image and that of the hotels would be destroyed in an instant.

That was just how it worked. The masses could make or break you, as Cyrus had always said. Grant was starting to realize just how true that statement was.

His gaze shot to the portraits that hung on the wall across from his desk, and he studied his grandfather's image thoughtfully. He wondered how the old man would have handled all of this had he chosen to stay alive. Would he have let Kennedy's kidnappers get the best of him? Or would he have called them on their bluff?

He had the sickening feeling that his grandfather, acting in one of his crueler moments, would have simply told them to go fuck themselves. In his lifetime, no other man had ever threatened him, either personally or in business. Grant had to wonder if that was because they had all known, as he did now, that Cyrus backed down for no one.

It was this trait that Grant saw in his own sister. He wanted to believe it was a sign of her strength, of her courage. But since she had shown him the letters she had received, the ones she had hidden from him for weeks, he had to wonder if she was just plain clueless.

Did she really value her ambition over her sister's life? Over his life? Over even her own?

It left a bitter taste in his mouth as he looked from his grand-father's painting to a photograph of him and his siblings when they were kids.

Madison looked so small beside him, her tiny hand in his, her length of dark hair framing her petite face. Even her eyes seemed innocent, her smile easy as most children's smiles were.

How had that little girl grown into the woman she was today? The woman who now ran an empire, who faced enormous obstacles and deadly threats with unyielding nerve.

Somewhere along the way, probably thanks to Cyrus, that little girl had gotten it into her head that she was capable of anything. Even if the entire world was against her, she would tirelessly build her fort and man it all on her own, with weapons of her own creation, beating back the enemy until she could no longer fight. And at that point, she would draw her dagger and stab her own heart, just to prevent them from having the satisfaction of killing her themselves.

That was just who she was, and who Cyrus had been. While he admired her for it in many ways, part of him was revolted by it as well.

There was a sudden, brisk knock on his door, startling him from his reverie. His eyes jolted to the door as his brows knit with caution.

"Come in," he called out, watching as the door swung open and a strange man walked in, dressed in a neatly pressed and expensively tailored suit.

The man smiled cheerfully, his white teeth flashing. "Sorry to just barge on in here, but I see your secretary is out to lunch."

Grant's face hardened. "She's in the hospital, actually."

"Oh, sorry to hear that," the stranger apologized in a smooth, southern accent. He shut the door and made his way into the room, hand extended. "My name is Jack Morgan."

Grant hesitated, recognition hitting him like a brick to the face. He rose to his feet and accepted the man's hand warily. "What can I do for you, Mr. Morgan?"

Morgan took a seat in one of the chairs across from Grant, crossing one leg over the other as he sat back casually. His head angled to the side as he continued to smile. "I came here to introduce myself, first and foremost, and to offer you my assistance."

"Why would I need your help?" Grant asked, taking a seat himself.

Morgan grinned, his blue eyes lit with charisma and spunk. "Well, I hear we have a common enemy."

Grant's eyes narrowed. "Who would that be?"

"Senator Warren Shaw," Morgan replied, an almost imperceptible hint of anger to his voice. "He is the current holder of the senate seat I hope to win in next year's election."

"I know who he is." Grant frowned, eyeing the man coldly. "I also know about your father and his connection to my family."

Morgan's eyes glittered. "I see...you know, that connection makes us distant relatives."

"Right," Grant said flatly, irritated by the notion that they were in any way related. "So what is it that you want from me?"

"Oh, nothing." Morgan grinned. "I'm only here to offer you my support in counterbalancing the lies Shaw has spread about your family."

"He's shut up for now; I'm not really worried about him."

"Yes, for now. But what about when he goes public with this little secret of mine that you and I both know is coming...you don't think he'll throw as much mud in your faces as he can? It's dirty politics at its best, and you, my friend, are caught in the crossfire."

"So you want to do what, exactly?"

Morgan rolled his shoulders, his eyes taking in the office around him as he continued to grin. "I want to become your new best friend, Grant. I'm going to throw my full weight behind your family so they are portrayed exactly the right way in the press. That way, when Shaw starts running his mouth again, we can denounce his claim together. He will be made a fool of, son. And you and I will come out on top, just where we belong."

Grant said nothing for a long moment, digesting the man's—*the politician's*—words. He certainly did not trust him, yet he could not see a downside to his plan. Shaw had wronged them, time and again, and although Lynette had tried to make a case for him, Grant just didn't buy it. Shaw didn't care if the Vasser reputation was damaged further by these claims. All he wanted was to win his re-election.

But Morgan was an entirely different animal. Grant could sense the cruel ambition in this man, the ruthlessness required to do whatever it took to win. While Shaw still had some redeeming qualities, this man was an unknown. Just what good was there to Jack Morgan? If anything?

So the real question here was should he stick to the devil he knew and stand with Shaw, or should he make a deal with the new devil sporting the fancy suit and sweet promises?

Grant disliked very much having to make that decision.

"Mr. Morgan—"

"Please, call me Jack," Morgan said genially. "Why be so formal?"

One of Grant's eyebrows rose as he continued, "Don't you think Shaw's claim will be difficult to deny given the Army's own documented case file?"

"That's been taken care of," Morgan assured him easily. "The only people out there who know the truth are Shaw and your family."

Grant frowned. Clearly Morgan was unaware that Marshall had secured a copy of the case file only days before it was destroyed. That crucial little fact suddenly made the whole situation a lot more interesting.

"So let me get this straight...Jack," Grant began, letting out a slow exhale as he met the man's eyes directly. "You intend to speak favorably about my family to combat Shaw's accusations, and when Shaw goes to the press with your secret, you intend to deny it and want us to deny the claim as well."

"You're right on the money." Morgan's lips spread in a toothy smile. "It's a win-win for us both. You can't escape that fact."

Grant nodded, conceding that point. It would be best for his family not to be dragged through a messy political battle, and by using denial they may be able to snuff it out before it got started. It was more than he could have hoped for when Shaw had first told him about his plans...

He rose to his feet and offered his hand. "I accept your terms, Mr. Morgan."

Morgan stood up as they shook hands, his expression both relieved and jovial. It was a mix that Grant recognized immediately as faked and wondered what Morgan's real feelings were at that moment.

"You made the right choice," Morgan said, his handshake bold and as earnest as any politician could make it. He reached into his suit jacket pocket and pulled out a business card, handing it to Grant. "Here's my office number. If you need anything, anything at all, don't hesitate to reach out to me. We're on the same team now."

He nodded and left, shutting the office door behind him.

Grant stared down at the business card, praying to God he'd just made the right decision.

Then again, what was the worst that could happen? He hadn't destroyed any files, hadn't tampered with any evidence. The police didn't even know he knew about Morgan's connection to his family.

So what could go wrong in trusting Morgan?

Of course, Grant reminded himself sternly, he knew very little about Jack Morgan. For all he knew, the man ate puppies for breakfast and worshipped the Devil before bed each evening.

Though he found that highly unlikely.

THE STREETS OF New York City in the spring were bustling with activity. The sun was shining, melting away the last lingering chills of winter.

Madison turned her own face toward the sun, her eyes shielded by large, dark sunglasses and her hair pulled back in a sleek tail. She smiled, the warmth of the rays soothing her skin.

As much as she hated the sun when it was scorching hot out, she couldn't help but enjoy it when there was a fresh breeze in the air, spring in full swing all around her. Even she couldn't deny the pleasantness of it, and she was eager to let it chase away just one second of the gloominess from her life.

Beside her, Wyatt slipped on his fedora and wrapped his arm over her shoulders. "I know you like walking to this place, sweetheart, but maybe we should take a car, given the circumstances."

Madison sniffed. "No. I enjoy the walk. Besides, it's a beautiful day."

"Suit yourself. Though I'd feel safer if we drove." Wyatt let her lead the way down the sidewalk toward her favorite Italian restaurant, which was just one block east. He glanced around them anxiously, his eyes scanning the crowds that swarmed all around them. It was definitely a busy day to be out and about. All he wanted to do was get back inside where he could be sure she was safe.

"Wyatt, when are you going to move out of the hotel?" Madison asked suddenly, lifting her face up to his. "I know you've been paying your way even though you don't have to. As my lover, I figure that entitles you to some perks."

He grimaced, furious that she would even bring it up. "What, like last time? You can't buy me, Madison. That's not why I stick around."

She bristled, irritated that he was upset over it. "Was it why you left, then?"

"No," he stated flatly, tightening his grip on her as a tall, burly looking man approached them. The man met eyes with him and scowled, and just before he could pass Madison, Wyatt pulled her away protectively. As the man continued on, Madison stared up at Wyatt in annoyance.

"What was that about?" she demanded, fixing her ruffled dress from where he had grabbed her.

Wyatt stared over his shoulder at the man, who had continued on like nothing was wrong. He shook his head wearily. "I don't know, I'm probably just losing my mind."

"Did you think that guy was going to knife me or something?" she asked, amused as she watched him. He looked flustered and bitter, a combination she found delightful. "Tell me, who else is going to kill me, Wyatt? That little old lady over there in the gabardine sweater? The young man with the briefcase? Oh! Do you think it's a bomb?" She whispered the last part, her smile wicked.

"Shut up." He glowered, though he still didn't let go of her. "I'm just being cautious. You don't know what it's like to live with danger."

"Oh, and you do?" she snorted, rolling her eyes. "Please, humor me, Wyatt. Where have you been that was so dangerous?"

He looked down at her then, his expression completely serious. "Bogotá, Columbia. I pissed off the leader of one of the cartels in a game of cards and they put a hit out on me."

She eyed him incredulously. "Sure you did."

"I'm not kidding, sweetheart," he replied, his eyes hardening to steel. "There's a lot of things about me you don't know."

That got her, and she pouted slightly as she looked away.

She lost herself in thought over his words and didn't see the stranger approach her head on. She saw a flash of red from the hoodie the person wore as they walked quickly toward her, head lowered and face hidden from sight by sunglasses. The crowd around them shifted and moved, distracting her so that she didn't see the gun when it was drawn.

But Wyatt did.

He yanked Madison out of the way and stepped in front of her the second the shot rang out, the resounding pop horrifyingly loud and unmistakable. The people all around them let out a collective shout and scream of shock, several people dropping to the ground while others ran. Some remained where they were, confused by the noise and unsure what had happened. Disorder reigned as the person in the red hoodie took off at a run, escaping up the street.

Wyatt didn't see if anyone bothered to follow them. Instead he felt a blinding, hot pain in his side and pressed his hand against his shirt, seeing the blood as he pulled it away. His vision went blurry from the throbbing shock of it as he fell to his knees.

Madison froze, the world around her in chaos as she felt Wyatt crumble beside her. She stared down at him, confused, and saw the blood. Her face went white as a sheet.

"Oh, my God," she managed as she collapsed down with him, her eyes on the blood that poured out of him and onto her hands, staining them a violent red. Her eyes met his for one sick, horrific moment, and she could have killed him for smiling at her.

"It's just a flesh wound," he huffed, his breathing labored and strained from the pain. He let her hold him, too shocked to do more than lay there.

"You goddamn bastard," she snarled, tears springing into her eyes as she glared at him. "You took a bullet for me."

"Don't get all sentimental on me, sweetheart. Just call 911." His head fell back against her shoulder, his eyes closing.

"Already doing it," she told him, her cell phone in her hand and a determined resolve forming in her eyes. She pushed back the shock, the panic, the tears, and did what she did best: she handled the situation.

She looked up at the crowd that was gaping at her in alarm and shock and sighed as more than a few photographs were snapped off.

She vowed to punch that bastard with the camera in the face the second Wyatt was safe.

EIGHTEEN

She rode with him in the ambulance. All it took was one molten-hot glare for the paramedics to throw up their hands and welcome her onboard.

Her bloodstained hand stayed in Wyatt's as the paramedics stemmed the bleeding, the bullet's entry point a neat hole in his left side. They would need to dig out the slug at the hospital. Until then, all they could do was stabilize him.

Madison avoided her lover's eyes, and instead stared pointedly at the two paramedics who worked on him. She followed their movements, her jaw clenched and her amber eyes harsh and measuring. One slip up, one accidental faltering of a hand that brought Wyatt more pain, and she'd kill them.

He squeezed her hand, albeit weaker than normal, and brought her eyes down to his. His cocky smile was enough to both piss her off and bring on a rush of relief. He wasn't dead. In fact, he was just as much of an asshole as ever.

"Are you going to hang out at my bedside day and night? Spoon feed me soup and sneak me beer?" he joked, pleased to see she hadn't shed a tear, hadn't broken down. She was too strong for that.

"No," she replied coolly, one eyebrow arching. "That beer might leak out of the bullet hole you took for me."

He only continued to smile, though there was an edginess to it now. "Better me than you, sweetheart."

"Better neither of us," she reasoned, anger flashing brilliantly over her face, darkening her eyes and curling her lips fiercely. Wyatt only watched her intently, wishing he had more to say. Wishing he could make the demons plaguing her disappear.

Minutes later, the ambulance came to a stop and the paramedics began to unload. Madison was forced to release his hand as they pulled out the stretcher, extending the legs down to the asphalt. They rushed him inside the hospital without a word to her, and she watched them go with murder in her eyes.

WITHIN AN HOUR, Grant and Linc were at her side in the hospital waiting room. They hovered over her protectively, nervously glancing around as if the boogeyman was going to come out of the walls with a knife and stab her in the heart. She let them be, pleased by their concern more than she was annoyed by it.

As much as she wanted to believe she could take care of herself, she had to acknowledge that she clearly couldn't. Had Wyatt not been walking with her, had he not seen the gun, would she have noticed it? Or would she have taken that fated bullet in the stomach and bled to death in the street while cameras flashed off all around her and people screamed in shock and fear?

Her breath rushed out of her lungs then as the thought hit her. The cameras. There had been people taking photographs during and after the shooting. It was very possible that someone caught a photo of the stranger in the red hoodie. It was also likely that the press had gotten ahold of one of these photos.

When she jumped to her feet and launched herself at the nearby wall mounted television set, currently showing *I Love Lucy* re-runs, her brothers watched her warily. She reached up and began flipping through the channels, searching for some kind of afternoon news. When she landed on one, she backed away and stared intensely at the screen.

The newscaster, a solidly built man with flawless olive skin and perfectly groomed jet black hair, was busy rattling on about an incident on the subway between two homeless men. She continued to watch impatiently as an image of her face suddenly popped up beside the reporter, and he launched into a discussion of the shooting.

"A shot was fired just outside The Vasser Hotel earlier today, in what police are presuming to be an assassination attempt on Madison Vasser, the hotel heiress who recently made headlines with her bold press conference where she admitted to knowing of her grandfather, Cyrus Vasser's, crimes.

"One man was wounded and was taken immediately to the hospital. The suspect fled the scene, but has been described as wearing a red hoodie sweatshirt. No arrests have been made at this time. We are waiting to learn more information from authorities, however, several witnesses managed to get pictures of the event, including this one of the suspect."

Madison's eyes narrowed as she watched a photograph flash over the screen, showing the shooter several yards away, running with their head down. She studied the image while the reporter continued on about how eyewitness accounts seemed to vary over whether the shooter was male or female, white or Hispanic, blonde or brunette.

They then shot to a reporter on the scene, who had managed to snag the old lady in the gabardine sweater that Madison had noticed right before the shot was fired. Madison clenched her teeth as she listened to the jittery and frail gray-haired woman recount the event as she remembered it.

"I-I saw Madison and that boyfriend of hers, but I didn't think any-th-thing of it. I'm staying at the Vasser Hotel for a week visiting my daughter...can't believe this happened...I should check out of the hotel..."

The reporter's eyes flashed with both sympathy and glee. *"Did you see the shooter? Can you describe him?"*

"Her...I saw her, briefly," the woman corrected him, shooting a nervous glance at the camera. *"The hood covered her face, but her hands were...delicate. It was a woman, I have no doubt."*

Madison felt a hand fall over her shoulder, squeezing gently. She turned her head and met Grant's gaze, rage a smoldering fire hot in her belly. His expression was hard to read, but she caught a trace of pity in his eyes.

"The police will find who did this," Grant told her, his voice calm and collected. It only infuriated her more.

"Like they found Kennedy?" she snapped coldly. "She's still out there somewhere, alive or dead, and all this has done is piss me off further. Quinn almost died, Wyatt's been shot, and it's all because someone out there has a vendetta against *me*. Not either of them, not you, not Linc, no one. Just me. And if that old woman is correct and isn't off her medication and the shooter is a woman, not a man, then there's only one likely suspect here."

"Who?" Linc came up beside Grant, his movements cagey and restless. "You can't mean..."

"Jorja," Madison confirmed, eyeing them both fiercely. "She may not be behind all of this, but I have to believe that she's at least a player in whatever the hell is going on."

Grant nodded, acknowledging her point, while Linc just looked furious. "Damnit. If this was her, I will never forgive myself."

He stalked off, leaving his siblings behind in the empty waiting room to wallow under the weight of this new revelation. Grant released a long, slow breath as he turned to face his sister.

"I'll go call the detective, have her round up Jorja." He placed both hands on Madison's shoulders, leveling his gaze with hers. "Go see Wyatt. He should be out of surgery by now."

"It's probably time you told Quinn about the brakes," Madison said curtly. "She deserves to know the truth."

He sighed. "Yes, she does. After I call the detective, I'll fill her in."

He turned and left, cell phone already to his ear. She watched him disappear around the corner and scowled.

The urge to hunt down that damn actress and strangle her herself was overwhelming, but Madison fought it back like one does a rabid dog. She clawed the feeling from her system and focused instead on the task at hand.

She would go to Wyatt. The cops would question Jorja. And the truth would, at last, be revealed.

"DO YOU KNOW who you are talking to?" Jorja hissed, blue eyes aflame as she stared Detective Tina Crawford directly in the eye.

Coolly indifferent to Jorja's question, Tina continued. "We have reason to believe that you may be involved in the shooting earlier today in front of the Vasser Hotel."

"That's ridiculous." Jorja crossed her arms, her low cut, red dress emphasizing the assets she'd made money from her entire life. She couldn't believe she was sitting in a horrid, metal chair at the police station, being questioned like a common criminal. It was degrading and downright humiliating. Those bastards would be hearing from her lawyer. "I didn't do *shit*."

"The Vasser family believes otherwise. We have records of you making a phone call to Madison Vasser's office recently. Ms. Vasser claims you were hostile."

Jorja scoffed, rolling her eyes. "That bitch can rot. So we have a feud; I didn't try to kill her."

"Most of the eyewitnesses confirm that the shooter was a female. Can you think of any other woman, besides yourself, who may have a motive to shoot Ms. Vasser?"

"How the hell should I know?"

Tina's face remained professionally detached as she jotted down a few notes in her pad. When she looked back up to Jorja, she tapped her pen on her palm thoughtfully. "Ms. Hale, where were you at 12 o'clock this afternoon?"

Panic noticeably flashed in Jorja's eyes. "At my apartment. I only stay there when I'm in the city."

"Why are you in the city, exactly?"

Jorja's hands wrung together in her lap, but she let her earlier anger chase the icy edge of fear from her expression. "Does it matter? It's not against the law to travel, is it?"

"I placed a phone call to your agent back in Los Angeles a few days ago. He says he hasn't heard from you, and that you had no audition or engagement in the city that he knew of. He was actually quite worried about you." Tina's head tilted ever so slightly to the side, her calm blue eyes unflinching as she watched Jorja. She mentally stored away every blink, every twitch, every flare of temper and jolt of alarm, thinking to herself that the woman was showing all the signs of a guilty conscience. Whether she was feeling guilty over having attempted to shoot Madison Vasser or if it was something else entirely, Tina couldn't be sure. But she was damn certain the woman was hiding something. "Do you have anything to say to that?"

Jorja's cheeks flushed angrily, arrogance and temper getting the best of her. "I wanted to prove that Madison was responsible for my boyfriend's death."

"Win Vasser," Tina confirmed, glancing down briefly at her notes. "He committed suicide."

"Yeah, yeah, so he did. That doesn't mean he *wanted* to. She drove him to it by keeping him locked up in that godforsaken room and for feeding him bad drugs. I told this to the other cops already, but they didn't give a shit. She probably bought them off."

"Did Win ever express a fear of his daughter to you? Give you reason to believe she may try to harm him?"

Jorja snarled, jumping on the statement. "Of course he did! He was terrified of her. I even saw her attack him at that fundraiser they had. Socked him right in the face. She had murder in her eyes, I'm telling you. She had wanted him dead ever since he went public with the little secret that she and Grandpa Vasser were hiding."

Tina jotted down a few more notes. "The murder of Winston Vasser that Win witnessed when he was a child."

"Yeah. Screwed poor Winnie up for life. And Queen Bitch couldn't give a rat's ass." Jorja snorted scathingly. She stared at the metal table before her, eyes unseeing. "I even heard she's been using Vicodin. That drug test was obviously faked. Eddie wouldn't lie to me."

"Eddie is the drug dealer?" Tina asked smoothly, the hairs on the back of her neck prickling as she quickly jotted down the name.

Jorja nodded. "Dumb Russian fool."

"Is that where you purchased the drugs for Win?"

Jorja's eyes widened in a sudden, wild flash as she realized she had said too much. "No!"

Tina flipped through her notepad absently, keeping her cool even as her adrenaline kicked into high gear. "The officers who questioned you following Win's suicide noted in their report that you claimed not to know the dealer. Are you changing your story now?"

Jorja hesitated, her face a contorted mess of rage, fear, and shock. "So I knew him, sue me. I picked up the drugs for Win, but I thought it was just pot. I didn't know it had hard shit mixed in."

"But Eddie told you later on that he had sprayed the marijuana with PCP at Win's request?" Tina pressed, leaning closer over the table toward Jorja.

Jorja's lips curled. "No, he said Queen Bitch told him to do it. Apparently she picked up her daily dose of pills and mentioned that Win was looking for something that would make him jump out of a window or something like that. So he spiked the pot and handed it right over to me when I showed up."

"He claims that Madison Vasser told him to tamper with the marijuana?"

"Yes," Jorja snapped viciously.

"And when you found out that Madison was responsible, you set out to get rid of her in an attempt to avenge your lover's death," Tina began, pulse jumping as the pieces began to fall into place. "You went to the press on your own to try and point the finger at her without endangering yourself, and when that didn't work, you acted as an anonymous informant to Senator Shaw, who played along with you and did his own stint with the press. When that still had no effect, you bumped up the stakes and anonymously accused Madison of being addicted to drugs *and* of knowing her grandfather's murderous secret."

"Wait one goddamn minute," Jorja stammered, blinking uncontrollably as she tried to formulate an argument, her lips moving soundlessly. She managed a few words laced with frenzied heat. "I didn't know that bitch knew about the murder before Win exposed the truth. That wasn't me."

Tina only continued, her voice still level even as her eyes sparked with knowledge and authority. "When that *still* didn't work, when she outsmarted you and became a hero in the public eye, you had to

change tactics, hit her where she would feel it. So you hired someone to kidnap her sister. You ordered in the ransom note that she
be thrown in prison for what she had done, not because you wanted
money, but because you wanted justice. Justice for Win. When she
refused to listen yet again, you tampered with the brakes on Grant
Vasser's town car to send a message. Then you upped the stakes one
last time when you decided to finally get rid of her yourself, so you
went where you knew she routinely walked and you attempted to
assassinate her."

"This is outrageous!" Jorja's eyes widened with panic as she
gaped at the detective. "What the fuck are you saying? That I did all
of this? I gave you the name of the dealer and suddenly *I'm* the one
who kidnapped the girl and tried to kill people?"

Tina's lips quirked up ever so slightly as she settled back in her
chair, jotting down a few notes in her pad. She didn't look up at Jorja
as she spoke. "Right now, it's all theory. A good one, in my opinion.
If you confess now, I can ask the DA to go lenient on your sentence."

"But I didn't do anything wrong!" Jorja's hands fluttered over her
face, her breath heaving out in quick, shuddering rasps as she realized the tables had been violently turned on her. She could seriously
go to prison.

Tina looked up from her writing and eyed Jorja with a cool stare.
"Tell me where Kennedy Vasser is."

Jorja started crying—heavy, gasping sobs that wracked her body
and propelled tears from her eyes. She slammed her fists down upon
the table in a sudden act of violence, her words hard to understand
through her sobbing. "I want my lawyer. Call my goddamn lawyer!"

Tina merely rose to her feet and left the room, the door slamming
with a hollow and desolate bang behind her.

MADISON STOOD IN the sterile, white walled hallway outside
Wyatt's room in the hospital, her arms folded over her chest as she
faced the detective. "So, it's true then? She did it? All of it?"

"I can only prove some of it, not all. Not the important things," Tina corrected, her demeanor detached and polite, her voice revealing none of her excitement, frustration, or eagerness. "She lawyered up, which means getting anything more out of her will be like pulling teeth unless she wants to confess."

"What about the letters I've been receiving, did she send them?" Though Madison doubted the very words as they came out of her mouth, she still had to ask.

Tina frowned. "I didn't get the chance to ask her, but I don't see any reason why she *couldn't* have sent them. She has a clear vendetta against you, a clear motive to want you out of the picture. Her alibi for her whereabouts during the shooting is shaky at best, and the simple fact that she withheld information from us the first time around paints her in a very bad light. We can hold her for obstructing justice on that alone for now until we can prove the rest of it. We'll need to search her apartment for the pistol that was used."

Madison nodded slowly, considering the detective's words. "There's one thing Jorja couldn't have done. It's not very important in light of everything else that has happened, but I think you should know."

"What's that?" Tina asked, pulling out her notepad so she could write it down.

Madison's spine straightened. "Whoever it was who went to the press with the accusation that I knew my grandfather's secret was a family member, one of only a few select men. I haven't figured out who it is yet, but no one outside the family knew that secret except them."

Tina eyed her thoughtfully. "Is Duke Vasser one of those men?"

Madison hesitated, her expression guarded and suspicious. "Yes, he is. Why?"

Tina made a quick notation and then closed her notebook. "Your brother Grant asked me to look into Duke right after the car accident. He wouldn't tell me why he was suspicious, but I did as he asked."

"And?"

"The only thing I could find out was that he rented a storage unit on the Lower East Side. Other than that, no strange phone calls from his suite here at the hotel and none of the hotel staff have seen him acting strangely—nothing."

Madison's eyes tightened as she processed this new information. If Grant was suspicious of Duke, then why hadn't he told her about it? Why had he kept her in the dark?

"Ms. Vasser, there's one more thing that Ms. Hale said that I need to ask you about." Tina shifted her weight, her well-practiced cop's expression impossible to read. "Ms. Hale gave me the name of the drug dealer who supplied the drugs your father consumed. She also stated that you know this man, that you buy drugs from him yourself."

Madison's brows rose in disbelief. "Excuse me?"

Tina gauged Madison's sincere-looking response, but kept on the offensive just in case. "According to Ms. Hale, this dealer is claiming that *you* were the one who told him to alter the drugs. If that's the case, then that makes both you and the dealer responsible for your father's death. You could be looking at manslaughter."

Fury flashed over Madison's face, then flickered away as quickly as it came. She replaced it with cool reason, her lips curving as she stared pointedly at the detective. "The woman's a liar, Detective. Anything she says should be taken with a grain of salt."

"By my account, Ms. Vasser, you have motive to have wanted your father out of the picture. I'm inclined to believe Ms. Hale in her accusation that you conspired with the dealer to harm your father. Once I track him down, I suspect he will confirm my belief."

"And until then?" Madison asked coldly, already sensing the detective's eagerness to arrest her. Tina's hand had subconsciously already reached for the handcuffs clipped to her belt.

"Until then, it's best that you come with me down to the station so we can get this all straightened out."

Madison laughed, bursting with the irony and the ridiculousness of it all. She shook her head, eyeing the detective with pity. "I'll have your badge, Detective."

She held out her wrists, side by side, daring the detective to cuff her. She wanted to watch the woman do it, and could already sense her hesitation. She had seemed so sure just a second ago, but now faced with Madison's easy compliance, she hesitated.

But she began to cuff Madison anyway, only to freeze as a voice called out from down the hallway.

"What is going on?" Charlene huffed, furiously racing toward them with her heels hammering over the linoleum floor. "Why are you arresting my daughter?"

Tina turned to face her smoothly. "I need to bring her in for questioning. I don't have to cuff her, but she insisted."

Charlene glared up at her daughter, righteous anger and disbelief blooming red in her ivory cheeks. "What is this about?"

Madison only shook her head with a sarcastic smile. "Apparently I'm addicted to Vicodin, after all. I must have been popping pills in my sleep, none the wiser. How ironic."

"I don't understand." Charlene vibrated with fury as she rounded on the detective. "Explain to me what's going on at once, or I will contact your superior."

Tina fought the instinct to snap back and instead remained coolly reserved. "Your daughter has been accused of conspiring with the drug dealer who supplied the drugs to Win Vasser."

"That's preposterous," Charlene barked, blue eyes violent. "Uncuff her at once."

"It's okay, mother," Madison said coldly. "This will all get straightened out. Soon Detective Crawford here will understand that she can't trust a word out of Jorja Hale's mouth."

Tina finished clicking the cuffs closed and pulled on Madison's shoulder. "Come on."

"Wait." Charlene stood in front of Tina, blocking her. "You're arresting the wrong woman."

"Am I?" Tina asked curtly, eyes narrowing.

Charlene lifted her chin, avoiding eye contact with her daughter as she eyed the detective. "I was the one who spoke with Eddie about the drugs. I get my pills through him, and knew Win would turn to him while he was in the city for his own vices. I told Eddie that if Win or his girlfriend Jorja came sniffing around for anything, that I would pay him extra to see to it that Win got something special. It was my very intent to see to it that Win fell off the wagon again, and I had hoped he would overdose. Instead he killed himself, which is just as well. I got the outcome I wanted."

Madison's heart plummeted into her gut as she heard the icy and unfeeling words. Her brows knit with resentment and anger as she tried to launch herself at her mother. "How *could* you?"

Charlene danced back a step as Tina restrained Madison. "I did it for you, Madison. And for your brothers. Until Win was out of the way, there would be no moving forward. He hurt you, all of you, and for that I had to get rid of him."

Madison registered her mother's words, but could do nothing more than stare at her in disgust. "Damn you."

Tina immediately released the handcuffs from Madison's wrists and turned to Charlene.

"Mrs. Vasser, you'll need to come with me. No cuffs, just come quietly and we won't make a scene."

Charlene's lower lip trembled, but she kept her composure as she shot one last look at her daughter. There was a brief hint of pain in her cold blue eyes, and Madison held on to that as she watched her mother be taken away.

She heard her mother snap at the detective, "Now, can you shut Jorja Hale up about my ex-husband and find my missing daughter?"

The detective only sighed.

NINETEEN

L inc stared out of the dark window of Lynette's apartment later that evening, eyes unseeing. She watched him from her seat on the sofa, brow creased with worry and a sick feeling in her gut.

They had received word from the detective that Jorja Hale had been arrested and was being questioned in connection with the various crimes that had taken place against the family: the slanderous leaks to the press, the kidnapping, the tampered brakes, the assassination attempt...

Also, Madison had just called to let Linc know that their mother had been arrested for conspiring with the dealer to tamper with the drugs. Lynette winced as she remembered Linc's outburst of fiery anger at the news, his temper in full swing as he nearly threw his cell phone against the wall. He had been fuming with disbelief, anger, and disappointment all at once. It had taken all she had to try and calm him down, to bring him back to reality.

Now he was quiet, too quiet, as she assumed he tried to figure all the angles in his head.

So she waited with bated breath, unsure what to do with herself, with him. Unsure just what was going to happen next.

"I just don't know," Linc mumbled suddenly to himself, his head shaking jadedly. "She's not smart enough..."

Feeling sorry for him, Lynette got to her feet and went to his side, wrapping her arm around his waist. She rested her head on his shoulder with a quiet sigh. "If Jorja is responsible, Linc, then at least she's with the police. She can't hurt us anymore."

He only continued to shake his head. "No, it just doesn't add up to me. She's vindictive and greedy, but I don't see her resorting to kidnapping and murder to get what she wants. She just doesn't think that way."

Lynette bristled, as she often did when remembering that he and Jorja had once been lovers. As close as two people can be...

"You know her best," she said quietly, pulling away from him to wander into her kitchen to make some tea.

He stared after her, a scowl darkening his features. "You're right, I do know her. And while I can see her going to the press and playing games with us, I don't see her committing multiple felonies."

"It was a woman who shot Wyatt," Lynette asserted smoothly, unearthing a tea bag and a mug from a cabinet. She poured water from the sink into the mug. "Jorja is very likely that woman."

He shoved his hands into his pockets restlessly as he turned back to the window. "I just don't believe it."

Lynette rolled her eyes but kept her comments to herself, knowing she wouldn't convince him. If he didn't want to see what was so plainly in front of their eyes, then she couldn't help that. But as far as she was concerned, if the police believed Jorja to be a suspect then she likely had some damning evidence against her.

Besides, the idea that Jorja really *was* responsible for everything lifted a weight from her shoulders. The weight of fearing that Linc may be the next target, that the assassin was still out there somewhere, primed for another shot at the Vasser family...

She heard Linc switch on the television and turn on the evening news. As she finished making her tea, she caught the name Vasser and immediately whirled around.

Linc was sitting on the sofa, eyes glued to the man on the screen.

"Who is that?" Lynette asked, moving over to sit beside him curiously.

"That's Jack Morgan." Linc's hands tightened over his knees, as tense as a predator cat primed to pounce.

Her eyes widened as she stared at the man, taking in his neatly trimmed hair and attractive smile. A politician's smile, one that she knew very well. One she knew could never be trusted.

"*The Vassers are wonderful people, down-to-earth, charitable. They do not deserve the havoc that has been wreaked upon them in recent weeks,*" Morgan was saying to the reporter, the nighttime view of the South Carolina capital city behind him. "*So much tragedy has befallen this great American family, and for anyone to make use of their heartache for personal gains...why, that's just barbaric.*"

Linc scoffed, shaking his head. "What the hell is going on?"

The reporter spoke then, a generously built blonde with sparkling blue eyes. "*Mr. Morgan, can you comment on the assassination attempt on Madison Vasser? The police have apprehended a suspect, but they won't release the information on who this person is.*"

"*And rightfully so. The investigation, as I understand it, is still being conducted,*" Morgan said with both sympathy and concern. "*All I can say is that hopefully the police have the correct individual, and the violence can stop. Hopefully, this arrest will lead them to the missing girl, as well. We all pray for her safe return.*"

"What a load of—" Linc began, only to pause as Lynette grabbed his arm hurriedly.

"Look! See his face?" she asked, pointing at the television.

They both watched the reporter say goodnight to Morgan, and they watched his face as the slightest of smiles curled over his lips and the subtlest flash of glee passed over his face. When he was gone and the reporter moved on to other topics, Lynette turned to Linc worriedly.

"He just lied." She frowned, worry creasing her brow. "This is all a show to him, he didn't mean any of it."

Linc shrugged. "Newsflash. Politicians, lawyers, men, women, whatever. They all lie. Why would you assume he gave a damn in the first place?"

"We know what he's hiding. Why would he want to associate himself with your family in any way? It just leads to more questions."

"Maybe that's the point. Maybe he knows that your dad's going to eventually break the news to the public about his father, so he wants to get on our good side so we can back him up. He wants to make us look better rather than worse, that way when the news hits, it's not that big of a deal."

Lynette chewed on her lower lip, processing his words. "That would make sense. But still, there's something fishy going on here. It doesn't sit right with me."

A grin flashed over Linc's face as he leaned in to kiss her forehead. "Talk some more of that good ol' southern talk, Lynette. It cheers me up."

A giggle escaped her throat as she pushed him away. "You put me back in the South, Yankee, and you'll see just how southern I can get."

"Mmm...maybe I should," he ventured, leaning in to kiss her then, his hands sliding over her hips as he pushed her back against the sofa. "You haven't been to my castle in New Orleans yet."

"You don't own a castle."

"A man's home is his castle, whether it be a cardboard box or a sprawling estate in Tuscany." He nipped at her ear, pleased when she shivered against him. "When all this is over, I'm going to take you down there and make love to you in every single goddamn room."

She snorted, though the idea had her mind exploding with ideas. "How many rooms are there again?"

"Not enough." He pressed against her, his mouth finding hers greedily as he took his fill of her. She arched, arms winding around his back as she gave, gave all she had, all she was. In these times of trouble, it was all she could do for him. When he needed her, she had to be there.

Her cell phone went off suddenly in her pocket. She let out a frustrated breath and pushed Linc aside as she reached for it. When she spotted her father's name on the screen, she shot Linc a knowing look.

"Hi, Daddy," she said as she answered the phone, her voice purposely void of emotion. She had not spoken to him since she had left her parent's home in South Carolina, ultimately having decided that he had nothing to do with Kennedy's disappearance. She questioned her judgment now, when she heard the liquor in his voice.

"*Lynette*," he mumbled, sounding sick with fear and stress. "*You need to get out of New York. Get somewhere safe, anywhere other than there.*"

"Why?" she demanded, alarmed. Linc leaned in to listen to her father speak.

"*I can't let you get hurt by politics, pumpkin...I can't do it anymore.*"

Fear licked at her insides as she met eyes with Linc.

"*It's Morgan...he's the one who had the brakes cut on that car. It's my goddamn fault, I should have never led him to Grant and Linc.*"

"But the police have Jorja Hale in custody for that," Lynette told him. "Didn't you know that?"

"*She didn't do it, damnit. Morgan did. I have a man inside Morgan's camp feeding me information; he confirmed that to me just today. And after the assassination attempt, I have to think that's Morgan's doing as well. You have to get out of there, Lynette.*"

Linc grabbed the phone from her and growled into the receiver. "Damnit, Shaw, what the hell are you talking about?"

There was a moment of tense silence before Shaw decided to speak. "*Hello, Linc.*"

"Yeah, hi. What's up?" Linc grunted mockingly. "What are you talking about with Morgan? Do you have any proof?"

He heard Shaw take a long sip of what he presumed to be an alcoholic beverage before speaking again. "*I have a recorded conversation. It won't hold up in court, but it can at least lead the police to Morgan.*"

"So why would Morgan try and kill my brother and sister?"

"*The man is insane, bipolar, an egotist...he can't be trusted. He probably figured that by hurting you more, he could generate more sympathy from the public. Soften the blow that I was planning to deliver, make it seem like I was the bad guy for bringing it up at such an awful time.*"

Anger flashed over Linc's face as he gripped the phone tighter in his hand. "And thereby discredit you, so no one would care what you had to say in regards to his father's connection to my grandfather."

"*Exactly.*" Shaw hiccupped, then could be heard taking another swig of alcohol. "*Get my daughter to safety, Linc. Tell your family about Morgan, keep an eye out. I won't be involved in this any longer, I've done enough damage."*

He hung up then, leaving Linc hanging onto the phone, a strange, pulsing sensation rushing over his body. Lynette pulled the phone from his hand and reached up to touch his face gently.

"You were right. It wasn't Jorja," she murmured, still dulled by the shock of her father's words.

Linc nodded slowly, then rose to his feet. He went straight to the door of Lynette's apartment and clicked the deadbolt shut. He then ran his hands over the door's surface, his breathing quickening as he suddenly felt enraged and vulnerable.

"I need to protect you," he whispered, resting his head against the door to try and cool his raging system. "I have to protect my family."

Troubled, Lynette got up to pull him away from the door. Without a word, she hugged him and tried desperately not to show how terrified she was.

If he knew, it would only make things worse.

"YOU FAILED," SAID the voice, warped and outraged. She shook uncontrollably against the bonds that held her.

"I-I tried..." Kennedy stammered, her heart hammering ferociously in her chest out of fear, out of desperation. "H-he blocked me."

"I told you what would happen if you failed to kill her!" the voice said again. Kennedy could hear the sound of feet shuffling over the concrete floor around her as the man circled her like a vulture circling a dead carcass—hungry and malicious.

"Why d-didn't you just set o-off the bomb you strapped to my chest? Or the bomb you planted at the hotel?" she asked, her tears warming her eyes behind the blindfold she wore. "Why did you grab me off the street and bring me back here?"

"I didn't realize you had hit the wrong target."

Her head whipped back violently as a gloved hand struck her in the face, blinding, hot pain shooting through her system. A sob built and exploded in her throat as she began to cry.

"And there weren't any bombs. I just told you that so you wouldn't try to run away. Foolish girl."

She shuddered and lowered her face, the pain on her cheek still throbbing through her body. She remained silent, certain now that he intended to kill her. Perhaps it had always been his plan, even if she had succeeded in killing her own sister. Why in the world this stranger wanted Madison dead, she would never know. Not now.

"Untie her. We need to get rid of her," the voice ordered. At first Kennedy was confused, unsure who he was talking to. But when she heard a second set of feet shuffle over the floor, she realized her captor wasn't alone.

She felt rough hands brush against her shoulder as the second captor untied the rope at her back, releasing her hands. He lifted her from the chair, not as roughly as she expected, and leaned in to whisper in her ear.

"Don't move."

She thought she recognized the voice, but couldn't be certain. Regardless, her instincts won over any common sense as she tried to swing her arm around and hit the man who stood beside her. She felt her fingers make contact with his arm and dug in, leaving what she hoped were deep scratches as he cursed under his breath and wrestled her arms behind her back again.

"Damnit, put her back in the chair," the warped voice said. "I don't have time for this. Kill her and get rid of the body. You know what I'll do to you if you don't."

Kennedy fell back into the chair, sobbing as the man tied her hands again. She heard a metal door open and shut with a hollow bang, and realized the man with the voice changer had left. Deciding she had only one chance left to survive, she began to plead with her remaining captor.

"Please, let me go. I won't go home; I'll disappear. I'll go to Florida, Canada, somewhere else. Please, just don't kill me."

The man said nothing, but she could hear him breathing and could sense he was deciding what step to take next. She prayed, though she didn't even believe in God, that the man would release her.

After a few minutes of silent deliberation, she felt him reach down and untie her bonds. Without saying anything else, he left the room and shut the door quietly behind him.

She waited, holding her breath and listening for any sound, any indication he may be returning to finish what he had abandoned. When all she heard was silence, she let out a frantic sob and reached up to remove her blindfold, blinking into the darkness of the room. She rose shakily from the chair, fear skittering down her spine and causing her body to shake uncontrollably, so much so that it was almost impossible to walk on her own.

Her hands extended out into the darkness, feeling the air, hoping to find the walls of the chamber and find the door. She had no clue what awaited her outside or just how far she was from home.

When she found the door, her hand gripped the handle weakly and she used whatever desperate strength she could muster to push open the door. She stumbled out into the sunlight and crumbled to her knees. Her eyes shut instantly from the glare of light, her arms coming up to shield her face. For a few moments, she hesitated, listening to the distant sounds of the city.

Her eyes opened slowly and saw buildings and streets she did not recognize; the whole world beyond her chamber foreign and frightening. Unable to do more, she broke down and wept, terrified and yet thankful for the unknown captor who had freed her.

AGAINST MEDICAL ADVICE, Wyatt insisted on leaving the hospital a day ahead of schedule. There was no way in hell they were going to keep him away from Madison or away from the hotel at a time like this. Not when there was this false sense of security in the air now that Jorja Hale had been arrested.

He couldn't believe the cops could be such fools. Then again, every time he'd had a run-in with the law, it seemed that they didn't care if they caught the right guy. They just needed to catch *a* guy, get him convicted by a jury of his peers, and then pat each other on the back for it. He'd seen more than one innocent man go down because of corrupt city officials, and while he couldn't give a shit about the fate of Jorja Hale, he knew there was a greater danger here.

The real bastard was still out there somewhere, and Wyatt was beginning to think his original assumption had been alarmingly accurate. The threat *had* come from inside the Vasser family, and it only put Madison in more danger.

His reluctance to tell her the truth about Vegas had put her in this position, and he understood now that he couldn't wait another second before telling her the truth. She had to know, consequences be damned, why he had left all those years before.

Once she did know...well, he hoped she would side with him when he accused a member of her family of kidnapping and attempted murder.

He slipped out of his hospital bed, intent on getting dressed and hightailing it out of there as quickly as possible. He had to stop short as his body revolted, dizzying his brain and sending spots sparking like fireworks out over his vision. Sitting back down on the bed, he shut his eyes and winced at the pain in his side where the bandage covered his bullet wound.

Damnit. With a labored sigh, he rested his head in his hands and fought to get his bearings back. He couldn't waste anymore time.

As he did so, his thoughts flashed back to the past and to his last memory of Vegas.

It had been the last time he had walked the halls of the casino, experienced the lights, the sounds, the thrill of it. It had also been the moment his life had, in many ways, ended.

It was a moment he knew he could never take back. He also knew he wouldn't change his reaction to it, even if he could relive the moment a thousand times.

LAS VEGAS, NEVADA
JULY 1ST 2004

When he woke up that morning, he had no idea his life was about to change. He felt his lover's hands slide over his chest, felt her lips warm on his cheek as her body curled against his own. Her hair trailed over his face as she rose up to kiss him, the words on her breath smooth as honeyed wine.

"*Je t'aime*, darling," Madison murmured, her heart beating softly against his, naked skin over naked skin.

A smile teased up the corners of Wyatt's mouth as he pulled her to him, his hands winding into her hair and holding her face over his. His eyes opened slowly as he took her in, the morning light accenting the soft angles of her face. He stared into her heavy-lidded, sultry eyes and felt his blood begin to race in his veins.

Without a word, he crushed her mouth with his and savored her, never fully sated. She was like a drug to him, an addiction he could never shake, never control.

Waking up beside her every morning was like shoving a box full of needles filled with heroin at an addict and expecting him not to shoot up. It was like dangling a bottle of whiskey over the head of a miserable alcoholic, desperate and greedy for that old familiar burn.

Little did he know that within the hour, he would decide to leave her.

She slipped from his grasp with a wink and went to shower, and he listened to her get ready. When she was set to go downstairs to her office, she kissed him one last time.

"Grant's flying in tonight. I expect you to play nice," she said with a grin, patting him on the cheek.

Wyatt chuckled. "Big brother doesn't much care for me, sweetheart. He thinks I'm a bad influence on you."

She shot him a curious look, lifting one sculpted eyebrow. "Funny. I thought *I* was the bad influence on *you*."

He rolled over onto his side, propping up on his elbow as the sheets slipped down to barely cover his waist. It took all the control she had to not slide back into bed with him and blow off the entire work day.

"I think we are both too set in our ways to be influenced by anyone," he told her, that trickster's grin flashing over his face. "We're originals, you and I."

"Yes, we are." She smiled then, and the effect it had on him was devastating. What should have been innocent beauty was tainted by Devil's fire. He wouldn't have wanted her if she didn't possess that distinct bite of wickedness.

She swept from the room without another word, leaving only the scent of her perfume to linger behind her.

With a grunt, he fell back against the pillows, wondering how in the hell he had ever managed to catch such good luck.

Then again, a seasoned gambler holds true that good luck always runs out given enough time to do so and knows to call it quits before the hammer falls. Perhaps that was why he had married her three weeks earlier, in a desperate, spontaneous attempt to keep a hold on her, to normalize whatever it was they had together. It was his way of quitting the game and making it real.

Even though she insisted it be their little secret for now, he still liked knowing he had taken every step possible to make her his and his alone.

There would be no one else for him, or for her.

It was those thoughts that stayed with him as he made his way downstairs into the casino to begin his day as pit boss. It was a position he liked to think he had earned off the sweat of his own brow, but his darker nature knew it was because of Madison. Just like the expensive, expertly tailored clothes he wore and the flashy Mercedes he drove...she had supplied it all. He knew it was part of that lucky streak he had been riding this last year, and he seriously wondered when the pieces of this castle he was building were going to fall out from beneath him.

When he received a phone call from Duke, asking him in for a meeting, a warning light clicked on in his head. He didn't know what caused it, but he tried to push back the uneasy feeling as he headed straight to his boss' office.

He walked past Duke's bubbly and well-endowed secretary with a wink and let himself in.

"What's going on, boss?" Wyatt greeted, putting on a cheerfully careless mask as he successfully swallowed his earlier bad feelings.

He watched as Duke turned in his desk chair to face him, his expression oddly somber.

"Have a seat," Duke requested, nodding at the chairs that sat before his wide, oak desk. Wyatt did as he was told and sat back casually, keeping an easy smile on his face.

The office around them was spacious and luxurious, typical of a Vegas showman like Duke. Presentation was everything in the business, and he kept his office as ostentatious as his upscale home in the wealthiest suburb of Vegas. Bold colors, oversized, plush furniture, expensive photographs of Vegas and the casino cluttered the two walls, while floor to ceiling windows graced the rest of the space. Outside, Wyatt could see Las Vegas baking in the rising sun.

"I wanted to ask you a question, Wyatt," Duke began, steepling his fingers together as he leaned back in his chair.

"Hit me." Wyatt could feel the tension in the air, could sense that he wasn't going to like whatever it was that came out of Duke's mouth.

Turned out he was dead right.

"Why do you feel the need to steal from me?"

Wyatt bristled. "Excuse me?"

Duke only managed a tight smile. "Why did you steal from me? After all I have given you, all Madison has given you. Yet you couldn't hold back your natural compulsions, could you? The renegade living within your heart couldn't let you live on the straight and narrow, could he?"

Wyatt's eyes narrowed. "I didn't steal from you, Duke. You've got the wrong guy."

"Do I?" Duke scoffed, shifting in his chair restlessly. "I'm afraid I don't. The evidence against you is quite damning."

"What the hell do you think I stole?"

"What does anyone steal in a casino, Wyatt?" Duke said with a sardonic grin. "Money. Cash. And a lot of it."

"Liar," Wyatt charged, jumping to his feet then as the disgust and anger barreled through him. "Let me see your proof."

Duke let out a measured breath, then reached for a file folder to his right that held a photograph. He tossed it across the desk to Wyatt.

"That's the money, stashed away in your employee locker downstairs."

Wyatt lifted the photograph and stared at it dully. "I never use that locker. You know that. Why would I if I live right upstairs?"

Duke shrugged indifferently. "I have no idea. I suppose you use it to hide stolen cash before you can dispose of it."

"This is fucking ridiculous and you know it. I'm being set up!" Wyatt growled, tossing the photograph back to his boss. He seriously considered throwing around a few more objects for good measure, but withheld the urge. It wouldn't do to lose control here, not now.

"Who in the world would possibly set you up?" Duke asked, eyebrows raised curiously. "I'm more inclined to believe that you just couldn't help yourself."

"Right. Because the opportunity never presented itself in the three years I've worked here." Wyatt shoved his hands into the pockets of his tailored slacks, his jaw tightening. "Tell me what this is really about, Duke."

"This is about you stealing from me and me giving you two solid options to choose from," Duke replied, sitting back in his chair again. "You see, I have not yet gone to the police with this matter. I felt it would be better, and less messy, to handle personally."

Wyatt's lips curled into a sneer, but he said nothing.

"Your first option is, of course, to leave the casino immediately. I want you out of the Vasser Hotel, out of Las Vegas, out of Nevada. You leave at once, and you say nothing of this to Madison. She does not need the pain of knowing you are a thief and a liar. Better that you break this clean and get out of her life, and our lives, for good."

Wyatt found for a long moment that he couldn't breathe. He relished in his initial impulse to strangle the man across from him, but knew that such a move would only make matters worse. No, it was better to hear him out. A deer in the crosshairs has no choice but to run, as it stands no chance against the hunter.

Duke smiled predatorily. "Your other option is to stay and take the fall. The police will arrest you, put you in prison. My cousin, your *wife*, will be shamed."

"How do you know about that?" Wyatt snarled, violence flashing in his eyes.

Duke laughed. "You think there's anything that goes on in my town that I don't know about?"

Wyatt only grimaced, knowing he was being painted into a corner. "I won't leave her."

"You won't convince her to leave with you, either. Her place is not with you, it's here with her family. I think both of us know she deserves better than to be the wife of a felon. Of a gambling addict, a drug pusher with ties to the cartels in South America—"

"That's a goddamn lie," Wyatt shouted, his control shattering in one explosive burst. "I never—"

He froze then as the door behind him opened and Raoul walked in, looking just as stunned to see Wyatt as Wyatt was to see him. Both men stared at each other for a long, heavy moment as silence filled the room.

Raoul blinked, straightened, and shifted his gaze to Duke. "You asked for me?"

A half laugh bubbled out from within Duke's throat as he watched the two men with dark amusement. It was clear he considered himself the clever cat, toying with two rabid mice and thoroughly enjoying it.

"I did, Raoul. Come in. Join us."

Raoul shot a look back at Wyatt, both cautious and aggressive, as he slipped into the room and shut the door. His sneer was instinctual and the hatred in his eyes spoke louder than his words ever could.

"Better to be alone than in bad company," he muttered under his breath.

Wyatt's jaw clenched as he glared at the man. "This is your doing, isn't it?"

Raoul only rolled his shoulders, sniffing disdainfully.

It was all Wyatt needed to see to confirm the truth. Before Raoul could even flinch, Wyatt had lunged at him full force and shoved him up against the door to the office, his forearm pressing underneath the man's chin. Raoul clawed at his arm, matching his rage as they stared forcefully into each other's eyes.

"She is blinded by your charms, but I see who you really are, snake," Raoul hissed. "*Veo lo malo en los ojos.*"

Wyatt bared his teeth in a fierce grin. "She'll never forgive you for this."

"She won't be finding out about it, Wyatt, because you're going to leave," Duke interrupted from safely behind his desk. "I assure you that is the best solution here. Otherwise, I'll have to turn over this evidence to law enforcement, and trust me, they will not give you such an easy out."

Wyatt released Raoul, his hands clenched into fists as he weighed the limited options he had, turning them over and over again in his head. His hands dove into his hair as he fought back the urge to scream, to rage, to destroy. None of that would help Madison. Nothing he did at this point would give her comfort, happiness. No, his only option was to decide which way he wanted to hurt her.

As much as it torc his ravaged heart to pieces, he knew that he couldn't allow her to be tangled up in a crime, despite how ludicrous it was. Duke was too powerful, too well connected in the city to give him any chance of fighting the charges. As for Raoul, who knew what kind of lies he would slip into Madison's ear to turn her against him as he stood trial for something he hadn't even done.

No. Leaving her was the only option he had. And leaving her was exactly what he was going to do.

He turned to his boss, calmer, his fury simmering to a slow boil now that he knew his path and had gotten over the shock. Eyes of molten steel bored into Duke's baby blues, and the threat, the violence, was clear as day.

"I'll play along, Duke. I'll leave the city, leave it all behind. But if I ever, *ever*, come across you again somewhere down the road, you can bet I'll beat your goddamn face in."

Duke's eyebrows rose as he tilted his head slightly. "I know you're upset, Wyatt, but a threat like that may make me change my mind about turning this over to the police."

Wyatt only scowled. "Burn it. I'll go."

He turned on his heel and got in Raoul's face one last time, eyes on fire. "I hope you understand what you're doing. This will cause her more pain than I think you realize."

Raoul's sneer deepened. "She is a survivor."

Shaking his head, Wyatt stormed from the room, slamming the door shut behind him. He took the back way up the stairs to get to the suite he shared with Madison and prepared himself for how he was going to get out without seeing her.

If he saw her, he knew he wouldn't have the strength to leave.

WYATT RUBBED HIS forehead with his hands, the old memory sickening to him. He knew what both Duke and Raoul were capable of, had known it all this time. Yet he had held back, biting his tongue and hiding his cards because he was so goddamn afraid of what Madison would say if she knew the truth.

How it would hurt her to know it was her friend's handiwork that led to the greatest heartbreak of her life. Now the time had come to play out the hand and see if it paid off. After all, he had his own revenge beating on the door that he had to answer for. He'd waited eight long years for this day to come.

He opened his eyes and stared around at the hospital room, the sanitary, white walls and the soft drapes over the windows that let in filtered light. Blue blankets covered the bed he sat on; flowers, red and black lilies, graced the table beside it.

This was the reality of his decision. He was here because he had failed to warn Madison ahead of time what her own blood was capable of doing. What her greatest confidant held in his heart, this raging jealousy, that took over his senses and in turn caused her harm.

But not any longer. He would tell her the truth, and he would hunt down Duke and Raoul, and demand answers.

Because it was clear to him now that all this wasted time had only given the men who had destroyed his life more time to commit heinous acts. Acts that had nearly killed him and Quinn, and quite possibly Madison's little sister as well.

He wasn't going to have that girl's blood on his hands.

TWENTY

"D o you have your cell phone?"

"Yes, boss."

"And is it charged?"

"Of course."

"Fully?"

"Grant. I'm fine." Quinn crossed her arms and stared up at him, eyebrows raised. She shook her head with an amused smile. "Want to check for monsters in the fridge, too? Or, maybe there's one hiding up under the range hood. Better make sure, I don't want to get eaten while I'm sautéing mushrooms for Raoul today."

Grant frowned. "That's not funny."

"What's not funny is you stressing yourself out over me," she corrected, motioning at the kitchen of *Cherir* with her arms. "What are you so afraid of, anyway? Jorja Hale is in custody. She can't hurt us anymore."

He sighed, running a hand over the back of his neck as he stared around the quiet kitchen. For whatever reason, he had been unable to shake the uneasy feeling he'd had ever since speaking with the detective about Jorja. While he wanted to be content that the matter was being settled, he couldn't. It still scratched at the back of his brain, burrowing there and hissing at him every time he tried to relax.

Quinn coming back to work only made things more complicated. Now he had to deal with the possibility that a bomb had been planted in the kitchen or arsenic slipped into the food. In his mind, he pictured the whole place exploding with flames and his entire future burning to death within.

He had to protect her. As foolish as he wanted to believe all those scenarios to be, he just couldn't help himself. If anything else happened to her, he would never forgive himself.

"If Raoul gives you any grief today for working slower because of your injuries, I want you to tell me."

Quinn snorted. "The day I can't handle myself in the kitchen, please shoot me."

When he paled and his left eye twitched, she promptly shoved her foot in her mouth.

"Okay, bad joke." She winced, reaching out to pull him into a hug. She rested her head under his chin and tried to be cheerful. "I'm going to be fine. You're going to be fine. The police have Jorja, and I'm sure she'll confess any day now. And then we're going to move on. You're going to get back on the right track with the company, Madison and Linc at your side. You'll open up those new hotels and expand, bringing the Vasser name to even more cities across the country. And life is going to be amazing, I promise."

"You forgot something important," Grant murmured, tightening his hold on her and pressing a kiss to the top of her head.

"What?"

"The part where I make you my wife."

"Oh." Quinn flushed, biting back a smile as she glanced up at him. "That is pretty important, isn't it?"

He nodded, framing her face in his hands and watching her, his gaze taking on a powerful intensity. He found himself at a loss for words as he silently absorbed the warmth of her eyes, the sunny beauty of her face. She was so alive, here before him, in his arms. No monster was going to take away his light, not while he was still alive and fighting.

"I should get upstairs," he said, running his thumb along her cheekbone tenderly.

She nearly melted into a useless puddle at his feet.

"In a minute." She rose up on her toes and caught his mouth with hers, her arms reaching out to circle his neck. One of her sore ribs protested but she ignored the pain, pushing it aside to instead embrace the exhilarating jolt from the feel of his lips raging over her own. That lightning bolt of thrill and need and desire pummeled into her like a speeding train, drowning out everything else.

Grant pulled back and met her eyes, as always battling against his own wants to try and be professional. "I'll come down to see you in a few hours."

She only smiled. "Okay. I promise to whack any monsters I see on the head with my frying pan, so don't you worry."

His lips twitched. "They better watch out."

"I also have a mean right hook." She showed him with a playful punch in the shoulder, eyes dancing. "Now, go upstairs and get to work."

"Yes ma'am." He kissed her forehead on impulse and shot her an amused look. She watched him go, leaving her alone in the kitchen.

Though she felt more than a little ridiculous, a chill ran over her skin and brought goose bumps to her arms. She ran her hands over them, trying to chase away the ominous feeling as she stared around the kitchen.

Everything looked normal. The stainless steel counters were meticulously clean; the glass door refrigerator neatly stocked with fresh vegetables and fruit. The florescent lights above gave a stark, white glow to everything, but that was how it always looked.

So, why did she seriously consider checking the range hood for a monster?

Deciding she was letting Grant's stress get the better of her, Quinn put a smile on her face and slipped on her white apron. She set about cleaning and slicing lettuce and carrots for the day's side salads, her movements quick and efficient.

There, everything is just like normal, she told herself, feeling better. She would spend some time down here, then make her way upstairs to help Grant out with any filing or paperwork he needed processed. Then they would go home, she would cook for him like she always did, and they could share a bottle of Cabernet on the balcony under the stars.

She was lost in her reverie and didn't hear Raoul enter the kitchen. It wasn't until he moved in her peripheral and she caught a glimpse of a dark figure that she nearly jumped out of her own skin. A small yelp escaped her throat as she whirled around to face him, her knife up and ready.

Raoul only scowled at her, mean-spirited as always. "I see my apprentice is feeling better."

Quinn let out a half laugh, her free hand flying up to her furiously beating heart as she lowered her other hand. "I'm so sorry, I thought you were—"

"A monster?" he asked, one dark eyebrow lifted.

She blinked, panic skittering down her spine for one brief moment. She fought it back, realizing it was stupid. He wasn't dangerous. He was Madison's best friend...

"Maybe." She shrugged, then attempted a small smile. "I know you've missed me a little, Raoul. It's okay to admit it."

He waved off her comment with a dispassionate grunt as he turned around to rummage through the refrigerator, pulling out containers filled with vegetables.

She watched him quietly, wondering if and when she would ever get him to like her.

"My mother is in town. I know she'd love to come by and see the kitchen and meet you," Quinn began, gauging his reaction as he slammed the refrigerator door shut and gathered up the containers filled with bell peppers and onions. He turned to set the containers on the counter she was working at, though he avoided her eyes.

"We are very busy," he replied, pushing up his sleeves as he snatched a couple of onions and started chopping.

She smiled knowingly and was about to argue with him, but her eyes landed upon his right forearm and the deep scratches that marred his skin.

"What happened to your arm?" she cried, concern clouding her features as she rounded the counter to inspect him.

He abruptly pulled his sleeve down and glared at her, eyes suddenly dark and violent. "It is nothing. Leave me alone."

Quinn froze, startled by the fierce hostility in his voice, in his expression.

"Okay..." Her mind raced with thoughts and suspicions as she returned to her workstation and continued cutting up carrots, instinctually keeping an eye on him. His movements seemed more abrupt, more angry, but he didn't say another word.

The simple fact that he was so touchy about the scratches meant that it was something serious, something he didn't want to share with her. She had to assume that if the scratches were caused by a cat, then he wouldn't be so hostile about them.

Which left only one other possibility. The scratches had been caused by a human, probably a woman.

Or a girl.

She felt sick to her stomach then as her hand trembled, her knife skipping off the surface of the carrot and smacking into the cutting board. Raoul glanced over at her, but said nothing as she attempted to recover and hide her nerves.

Realizing she couldn't fake it any longer, Quinn dropped her knife onto the cutting board and cleared her throat.

"I have to use the restroom," she lied, not even sparing him a look as she fled from the room, the stainless steel doors swinging closed behind her. She tore through the restaurant and out into the lobby, then hopped on an already full to capacity elevator on its way up.

She reached over and punched the button for the second floor just moments before they nearly passed it, then hopped off and raced toward Madison's office.

Carrie looked up curiously as she walked past, but Quinn ignored her and shoved open Madison's door unannounced.

Madison was seated at her desk, eyes narrowed as she looked over a contract. She glanced up at Quinn as the door clicked shut.

"I have to tell you something," Quinn said breathlessly, approaching the desk. Her hands twisted together in front of her, a sure sign she was anxious.

Madison's brow lifted. "What is it?"

Quinn took a deep, measured breath, then launched into her explanation. "I was downstairs in the kitchen slicing some carrots and lettuce for today's salads, and Raoul came in. He started working on cutting the onions and was across from me at the counter, and I started talking to him and he rolled up his sleeves, and I noticed scratches on his arm. When I asked him about it, he got angry with me and—"

"Get to the point, Quinn," Madison said firmly, coldly.

Quinn sighed. "I think Raoul has Kennedy."

For a brief moment, the two women held eyes and neither seemed to breathe. The office around them was hauntingly quiet. The damning words just spoken were hanging like a noose in the air, anxiously awaiting a soul to squeeze the life out of.

When Madison did speak, Quinn noticed the disdain in her voice. "Because of a few scratches, you assume Raoul kidnapped my sister?"

"He was very defensive about it," Quinn argued, resting her hands on her hips. "I know you don't want to believe it, but please just consider the possibility. How else would he have gotten scratches like that on his arm?"

"A cat."

"Does he own a cat?"

Madison's heart panged once, hard and hollow. "No."

Quinn felt sorry to have to even bring this to Madison. But if she didn't, and Raoul really *did* have Kennedy, then not acting could result in the girl's death. That is, if she was still alive at all.

"Just go talk to him. Ask him about the scratches," Quinn pleaded, brow creasing with distress. "He wouldn't tell me. But he might tell you."

"What reason would Raoul have to kidnap my sister?" Madison hissed, cold fury icing her veins. "I think you're overreacting."

"I hope I am." Quinn shook her head sadly, her hands falling to her sides. "But if I'm not, then you owe it to Kennedy to find out the truth."

Leaving it at that, she turned and left the room, shutting the door behind her.

Madison hesitated, sincerely wanting to blow off Quinn's concerns. After all, the notion of Raoul doing something like that was ludicrous. He was loyal to her, her greatest friend and confidant. What reason would he have to kidnap her little sister?

To scare her. To get her to back down, to get out of harm's way. Her breath quickened as she remembered what he said to her when she told him about the letters.

You should heed those warnings. There is only so much I can do to help you.

Had he sent her all those letters, including the ransom note for Kennedy?

She held on to that thought as she stormed from her office and down to the kitchen of *Cherir*, shaking with suspicion and primed for a fight.

When she stepped into the empty kitchen and understood that he had fled, her heart plummeted to the floor and her eyes filled immediately with furious tears.

Good Lord, what had he done?

GRANT HUNG UP the phone, his expression hard to read as he met eyes with Quinn.

"The detective didn't answer," he told her quietly. "I'll try again in a few minutes."

"She's probably still questioning Jorja." Quinn reached out to run her hand over his shoulder comfortingly. "We'll get this straightened out."

Madison stood as still as a statue beside the wide windows of Grant's office, arms crossed tightly as if to ward off a chill. Her eyes took in the sunny, mid-morning view of the city outside, though she found no enjoyment in it. All she could think about was Raoul. "I should go find him, talk to him first."

"He could be dangerous," Grant growled. "I don't want you going near him."

Her fingernails dug deep into her forearms as she resisted the urge to reach out and strike her own brother. "He would never hurt me."

"You don't know that." Grant let out an impatient sigh and stared up at Quinn. "You are not leaving my sight until the police arrest Raoul."

Quinn started to protest, but held back at the fierce look he gave her. She instead left him and went to Madison's side, careful not to give into her instinct to soothe, to comfort. The woman looked ready to explode at any moment.

"Are you sure Raoul is the one who sent you the letters?"

Madison stiffened, but nodded. "Those letters were personal, more personal than I even realized. But he knew I would never suspect him."

"Do you think he's hurt your sister?" Quinn asked, knowing the possibility needed to be discussed. Finding Kennedy had to be their number one priority now.

"No." Madison avoided looking at her, knowing that no matter what defense she made for Raoul, the two of them wouldn't believe her. They didn't know him like she did and even though she was wary of his possible role in her sister's kidnapping, she knew better than to doubt his intentions.

The door to the office burst open suddenly and Linc and Lynette swept in, both looking edgy and troubled.

"You are not going to believe what we found out," Linc announced, holding up a CD and waving it around. He was about to launch into his explanation of what Shaw had said about Morgan, but paused at the looks on his siblings' faces. "What happened?"

"We think that Raoul might have Kennedy," Quinn filled him in, attempting to ignore the fury vibrating off Madison at her words. "Madison thinks he's the one who wrote those threatening letters she's been getting, and this morning I saw scratches on his arm."

Linc's eyes widened. "No shit?"

Beside him, Lynette piped in. "Well, *we* have reason to believe that Jack Morgan is behind the kidnapping. We have proof that he tampered with the brakes on Grant's car."

Grant's face immediately turned to stone. "Jack Morgan? Your father's opponent?"

"Yes." Lynette nodded, taking the disc from Linc's hands and handing it to Grant. "My father had a man on the inside spying on Morgan. He managed to record Morgan ordering that the brakes be cut. It won't be admissible in court, but at least we can point the police in his direction..."

Grant stared down at the disc, enraged at the sudden realization that the man who had tried to kill him had also sat before his desk and offered his support just days later.

"Why would Morgan do this?" Grant asked, glancing around at the others doubtfully.

"Shaw thinks that Morgan wanted to drum up more sympathy for the family," Linc supplied, crossing his arms furiously. "That way he could be the good guy and go around singing our praises, making Shaw the bad guy the second he wanted to unveil Morgan's secret."

"And my father has decided to let that go, by the way," Lynette told them. "He won't go public with the information on Morgan's father."

Grant nodded, pleased to hear it. "So if Morgan is responsible for the brakes, isn't it possible that he kidnapped Kennedy, and not Raoul, and that he also tried to have Madison shot?"

"Morgan didn't write those letters," Madison said suddenly, her voice bitter. All eyes turned to her as she continued. "Raoul is involved in this, but I doubt he has any knowledge of Morgan. And he wouldn't team up with Jorja, so there must be someone else involved."

Both she and Grant thought of the same person at that moment, but neither voiced the name.

"But would Morgan team up with Jorja?" Quinn asked, reaching for the newspaper on Grant's desk that had a photograph of the hoodie-wearing assailant on it. "Can we be sure that this is her?"

"I don't think it is her," Linc sniffed, irritated. "Morgan probably just hired someone to do it."

"Who hires a woman to do a hit?" Lynette asked, eyebrows raised.

Madison snorted. "The right woman wouldn't have missed."

Quinn's eyes narrowed as she stared intently at the photograph. "You know, this is going to sound really crazy...but I swear that this woman has the same build as Kennedy. And look, you can see a little bit of hair sticking out from under the hood. Doesn't it look light brown?"

"Christ, Quinn, what the hell are you saying?" Linc stared at her in disbelief. "You think *Kennedy* tried to kill Madison? She's just a kid."

"She's nineteen," Quinn defended. "Look, it sounds bizarre, but maybe the kidnapper forced her to."

Madison stared at Quinn coldly. "It doesn't sound that bizarre. We all know she hates me."

Linc couldn't help but laugh at her. "Are you serious? You think she hates you so much that she'd try and *murder* you?"

Madison stiffened. "Why the hell wouldn't she?"

He only shook his head and turned back to Quinn. "Look, there's no point in even thinking about it anymore. It wasn't Kennedy. Okay?"

Quinn eyed him carefully, understanding that she had crossed some line with him. She wisely chose to beat back her stubborn nature and back off for the time being. "Okay."

Grant watched Quinn, tapping his fingers over his desk as he gave her idea some thought. On instinct he wanted to revolt the way that Linc was, but he knew she wouldn't voice something so horrific if she didn't have reason to believe it may be true.

"Let me see that." Grant took the paper from her, then looked at the photograph himself. It showed a glimpse of the shooter's back as she ran away, partially blocked by the surrounding crowd as confusion reigned. His eyes took in the assailant's slender, lanky figure, and he spotted the tuft of hair Quinn had seen. Seeing it dropped a sick ball of revulsion into his stomach.

Saying nothing, he set the newspaper back on his desk just as Wyatt came into the room.

All eyes turned to him curiously as he shut the door at his back with a quiet click. He did a quick glance around at everyone, but when his gaze landed on Madison he paused.

"I have some news you're not going to want to hear, sweetheart," he said, voice void of emotion. He stuffed his hands into his pockets.

"What could be worse than what I already know?" Madison retorted, fighting back the rush of emotions she felt. "Raoul wrote those letters. He has scratches on his arm, which leads us to believe he has Kennedy."

Wyatt nodded. "I know."

Before Linc or Quinn could launch themselves at him and barrage him with questions, Wyatt held up his hands to stop them. "But before you all jump to conclusions, I think you should know why he did it."

"How the hell do you know why he did it?" Madison asked, fire breaking out in her eyes to burn violently.

Wyatt's lips curled in a well practiced sneer. "I know because this shit got started in Vegas, eight years ago."

Madison said nothing as she continued to stare at him. Her insides went a bit queasy and her knees felt weak, but she held her ground.

Wyatt continued, "The short of it is, Duke is blackmailing Raoul and using him to get rid of you. In essence, your asshole cousin wants what your grandpa gave you and will do anything to get it. Even resort to killing you."

Because part of her had expected this, Madison barely flinched. "And the long of it?"

Wyatt sighed. "The long of it started in Las Vegas. The day I left, Duke called me into his office. He claimed that I had stolen a large sum of cash from the casino and that it had been discovered in my employee locker. He insisted that he could have me arrested, unless I left the city. Unless I left you and my job behind without a word.

"Then Raoul came in, and I understood at that moment that he had framed me. He had stolen the money and planted it in my locker, in the hopes that I would get caught. And Duke clearly knew about it because he made no secret of his desire for me to leave town. None of your family ever approved of us, sweetheart. Duke held that over my neck like a goddamn axe. As my wife, a scandal like that would have ruined you. He knew I would have no choice but to leave."

"Wife?" Linc cut in, eyes wide as he stared back and forth between Wyatt and Madison. "You guys are married?"

Madison's jaw clenched with fierce intensity as she tried to hold the flooding emotions in, to keep from exploding. She shot her brother a nasty look. "Not really."

Grant cleared his throat and looked up at Wyatt expectantly. "So how does this all relate to what's happening now?"

Wyatt turned to him, teeth bared in a cynical grin. "Duke comes to New York City eight years later, furious that Madison got the position he feels is rightfully his. He turns to his old buddy Raoul, knowing he can blackmail the poor bastard into helping get rid of her."

Grant frowned. "So he sends her letters to scare her, and helps Duke kidnap Kennedy, hoping to convince her to back down. When that didn't work, he arranged to have her killed."

"*No!*" Madison snarled, face contorted with rage as she stormed up to Wyatt and grabbed him by his shirt, shaking him forcefully. "Raoul wouldn't hurt me, damnit. He had his reasons for trying to scare me away, I can deal with that. But he would never be part of a plot to kill me."

Wyatt grabbed her wrists tightly to hold her in place, his eyes meeting hers fiercely. "You underestimate the power of blackmail, sweetheart."

"What the hell is he so afraid of that he'd resort to this?" she hissed, trying to free herself from his grasp.

He just pulled her in closer and with one, sinister look stopped her struggling. "Tell me you don't hate him for what he did to me? To you?"

Her lips parted as she processed his words, absorbed the betrayal. Yes, it was true. She did hate him for it. And with that hatred came the sickness, the shock. The pain.

Wyatt softened his hold on her, sensing her acceptance. He brushed at the single tear that fell from her eye and let the relief pulse through him. At last, the truth was out.

"He made the choice to guard his secret and help Duke destroy your life, versus facing you with the truth."

"So did you," she murmured, staring at him as if he were a stranger. "Why did you wait so long to tell me this? We could have stopped them."

Wyatt watched as she backed away from him, as Linc slid his arm around her protectively.

An old familiar pain slipped in to mix with the fury he felt.

"Would you have believed me, Madison, if you hadn't known for yourself that Raoul was involved?" he asked frostily. "In any event, I held my cards to my chest because I knew it wasn't the right time to lay them down. Now it is."

"Now that you've taken a bullet," Madison spat, furious tears in her eyes.

"A bullet that was meant for you," Wyatt corrected. "And yes, I suppose the shooting opened my eyes to the seriousness of the situation. You can stand up to many things, sweetheart, but a bullet isn't one of them."

Grant's face tightened with concern as he looked at Wyatt. "Shaw confirmed that his opponent, Jack Morgan, is responsible for cutting the brakes on my car. Could Duke be working with him?"

Wyatt's eyes narrowed at this information, but he shook his head. "I doubt it. In my opinion, you've got threats coming in from all sides. That's the price you pay for being notorious."

Madison straightened, shaking the initial shock and resentment from her system. She didn't have the time for it now. She had to act.

"Call the detective again, Grant. Have them arrest Duke," she ordered. "Raoul's involvement in this does not leave this room. Do not mention his name to the police until I have had a chance to speak to him."

She swept up to Wyatt, let out a restless huff of breath, then reached up to grab his shirt and pull his face down to hers for a hard and fast kiss. When he stared at her with a confused expression, she tried on an edgy smile. "When I get back, we're going to settle this once and for all."

"Where are you going?" He wanted to hold her back, to keep her safe, but knew better than to try.

She lifted her chin defiantly. "To find my chef."

THEY LOUNGED ON one of the long sofas in *Amoureux,* sipping whiskey and talking bullshit. It was one of Cy's favorite pastimes, but lately he'd gotten less and less enthusiastic about it.

Especially since the only person who would give him the time of day was Duke, and he was pretty sure his cousin had lost his damn mind.

Which was exactly why he had booked a flight out to Los Angeles the following morning. He was done putting up with Duke's coded statements and blatant arrogance, especially since the shooting. Things had really gotten strange after that...

"Knicks game on tonight," Cy muttered conversationally, swirling the whiskey in his glass and watching it catch the light. The game was on one of the flat screen televisions across the room, the sound muffled by the infectious pop music that reminded him nostalgically of Los Angeles.

Beside him, Duke scoffed. "I'll never understand your fascination with sports."

"And I'll never understand your fascination with Madison," Cy shot back.

Duke let out a dark laugh, sipping at his drink and eyeing a leggy blonde that walked past. "I don't see how you can't, my friend. She's as much a thorn in your side as she is in mine."

"Except that I only want to pluck out the thorn. You want to pluck out the thorn, smash it into little pieces, then burn it to ash."

Duke smiled, amused by the analogy despite the circumstances. "We all have our methods."

Disturbed by the look in his cousin's eyes, Cy turned away and downed the last of his whiskey. He started to stand up, deciding he'd had enough conversation for the time being. "I gotta go take a leak."

He was about to leave when he spotted a couple of cops enter the bar and scan the crowd, searching for someone. A lump formed hot in his throat as he stared immediately down at Duke.

Duke rose to his feet as Detective Crawford and another cop saw him and approached.

"Duke Vasser?" Tina asked, flashing her badge at him.

"That's right." Duke sipped at his drink casually, a sly grin on his face. "How can I help you?"

"We need to talk with you regarding your cousin's kidnapping. It may be best if you come with us down to the station."

Duke's eyes narrowed, anger flashing in them. "Why don't we start in the lobby. You can ask your questions there."

"I should let you know that we learned you rented a storage locker down in the East Village. I have a squad car on its way right now to search the area. We can have a warrant within hours if we suspect the missing girl may be there."

Duke nearly dropped the glass in his hand. "I rented that unit to store some of my belongings while I stay here in the city. You call off your men or I'm going to call my lawyer."

"You probably should contact your lawyer, Mr. Vasser," Tina said dispassionately. "But I will not call off that squad car."

"You have no right!" Duke charged, looking like he was going to punch her in the face. She stepped back as he suddenly lunged at her, his glass shattering to the floor. Within seconds she had whipped out her handcuffs and her partner was restraining Duke's arms.

"Duke Vasser, you are under arrest. You have the right to remain silent..."

She spun him around to slip the cuffs on his wrists, and Duke started laughing.

"I don't believe this." He shook his head, grinning cynically at his cousin before turning his head to glare at the detective. "My fucking lawyer will have your badge, bitch."

She only continued to read him his rights until she was interrupted by her cell phone. When she answered it, her face visibly softened with both relief and thrill. She hung up, then turned to Duke.

"My squad car picked up the girl three blocks from your storage unit, Mr. Vasser. She led them right back to your unit when asked where she was held."

Duke paled and suddenly gnashed his teeth in panic. "I gave Raoul García a key. He must have taken her. Why would I kidnap my own cousin? Where the fuck is my phone? My lawyer is going to be so far up your ass..."

Tina said nothing as she read him his rights all over again and led him from the bar.

Cy watched them go, eyes wide. He blinked a few times, hoping what he had just witnessed had actually occurred and had not just been a side effect of the whiskey.

When he understood that Duke was really gone, he plopped back onto the sofa and laughed like a fool.

TWENTY ONE

After knocking on the door, she took a second to wonder if he would even open it for her. She figured that if he didn't, then she would find the nearest hard and heavy object and batter down the door herself. It would certainly help relieve some of the tension.

She was saved the trouble as the door slid back and Raoul's head appeared behind it.

Madison studied the dark shadows under his eyes, the messy waves of raven hair that fell over his ashen face, the harsh curl of his mouth. He looked like a man who'd been down to Hell and managed to claw his way back to the surface, only to fear being dragged under again.

She supposed that was exactly how he should feel, how she wanted him to feel, given the circumstances.

"Can I come in?" she asked, keeping her emotions tightly coiled up inside of her, knowing they spit and riled like deadly snakes, aching to strike. But the moment to attack was not now, not when she knew she owed him at least a moment to explain himself.

Raoul said nothing and backed away from the door, leaving it open. She followed him inside and shut it at her back.

His apartment was large and spacious, yet he had all the windows covered so that it felt like a cave. A few candles flickered on the coffee table, where a tall bottle of Spanish red wine stood, half empty. The glass beside it was also empty.

Some kind of heavy and violent instrumental music played in the background, and she saw him touch a panel on the wall to turn down the volume.

He rummaged around in his state-of-the-art stainless steel kitchen, looking for what she assumed was another wine glass.

Deciding she was going to have to speak first, she stepped up to him and placed her hand firmly on his arm.

"Darling, we both know you have a few things to confess." She kept her voice level, distanced, even as the fire in her gut surged. She wanted an explanation, needed a reason, any reason, not to hate him.

Raoul cursed in Spanish under his breath, then turned to face her. He handed her a wine glass with a grunt, then motioned for her to follow him to his expansive, black leather sofa.

She took a seat beside him silently as he poured wine into her glass.

"My apprentice told you what she saw, no?" he grumbled, setting aside the bottle after pouring himself more wine as well. He kept his eyes averted from hers as he sipped.

Without speaking, Madison reached over and lifted up the sleeve of his right arm, exposing the scratches. She bit down on her tongue to keep from clawing at him herself.

"The police picked up Kennedy as I was on my way over here. She was found on the Lower East Side near a storage unit that was rented in my cousin's name."

Raoul chuckled darkly, then knocked back the rest of his wine and set aside the glass.

"She'll have quite the story to tell," he told her with a heavy sigh, somber now. "Poor girl stood no chance against the monster that lies in that man's heart."

"She told the police she managed to escape on her own, but somehow I find that unlikely." Madison's heart stumbled, torn between fury and gratitude. "Did you free her?"

Raoul shrugged even as his hands clenched into fists. "I should have known he would try and kill you, but I was certain I could make you back down. After he put a gun in your sister's hand and ordered her to shoot you, I prayed to God for the strength to defy him. So I did."

Madison winced, pain lashing out to stab her in the chest. "So it was Kennedy."

"He did that on his own. I didn't know of it, *cariño*." Eyes oddly haunted and wet with tears, he angled his head to face her. "If I had, I would have killed him."

For a few moments, she said nothing. She looked him directly in the eye and measured his statement against everything she knew of him. She saw her closest friend, one of the few she had in this world. Yet he had betrayed her, just like all the others. Loyalty was the one thing she required in any association.

"I believe that you didn't want me dead, Raoul. However, I'm still trying to come to terms with the fact that you drove my lover away and consequently helped Duke kidnap my sister."

At the mention of Wyatt, fury flashed vividly over Raoul's face. "So he told you the truth about Las Vegas."

She nodded, letting the burning pain she felt show, unable to hold it back any longer. "You knew I loved him. Yet you framed him and took him from me. Why?"

When he said nothing, violent rage hit her like a slap across the face. "*Goddamnit, answer me!*"

Raoul's nostrils flared with his own fiery anger. "Because he is a bad man. He has secrets you don't know, a past he keeps from you. I needed to protect you from him."

She actually started laughing. "With what you know of my past, darling, don't you think I have more skeletons in my closet than he does?"

"Your past is noble, *cariño*. His is not." Raoul reached for the wine again and this time took a swig straight from the bottle.

She watched the bitterness haunt his expression, could feel the resentment he carried. While part of her understood it, the other part considered it useless.

"Even if Wyatt has a checkered past, don't you see that it was the mystery of him that I loved from the very start? You had no right taking that from me."

Raoul shot her a dark look. "If I could do it over a thousand times, I would do the same."

A distinct coldness fell over her face. "So what is it exactly that Wyatt's done that's so awful, Raoul? So awful that even the grand-daughter of a killer couldn't be with him?"

He reached for the bottle again, but this time just rolled it between his slender hands, lost in thought. When he spoke, his voice was as cold as her own.

"He was involved in drug deals in Columbia, with the cartels. Dangerous men, with a distaste for arrogant Americans. There is a bounty on his head that has yet to be collected. One day, it will catch up with him. If you are there, they will kill you, too."

She sighed. "He told me some of that. In any event, I clearly have a more pronounced target on my back than he does. If anything, I am more of a danger to him than he is to me."

Raoul scowled. "There are other things, whisperings of bad things that follow his path through Europe." He reached over to take her hand in his, eyes meeting hers. "I know I cannot keep you from him, not now. But at the very least, take care, *cariño*. I only ever wanted to protect you. *Mi familia*."

Her heart constricted in her chest, stifling her breath as she stared into his eyes. Tears threatened her as she tried to hold on to her anger.

"I can't forgive you," she whispered, pulling her hand from his grasp and rising to her feet. She glared down at him, filled with conviction. "I know you wrote those letters. Only someone who knew where to hit could have written something so eloquent."

Pain contorted his features, and she bit back the urge to go to him. All these years, he had stayed by her side through thick and thin, always there no matter the storms she faced. Although he had caused arguably the worst storm of her life, she couldn't discount the years that had followed. For that, and for defying Duke and releasing her sister, she now knew what she had to do.

"Did Duke see Kennedy scratch you?"

Raoul shook his head dully. "No. It happened too fast."

"Good. I'm going to talk with Kennedy. We will make sure the kidnapping falls on Duke, and Duke alone." Defiance glittered in her eyes as her lips curled. "I want that bastard to pay for what he's done."

She started to leave, but paused as he said something under his breath that sent a jolt of recognition, of love, straight through her.

"*Hasta siempre, cariño.*"

Her entire face softened. "Until forever, darling."

ALTHOUGH HER EMOTIONAL injuries were far worse than her physical ones, Kennedy was taken to the hospital. Madison went straight there, knowing her family, including her mother, would already be waiting.

Charlene had been released after the police failed to get anymore information out of Jorja, including the full name of the dealer who she supposedly had purchased the drugs from. Without the dealer, no conspiracy to commit murder could be established. With the powerful weight of the Vasser family lawyer bearing down on their backs, they had no choice but to let Charlene go on the promise that the instant more information came to light, she could be arrested again.

But until then, she was a free woman. Not a very well liked woman, but a free one.

Madison walked into Kennedy's hospital room, her eyes landing first on her brothers. Linc was seated on the bed with his arm wrapped around Kennedy and a pleased smile on his face. Grant stood on the other side of the bed, hands tucked in the pockets of his slacks and his eyes filled with quiet relief.

Charlene stood near the window with Marshall, cell phone to her ear as she barked orders into it, most likely to the lawyer.

They all glanced over at Madison as she approached her little sister's bed.

"Hey Mads," Linc greeted, feeling Kennedy tense against him. He put on a cheerful grin to help ease the mood. "Get everything straightened out with you-know-who?"

Madison nodded, unable to speak. Instead, she just stared at her sister and tried to imagine the girl with a gun in her hand, aimed right for her heart.

Kennedy looked worse for the wear, her long chestnut hair tangled and messy, her face pale and her lovely blue eyes dulled and frightened. She looked like some fragile porcelain doll that had been tossed around the playground by a big bully, then left outside to weather a torrential storm.

Madison understood at that moment what her sister had been through because of her, and it sent a hot bullet of shame to burn straight through her heart.

Grant stepped to Madison and laid his hand on her shoulder comfortingly, a knowing look in his eyes. "We'll give you two some time alone."

He motioned with his head for Linc to follow him out, then looked to Marshall and his mother as well. The four of them left the room, Marshall pressing a kiss to Madison's forehead as he walked past.

When the door shut behind them with a quiet click, she turned to face her sister. For a moment, neither of them spoke. The only sound was the ticking clock on the wall and the distant hospital sounds beyond the door.

Madison released a long breath, crossing her arms protectively. It was all she could do to keep from exploding with the anguish, the rage, the stunned relief...

By contrast, her face was cold and remote.

"Duke is the one who took you, did they tell you that?"

Kennedy nodded slowly, her lower lip quivering.

"I have yet to speak with him, but I imagine his reasons for doing so were because of me." Madison frowned, annoyed that her words felt so hollow, so pointless. How could she really convey to Kennedy just how she felt? How the guilt and the misery were eating away at her?

Kennedy averted her eyes, her fingers toying with the soft, blue blanket that covered her legs. "He told me you had left me there to die, that you wouldn't meet his demands," she whimpered, tears falling freely from her eyes. "Considering no one ever came to find me, I guess he was right."

"We did all we could to find you," Madison snapped in irritation.

Kennedy looked up at her then, an odd sort of fury in her eyes. "Except back down, right? Wasn't that what he wanted?"

Madison said nothing, her emotions carefully concealed as she weighed her sister's statement in her mind. Though she didn't want it to, it hurt to know that Kennedy did in fact blame her.

"Even if I had conceded, who's to say that he would have released you?"

"But you didn't even want to try!" Kennedy cried out miserably. "You care more about yourself and the stupid hotels than you do me! I sat there in that stupid storage unit and gave up hope that I'd ever get out because I knew my family couldn't care less if I lived or died. And now you all *pretend* to be relieved, but you're already moving on with your stupid lives. I never mattered to you; I *still* don't matter to you!"

The urge to argue, to strike out in anger, to turn around and walk out, all raced through Madison's mind in a mad rush. But all lost the battle as she realized it was true. She did care more about the business, and her own life, than she did Kennedy's. Understanding that brought even more shame to her shadowed heart.

"You're right, darling. I have been selfish," Madison admitted, swallowing her pride as she took a seat on Kennedy's bed and reached for her sister's hand. If Kennedy hadn't been so shocked, she may have batted Madison's hand away. Instead, she accepted it numbly as Madison continued, "I could make the case to you that I've been under stress and pressure, and that seeing the toll our grandfather's crimes has taken on our family has hurt me. I could tell you that I won't forgive you for trying to kill me; that the bullet you had aimed at my heart ended up in the one person I love above all else in this world, and I will always, always despise you for it. I could say that I don't see one ounce of what makes the Vasser family extraordinary in you, that you have been disappointing to me in nearly every way. And I suppose I could also let you know that the hatred you have shown me nearly our entire lives has destroyed me, bit by horrible bit, until you gave me no choice but to give up on ever trying to love you."

Tears spilled from Kennedy's eyes as she winced at Madison's words, mortified. Madison only attempted a sad smile as she continued.

"But I see now that you have many reasons to hate me, and the only thing I can do is to try and win over your trust, as difficult as that might be." She squeezed her sister's hand, letting her face soften with honesty. "It isn't easy being me, darling. But I imagine I've forgotten that it isn't easy being you, either."

Kennedy shook her head slowly, a dark laugh escaping her throat. "Being a Vasser in general sucks."

"A few months ago I would have disagreed with you," Madison admitted, a shadow passing over her face. "Now, I'm not so sure that you aren't dead right."

Kennedy sniffled, squeezing Madison's hand in a show of peace, of understanding. "When dad died, I felt like I was the only one who cared that he was gone. The three of you, you never even asked me how I was doing or cared about how I felt over it. I guess it's kind of been that way my whole life. With the age difference, I've always just been the little kid, hanging out with mom in the shadows of her older siblings while they took on the world."

Madison felt her throat tighten as she realized she had never even noticed. Never cared to notice. "Our father made many mistakes in his life. We sheltered you from them; I suppose because we felt you weren't ready to hear the truth."

"What? That he did drugs? That he was an alcoholic?" Kennedy asked, frustration heating her voice. "I'm not stupid, Madison. I have eyes."

"I know," Madison conceded, bowing her head slightly. "And the three of us failed to notice when you stopped being a child and became a young woman, capable of all the same things we were."

Kennedy snorted. "Well, I don't think I'm nearly as smart as you guys, but I'm not completely useless. I can learn."

Madison eyed her curiously for a moment, seeing her sister in a much different light than she ever had before. Perhaps it was a result of finally having a conversation lasting longer than two minutes that made her see just how wrong she may have been all this time...

"Do you want to help out with the hotel?" Madison asked.

Kennedy nodded. "I always have. But mom says I'm not ready. I think she believes I'll get in your way."

At the mention of their mother, Madison grimaced. "Well, I think we can both agree that our mother needs some time to reflect on her actions for awhile before giving us a well deserved apology for what she's done."

"The drugs...dad." Kennedy's face fell, the old grief resurfacing. "I blamed you. I wanted so badly to blame you..."

Madison waved off the comment. "Water under the bridge, darling," she said with a smile, putting as much warmth into it as she could. That wound was still fresh. "I want us to have a new beginning now, a fresh start. I know Grant and Linc feel the same. You should have seen how distraught they were when you went missing."

Kennedy smiled, the thought somewhat comforting. "Really? You guys were upset about it?"

Madison's heart shattered at the hopeful look on her sister's face. "Of course we were. And now we will fight for vindication on your behalf. That bastard cousin of ours is lucky I don't put his balls in a vice."

Kennedy snorted out a laugh, shocked to hear her proper, older sister utter such a derogatory phrase. "Ouch."

"Or, perhaps we can tie him to a chair for a week and let him starve, eye for an eye," Madison ventured with a wicked grin.

"No. No, that wouldn't be right." Kennedy sighed, pity flashing over her face. "When I think back to what he said to me, he sounded so desperate, so insane...I don't think he's been in his right mind lately."

Madison frowned, one eyebrow raised in disbelief. "Even still, he hurt you. He hurt all of us. He deserves to be punished."

"I'm not vindictive like you," Kennedy told her, shaking her head. "I feel sorry for him, in some way. I know what he put me through sucks but he was just desperate. He didn't know what else to do."

Madison couldn't help but roll her eyes and laugh. "Alright, if that helps you sleep at night. Either way, he's at the very least going to prison for this. The evidence against him is too damning."

"Prison is fair," Kennedy said with a nod.

"Speaking of evidence..." Madison began, her smile fading as Raoul's role in the kidnapping came back to her. "You scratched one of your captors."

Kennedy's eyes widened. "How did you know about that?"

Madison tensed, but knew she couldn't risk telling Kennedy about Raoul just in case her sister didn't agree with the plan. "Let's just say a little bird told me. Have you told the police about it? About there being a second man involved?"

"No, I didn't even think of it..." Kennedy's brow furrowed as she considered. "I mean, he saved me. He let me go even after Duke ordered him to kill me. I guess I wasn't planning on ratting him out."

Madison smiled. "Good. I don't want you to, Kennedy. It's important that you tell the police that there was only one man who kidnapped you."

Kennedy frowned. "Do you know who it is? Is that why you don't want me to say anything?"

Without saying the word, Madison nodded.

"Okay. I won't say anything," Kennedy assured her, easy acceptance flashing over her face. Madison marveled at it, just as she had when Quinn had held the same expression just days earlier. It was something that Madison knew she would never be capable of.

"Thank you." She leaned in to press a kiss to her sister's forehead, smiling as she pulled away. "I have to go talk to the police."

"Before you go, I'm really sorry, okay?" Kennedy apologized sadly, her lower lip trembling again.

Madison rose to her feet. "For what?"

"For shooting Wyatt...for trying to shoot you." A tear fell down Kennedy's cheek, though her expression was haunted, frozen. "I barely remember that moment, it's so surreal to me now. The gun, the shot; I didn't even look up at your faces. I just aimed and pulled the trigger. I'm so sorry. He strapped what I thought was a bomb to my chest, and he said he planted one at the hotel, too. If I didn't do it, innocent people would die. I was just so scared..."

Heartbroken, Madison leaned in to pull Kennedy into a hug, tears filling her own eyes. "More water under the bridge, darling."

When she pulled away, she brushed at the tears that fell from her eyes. Kennedy saw them, and Madison noticed the surprise on her sister's face.

"But you never cry," Kennedy managed.

Madison smiled. "Family is my weakness."

Leaving it at that, she turned and left the room, knowing for the first time in her entire life that her sister no longer hated her.

THE SCENE AT the police station was chaotic to say the least.

When Madison pulled up in her town car, her eyes took in the swarming reporters, flashing cameras, shouting voices, and the stern faced guards protecting the doors.

Clearly, the entire situation had been mysteriously leaked to the media, most likely Jorja's doing. She would want every person in the country to witness just how wronged she had been, yet again, by the Vasser family. It heated Madison's blood just to imagine the headlines that would grace the papers the following morning once Jorja was released and had her chance to gossip.

Until then, she had to put the woman out of her mind and focus instead on making sure her cousin suffered the fate he deserved.

As she exited the car, cameras burst with light in her face as the paparazzi lunged at her.

"Madison! Is it true that Jorja Hale was framed by your family for the kidnapping?"

"Can you comment on the man the police have in custody? Is it one of your brothers?"

"Madison, how do you feel now that your sister has been found? Will you be pressing charges?"

She merely kept her chin held high and an expression of dignified fury on her face as she ignored their questions and made her way to the entrance.

The policemen let her inside and shut the doors behind her.

Inside the police station was nearly as hectic as outside had been. Uniformed men and women in blue shot in and out of offices and through the hallway that led into a large room filled with desks and even more officers. Voices carried as conversations were held, some hurried, some amused, some distracted, and others stressed. It was obvious that Duke's arrest and Jorja's wagging tongue were hot topics at the precinct that day.

Madison took note of the curious looks she received as she walked through the corridor, searching for Detective Crawford.

She spotted the detective near the back, standing beside a glass walled interrogation room, cell phone to her ear and exasperation in her eyes. As Madison approached, Tina glanced up and gave a curt nod in acknowledgment.

"I don't care what you have to do; you find out who we have to talk to in South Carolina and have them pay Mr. Morgan a visit," Tina grunted into the phone before snapping it shut. She let out an impatient sigh as she looked up at Madison. "Ms. Vasser. How's your sister doing?"

"As fine as she can be, considering the circumstances," Madison replied coolly.

"Your brother Linc called a little while ago, sent over a copy of that recording of Jack Morgan talking about tampering with the brakes on your brother's car. I can't use it, but I can have him brought in for questioning."

"Good. I will sleep better knowing he won't be able to harm my family further," Madison said. "Speaking of harming my family, where is my cousin?"

Tina nodded in the direction of the room behind her, the glass covered by closed blinds. "He lawyered up. I had a unit search his room at the hotel, found a voice changer. Coincides with what your sister told us. Your cousin has wisely chosen to keep his mouth shut."

"Of course he has." Madison frowned, one eyebrow raised. "I would like to speak with him."

Eyes narrowed, Tina considered the request. "I don't think that's a good idea."

"I promise not to kill him," Madison insisted, wickedness tinting her words. "I just need to ask him a few questions."

Tina sighed, then nodded to the guard protecting the door to the interrogation room. The guard opened it, and Madison slipped inside.

Duke was sitting calmly at a spotlessly clean metal table, hands folded in front of him. He looked up as she entered, and a scowl darkened his face.

"I can't believe they let you in," he commented dryly, his hands tightening until his knuckles turned white. His dark waves of hair were slightly mussed, the gray strands stark in the fluorescent light of the room. The stress lines on his handsome face deepened as he stared at her, the anger in his blue eyes flaring.

"I promised the detective that I wouldn't kill you," Madison replied smoothly, legs winding as she wandered over to the table and rested her hands upon its surface. Her eyes met his, intense and filled with a carefully composed rage. She enjoyed the way he ever so slightly leaned back from her, intimidated by her presence. "I'm impressed at the lengths you were willing to go to just to have my job, Duke. Blackmail, slander, kidnapping, murder...you make Cyrus look like a saint."

Duke sneered. "None of that can be proved."

"Oh?" Madison's lips upturned in a half smile, dripping in malice. "Tell me, darling. How do you plan to get away with all of this? Unfortunately, blaming Raoul isn't going to work. No one will believe you, and no one will corroborate your story. Not even Kennedy."

His eyes narrowed in disgust as he shook his head. "You're nothing but a rotten, manipulative little bitch, aren't you?"

She only laughed, amused by his statement. "You've known me for a very long time. You know what I do to those who betray me."

Duke glared at her. "How the hell are you going to run this company? You have no idea what you're doing. This family needs real leadership and only I can provide that."

"So you thought the best way to get it would be to have me shamed, destroyed, and killed?" Madison asked, lips twisting with revulsion. "I have a newsflash for you, darling. I am this company and this company is me. In your attempts to ruin *me*, you have cost this family a far greater loss. Pain and suffering cannot be reversed, and you can be damn sure that I will never forget what you have done. So while you rot miserably in prison, I will take our company in the direction *I* think it should go, the direction Cyrus wanted it to go, and we will be victorious. In fact, I may even send Kennedy to Las Vegas to learn the ropes and one day take over your job. Isn't that just wonderfully ironic?"

Duke's anger boiled up inside of him at her words, fury reddening his face. He shot suddenly to his feet and reached out with one hand to latch violently around her throat. He dragged her over the table, his face inches from her own as her hands came up to claw at his wrist.

Fear tore through her at the look of sheer madness in his eyes, the haze of red that seemed to filter down over the blue, darkening with hatred. It was like staring into the eyes of the Devil himself, and she found herself furiously praying for her grandfather's strength as she struggled.

His next words had the blood in her veins freezing to ice, and her limbs went weak with it. Her own brutality beat frantically at the doors of her mind, but she found she couldn't let it in. She could do nothing but stare into his eyes and witness the madman within.

"There's a special place in Hell reserved for you, Madison. I'm only trying to get you there faster."

His hand tightened on her throat until her breath cut off completely and her vision began to dim. Before she could reach out and claw his eyes or attempt to pry his hands from her neck, the guard rushed in and tore Duke from her, slamming him down upon the table and cuffing his hands behind his back.

Madison stumbled backward, her hands covering her throat as she sucked in air, an insane fury in her eyes. She glared at her cousin, both horrified and disgusted by what she had seen, what he had tried to do to her. When had he become so unstable? How had he hidden his madness so well?

The detective came in and helped haul Duke from the room and to a cell. Madison found she couldn't look at him and simply dropped down into one of the metal chairs at the table. She rested her face in her hands, furious tears in her eyes as she tried to settle her raging heart.

TWENTY TWO

For the first time in several weeks, Linc settled down into his desk chair at the hotel and breathed an honest-to-God sigh of relief.

His head fell back against the chair as he let his blood settle, his heart cooling to a simmer as his breathing begin to slow. Kennedy was safe, Duke was with the police, Morgan was being questioned, and things finally seemed to be moving in a positive direction.

Jorja was still a wild card, of course, but Linc found he didn't have the strength to give a rat's ass about her anymore. Now that he knew for certain that she wasn't behind anything more than talking trash, he was content to let her go live her life. Which, according to what had been released of her tell-all to the media, included her flying immediately back to Los Angeles and resuming her acting career. She also mentioned plans to write an exploitative book, detailing her horrific experiences with the horrid Vasser family.

Of course, that might change. Linc recalled spotting his own cousin Cy hovering behind Jorja as she gushed to the reporters outside the police station earlier that day. The glimpses of them climbing into a car together, aimed at the airport, had raised some eyebrows and fired up some gossip, including rumors that Jorja had at last found a Vasser man she could hang on to.

Linc silently wished Cy the best of luck, knowing the poor bastard was desperately going to need it.

Kennedy had been released from the hospital and taken straight home by Charlene, who was doting over her like an injured little lamb. He imagined his poor sister wouldn't see the light of day for quite some time with Charlene's chains wrapped so tightly around her.

Linc grimaced at the memory of confronting his mother at the hospital, the first time he had seen her since he'd found out about the drugs. She had wanted his father dead and, as much as he tried to see her side of it, he couldn't. It was all too morbid, too cold and calculating. Forgiving her would take time. Lots of time.

Until then, he had to focus on ensuring Morgan would be brought to justice for his scheming attempts at both becoming a confidant of the Vasser family and destroying them in turn. With Shaw's help and the testimony provided by the witness, they should be able to piece together enough evidence to at least go to trial. Then it would be up to a jury.

And juries never really went easy on politicians. Especially when they saw the photographs of Quinn's injuries after the accident, and her brave, innocent face. In essence, Morgan was toast, nice and burnt.

So was Duke, apparently. Linc rubbed his face with his hands tiredly as he tried to wrap his mind around how his cousin, his blood, could have done so many rotten things. Things that brought so much pain, so much trauma. All the while he had stood with them, playing concerned and sympathetic to their distress.

If only he had believed Cy when the poor bastard had tried to warn him and Grant...maybe they could have found Kennedy sooner. Instead, he had let his loyalty to family cloud his judgment, never wanting to believe for one second that it was an inside job. No, it had been easier to assume that the monster responsible for everything heinous that had occurred was in fact an outsider, a stranger, even. He would have been able to accept that.

Especially because the wounds of Cyrus' sins were still so fresh, so bloody. To know that yet another member of his family was willing to resort to murder in order to claim power rattled his very bones.

He just had to hope that the bad genes died out with Duke and never again resurfaced within his bloodline. After all, he himself wanted to start a family someday, and the empire needed to be preserved so he could pass it on to his kids.

The Vasser legacy was, and would always be, timeless. And with the restructuring of the company and the expansion into other types of hotels, Linc knew it would only get better. His kids would know a Vasser empire without murder, without sin and grief. They would inherit a company worth fighting for. Worth being proud of.

That would be his mission from here on out, he decided. His eyes opened to stare around at his office, hopelessly cluttered with charts and maps but bursting with his ideas, his passions, and his dreams. Yes, he and his siblings were going to succeed, and succeed big.

His desk phone rang suddenly, shocking him out his reverie. He grunted impatiently as he grabbed the receiver.

"Yeah?"

"*Hi there, Linc,*" Shaw greeted cheerfully.

Linc shifted the receiver onto his shoulder and sat back in his chair. "What's up, Senator? Any updates on Morgan?"

"*No, that's not why I'm calling. Although, you can imagine how delighted I am that he's being held accountable for his actions. It's such a relief to know that now the world will see him for what he really is.*"

"Yeah, yeah. I can't wait to hear what he says when the cops hand him our copy of his dad's Army file. He'll be shitting bricks."

"*I imagine he will be,*" Shaw replied, amusement in his voice. "*Linc, a little bird told me that you want to marry my daughter.*"

Linc paused, taken aback. "Oh. Well, yeah, I do."

"*You have my blessing, son. I know that probably doesn't mean anything to you, but I just thought I'd let you know anyway.*"

Linc sat up in his chair, his hand now gripping the receiver as his eyebrows rose. "Wow. Thank you, Senator. It does mean something to me, but it will mean a lot more to Lynette. She doesn't like us to fight."

"*We were friendly once; I imagine we can be that way again,*" Shaw chuckled. "*The wedding will be here, of course, in our church. Y'all set the date, I'll just show up in my tux and give you my little girl. I trust you'll be good to her, Linc. Don't think I won't wring your neck if she ever sheds one tear over you."*

"Got it. No crying," Linc agreed, a wide grin spreading over his face. "Thanks again. I'll be in touch."

As he hung up the phone, he let Shaw's words sink in, both awed and exhilarated. Not only was he going to transform the family business, he was also going to marry the girl of his dreams. Who knew he'd ever be so committed to settling down?

There was a knock on the door that shook him from his thoughts. He looked up as Walter shoved open the door.

"Hey dude, your girlfriend is here."

"Fiancé," Linc replied with a grin, rising to his feet eagerly. He reached for Walter's hand to shake it happily. "I'm gonna make that ballerina out there my wife."

"That's...cool. Congrats, man." Walter smiled a little as he watched his boss take off, sparking with energy. Before Linc could push open the door that led to the front desk, Walter called out to him. "Hey, does she have a sister?"

Linc snorted out a laugh and shot his assistant a wicked look. "Come to the wedding, buddy. I'll find you a southern princess."

He burst out the door and raced straight to Lynette, who was standing patiently by the desk. Saying nothing, he swept her off her feet and spun her around. He kissed her boldly, fiercely, the second he set her feet back on the ground.

She curved into him, startled by his urgency, his energy. It was vibrating off him in explosive waves that shot through her like dynamite.

"Linc," she breathed, her hands gently pushing back against his shoulders as she met his eyes. "What's gotten into you?"

"I love you."

"I know."

"No, I really mean it, Lynette," Linc told her, framing her face with his hands. "You've got to compete with Quinn now."

Her eyebrows rose. "Excuse me?"

"You're both going to be Mrs. Vasser. But *you* are going to outshine her. In fact, we should get married as soon as possible so you can claim you had the title first."

Lynette was speechless for a long moment, warring between insult, laughter, and disbelief all at once. When she could speak, she let her wit guide her tongue. "Who says I want to change my last name? I am partial to Shaw. That is my stage name, after all. I have a reputation to uphold."

Linc frowned. "My name's more famous."

"Your name is more *notorious*," she corrected, though a smile teased her lips as her eyes brightened with sudden tears. "Then again, refusing you has never been my strong suit, so I suppose I'll have to cave."

He smiled, one hand sliding back into her hair possessively, his eyes intent on hers. "Your father wants us to get married in your church back home. I told him that was perfect. He also told me that you're not allowed to cry anymore; so stop it, before he comes up here and kicks my ass."

Lynette started laughing, only to pause as she realized what he had said. "You spoke to my father about us getting married?"

"He called me up just now and gave me his blessing," Linc told her. "It was his first stab at being friendly with me again."

She shook her head. "I don't even know what to say."

"How about, 'Oh, Linc, I'm so happy I could take you home and screw your brains out'?"

Lynette smacked him on the arm. "Smartass."

He only grinned. "But you love me."

"For some insane reason, I let you *convince* me to love you," she said, wrapping her arms around his neck then and pressing a soft kiss to his mouth. Her smile fell as the kiss became more urgent, and her heart began to race with the thrill of loving him.

He broke the kiss and held her back, a dark laugh escaping his throat. "I didn't mean you should make good on that 'screwing my brains out' thing right now, but my office back there does have a convenient little lock on it."

"As does my apartment," she reminded him, kissing his nose playfully. "I have to get to rehearsal. I'll see you tonight?"

"And every night," he replied as she broke free of his grasp, her eyes on his as she started to leave.

"I'll hold you to that, Yankee." She grinned, and the last dying rays of the sun shot through the glass windows flanking the lobby doors, glowing bright gold in her copper hair. It created a glittering halo around her heavenly face, and he held on to that image as she turned and left.

She was truly an angel, come down from heaven to rescue his soul from the scandal, murder, and deceit. Without her, he wondered just how in the hell he could have survived it all.

He knew he'd be thanking God for her every day for the rest of his life.

MADISON'S FINGERS TRACED over the tender skin of her neck, and she wondered if there would be bruises. Before she left, she had examined herself in the bathroom mirror at the police station and had seen only redness. Hopefully, she would be spared the agony of having to explain to her family what Duke had attempted to do to her.

Though in retrospect, it had not been a surprise. The man had tried to kill her before. Not by his own hand, but it still showcased the hate he held in his heart. Hate for her and for what she had become. Thankfully, he would be locked away for many years because of his actions, sparing her family any further pain.

As for Raoul...well, that situation was entirely more complicated. She'd given a lot of thought to what she should do with him, whether or not she'd allow him to remain a part of her life. In the end, she knew she couldn't bear to live without him. She'd never been one to judge a man for his sins, so why should her closest friend be any different?

Despite the doubts she knew her family and Wyatt would have, it was ultimately her decision. Raoul was going to remain on with her at the hotel, and no one would ever speak of his involvement in Kennedy's kidnapping again.

She knew that, in a way, her decision showed her weakness. Yet, she also felt it showed the humility she was fighting so hard to learn. The humility that had never come naturally for her, because Cyrus had never allowed for it.

She shivered, turning her attention to the glittering city lights outside the window of her town car as she made her way home. Thinking of her grandfather had her turning over her wrist and staring at the mark she had taken for him. The symbol of her loyalty, of her dedication, to the man who had made her into what she was.

The man who, consequently, was a killer. A man who had done everything in his life with cold blood. He had killed with it, cursed with it, ruled with it, and at last he had died with it. That was who Cyrus Vasser had been, and his legacy was now hers to transform.

She had no intention of letting his sins mar the polish of that legacy. Instead, she would take everything awful that had happened these last few months and use them to her advantage. Much like she had done with the press conference, she would utilize her and her family's notoriety and step forward anew, focused on the future and exploding with tireless ambition.

The list Cyrus had given her would finally be enacted, now that no one and nothing stood in her way. The company would flourish and expand, shedding the skin of the past.

No longer would the Vasser name only be associated with murder, suicide, and scandal. She would make sure they made all the right headlines and captured all the right opportunities.

When the world heard the word hotel, she was going to make damn sure they thought the name Vasser.

Her car pulled up in front of her town house, and she spotted Wyatt waiting on the front steps.

"Didn't I give you a key?" she asked teasingly as she slipped from the car, eyes lit with triumph. She ascended the steps and went straight into his arms.

"You must have forgotten my key while you were busy slaying dragons and taking on the world," Wyatt murmured, holding her close. He reveled in the warm feel of her body and the soft, quiet way she sighed.

"We still have things to settle," Madison reminded him as she pulled away, a strange mix of sadness and frustration on her face. "I have a bottle of Pinot Noir inside. Why don't you open it while I change into something more comfortable? Then we can talk."

He nodded, saying nothing as she opened the door to her home and welcomed him inside. She pointed in the direction of the kitchen, where he spotted her wine rack filled with bottles. Then she disappeared into her bedroom and left him alone.

The silence of her town house hung heavy with some kind of strange finality. He wondered over it as he opened the wine, his eyes taking in her rich black and scarlet furnishings, seeing so much of her in the things she surrounded herself with.

Things both modern and antique, chicly sophisticated yet classically timeless. It spoke as much about her as her own personality and actions did.

And Lord, did that woman's actions speak louder than any words.

He let out a heavy sigh as he reached for two glasses and carried them and the wine over to her coffee table. He lit a fire in her fireplace, then settled onto her sofa.

She knew the truth now, all of it. Why he had left her, why he couldn't tell her all these years. Now the big question was, could she ever fully forgive him for it?

Not that it mattered. He had no intention of letting her shut him out of her life. He wasn't going back to the way things were. In fact, he would never set foot in Maine again if it meant she might shut her doors for good.

No, he was staying right where he was. If she could be a thousand ton rock, then he could be the immovable mountain. If her temper and righteousness erupted in his face like a brutal volcano, then he would just have to combat her like the fiercest, wildest tornado. And if her frustration and sorrow pooled at his feet like the cold sea foam waves of the ocean, then he would have to lift her up on his boat and guide her back to dry land.

They were made for each other; two pieces of this perfect puzzle that had for too long been broken by greed, deceit, ignorance, and pride. It was time they forfeited all of that and let themselves be free.

He looked up as Madison came into the room, body dipped in a silk nightgown the color of almonds. The rich brown of it was just shades lighter than her hair, and it shifted seductively over her slender body as she sat beside him and reached for her wine.

Her eyes met his as she took the first sip.

"You know, I have hated you for longer than I have loved you," she mused, a hint of regret in her voice. "I used to envision the ways I was going to make you pay if I ever saw your face again. Imagine my surprise when you actually showed up at my office, all rugged and cocky, just like you had been then." She paused, measuring him quietly. "But there was something different about you. Time had done a number on your spirit, but I let my hate get in the way of actually seeing you. Until you forced my eyes open and demanded I look at you for the first time in eight years."

"I don't regret my choices," Wyatt informed her easily, knowing it was true. "I did what was best for you, sweetheart."

She arched one sculpted brow curiously. "Isn't it odd how what's best for us tends to hurt the worst?"

His mouth twisted into a half smile. "I never stopped thinking about you. The few times I met up with Linc, it took all I had to not ask him about you, to not find out if you were okay. I wanted you to be happy, to know that my decision, while it had destroyed me, had in fact benefited you. I can honestly say that it has."

Confused anger came over her eyes. "Has it?"

He reached out to lift up her chin, to admire her face in the soft glow of the fireplace. "Just look at you, Madison. You always had greatness, but now you embody the word like it was created just for you."

Tears formed in her eyes, both from the rich ache of love in her heart and from the heavy weight behind his words. "The pain made me cold."

"The pain made you strong," he corrected, determined to make her see. "And now I'm here, the truth is out, and we can start over."

"I suppose every queen should have a king at her side," she decided, fighting back the tears with a bold smile. "Though I should remind you that ours will always be a volatile love. I'll fight you, hurt you, love you, and worship you. There will be days when I'll want to destroy you, and other days when I'll need you more desperately than any woman has ever needed a man. Can you weather those storms with me, Wyatt? Or should I find someone who can?"

The steel of his eyes sharpened enough to slice her, his face lit with purpose and passion. "If not me, than who? No one else will ever be able to handle you the way I can."

"I know," she whispered, leaning in to capture his mouth with her own, her hands grasping at the black t-shirt he wore. "Damnit, if you ever leave me again I swear I'll kill you."

"The only way I'm leaving you is if I'm already dead," Wyatt told her, holding her against him possessively as his lips roamed over hers, suddenly taking on a tenderness that startled them both. His hand came up to trail over her cheek, brushing strands of her hair away from her face. "You realize that I have to make you my wife now."

"For the second time," she murmured, smiling as her eyes met his.

"Sweetheart, with the way we go at each other, I'm sure we'll be marrying and divorcing each other once a year, at least."

She laughed, eyes bright as she shook her head. "We will never be apart again. They'll have to poison us, drown us, burn us and tear off our limbs before we'll ever let go. And by then we'll be dead."

"And dancing in the flames of Hell together," Wyatt grinned, kissing her again.

When he pulled away, Madison's answering smile was every bit as sinful as the laugh that accompanied it. "Until then, we'll just have to raise hell right here."

He reached for her hands, linking his fingers with hers. "The world isn't going to know what hit them."

GRANT STOOD, AS he often did, at the wide windows of his office, admiring the city outside that exploded with light. Reds, yellows, blues, and whites all shifted and glittered against the darkness, highlighting the buildings and cascading upward to the sky to block out any trace of what stars may be hiding.

He didn't mind. He would take the stars of city lights any day over the real thing. City lights meant that he was home.

The door to his office opened, and he turned to see Quinn step in and close the door behind her. She smiled, slow and knowing, as she walked up to him.

Mesmerized by the look of longing in her eyes, Grant found he nearly forgot to breathe. Seeing her, dressed in a soft white dress with her hair loose to her shoulders and her gypsy eyes only for him, had him remembering the first time he had kissed her, right there before that very window. That had been when the storm had just begun, when his life was still somewhat intact, somewhat still structured and uncluttered.

Now what was it? he wondered as he watched her lift her arms to wrap around his neck, as her face tilted up to his for a kiss.

It was extraordinary.

He kissed her, greedy to the feel of her body pressing into his own. Her hair filled his hands as he took, took, and took all she was willing to give, all she was offering. Quinn had given him so much since she had walked into his life. Now it was time he gave her something in return.

As he pulled away, he reached into his jacket pocket and unearthed a small, black box. Quinn stared at it blankly for a moment before realizing what it was.

"Oh, my God." A brilliant smile burst over her face as she looked up at him, her hands coming up to cover her mouth.

He only smiled in return as he opened the box, took out the old fashioned gold ring with its intricate leaf patterns and single, rose colored stone, and reached for her hand.

"This ring was my great-grandmother's," he explained as he slipped it onto her ring finger, pleased that it fit better than he had hoped. "Fern Vasser. She was married to Winston."

Quinn stared down at the ring, speechless. Her mouth opened and closed as she tried to find the words to say, but instead she simply threw her arms around him.

"Thank you," she whispered, tears falling from her eyes. "It's perfect, Grant."

He held onto her, surprised by how moved he was by her reaction. He had hoped she would appreciate an antique; a ring that may not glitter, but an heirloom that carried with it the history of times past and the traditions he held so dear to his heart.

She backed away and beamed up at him, wiping away the tears. "Great, now I'm a hot mess. How romantic, huh? Ma would be so ashamed."

He silently reached into his jacket pocket, pulled out a handkerchief, and handed it to her. She stared down at it and immediately started laughing.

"I swear you were born in the wrong century," she said as she wiped at her face, looking up at him adoringly. "Next you'll tell me you have a top hat in your closet that you wear on special occasions."

His eyebrows rose curiously. "And if I did?"

She grinned. "I'd tell you to get the horse and buggy, and take me for a ride."

"That can be arranged, if you want."

When she realized he was serious, she bit back another laugh. "That's okay. Though I would love to take my family on a tour of the city. This is the first time they've been here."

Grant fought back a wince. "Your whole family?"

She nodded. "The boys want to see the Statue of Liberty, and my sisters want to hit up Broadway. Ma wants to see the Empire State Building, and dad just wants to find the most authentic pizza parlor in town and sample everything they've got." She smiled again, amused by the flicker of panic in his eyes. "I know my family is a lot to handle, Grant. But I promise we are the most loving bunch of people you'll ever meet. And they adore you, seriously. My sisters are already scheming how to steal you away from me."

"Ah…" he frowned, brows furrowed as he tried to think of what to say.

Quinn reached up to cup his face. "It's a joke. They know you're nuts about me."

Warmth flashed in his eyes to chase away the anxiety. "Good. I suppose it would be hypocritical of me to dislike your family while asking you to accept my own. No one in your family ever killed anyone."

Her hand fell as she sighed. "You forgot about my father, the mobster."

"You said that was a joke."

"Please. After meeting my dad, don't you think he could pass for a gangster?" she asked playfully, nudging him in the arm. "He can do serious pretty well until you make him laugh. Then he's nothing but a big softie. Kind of like you, actually."

"I am not soft," Grant countered.

"Uh huh," she teased, wrapping her arms around his waist and staring up at him. "The first time you smiled at me, I knew my oh-so-serious boss had a soft side. You just needed someone pushy to get it out of you."

"Pushy..." Grant repeated, holding her close as his mouth twitched. "That's a fitting word for you."

She snorted. "Oh, shut up and kiss me again before I smack you."

He obliged her, relishing in the feel of her melting against him, as caught up in the moment as he was. Her hands weakened as she tried to hold on to him, but he felt her giving in to him, conceding the battle as he stripped her of her wit and her ability to think.

He wanted to spend the rest of his life doing just that.

"Are you sure you still want to marry into my family?" he asked, suddenly feeling as though he were trapping her, stealing her away. What if his family really did destroy her?

"Such a stupid question," she replied, kissing his cheek, his jawline, the curve of his throat. "The future is ours, Grant. We can make it whatever we want. I say we make it spectacular."

"How?" he managed, consumed by her as her lips trailed over his once again.

She smiled, meeting his eyes. "Together. We do it together."

Grant absorbed her words, let her confidence and her strength sink in and penetrate his doubts, his worries for the future. She was right. As long as they all stood together now, there would be no stopping them.

And at last, the real work could begin.

"Do not let your fire go out, spark by irreplaceable spark. In the hopeless swamps of the not quite, the not yet, and the not at all, do not let the hero in your soul perish and leave only frustration for the life you deserved, but never have been able to reach. The world you desire can be won, it exists, it is real, it is possible, it is yours."

— AYN RAND —

Acknowledgements

Kudos to the creative team at Blue Harvest Creative for making all my books true works of art. Thank you for everything you do, and most importantly, thank you for being the best of friends to me.

Another big thank you to my support team of fellow authors...you know who you are. You have made this journey a truly extraordinary one.

Fantasy Awaits You

NOW GET ALL FOUR DRYAD QUARTET BOOKS IN
ONE VERY SPECIAL EDITION

ENJOY EXTRA SPECIAL FEATURES INCLUDING
BEAUTIFUL ILLUSTRATIONS AND A BONUS STORY

ALL TITLES ALSO AVAILABLE SEPARATELY
IN BOTH PRINT AND EBOOK

About the Author

Nothing can compare to the exhilaration of discovering, at last, a mode of release for the imagination. Mine came, after years of struggling to visualize my creativity, in the form of the written word. I found myself with my nose constantly in a book, absorbing the life of the characters and the beauty of the setting. It was intoxicating, to say the least, and the only thing I knew was that I wanted to give writing a shot, and take the thousands of characters and storylines in my head and put them down on paper and form them into something real and compelling.

In truth, I'm just a girl from a small town north of Los Angeles with an imagination for days and thank goodness a keyboard at my fingertips. And even though my husband thinks I'm a nerd and my mom is undoubtedly my biggest fan, at the end of the day I'm loving life and enjoying giving breath to the characters living in my heart and sharing with others all of the creativity I can harness.

I believe in true love and I've always believed in happy endings. And that is just the beginning of the story.